ALMOST AN ESCAPE...

"Bribery, Zakalwe?" Tsoldrin Beychae said, smiling.

"Hey, it was just a thought. And it'd be a payment, not a bribe. And they wouldn't force renewed youth on you. But it's academic, anyway." He paused, nodding to the sky. "Completely academic now. Here comes a plane."

Beychae looked out to the red clouds of sunset. He couldn't see any aircraft.

"A Culture one?" Beychae asked cautiously.

Zakalwe smiled. "In the circumstances, Tsoldrin, if you can see it, it isn't a Culture one." He turned and walked quickly, picking up his suit helmet and putting it on. Suddenly the dark figure became inhuman behind the armored, sensor-studded faceplate of the suit. He took a large pistol from the suit holster.

"Tsoldrin," his voice came booming from the speaker set in the suit chest as he checked the settings on the gun. "If I were you I'd get back to the capsule or just plain run away and hide." The figure turned to face Beychae like some gigantic, fearsome insect.

"I'm fixing to give these folks a fight, just for the sheer hell of it, and it might be best if you weren't nearby. . . .

BOOKS BY THE SAME AUTHOR

The Player of Games
The Bridge
The Wasp Factory
Canal Dreams
Consider Phlebas
Against a Dark Background

USE
OF
WEAPONS

Iain M. Banks

BANTAM BOOKS
NEW YORK · TORONTO · LONDON · SYDNEY · AUCKLAND

USE OF WEAPONS
A Bantam Spectra Book / April 1992

PRINTING HISTORY
First Published in Great Britain by Macdonald & Co.

ISBN 0-553-29224-2

Published simultaneously in the United States and Canada

Bantam Books are published by Bantam Books, a division of Bantam Doubleday Dell Publishing Group, Inc. Its trademark, consisting of the words "Bantam Books" and the portrayal of a rooster, is Registered in U.S. Patent and Trademark Office and in other countries. Marca Registrada. Bantam Books, 1540 Broadway, New York, New York 10036.

PRINTED IN THE UNITED STATES OF AMERICA
OPM 0 9 8 7 6 5 4 3 2

FOR MIC.

ACKNOWLEDGMENT

I blame Ken MacLeod for the whole thing. It was his idea to argue the old warrior out of retirement, and he suggested the fitness program, too.

CONTENTS

"Slight Mechanical Destruction"

Zakalwe enfranchised;
Those lazy curls of smoke above the city,
Black wormholes in the air of noontime's bright Ground Zero;
Did they tell you what you wanted to be told?
Or rain-skinned on a concrete fastness,
Fortress island in the flood;
You walked among the smashed machines,
And looked through undrugged eyes
For engines of another war,
And an attrition of the soul and the device.
With craft and plane and ship,
And gun and drone and field you played, and
Wrote an allegory of your regress
In other people's tears and blood;
The tentative poetics of your rise
From a mere and shoddy grace.
And those who found you,
Took, remade you
("Hey, my boy, it's you and us knife missiles now,
Our lunge and speed and bloody secret:
The way to a man's heart is through his chest!")
—They thought you were their plaything,
Savage child; the throwback from wayback
Expedient because
Utopia spawns few warriors.
But you knew your figure cut a cipher
Through every crafted plan,
And playing our game for real
Saw through our plumbing jobs
And wayward glands
To a meaning of your own, in bones.

—The catchment of these cultured lives
Was not in flesh,
And what we only knew,
You felt,
With all the marrow of your twisted cells.

Rasd-Coduresa Diziet Embless Sma da' Marenhide.
c/o SC, Year 115 (Earth, Khmer calendar).
Marain original, own translation. Unpublished.

Prologue

"Tell me, what is happiness?"

"Happiness? Happiness . . . is to wake up, on a bright spring morning, after an exhausting first night spent with a beautiful . . . passionate . . . multi-murderess."

". . . Shit, is *that* all?"

In his fingers, the glass lay like something trapped, sweating light. The liquid it contained was the same color as his eyes, and swilled around lethargically in the sunlight under his heavy-lidded gaze, the glinting surface of the drink throwing highlights onto his face like veins of quick gold.

He drained the glass, then studied it as the alcohol made its way down his throat. His throat tingled, and it seemed to him that the light tingled in his eyes. He turned the glass over in his hands, moving it carefully and smoothly, seemingly fascinated by the roughness of the ground areas and the silky slickness of the unetched parts. He held it up to the sun, his eyes narrowing. The glass sparkled like a hundred tiny rainbows, and minute twists of bubbles in the slender stem glowed golden against the blue sky, spiraling about each other in a fluted double helix.

He lowered the glass, slowly, and his gaze fell upon the silent city. He squinted out over the roofs and spires and towers, out over the clumps of trees marking the sparse and dusty parks, and out over the distant serrated line of the city walls to the pale plains and the smoke-blue hills shimmering in the heat haze beyond, beneath a cloudless sky.

Without taking his eyes from the view, he suddenly jerked his arm, throwing the glass over his shoulder, back into the cool hall, where it vanished into the shadows and shattered.

"You bastard," said a voice, after a slight pause. The voice sounded both muffled and slurred. "I thought that was the heavy artillery. I nearly crapped myself. You want to see the place covered with shit? . . . Oh hell; I've bit the glass, too . . . mmm . . . I'm bleeding." There was another pause. "You hear?" The muffled, slurred voice increased a little in volume. "I'm bleeding . . . You want to see the floor covered with shit and pedigree blood?" There was a scraping, tinkling sound, then silence, then, "You bastard."

The young man on the balcony turned away from the view over the city and walked back inside the hall, only a little unsteadily. The hall was echoing and cool. The floor was mosaic, millennia old, veneered over in more recent times with a transparent, scratch-proof covering to protect the tiny ceramic fragments. In the center of the hall there was a massive, elaborately carved banqueting table, surrounded by chairs. Around the walls were scattered smaller tables, more chairs, low chests of drawers, and tall sideboards, all made from the same dark, heavy wood.

Some of the walls were painted with fading but still impressive murals, mostly of battlefields; other walls, painted white, supported huge mandalas of old weapons; hundreds of spears and knives, swords and shields, pikes and maces, bolas and arrows all arranged in great whorls of pitted blade like the shrapnel of impossibly symmetrical explosions. Rusting firearms pointing importantly at each other above blocked-off fireplaces.

There were one or two dulled paintings and frayed tapestries on the walls, but vacant spaces for many more. Tall triangular windows of colored glass threw wedges of light across the mosaic and the wood. The white stone walls rose to red piers at the top, supporting huge black beams of wood that closed over the length of the hall like a giant tent of angular fingers.

The young man kicked an antique chair the right way up and collapsed into it. "What pedigree blood?" he said. He rested one hand on the surface of the great table, and put the other up to and over his scalp, as if through thick long hair, though in fact his head was shaved.

"Eh?" said the voice. It appeared to come from somewhere beneath the great table the young man sat beside.

"What aristocratic connections have you ever had, you drunken old bum?" The young man rubbed his eyes with clenched fists, then, with his hands open, massaged the rest of his face.

There was a lengthy pause.

"Well, I was once bitten by a princess."

The young man looked up at the hammer-beamed ceiling and snorted. "Insufficient evidence."

He got up and went out onto the balcony again. He took a pair of binoculars from the balustrade and looked through them. He tutted, swaying, then retreated to the windows, bracing himself against the frame so that the view steadied. He fiddled with the focus, then shook his head and put the binoculars back on the stonework and crossed his arms, leaning against the wall and gazing out over the city.

Baked; brown roofs and rough gable ends, like crusts and ends of bread; dust like flour.

Then, in an instant, under the impact of remembrance, the shimmering view before him turned gray and then dark, and he recalled other citadels (the doomed tent city in the parade-ground below, as the glass in the windows shook; the young girl—dead now—curled up in a chair, in a tower in the Winter Palace). He shivered, despite the heat, and shoved the memories away.

"What about you?"

The young man looked back into the hall. "What?"

"You ever had any, umm, connections, with our, ah . . . betters?"

The young man looked suddenly serious. "I once . . ." he began, then hesitated. "I once knew someone who was . . . nearly a princess. And I carried part of her inside me, for a time."

"Say again? You carried . . ."

"Part of her inside me, for a time."

Pause. Then, politely: "Wasn't that rather the wrong way round?"

The young man shrugged. "It was an odd sort of relationship."

He turned back to the city again, looking for smoke, or people, or animals, or birds, or anything that moved, but the view might as well have been painted on a backdrop. Only the air moved, shimmering the view. He thought about how you could make a backdrop tremble just so to produce the same effect, then abandoned the thought.

"See anything?" rumbled the voice under the table.

The young man said nothing, but rubbed his chest through the shirt and open jacket. It was a general's jacket, though he wasn't a general.

He came away from the window again and took up a large pitcher that stood on one of the low tables by the wall. He lifted the pitcher above his head and carefully up-ended it, his eyes closed, his face raised. There was no water in the pitcher, so nothing happened. The young man sighed, gazed briefly at the painting of a sailing ship on the side of the empty jug, and gently replaced it on the table, exactly where it had been.

He shook his head and turned away, striding up to one of the hall's two giant fireplaces. He hauled himself up onto the broad mantelpiece, where he stared intently at one of the ancient weapons mounted on the wall; a huge wide-mouthed gun with an ornamental stock and open firing mechanism. He started trying to prise the blunderbuss away from the stonework, but it was too firmly attached. He gave up after a while and jumped to the floor, staggering a little as he landed.

"See anything?" said the voice again, hopefully.

The young man walked carefully from the fireplace toward one corner of the hall, and a long, ornate sideboard. Its top was covered by a profusion of bottles, as was a considerable area of the nearby floor. He searched through the collection of mostly broken, mostly empty bottles until he found one that was intact and full. When he found it he sat carefully on the floor, broke the bottle open against the leg of a nearby chair, and emptied into his mouth the half of the bottle's contents that hadn't spilled over his clothes or splashed across the mosaic. He coughed and spluttered, put the bottle down, then kicked it away under the sideboard as he got up.

He made his way toward another corner of the hall, and a tall pile of clothes and guns. He picked up a gun, untangling it from a knot of straps, sleeves and ammunition belts. He inspected the weapon, then threw it down again. He swept several hundred small empty magazines aside to get at another gun, but then discarded that one too. He picked up two more, checked them and slung one round his shoulder while placing the other on a rug-covered chest. He went on through the weapons until he had three guns slung about him, and the chest was nearly covered with various bits and pieces of hardware. He swept the gear on the chest into a tough, oil-stained bag and dumped that on the floor.

"No," he said.

As he spoke, there was a deep rumble, unlocated and indeterminate, something more in the ground than in the air. The voice under the table muttered something.

The young man walked over to the windows, setting the guns down on the floor.

He stood there a while, looking out.

"Hey," said the voice under the table. "Help me up, will you? I'm under the table."

"What're you doing under the table, Cullis?" said the young man, kneeling to inspect the guns; tapping indicators, twisting dials, altering settings and squinting down sights.

"Oh, this and that; you know."

The young man smiled, and crossed to the table. He reached underneath and with one arm dragged out a large, red-faced man who wore a field-marshal's jacket a size too big for him, and who had very short gray hair and only one real eye. The large man was helped up; he stood carefully, then slowly brushed one or two bits of glass off the jacket. He thanked the young man by slowly nodding his head.

"What time is it, anyway?" he asked.

"What? You're mumbling."

"Time. What time is it?"

"It's daytime."

"Ha." The large man nodded wisely. "Just as I thought." Cullis watched the young man go back to the window and the guns, then heaved himself away from the great table; he arrived, eventually, at the table holding the large water-pitcher which was decorated with a painting of an old sailing ship.

He lifted the pitcher up, swaying slightly, turned it upside down over his head, blinked his eyes, wiped his face with his hands and flapped the collar of his jacket.

"Ah," he said, "that's better."

"You're drunk," said the young man, without turning away from the guns.

The older man considered this.

"You almost manage to make that sound like a criticism," he replied, with dignity, and then tapped his false eye and blinked over it a few times. He turned as deliberately as possible and faced the far wall, staring at a mural of a sea battle. He fixed on one particularly large warship portrayed there and seemed to clench his jaw slightly.

His head jerked back, there was a tiny cough and a whine that terminated in a miniature explosion; three meters away from the warship in the mural, a large floor-standing vase disintegrated in a cloud of dust.

The large gray-haired man shook his head sadly and tapped his false eye again. "Fair enough," he said, "I'm drunk."

The young man stood up, holding the guns he had selected, and turned to look at the older man. "If you had two eyes you'd be seeing double. Here; catch."

So saying, he threw a gun toward the older man, who stretched out one hand to catch it at just the same time as the gun hit the wall behind him and clattered to the floor.

Cullis blinked. "I think," he said, "I would like to go back under the table."

The young man came over, picked up the gun, checked it again, and handed it to the older man, wrapping his large arms around it for him. Then he maneuvered Cullis over to the pile of weapons and clothes.

The older man was taller than the young man, and his good eye and the false eye—which was in fact a light micropistol—stared down at the young man as he pulled a couple of ammunition belts from the floor and slung them over the older man's shoulders. The young man grimaced as Cullis looked at him; he reached up and turned the older man's face away, then from a breast pocket in the too-big field-marshal's jacket extracted what looked like—and was—an armored eye-patch. He fitted the strap carefully over the taller man's gray, crew-cut head.

"My god!" Cullis gasped, "I've gone blind!"

The young man reached up and adjusted the eye patch. "Your pardon. Wrong eye."

"That's better." The older man drew himself up, taking a deep breath. "Where are the bastards?" his voice was still slurred; it made you want to clear your throat.

"I can't see them. They're probably still outside. The shower yesterday is keeping the dust down." The young man put another gun into Cullis' arms.

"The bastards."

"Yes, Cullis." A couple of ammunition boxes were added to the guns cradled in the older man's arms.

"The filthy bastards."

"That's right, Cullis."

"The . . . Hmm, you know, I could do with a drink." Cullis swayed. He looked down at the weapons cradled in his arms, apparently trying to puzzle out how they had appeared there.

The young man turned round to lift more guns from the pile, but changed his mind when he heard a large clattering, breaking noise behind him.

"Shit," Cullis muttered, from the floor.

The young man went over to the bottle-strewn sideboard. He loaded up with as many full bottles as he could find and returned to where Cullis was snoring peacefully under a pile of guns, boxes, ammunition belts and the dark-splintered remains of a formal banqueting chair. He cleared the debris off the older man and undid a couple of buttons on the too-large field-marshal's jacket, then stuffed the bottles inside, between jacket and shirt.

Cullis opened his eye and watched this for a moment. "*What* time did you say it was?"

He buttoned Cullis' jacket up halfway. "Time to go, I think."

"Hmm. Fair enough. You know best, Zakalwe." Cullis closed his eye again.

The young man Cullis had called Zakalwe walked quickly to one end of the great table, which was covered by a comparatively clean blanket. A large, impressive gun lay there; he picked it up and returned to the large, unimpressive form snoring on the floor. He took the old man by the collar and backed off toward the door at the end of the hall, dragging Cullis with him. He stopped to pick up the oil-stained bag full of weaponry he'd sorted out earlier, slinging that over one shoulder.

He'd dragged Cullis halfway to the door when the older man woke up, and with his one good eye fixed him with an upside-down bleary stare.

"Hey."

"What, Cullis?" he grunted, heaving him another couple of meters.

Cullis looked round the quiet white hall as it slid past him. "Still think they'll bombard this place?"

"Mm-hmm."

The gray-haired man shook his head. "Na," he said. He took a deep breath. "Na," he repeated, shaking his head. "Never."

"Cue incoming" the young man muttered, glancing around.

Nevertheless the silence continued as they reached the doors and he kicked them open. The stairs that led down to the rear entrance hall and out into the courtyard were of brilliant green marble edged with agate. He made his way down, armaments and bottles clinking, gun bumping, dragging Cullis down step after step, the big man's heels thumping and scraping as he went.

The old man grunted with each step, and once mumbled. "Not so damn hard, woman." The young man stopped at that point and looked at the old man, who snored and dribbled saliva from the corner of his mouth. The young man shook his head and continued.

On the third landing he stopped for a drink, allowing Cullis to snore on, then felt sufficiently fortified to continue the descent. He was still licking his lips and had just grabbed Cullis' collar when there came an increasing, deepening, whistling noise. He dropped to the floor and hauled Cullis half on top of him.

The explosion was close enough to crack the high windows and loosen some plaster, which fell gracefully down through the triangular wedges of sunlight and pattered delicately on the stairs.

"Cullis!" He grabbed the other man's collar again and

leapt backward down the stairs. "Cullis!" he yelled, skidding round the landing, almost falling. "Cullis, you dozy old prick! Wake up!"

Another falling howl split the air; the whole palace shuddered to the detonation and a window blew in overhead; plaster and glass showered down the stairwell. Half crouched and still pulling Cullis, he staggered and cursed down another flight of stairs. "CULLIS!" he roared, tearing past empty alcoves and exquisitely rendered murals in the pastoral style. "Fuck your geriatric ass, Cullis; WAKE UP!"

He skidded round another landing, the remaining bottles clanking furiously and the big gun knocking chunks out of decorative panels. The deepening whistle again; he dived as the stairs leapt up at him and glass burst overhead; everything was white as the dust whirled. He staggered to his feet and saw Cullis sitting upright, scattering plaster shards from his chest and rubbing his good eye. Another explosion, rumbling further away.

Cullis looked miserable. He waved one hand through the dust. "This isn't fog and that wasn't thunder, right?"

"Right," he shouted, already leaping downstairs.

Cullis coughed and staggered after him.

More shells were arriving as he reached the courtyard. One burst to his left as he emerged from the palace; he jumped into the half-track and tried to start it. The shell blew the roof off the royal apartments. Showers of slates and tiles hammered into the courtyard, turning into little dusty clouds in their own tributary explosions. He put one hand over his head and rummaged in the passenger's footspace for a helmet. A large chunk of masonry bounced off the engine cover of the open vehicle, leaving a sizeable dent and a cloud of dust. "Oh . . . shiiiiit," he said, finally finding a helmet and jamming it onto his head.

"Filthy Ba . . . !" yelled Cullis, tripping over just before he reached the half-track and tumbling into the dust. He swore, then dragged himself into the machine. Another shell and another ploughed into the apartments to their left.

The clouds of dust kicked up by the bombardment were drifting across the faces of the buildings; sunlight sheared a gigantic wedge through the chaos of the courtyard, edging shadow with light.

"I honestly thought they'd go for the parliament buildings,'' Cullis said mildly, gazing at the burning wreck of a truck on the far side of the courtyard.

"Well, they didn't!'' He punched the starter again, shouting at it.

"You were right,'' Cullis sighed and looked puzzled. "What was the bet we had again?''

"Who cares?'' he roared, kicking somewhere beneath the dashboard. The half-track's motor stumbled into life.

Cullis shook flaked tile from his hair while his comrade strapped on his own helmet and handed a second one to him. Cullis accepted it with relief and began to fan his face with it, patting the area of his chest over his heart as if in encouragement.

Then he drew his hand away, staring in disbelief at the warm red liquid on it.

The engine died. Cullis heard the other man bellow abuse and slam the starter again; the engine coughed and spluttered, to the accompaniment of whistling shells.

Cullis looked down to the seat beneath him as more explosions thundered, far away in the dust. The half-track shuddered.

The seat below Cullis was covered in red.

"Medic!'' he yelled.

"What?''

"Medic!'' Cullis screamed over another explosion, holding his red-stained hand out. "Zakalwe! I'm hit!'' His good eye was wide with shock. His hand trembled.

The young man looked exasperated and slapped Cullis' hand away. "That's wine, you cretin!'' He lunged forward, hauled a bottle out of the older man's tunic and dropped it in his lap.

Cullis looked down, surprised. "Oh,'' he said. "Good.'' He peered inside his jacket and carefully extracted a few pieces of broken glass. "Wondered why it was fitting so well,'' he mumbled.

The engine caught suddenly, roaring like something made furious by the shaking ground and the swirling dust. Explosions in the gardens sent brown sprays of earth and pieces of shattered statuary over the courtyard wall, landing spattering and chunking all around them.

He wrestled with the gear-lever until the drive engaged and nearly threw him and Cullis out of the half-track as it leapt forward, out of the courtyard and into the dusty road beyond. Seconds later the major part of the great hall collapsed under the combined zeroed-in weight of a dozen or so heavy artillery pieces, and smashed down into the courtyard, filling it and the surrounding area with splintered wood and masonry and yet more tumbling clouds of dust.

Cullis scratched his head and muttered into the helmet he had just been sick into.

"The bastards," he said.

"That's right, Cullis."

"The filthy bastards."

"Yes, Cullis."

The half-track turned a corner and roared away, toward the desert.

1:

THE
GOOD
SOLDIER

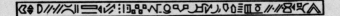

1

She made her way through the turbine hall, surrounded by an ever-changing ring of friends, admirers and animals—nebula to her attractive focus—talking to her guests, giving instructions to her staff, making suggestions and offering compliments to the many and various entertainers. Music filled the echoing space above the ancient, gleaming machines, sitting silently among the chattering throng of gaily dressed party-goers. She bowed graciously and smiled to a passing Admiral and twirled a delicate black flower in her hand, putting the bloom to her nose to draw in its heady fragrance.

Two of the hralzs at her feet leapt up, yelping, fore-paws attempting to find purchase on the smooth lap of her formal gown, their glistening snouts raised to the flower. She bent, tapping both animals gently on the nose with the bloom, making them bounce down to the floor again, sneezing and shaking their heads. The people around her laughed. Stooping, gown belling, she rubbed her hands through the pelt of one of the animals, shaking its big ears, then raised her head to the major-domo as he approached, deferentially threading his way through the crowd around her.

"Yes, Maikril?" she said.

"The System Times photographer," the major-domo said quietly. He straightened as she rose, until he was looking up at her, his chin level with her bare shoulders.

"Admitting defeat?" She grinned.

"I believe so, ma'am. Requesting an audience."

She laughed. "So well put. How many did we get this time?"

The major-domo sidled a little closer, looking nervously at one of the hralzs when it snarled at him. "Thirty-two moving-picture cameras ma'am; over a hundred still."

She brought her mouth conspiratorially close to the major-domo's ear and said, "Not counting the ones we found on our guests."

"Quite, ma'am."

"I'll see . . . him? Her?"

"Him, ma'am."

"Him, later. Tell him ten minutes; remind me in twenty. West atrium." She glanced at the single platinum bracelet she wore. Recognizing her retinas, a tiny projector disguised as an emerald briefly displayed a holo plan of the old power station in twin cones of light aimed straight at her eyes.

"Certainly, ma'am," Maikril said.

She touched his arm and whispered, "We're heading over to the arboretum, all right?"

The major-domo's head barely moved to indicate he had heard. She turned regretfully to the people around her, her hands clasped as though in pleading. "I'm sorry. Will you all excuse me, just a moment?" She put her head to one side, smiling.

"Hi. Hello. Hi there. How are you." They walked quickly through the party, past the gray rainbows of drugstreams and the plashing pools of the wine fountains. She led, skirts rustling, while the major-domo struggled to keep up with her long-legged gait. She waved to those who greeted her; government ministers and their shadows, foreign dignitaries and attachés, media stars of all persuasions, revolutionaries and Navy brass, the captains of industry and commerce and their more extravagantly wealthy shareholders. The hralzs snapped perfunctorily at the heels of the major-domo, their claws skittering on the polished mica floor, all ungainly, then bounding forward when they encountered one of the many priceless rugs scattered throughout the turbine hall.

At the steps to the arboretum, hidden from the main hall by the easternmost dynamo housing, she paused, thanked the major-domo, shooed the hralzs away, patted her perfect hair, smoothed her already immaculately smooth gown and checked that the single white stone on the black choker was centered, which it was. She started down the steps toward the tall doors of the arboretum.

One of the hralzs whined from the top of the steps, bouncing up and down on its forelegs, eyes watering.

She looked back, annoyed. "Quiet, Bouncer! Away!"

The animal lowered its head and snuffled off.

She closed the double doors quietly behind her, taking in the quiet extent of luxuriant foliage the arboretum presented.

Outside the high crystal curve of the partial dome, the night was black. Small sharp lights burned on tall masts inside the arboretum, casting deep jagged shadows among the crowded plants. The air was warm and smelled of earth and sap. She breathed deeply and walked toward the far side of the enclosure.

"Hello there."

The man turned quickly to find her standing behind him, leaning against a light-mast, her arms crossed, a small smile on her lips and in her eyes. Her hair was blue-black, like her eyes; her skin was fawn and she looked slimmer than she did on newscasts, when for all her height she could seem stocky. He was tall and very slim and unfashionably pale, and most people would have thought his eyes were too close together.

He looked at the delicately patterned leaf he still held in one fragile-looking hand, then let it go, smiling uncertainly, and stepped out of the extravagantly flowered bush he'd been investigating. He rubbed his hands, looked bashful. "I'm sorry, I . . ." he gestured nervously.

"That's all right," she said, reaching out. They clasped hands. "You're Relstoch Sussepin, aren't you?"

"Umm . . . yes," he said, obviously surprised. He was still holding her hand. He realized this, and looked even more discomforted, quickly letting go.

"Diziet Sma." She bowed her head a little, very slowly,

letting her shoulder-length hair swing, keeping her eyes on him.

"Yes, I know, of course. Umm . . . pleased to meet you."

"Good," she nodded. "And I you. I've heard your work."

"Oh." He looked boyishly pleased and clapped his hands in a gesture he didn't seem to notice himself making. "Oh. That's very . . ."

"I didn't say that I liked it," she said, the smile hovering only on one side of her mouth now.

"Ah." Crestfallen.

So cruel. "But I do like it, very much," she said, and suddenly she was communicating amused—even conspiratorial—contrition through her expression.

He laughed and she felt something relax inside her. This was going to be all right.

"I did wonder why I'd been invited," he confessed, the deep-set eyes somehow bright. "Everybody here seems so . . ." he shrugged, " . . . important. That's why I . . ." he waved awkwardly behind him at the plant he'd been inspecting.

"You don't think composers should be regarded as important?" she asked, gently chiding.

"Well . . . compared to all these politicians and admirals and business people . . . in terms of power, I mean . . . And I'm not even a very well-known musician. I'd have thought Savntreig, or Khu, or . . ."

"They've composed their careers very well, certainly," she agreed.

He paused for a moment, then gave a small laugh and looked down. His hair was very fine, and glinted in the high mast light. It was her turn to fall in with his laugh. Maybe she ought to mention the commission now, rather than leaving it to their next meeting, when she would reduce the numbers—even if they were distant numbers, at the moment—to something a little more friendly . . . or even leaving it to a private rendezvous, later still, once she was sure he had been captivated.

How long should she spin this out? He was what she wanted, but it would mean so much more after a charged friendship; that long, exquisite exchange of gradually more intimate confidences, the slow accumulation of shared experiences, the languorous spiraling dance of attraction, coming and going and coming and going, winding closer and closer, until that laziness was sublimed in the engulfing heat of requital.

He looked her in the eyes, and said, "You flatter me, Ms. Sma."

She returned his gaze, raising her chin a little, acutely aware of each nuance in her carefully translated body language. There was an expression on his face she did not think so childish, now. His eyes reminded her of the stone on her bracelet. She felt a little light-headed, and took a deep breath.

"Ahem."

She froze.

The word had been pronounced from behind and to one side of her. She saw Sussepin's gaze falter and shift.

Sma kept her expression serene as she turned, then glared at the gray-white casing of the drone as though attempting to melt holes in it.

"*What?*" she said, in a voice that might have etched steel.

The drone was the size—and near enough the shape—of a small suitcase. It floated in toward her face.

"Trouble, toots," it said, then moved briskly to one side, angling its body so that it appeared to be contemplating the inky heights of sky beyond the crystal semisphere.

Sma looked down at the brick floor of the arboretum, her lips pursed. She allowed herself the tiniest of shakes of the head.

"Mr. Sussepin," she smiled, and spread her hands. "This pains me, but . . . will you . . . ?"

"Of course." He was already moving, and went quickly past, nodding once.

"Perhaps we can talk later," she said.

He turned, still backing off. "Yes; I'd . . . that would . . ." He seemed to lose inspiration, and nodded nervously again, walking quickly to the doors at the far end of the arboretum. He left without looking back.

Sma whirled round to the drone, which was now humming innocently and apparently staring into the depths of a gaudily colored flower, its stubby snout half buried in the bloom. It noticed her and looked up. She stood with legs apart, put one fist on her hip and said, " '*Toots?*' "

The drone's aura field flashed on; the mixture of purple

regret and gunmetal puzzlement looked distinctly unconvincing. "I don't know, Sma . . . just slipped out. Alliteration."

Sma kicked at a dead branch, fixed the drone with a glare and said, "Well?"

"You're not going to like this," the drone said quietly, retreating a little and going dark with sorrow.

Sma hesitated. She looked away for a moment, shoulders suddenly slumping. She sat down on one of the tree roots. The gown crumpled around her. "It's Zakalwe, isn't it?"

The drone flashed rainbow in surprise; so quickly—she thought—it might even have been genuine. "Good grief," it said. "How . . . ?"

She waved the question away. "I don't know. Tone of voice. Human intuition . . . Just that time again. Life was getting to be too much fun." She closed her eyes and rested her head against the rough dark trunk of the tree. "So?"

The drone Skaffen-Amtiskaw lowered itself to the same height as the woman's shoulder and floated near her. She looked at it.

"We need him back again," it told her.

"I sort of thought so," Sma sighed, flicking away an insect which had just landed on her shoulder.

"Well, yes. I'm afraid nothing else will work; it has to be him personally."

"Yeah, but does it have to be *me* personally?"

"That's . . . the consensus."

"Wonderful," Sma said sourly.

"You want the rest?"

"Does it get any better?"

"Not really."

"Hell," Sma clapped her hands on her lap and rubbed them up and down. "Might as well have it all at once."

"You would have to leave tomorrow."

"Aw drone, come *on*!" She buried her head in her hands. She looked up. The drone was fiddling with a twig. "You're kidding."

" 'Fraid not."

"What about all this?" She waved toward the turbine hall doors. "What about the peace conference? What about all the froth out there with their greased-up palms and their beady eyes? What about three years' work? What about an entire fucking planet . . . ?"

"The conference will go ahead."

"Oh sure, but what about this 'pivotal role' I was supposed to be playing?"

"Ah," said the drone, bringing the twig right up to the sensing band on the front of its casing, "well . . ."

"Oh no."

"Look, I know you don't like . . ."

"No, drone; it's not . . ." Sma got up suddenly and went to the edge of the crystal wall, looking out into the night.

"Dizzy . . ." the drone said, drifting closer.

"Don't you 'Dizzy' me."

"Sma . . . it isn't real. It's a stand-in; electronic, mechanical, electrochemical, chemical; a machine; a Mind-controlled machine, not alive in itself. Not a clone or . . ."

"I know what it is, drone," she said, clasping her hands behind her.

The drone floated closer to her, putting its fields to her shoulders, squeezing gently. She shook its grip off, looked down.

"We need your permission, Diziet."

"Yeah, I know that, too." She looked up for stars that were twice hidden, by cloud and by the lights of the arboretum.

"You can, of course, stay here if you want to." The drone's voice was heavy, remorseful. "The peace conference is certainly important; it needs . . . somebody to smooth things through. No doubt about that."

"And what's so goddamn crucial I have to high-tail it tomorrow?"

"Remember Voerenhutz?"

"I remember Voerenhutz," she said, voice flat.

"Well, the peace lasted forty years, but it's breaking down now. Zakalwe worked with a man called . . ."

"Maitchigh?" she frowned, half turning her head to the drone.

"Beychae. Tsoldrin Beychae. He became president of the Cluster following our involvement. While he was in power he held the political system together, but he retired eight years ago, long before he had to, to pursue a life of study and contemplation." The drone made a sighing noise. "Things have slipped back since, and at the moment Beychae lives on a planet whose leaders are subtly hostile to the forces Zakalwe and Beychae represented and we backed, and who are taking a leading part in the factionalizing of the group. There are several small conflicts under way and many more brewing; full-scale war involving the entire Cluster is, as they say, imminent.''

"And Zakalwe?''

"Basically, it's an Out. Down to the planet, convince Beychae he's needed, and at the very least get him to declare an interest. But it may mean a physical spring, and the added complication is Beychae may require a lot of convincing.''

Sma thought it through, still regarding the night. "No tricks we can play?''

"The two men know each other too well for anything other than the real Zakalwe to work . . . likewise Tsoldrin Beychae and the political machine throughout the entire system. Too many memories involved altogether.''

"Yeah," Sma said quietly. "Too many memories." She rubbed her bare shoulders, as though she was cold. "What about big guns?''

"We've a nebula fleet assembling; a core of one Limited System Vehicle and three General Contact Units stationed around the cluster itself, plus eighty or so GCUs keeping their tracks within a month's rush-in distance. There ought to be four or five GSVs within a two- to three-months' dash for the next year or so. But that's very, very much a last resort.''

"Megadeath figures looking a bit equivocal are they?'' Sma sounded bitter.

"If you want to put it that way," Skaffen-Amtiskaw said.

"Oh goddamn," Sma said quietly, closing her eyes. "So; how far away is Voerenhutz? I've forgotten.''

"Only about forty days, but we have to pick Zakalwe up first; say . . . ninety for the whole outward journey.''

She turned around. "Who's going to control the stand-in if the ship's taking me?'' Her gaze flicked skyward.

"The *Just Testing* will remain here in any event," the drone said. "The very fast picket *Xenophobe* has been put at your disposal. It can uplift tomorrow, a little after noon, earliest . . . should you wish.''

Sma stood still for a moment, feet together and arms crossed, her lips pursed and face pinched. Skaffen-Amtiskaw introspected for a moment, and decided it felt sorry for her.

The woman was immobile and silent for a few seconds;

then, abruptly, she was striding toward the turbine hall doors, heels clattering on the brick pathway.

The drone swooped after her, falling in at her shoulder.

"What I wish," Sma said, "is that you had a better sense of timing."

"I'm sorry. Did I interrupt something?"

"Not at all. And what the hell's a 'very fast picket' anyway?"

"New name for a (Demilitarized) Rapid Offensive Unit," the drone said.

She glanced at it. It wobbled, shrugging.

"It's supposed to sound better."

"And it's called the *Xenophobe*. Well that's just fine. Can the stand-in pick up immediately?"

"Noon tomorrow; can you debrief up to . . . ?"

"Tomorrow morning." Sma said, as the drone flicked round in front of her and sucked the tall doors open; she strode through and leapt up the steps into the turbine hall, skirts gathered in front of her. The hralzs came skidding round the corner from the hall and gathered yelping and bouncing around her. Sma stopped, while they milled around her, sniffing her hems and trying to lick her hands.

"No," she told the drone. "On second thoughts, scan me tonight, when I tell you. I'll get rid of this lot early if I can. I'm going to find Ambassador Onitnert now; have Maikril tell Chuzleis she's to get the minister over to the bar at turbine one in ten minutes. Make my apologies to the System Times hacks, have them taken back to the city and released; give them a bottle of nightflor each. Cancel the photographer, give him one still camera and let him take . . . sixty-four snaps, strictly full permission required. Have one of the male staff find Relstoch Sussepin and invite him to my apartments in two hours. Oh, and—"

Sma broke off suddenly and went down on her haunches to cradle the long snout of one of the whimpering hralzs in her hands. "Gainly, Gainly, I know, I know," she said, as the big-bellied animal keened and licked at her face. "I wanted to be here to see your babies born, but I can't . . ." she sighed, hugged the beast, then held its chin in one hand. "What am I to do, Gainly? I could have you put to sleep until I come back, and you'd never know . . . but all your friends would miss you."

"Have them all put to sleep," the drone suggested.

Sma shook her head. "You take care of them till I get back," she told the other hralz. "All right?" She kissed the animal's nose and got up. Gainly sneezed.

"Two other things, drone," Sma said, walking through the excited pack.

"What?"

"Don't call me 'Toots' again, all right?"

"All right. What else?"

They rounded the gleaming bulk of the long-stilled number six turbine, and Sma stopped for a moment, surveying the busy crowd in front of her, taking a deep breath and straightening her shoulders. She was already smiling as she started forward and said quietly to the drone, "I don't want the stand-in screwing anybody."

"Okay," the drone said as they went toward the partying people. "It is, after all, in a sense, your body."

"That's just it, drone," Sma said, nodding to a waiter, who scurried forward, drinks tray proffered. "It *isn't* my body."

Aircraft and ground vehicles floated and wound away from the old power station. The important people had departed. There were a few stragglers left in the hall, but they didn't need her. She felt weary, and glanded a little *snap* to lift the mood.

From the south balcony of the apartments fashioned from the station's admin block, she looked down to the deep valley and the line of taillights strung out along Riverside Drive. An aircraft whistled overhead, banking and disappearing over the tall curved lip of the old dam. She watched the plane go, then turned toward the penthouse doors, taking off the small formal jacket and slinging it over her shoulder.

Music was playing, deep inside the sumptuous suite beneath the roof garden. She headed instead for the study, where Skaffen-Amtiskaw was waiting.

The scan to update the stand-in took only a couple of minutes. She came round with the usual feeling of dislocation, but it passed quickly enough. She kicked off her shoes and padded through the soft dark corridors toward the music.

Relstoch Sussepin drew himself out of the seat he'd been

occupying, still holding a softly glowing glass of nightflor. Sma stopped in the doorway.

"Thank you for staying," she said, dropping the little jacket onto a couch.

"That's all right." He brought the glass of glowing drink toward his lips, then seemed to think the better of it, and cradled it in both hands instead. "What, ah . . . was there anything, in particular you . . . ?"

Sma smiled, somehow sadly, and put both hands on the wings of a big revolving chair, which she stood behind. She looked down at the hide cushion. "Perhaps, now, I'm flattering myself," she said. "But, not to put too fine a point on it . . ." She looked up at him. "Would you like to fuck?"

Relstoch Sussepin stood stock still. After a while he raised the glass to his lips and took a long slow drink, then brought the glass slowly back down again. "Yes," he said. "Yes, I wanted to . . . instantly."

"There's only tonight," she said, holding up one hand. "Just tonight. It's difficult to explain, but from tomorrow onward . . . for maybe half a year or more, I'm going to be incredibly busy; two-places-at-once sort of busy, you know?"

He shrugged. "Sure. Anything you say."

Sma relaxed then, and a smile grew gradually on her face. She pushed the big chair round and slid the bracelet from her wrist to let it fall into the seat. Then she gently unbuttoned the top of her gown, and stood there.

Sussepin drained his glass, placed it on a shelf, and walked toward her.

"Lights," she whispered.

The lights slowly dimmed, right down, until eventually the softly glowing dregs of the finished drink made the glass on the shelf the brightest thing in the room.

XIII

"Wake up."
He woke up.

Dark. He straightened, beneath the covers, wondering who had talked to him like that. Nobody talked to him in that tone, not anymore; even half asleep, coming unexpectedly awake in what must be the middle of the night, he heard something in that tone he hadn't heard for two, maybe three decades. Impertinence. Lack of respect.

He brought his head out of the sheltering cover, into the warm air of the room, and looked round in the one-light gloom, to see who had dared address him like that. An instant of fear—had somebody got past the guards and security screens?—was replaced by a furious hunger to see who had the effrontery to speak like that to him.

The intruder sat in a chair just beyond the end of the bed. He looked odd in a way which was itself odd; a very new sort of unusualness, unplaceable, even alien. He gave the impression of being a slightly skewed projection. The clothes looked strange too; baggy, brightly colored, even in the dim light of the bedside lamp. The man was dressed like a clown or a jester, but his somehow too symmetrical face looked . . .

grim? Contemptuous? That . . . *foreignness* made it difficult to tell.

He started to grope for his glasses, but it was just sleep in his eyes. The surgeons had given him new eyes five years ago, but sixty years of shortsightedness had left him with an ingrained reaction to reach for glasses which were not there, whenever he first woke up. A small price to pay, he had always thought, and now, with the new retro-aging treatment . . . The sleep cleared from his eyes. He sat up, looking at the man in the chair, and began to think he was having a dream, or seeing a ghost.

The man looked young; he had a broad, tanned face and black hair tied back behind his head, but thoughts of spirits and the dead came into his head not because of that. It was something about the dark, pit-like eyes, and the alien set of that face.

"Good evening, Ethnarch." The young man's voice was slow and measured. It sounded, somehow, like the voice of someone much older; old enough to make the Ethnarch feel suddenly young in comparison. It chilled him. He looked around the room. Who was this man? How had he got in here? The palace was meant to be impregnable. There were guards everywhere. What was going on? The fear came back.

The girl from the previous evening lay still on the far side of the wide bed, just a lump under the covers. A couple of dormant screens on the wall to the Ethnarch's left reflected the bedside light's weak glow.

He was frightened, but fully awake now and thinking quickly. There was a gun concealed in the bed's headboard; the man at the end of the bed didn't seem to be armed (but then why was he here?). But the gun represented a desperate last resort. The voice code was the thing. The mikes and cameras in the room were on standby, their automatic circuits waiting for a specific sentence to activate them; sometimes he wanted privacy in here, other times he wanted to record something only for himself, and of course he'd always known there was a possibility that somebody unauthorized might get in here, no matter how tight the security was.

He cleared his throat. "Well, well, this is a surprise." His voice was even, he sounded calm.

He smiled thinly, pleased with himself. His heart—the heart of an athletic young anarchist woman up until eleven

years ago—was beating quickly, but not worryingly so. He
nodded. "This *is* a surprise," he repeated. There; it was
done. An alarm would already be ringing in the basement
control room; the guards would come piling through the door
in a few seconds. Or they might not risk that, and instead
release the ceiling gas cylinders, blasting them both into un-
consciousness in a blinding fog. There was a danger that
would rupture his eardrums (he thought, swallowing), but he
could always take a new pair from a healthy dissident. Maybe
he wouldn't even have to do that; the rumor was that the
retro-aging might include the possibility of body parts regrowing. Well, nothing wrong with strength in depth; back-
ups. He liked the feeling of security that gave one. "Well,
well," he heard himself say, just in case the circuits hadn't
picked up the code first or second time round, "this is indeed
a surprise." The guards should be here any second . . .

The brightly dressed young man smiled. He flexed oddly,
and leaned forward until his elbows rested on the top of the
bed's ornate footboard. His lips moved, to produce what
might have been a smile. He reached into one pocket of the
baggy pantaloons and produced a small black gun. He pointed
it straight at the Ethnarch and said, "Your code won't work,
Ethnarch Kerian. There won't be any more surprises that
you're expecting and I'm not. The basement security center
is as dead as everything else."

The Ethnarch Kerian stared at the little gun. He'd seen
water pistols that looked more impressive. *What is going on?
Can he really have come to kill me?* The man certainly didn't
dress like an assassin, and surely any serious assassin would
just have killed him in his sleep. The longer this fellow sat
here, talking, the more danger he was in, whether he had
knocked out the links to the security center or not. So he
might be mad, but he probably wasn't an assassin. It was
simply ludicrous that a real, professional assassin would behave like this, and only an extremely able and completely
professional assassin could have penetrated the palace security . . . Thus, the Ethnarch Kerian tried to convince his suddenly wildly beating, mutinous heart. Where *were* the damn
guards? He thought again about the gun hidden in the ornamental headboard behind him.

The young man folded his arms, so that the little gun was

no longer pointing at the Ethnarch. "Mind if I tell you a little story?"

He must be mad. "No; no; why don't you tell me a story?" the Ethnarch said, in his most friendly and avuncular voice. "What's your name, by the way; you appear to have the advantage over me."

"Yes, I do, don't I?" the old voice from the young lips said. "Actually there are two stories, but you know most of one of them. I'll tell them at the same time; see if you can tell which is which."

"I—"

"Ssh," the man said, putting the little gun to his lips.

The Ethnarch half glanced at the girl on the other side of the bed. He realized he and the intruder had been talking in quite low tones. Maybe if he could get the girl to wake, she might draw his fire, or at least distract him while he grabbed for the gun in the headboard; he was faster than he had been for twenty years, thanks to the new treatment . . . *where the hell were those guards*?

"Now look here, young man!" he roared. "I just want to know what you think you're doing here! Eh?"

His voice—a voice that had filled halls and squares, without amplification—echoed through the room. Dammit, the guards in the basement security center ought to be able to hear it without any microphones. The girl on the other side of the bed didn't even stir.

The young man was smirking. "They're all asleep, Ethnarch. There's just you and me. Now; this story . . ."

"What . . ." the Ethnarch Kerian gulped, drawing his legs up under the covers. "What *are* you here for?"

The intruder looked mildly surprised. "Oh, I'm here to take you out, Ethnarch. You are going to be removed. Now . . ." he laid the gun on the broad top of the bed footboard. The Ethnarch stared at it. It was too far away for him to grab, but . . .

"The story," the intruder said, settling back in the chair. "Once upon a time, over the gravity well and far away, there was a magical land where they had no kings, no laws, no money and no property, but where everybody lived like a prince, was very well-behaved and lacked for nothing. And these people lived in peace, but they were bored, because paradise can get that way after a time, and so they started to carry out missions of good works; charitable visits upon the less well-off, you might say; and they always tried to bring with them the thing that they saw as the most precious gift of all; knowledge; information; and as wide a spread of that information as possible, because these people were strange, in that they despised rank, and hated kings . . . and all things hierarchic . . . even Ethnarchs.'' The young man smiled thinly. So did the Ethnarch. He wiped his brow and shifted back a little in the bed, as though getting more comfortable. Heart still pounding.

''Well, for a time, a terrible force threatened to take away their good works, but they resisted it, and they won, and came out of the conflict stronger than before, and if they had not been so unconcerned with power for its own sake, they would have been terribly feared, but as it was they were only slightly feared, just as a matter of course given the scale of their power. And one of the ways it amused them to wield that power was to interfere in societies they thought might benefit from the experience, and one of the most efficient ways of doing that in a lot of societies is to get to the people at the top.

''Many of their people become physicians to great leaders, and with medicines and treatments that seem like magic to the comparatively primitive people they're dealing with, ensure that a great and good leader has a better chance of surviving. That's the way they prefer to work; offering life, you see, rather than dealing death. You might call them soft, because they're very reluctant to kill, and they might agree with you, but they're soft the way the ocean is soft, and, well; ask any sea captain how harmless and puny the ocean can be.''

''Yes, I see,'' the Ethnarch said, sitting back a little further, shifting a pillow into place behind his back, and checking just where he was in relation to the section of headboard that concealed the gun. His heart was thrashing in his chest.

''Another thing they do, these people, another way they deal in life rather than death, is they offer leaders of certain societies below a certain technological level the one thing all the wealth and power those leaders command cannot buy them; a cure for death. A return to youth.''

The Ethnarch stared at the young man, suddenly more intrigued than terrified. Did he mean the retro-aging?

"Ah; it's starting to click into place now, isn't it?" the young man smiled. "Well, you're right. Just that process that you've been going through, Ethnarch Kerian. Which you've been paying for, this last year. Which you did—if you re-member—promise to pay for with more than just platinum. *Do* you remember, hmmm?"

"I . . . I'm not sure." The Ethnarch Kerian stalled. He could see the panel in the headboard where the gun was from the corner of his eye.

"You promised to stop the killings in Youricam, remember?"

"I may have said I'd review our segregation and resettlement policy in the—"

"No," the young man waved his hand, "I mean the kill-ings, Ethnarch; the death trains, remember? The trains where the exhaust comes out of the rear carriage, eventually." The young man made a sort of sneer with his mouth, shook his head. "Trigger any memories, that? No?"

"I have no idea what you're talking about," the Ethnarch said. His palms were sweating, cold and slick. He rubbed them on the bedclothes; the gun mustn't slip, if he got to it. The intruder's gun was still lying on the bed's footboard.

"Oh, I think you do. In fact, I know you do."

"If there have been any excesses by any members of the security forces, they will be thoroughly—"

"This isn't a press conference, Ethnarch." The man tipped slightly back in his seat, away from the gun on the footboard. The Ethnarch tensed, quivering.

"The point is, you made a deal and then didn't stick to it. And I'm here to collect on the penalty clause. You were warned, Ethnarch. That which is given can also be taken away." The intruder tipped further back in his seat, glanced around the dark suite, and nodded at the Ethnarch, while putting his hands clasped behind his head. "Say goodbye to all this, Ethnarch Kerian. You're—"

The Ethnarch turned, banged the hidden panel with his elbow, and the section of headboard flicked round; he tore the gun from its clips and swung it at the man, finding the trigger and pulling.

Nothing happened. The young man was watching him, hands still behind his neck, body rocking slowly back and forward in the chair.

The Ethnarch clicked the trigger a few more times.

"Works better with these," the man said, reaching into a shirt pocket, and throwing a dozen bullets onto the bed at the Ethnarch's feet.

The gleaming bullets snicked as they rolled and gathered in a fold in the bedclothes. The Ethnarch Kerian stared at them.

". . . I'll give you anything," he said, over a thick and dry tongue. He sensed his bowels start to relax, and squeezed desperately, feeling suddenly like a child again, as though the retro-aging had taken him even further back. "Anything. Anything. I can give you more than you ever dreamed of; I can—"

"Not interested in that," the man said, shaking his head. "The story isn't finished yet. You see, these people; these nice kind people who are so soft and prefer to deal in life . . . when somebody goes back on a deal with them, even when somebody kills after they've said they wouldn't, they still don't like to kill in return. They'd rather use their magic and their precious compassion to do the next best thing. And so people disappear."

The man sat forward again, leaning on the footboard. The Ethnarch stared, shaking, at him.

"They—these nice people—they disappear bad people," the young man said. "And they employ people to come and collect these bad men and take them away. And these people—these collectors—they like to put the fear of death into their collectees, and they tend to dress . . ." he gestured at his own colorfully motley clothes, ". . . casually; and of course—thanks to the magic—they never have any problems getting into even the most heavily guarded palace."

The Ethnarch swallowed, and with one furiously shaking hand, finally put down the useless gun he was holding.

"Wait," he said, trying to control his voice. His sweat soaked the sheets. "Are you saying—"

"We're nearly at the end of the story," the young man interrupted. "These nice people—who you would call soft, like I say—they remove the bad people, and they take them away. They put them somewhere they can't do any harm. Not a paradise, but not somewhere that feels like a prison, either. And these bad people, they might have to listen sometimes to the nice people telling them how bad they've been, and they never again get the chance to change histories, but they live a comfortable, safe life, and they die peacefully . . . thanks to the nice people.

"And though some would say the nice people are too soft, the soft, nice people would say that the crimes committed by the bad people are usually so terrible there is no known way of making the bad people start to suffer even a millionth of the agony and despair they have produced, so what is the point in retribution? It would be just another obscenity to cap the tyrant's life with his own death." The young man looked briefly troubled, then shrugged. "Like I say; some people would say they're too soft." He took the little gun from the footboard and put it into a pocket of his pantaloons.

The man stood slowly. The Ethnarch's heart still pounded, but in his eyes there were tears.

The young man leaned down, picked up some clothes and threw them at the Ethnarch, who grabbed at them, held them to his chest.

"My offer stands," the Ethnarch Kerian said. "I can give you—"

"Job satisfaction," the young man sighed, staring at one set of fingernails. "That's all you can give me, Ethnarch. I'm not interested in anything else. Get dressed; you're leaving."

The Ethnarch started to pull on his shirt. "Are you sure? I believe I have invented some new vices even the old Empire didn't know about. I'd be willing to share them with you."

"No, thank you."

"Who are these people you're talking about, anyway?" The Ethnarch fastened his buttons. "And may I yet know your name?"

"Just get dressed."

"Well, I still think we can come to some sort of arrangement . . ." The Ethnarch secured his collar. "And this is all really quite ridiculous, but I suppose I ought to be thankful you're not an assassin, eh?"

The young man smiled, seemed to pick something from a fingernail. He put his hands in the pantaloon pockets as the Ethnarch kicked the bedclothes down and picked up his britches.

"Yes," the young man said. "Must be rather awful, thinking you're about to die."

"Not the most pleasant experience," agreed the Ethnarch, putting one leg, then another, into his trousers.

"But such a relief, I imagine, when you get the reprieve."

"Hmm." The Ethnarch gave a small laugh.

"A bit like being rounded up in a village and thinking
you're going to be shot . . ." the young man mused, facing
the Ethnarch from the foot of the bed. ". . . and then being
told your fate is nothing worse than resettlement." He smiled.
The Ethnarch hesitated.

"Resettled; by train," the man said, taking the little black
gun out of his pocket. "By a train which contains your family; your street; your village . . ."

The young man adjusted something on the small black
gun. ". . . And then ends up containing nothing but engine
fumes, and lots of dead people." He smiled, thinly. "What
do you think, Ethnarch Kerian? Something like that?"

The Ethnarch stopped moving, staring wide-eyed at the
gun.

"The nice people are called the Culture," the young man
explained. "And I always did think they were too soft." He
stretched his arm out, holding the gun. "I stopped working
for them some time ago. I'm freelance now."

The Ethnarch looked, speechless, into the dark, ancient
eyes above the barrel of the black gun.

"I," said the man, "am called Cheradenine Zakalwe."
He leveled the gun at the Ethnnarch's nose. "You are called
dead."

He fired the gun.

. . . The Ethnarch had put his head back and started to
scream; so the single shot pierced the roof of his mouth before it exploded inside his skull.

Brains splattered over the ornate headboard. The body
thumped into the skin-soft bedclothes and twitched once,
spreading blood.

He watched the blood as it pooled. He blinked, a couple of
times.

Then, moving slowly, he peeled off the gaudy clothes. He
put them in a small black rucksack. Underneath, the one-
piece suit was shadow-dark.

He took the mat-black mask from the rucksack and put it

round his neck, though not yet over his face. He moved to the head of the bed and peeled a little transparent patch from the neck of the sleeping girl, then went back into the dark depths of the room, slipping the mask over his face as he did so.

Using the nightsight, he unclipped the panel over the security systems control unit, and carefully removed several small boxes. Then, walking very softly and slowly now, he crossed to the wall-sized pornographic painting which concealed the door to the Ethnarch's emergency escape route to the sewers and the palace roof.

He turned back, before he slowly closed the door, and looked at the bloody mess on the curved carved surface of the headboard. He smiled his thin smile, a little uncertainly.

Then he slipped away into the stone-black depths of the palace, like a piece of the night.

2

The dam lay wedged between the tree-studded hills like a fragment from some enormous shattered cup. The morning sunshine shone up the valley, hit the concave gray face of the dam, and produced a white reflecting flood of light. Behind the dam, the long diminished lake was dark and cold. The water came less than halfway up the massive concrete bulwark, and the forests beyond had long since reclaimed over half the slopes the dam's rising water had once drowned. Sailboats lay tethered to jetties strung along one side of the lake, the chopping waters slapping at their glistening hulls.

High overhead, birds carved the air, circling in the warmth of the sunlight above the shadow of the dam. One of the birds dipped and swooped, gliding down toward the lip of the dam and the deserted roadway which ran along its curved summit. The bird pulled its wings in just as it seemed it was about to collide with the white railings which ran on either side of the road; it flashed between the dew-sparkled stanchions, executed a half roll, partially opened its wings again, and plummeted toward the obsolete power station that had become the grandly eccentric—not to mention pointedly symbolic—home of the woman called Diziet Sma.

The bird settled belly-down to the swoop, and, level with

the roof garden, flung out its wings, grasping at the air and fluttering to a precipitous halt, talons tacketing down on a window ledge set in the highest story of the old admin block apartments.

Wings folded, soot-dark head to one side, one beady eye reflecting the concrete light, the bird hopped forward to a slid-open window, where soft red curtains rippled out into the breeze. It stuck its head under the fluttering hem of the material and peered into the darkened room beyond.

"You missed it." Sma said with quiet scorn, happening to pad past the window just at that moment. She sipped from a glass of water she held. Droplets from her shower beaded her tawny body.

The bird's head swiveled, following her as she crossed to the closet and commenced to dress. Swiveling back, the bird's gaze shifted to the male body lying in the air a little less than a meter above the floor-mounted bed-base. Inside the dim haze of the bed's AG field, the pale figure of Relstoch Sussepin stirred, and rolled over in midair. His arms floated out to either side, until the weak centering field on his side of the bed brought them slowly back in toward his body again. In the dressing room, Sma gargled with some water, then swallowed it.

Fifty meters east, Skaffen-Amtiskaw floated high in the air above the floor of the turbine hall, surveying the wreckage of the party. The section of the drone's mind that was controlling the guard-drone disguised as a bird took a last look at the filigree of scratches on Sussepin's buttocks, and the already fading bitemarks on Sma's shoulders (as she covered them with a gauzy shirt), and then released the guard-drone from its control.

The bird squawked, jumped back from the curtain, and fell fluttering and frenzied off the ledge, before opening its wings and beating back up past the gleaming face of the dam, its shrill alarm-cries echoing back from the concrete slopes and disturbing it further. Sma heard the distant feedback of commotion as she buttoned her waistcoat, and smiled.

"Good night's sleep?" Skaffen-Amtiskaw inquired as it met her at the portico of the old admin block.

"Good night, no sleep," Sma yawned, shooing the whin-

ing hralzs back into the building's marble hall, where Maikril
the major-domo stood unhappily with a bunch of leads. She
stepped out into the sunlight, pulling on gloves. The drone
held the car door open for her. She filled her lungs with the
fresh morning air and ran down the steps, boot heels clattering. She jumped into the car, winced a little as she settled in
the driver's seat, then flicked a switch that started the roof
folding back, while the drone loaded her luggage into the
trunk. She tapped the battery gauges on the vehicle's dash
and blipped the accelerator, just to feel the wheel motors
strain against the brakes. The drone secured the trunk and
floated into the rear seats. She waved to Maikril, who was
chasing one of the hralzs along the steps outside the turbine
hall, and didn't notice. Sma laughed, stood on the throttle
and slipped the brakes.

The car leapt off in a spray of gravel, took the right-
hander beneath the trees with centimeters to spare, shot out
through the station's granite gates with a farewell shimmy of
its rear end, and accelerated hard down Riverside Drive.

"We could have flown," the drone pointed out, over the
rush of air.

But it suspected Sma wasn't listening.

The semantics of fortification were pan-cultural, she thought,
as she descended the stone steps from the curtain wall of the
castle, gazing up at the drum-shaped keep, hazy in the distance on its hill behind several more layers of walls. She
walked across the grass, Skaffen-Amtiskaw at her shoulder,
and exited the fort through a postern.

The view led down to the new port and the straits, where
sea ships passed smoothly in the late morning sunlight, heading for ocean or inland sea, according to their lanes. From
the other side of the castle complex, the city revealed its
presence with a distant rumble and—because the light wind
came from that direction—the smell of . . . well, she just
thought of it as City, after three years here. She supposed all
cities smelled different, though.

Diziet Sma sat on the grass with her legs drawn up to her
chin, and looked out across the straits and their arching suspension bridges to the sub-continent on the far shore.

"Anything else?" the drone asked.

"Yeah; take my name off the judging panel for the Academy show . . . and send a stalling letter to that Petrain guy." She frowned in the sunlight, shading her eyes. "Can't think of anything else."

The drone moved in front of her, teasing a small flower from the grass in front of her and playing with it. "*Xenophobe*'s just entered the system," it told her.

"Well happy days," Sma said sourly. She wetted one finger and rubbed a little speck of dirt from the toe of one boot.

"And that young man in your bed just surfaced; asking Maikril where you've got to."

Sma said nothing, though her shoulders shook once and she smiled. She lay back on the grass, one arm behind her.

The sky was aquamarine, stroked with clouds. She could smell the grass, and taste the scent of small, crushed flowers. She looked back up over her forehead at the gray-black wall towering behind her, and wondered if the castle had ever been attacked on days like this. Did the sky seem so limitless, the waters of the straits so fresh and clean, the flowers so bright and fragrant, when men fought and screamed, hacked and staggered and fell and watched their blood mat the grass?

Mists and dusk, rain and lowering cloud seemed the better background; clothes to cover the shame of battle.

She stretched, suddenly tired, and shivered with a little flashback of the night's exertions. And, like somebody holding something precious, and it slipping from their fingers, but them having the speed and the skill to catch it again before it hit the floor, she was able—somewhere inside herself—to dip down and retrieve the vanishing memory as it slipped back into the clutter and noise of her mind, and glanding *recall* she held it, savored it, reexperienced it, until she felt herself shiver again in the sunlight, and came close to making a little moaning noise.

She let the memory escape, and coughed and sat up, glancing to see if the drone had noticed. It was nearby, collecting tiny flowers.

A party of what she guessed where schoolchildren came chattering and squealing up the path from the metro station, heading toward the postern. Heading and tailing the noisy column were adults, possessed of that air of calmly tired wariness she'd seen before in teachers and mothers with many children. Some of the kids pointed at the floating drone as they passed, wide-eyed and giggling and asking questions, before they were ushered through the narrow gate, voices disappearing.

It was, she'd noticed, always the children who made a fuss like that. Adults just assumed that there was some trick behind the apparently unsupported body of the machine, but children wanted to know how it worked. One or two scientists and engineers had looked startled, too, but she guessed a stereotype of unworldiness meant nobody believed them that there must be something odd going on. Antigravity was what was going on, and the drone in this society was like a flashlight in the stone age, but—to her surprise—it was almost disappointingly easy just to brazen it out.

"The ships just met up," the drone informed her. "They're transferring the stand-in for real, rather than displacing it."

Sma laughed, plucked a blade of grass and sucked on it. "Old *JT* really doesn't trust its displacer, does it?"

"I think the thing's senile, myself," the drone said sniffily. It was carefully slicing holes in the barely more than hair-thin stems of the flowers it had picked, then threading the stems through each other, creating a little chain.

Sma watched the machine, its unseen fields manipulating the little blossoms as dexterously as any lace-maker flicking a pattern into existence.

It was not always so refined.

Once, maybe twenty years ago, far away on another planet in another part of the galaxy altogether, on the floor of a dry sea forever scoured by howling winds, beneath the mesa that had been islands on the dust that had been silt, she had lodged in a small frontier town at the limit of the railway's reach, preparatory to hiring mounts to venture into the deep desert and search out the new child messiah.

At dusk, the riders came into the square, to take her from the inn; they'd heard her strangely colored skin alone would fetch a handsome price.

The innkeeper made the mistake of trying to reason with the men, and was pinned to his own door with a sword; his daughters wept over him before they were dragged away.

Sma turned, sickened, from the window, heard boots thunder on the rickety stairs. Skaffen-Amtiskaw was near the door. It looked, unhurried at her. Screams came from the square outside and from elsewhere inside the inn. Somebody battered at the door of her room, loosing dust and shaking the floor. Sma was wide-eyed, bereft of stratagems.

She stared at the drone. "Do something," she gulped.

"My pleasure," murmured Skaffen-Amtiskaw.

The door burst open, slamming against the mud wall. Sma flinched. The two black-cloaked men filled the doorway. She could smell them. One strode in toward her, sword out, rope in the other hand, not noticing the drone at one side.

"Excuse me," said Skaffen-Amtiskaw.

The man glanced at the machine, without breaking stride.

Then he wasn't there anymore, and dust filled the room, and Sma's ears were ringing, and pieces of mud and paper were falling from the ceiling and fluttering through the air, and there was a large hole straight through the wall into the next room, across from where Skaffen-Amtiskaw—seemingly defying the law concerning action/reaction—hovered in exactly the same place as before. A woman shrieked hysterically in the room through the hole, where what was left of the man was embedded in the wall above her bed, his blood spattered copiously over ceiling, floor, walls, bed and her.

The second man whirled into the room, discharging a long gun point-blank at the drone; the bullet became a flat coin of metal a centimeter in front of the machine's snout, and clunked to the floor. The man unsheathed and swung his sword in one flashing movement, scything at the drone through the dust and smoke. The blade broke cleanly on a bump of red-colored field just above the machine's casing, then the man was lifted off his feet.

Sma was crouched down in one corner, dust in her mouth and hands at her ears, listening to herself scream.

The man thrashed wildly in the center of the room for a second, then he was a blur through the air above her, there was another colossal pulse of sound, and a ragged aperture appeared in the wall over her head, beside the window looking out to the square. The floorboards jumped and dust choked her. "Stop!" she screamed. The wall above the hole cracked and the ceiling creaked and bowed down, releasing lumps of mud and straw. Dust clogged her mouth and nose and she struggled to her feet, almost throwing herself out of the window in her desperate attempt to find air. "Stop," she croaked, coughing dust.

The drone floated smoothly to her side, wafting dust away from Sma's face with a field-plane, and supporting the sagging ceiling with a slender column. Both field components were shaded deep red, the color of drone pleasure. "There, there," Skaffen-Amtiskaw said to her, patting her back, Sma choked and spluttered from the window and stared horrified at the square below.

The body of the second man lay like a sodden red sack under a cloud of dust in the midst of the riders. While they were still staring, before most of the raiders could raise their swords, and before the innkeeper's daughters—being lashed to two of the mounts by their captors—realized what the almost unrecognizable lump on the ground in front of them was and started screaming again, something thrummed past Sma's shoulder and darted down toward the men.

One of the warriors roared, brandishing his sword and lunging toward the door of the inn.

He managed two steps. He was still roaring when the knife missile flicked past him, field outstretched.

It separated his neck from his shoulders. The roar turned to a sound like the wind, bubbling thickly through the exposed windpipe as his body crashed to the dust.

Faster—and turning more tightly—than any bird or insect, the knife missile made an almost invisibly quick circle round most of the riders, producing an odd stuttering noise.

Seven of the riders—five standing, two still mounted—collapsed into the dust, in fourteen separate pieces. Sma tried to scream at the drone, to make the missile stop, but she was still choking, and now starting to retch. The drone patted her back. "There, there," it said, concernedly. In the square, both of the innkeeper's daughters slipped to the ground from the mounts they had been tied to, their bonds slashed in the same cut that had killed all seven men. The drone gave a little shudder of satisfaction.

One man dropped his sword and started to run. The knife missile plunged straight through him. It curved like red light shining on a hook, and slashed across the necks of the last two dismounted riders, felling both. The mount of the final rider was rearing up in front of the missile, its fangs bared, forelegs lashing, claws exposed. The device went through its neck and straight into the face of its rider.

On emerging from the resulting detonation, the machine

slammed to a stop in midair, while the rider's headless body slid off his collapsing, thrashing animal. The knife missile spun slowly about, seemingly reviewing its few seconds' work, then it started to float back toward the window.

The innkeeper's daughters had fainted.

Sma vomited.

The frenzied mounts leapt and screamed and ran about the courtyard, a couple of them dragging bits of their riders with them.

The knife missile swooped and butted one of the hysterical mounts on the head, just as the animal was about to trample the two girls lying still in the dust, then the tiny machine dragged them both out of the carnage, toward the doorway where their father's body lay.

Finally, the sleek, spotless little device rose gently to the window—daintily avoiding Sma's projected bile—and snicked back into the drone's casing.

"Bastard!" Sma tried to punch the drone, then kick it, then picked up a small chair and smashed it against the drone's body. "Bastard! You fucking murderous *bastard*!"

"Sma," the drone said reasonably, not moving in the slowly settling maelstrom of dust, and still holding the ceiling up. "You said do something."

"Meatfucker!" She smashed a table across its back.

"Ms. Sma; language!"

"You split-prick shit, I told you to *stop*!"

"Oh. Did you? I didn't quite catch that. Sorry."

She stopped then, hearing the utter lack of concern in the machine's voice. She thought very clearly that she had a choice here; she could collapse weeping and sobbing and not get over this for a long time, and maybe never be out of the shadow of the contrast between the drone's cool and her breakdown; or.

She took a deep breath, *calmed* herself.

She walked up to the drone and said quietly, "All right; this time . . . you get away with it. Enjoy it when you play it back." She put one hand flat on the drone's side. "Yeah; enjoy. But if you ever do anything like that again . . ." she slapped its flank softly and whispered, "you're ore, understand?"

"Absolutely," said the drone.

"Slag; components; motherjunk."

"Oh, please, no," Skaffen-Amtiskaw sighed.

"I'm serious. You use minimum force from now on. Understand? Agree?"

"Both."

She turned, picked up her bag and headed for the door, glancing once into the adjoining room through the hole the first man had made. The woman in there had fled. The man's body was still cratered into the wall, blood like rays of ejecta.

Sma looked back to the machine, and spat on the floor.

"The *Xenophobe*'s heading this way," Skaffen-Amtiskaw said, suddenly there in front of her, its body shining in the sunlight. "Here." It stretched a field out, offering her the little chain of bright flowers it had made.

Sma bowed toward it; the machine slipped the chain over her head like a necklace. She stood up and they went back into the castle.

The very top of the keep was out of bounds to the public; it bristled with aerials and masts and a couple of slowly revolving radar units. Two floors below, once the tour party had disappeared round the curve of the gallery, Sma and the machine stopped at a thick metal door. The drone used its electromagnetic effector to disable the door's alarm and open the electronic lock, then inserted a field into a mechanical lock, jiggled the tumblers and swung the door wide. Sma slipped through, immediately followed by the machine, which relocked the door. They ascended to the broad, cluttered roof, beneath the vault of turquoise sky; a tiny scout missile the drone had sent ahead sidled up to the machine and was taken back inside.

"When's it get here?" Sma said, listening to the warm wind hum through the jagged spaces of the aerials around her.

"It's over there," Skaffen-Amtiskaw said, jabbing forward. She looked in the direction it had indicated, and could just make out the spare, curved outline of a four-person module, sitting nearby; it was giving a very good impression of being transparent.

Sma looked around the forest of masts and stays for a

moment, the wind ruffling her hair, then shook her head. She walked to the module-shape, momentarily dizzied by the sensation that there wasn't anything there, then that there was. A door swung up from the module's side, revealing the interior as though opening a passageway into another world, which was—in a sense, she supposed—exactly what it was doing.

She and the drone entered. "Welcome aboard, Ms. Sma," said the module.

"Hello."

The door closed. The module tipped back on its rear end, like a predator preparing to pounce. It waited a moment for a flock of birds to clear the airspace a hundred meters above, then it was gone, powering into the air. Watching from the ground—if they hadn't blinked at the wrong moment—a very keen-eyed observer might just have seen a column of trembling air flick skyward from the summit of the keep, but would have heard nothing; even in high supersonic the module could move more quietly than any bird, displacing tissue-thin layers of air immediately ahead of it, moving into the vacuum so created, and replacing the gases in the skin-thin space it had left behind; a falling feather produced more turbulence.

Standing in the module, gazing at the main screen, Sma watched the view beneath the module shrink rapidly, as the concentric layers of the castle's defenses came crashing in like time-reversed waves from the edges of the screen; the castle became a dot between the city and the straits, and then the city itself disappeared and the view began to tip as the module angled out for its rendezvous with the very fast picket *Xenophobe*.

Sma sat down, still watching the screen, eyes searching in vain for the valley on the outskirts of the city where the dam and the old power station lay.

The drone watched too, while it signaled to the waiting ship and received confirmation the vessel had displaced Sma's luggage out of the trunk of the car and into the woman's quarters on board.

Skaffen-Amtiskaw studied Sma, as she stared—a little glumly, it thought—at the hazing-over view on the module screen, and wondered when the best time would be to give her the rest of the bad news.

Because, despite all this wonderful technology, somehow (incredibly; uniquely, as far as the drone knew . . . how in the name of chaos did a lump of meat outwit and destroy a *knife missile*?), the man called Cheradenine Zakalwe had shaken off the tail they'd put on him after he'd resigned the last time.

So, before they did anything else, Sma and it had to find the damn human first. If they could.

The figure slipped from behind a radar housing and crossed the keep's roof, beneath the wind-moaning aerials. It went down the spiral of steps, checked all was clear beyond the thick metal door, then opened it.

A minute later, something that looked exactly like Diziet Sma joined the tour party, while the guide was explaining how developments in artillery, heavier-than-air flight and rocketry had made the ancient fortress obsolete.

XII

They shared their eyrie with the state coach of the Mytho-clast, a cluttered army of statues, and a jumble of assorted chests, cases and cupboards packed with treasure from a dozen great houses.

Astil Tremerst Keiver selected a roquelaure from a tall chiffonier, closed the cabinet's door and admired himself in the mirror. Yes, the cloak looked very fine on him, very fine indeed. He flourished it, pirouetting, drew his ceremonial rifle from its scabbard, and then made a circuit of the room, around the grand state coach, making a "ki-shauw, ki-shauw!" noise, and pointing the gun at each black-curtained window in turn as he swept by them (his shadow dancing gloriously across the walls and the cold gray outlines of the statues), before arriving back at the fireplace, sheathing the rifle, and sitting suddenly and imperiously down on a highly-wrought little chair of finest bloodwood.

The chair collapsed. He thumped into the flagstones and the holstered gun at the side fired, sending a round into the angle between the floor and the curve of wall behind him.

"Shit, shit, shit!" he cried, inspecting his breeches and cloak, respectively grazed and holed.

The door of the state coach burst open and someone flew

out, crashing into an escritoire and demolishing it. The man was still and steady in an instant, presenting—in that infuriatingly efficient martial way of his—the smallest possible target, and pointing the appallingly large and ugly plasma cannon straight at the face of deputy vice-regent-in-waiting Astil Tremerst Keiver the Eighth.

"Eek! Zakalwe!" Keiver heard himself say, and threw the cloak over his head. (Damn!)

When Keiver brought the cloak down again—with, he felt, all the not inconsiderable dignity he could muster—the mercenary was already rising from the debris of the little desk, taking a quick look round the room, and switching off the plasma weapon.

Keiver was, naturally, immediately aware of the hateful similarity of their positions, and so stood up quickly.

"Ah. Zakalwe. I beg your pardon. Did I wake you?"

The man scowled, glanced down at the remains of the escritoire, slammed shut the door of the state coach, and said, "No; just a bad dream."

"Ah. Good." Keiver fiddled with the ornamental pommel of his gun, wishing that Zakalwe didn't make him feel— so unjustifiably, dammit—inferior, and crossed in front of the fireplace to sit (carefully, this time) on a preposterous porcelain throne stationed to one side of the hearth.

He watched the mercenary sit down on the hearthstone, leaving the plasma cannon on the floor in front of him and stretching. "Well, a half watch's sleep will have to suffice."

"Hmm," Keiver said, feeling awkward. He glanced at the ceremonial coach the other man had been sleeping in, and so recently vacated. "Ah." Keiver drew the roquelaure about him, and smiled. "I don't suppose you know the story behind that old carriage, do you?"

The mercenary—the so-called (Ha!) War Minister— shrugged. "Well," he said. "The version I heard was that in the Interregnum, the Archpresbyter told the Mythoclast he could have the tribute, income and souls of all the monasteries he could raise his state coach above, using one horse. The Mythoclast accepted, founded this castle and erected this tower with foreign loans, and using a highly efficient pulley system powered by his prize stallion, winched the coach up here during the Thirty Golden Days to claim every monastery in the land. He won the bet and the resulting war, disestab-

lished the Final Priesthood, paid off his debts, and only per-
ished because the groom in charge of the prize stallion objected to the fact that the beast died of its exertions, and
strangled him with its blood and foam-flecked bridle . . .
which, according to legend, is immured within the base of
the porcelain throne you're sitting on. So we're told.'' He
looked at the other man and shrugged again.

Keiver was aware that his mouth was hanging open. He
closed it. ''Ah, you know the story.''

''No; just a wild guess.''

Keiver hesitated, then laughed loudly.

''By hell! You're a rum chap, Zakalwe!''

The mercenary stirred the remains of the bloodwood chair
with one heavily-booted foot, and said nothing.

Keiver was aware that he ought to do something, and so
stood. He wandered to the nearest window, drew back the
drape and unlocked the interior shutters, levered the external
shutters aside and stood, arm against the stones, gazing out
at the view beyond.

The Winter Palace, besieged.

Outside, on the snow-strewn plain, among the fires and
trenches, there were huge wooden siege structures and missile launchers, heavy artillery and rock-throwing catapults;
juried field projectors and gas-powered searchlights; a hei-
nous collection of blatant anachronisms, developmental par-
adoxes and technological juxtapositions. And they called it
progress.

''I don't know,'' Keiver breathed. ''Men fire guided missiles, from their mounts' saddles; jets are shot down by guided
arrows; throw knives explode like artillery shells, or like as
not get turned back by ancestral armor backed by these
damned field projectors . . . where's it all to end, eh, Zakalwe?''

''Here, in about three heartbeats, if you don't close those
shutters or pull the blackout drapes behind you.'' He stabbed
at the logs in the grate with a poker.

''Ha!'' Keiver withdrew rapidly from the window, half
ducking as he pulled the lever to close the external shutters.
''Quite!'' He hauled the drape across the window, dusting
down his hands, watching the other man as he prodded at the
logs in the fire. ''Indeed!'' He took his place on the porcelain
throne again.

Of course, Mr. so-called War Minister Zakalwe liked to pretend he did have an idea where it was all going to end; he claimed to have some sort of explanation for it all, about outside forces, the balance of technology, and the erratic escalation of military wizardry. He always seemed to be hinting at greater themes and conflicts, beyond the mere here-and-now, forever trying to establish some—frankly laughable—otherworldly superiority. As though that made any difference to the fact that he was nothing more than a mercenary—a very lucky mercenary—who'd happened to catch the ear of the Sacred Heirs and impress them with a mixture of absurdly risky exploits and cowardly plans, while the one he'd been paired with—him, Astil Tremerst Keiver the Eighth, deputy regent-in-waiting, no less—had behind him a thousand years of breeding, natural seniority and—indeed, for that was just the way things were, dammit—superiority. After all, what sort of War Minister—even in these desperate days—was so incapable of delegating that he had to sit on a watch up here, waiting for an attack that would probably never come?

Keiver glanced at the other man, sitting staring into the flames, and wondered what he was thinking.

I blame Sma. She got me into this crock of shit.

He looked around the cluttered spaces of the room. What had he to do with idiots like Keiver, with all this historical junk, with any of this? He didn't feel part of it, could not identify with it, and he did not entirely blame them for not listening to him. He supposed he did have the satisfaction of knowing that he had warned the fools, but that was little enough to warm yourself with, on a cold and closing night like this.

He'd fought; put his life at risk for them, won a few desperate rear-guard actions, and he had tried to tell them what they ought to do; but they'd listened too late, and given him some limited power only after the war was already more or less lost. But that was just the way they were; they were the bosses, and if their whole way of life vanished because it was a tenet of that way that people like them automatically knew how to make war better than even the most experienced commoners or outsiders, then that was not unjust; everything came level in the end. And if it meant their deaths, let them all die.

In the meantime, while supplies held out, what could be

more pleasant? No more long cold marches, no boggy excuses for camps, no outside latrines, no scorched earth to try and scrape a meal from. Not much action, and maybe he would get itchy feet eventually, but that was more than compensated for by being able to satisfy the more highly-placed itches of some of the noble ladies also trapped in the castle.

Anyway, he knew in his heart that there was a relief in not being listened to, sometimes. Power meant responsibility. Advice unacted upon almost always *might* have been right, and in the working out of whatever plan was followed, there was anyway always blood; better it was on their hands. The good soldier did as he was told, and if he had any sense at all volunteered for nothing, especially promotion.

"Ha," Keiver said, rocking in the china chair. "We found more grass seed today."

"Oh, good."

"Indeed."

Most of the courtyards, gardens and patios were already given over to pasture; they'd torn the roofs off some of the less architecturally important halls and planted there as well. If they weren't blown to bits in the meantime, they might—in theory—feed a quarter of the castle's garrison indefinitely.

Keiver shivered, and wrapped the cloak more tightly about his legs. "But this is a cold old place, Zakalwe, isn't it?"

He was about to say something in reply when the door at the far end of the room opened a crack.

He grabbed the plasma cannon.

"Is . . . is everything all right?" said a quiet, female voice.

He put the gun down, smiling at the small pale face peering from the doorway, long black hair following the line of the door's studded wood.

"Ah, Neinte!" Keiver exclaimed, rising only to bow deeply to the young girl (princess, indeed!) who was—technically, at least, not that that precluded other, more productive, even lucrative, relationships in the future—his ward.

"Come on in," he heard the mercenary tell the girl.

(Damn him, always taking the initiative like that; who did he think he was?)

The girl crept into the room, gathering her skirts in front of her. "I thought I heard a shot . . ."

The mercenary laughed. "That was a little time ago," he said, rising to show the girl to a seat near the fire.

"Well," she said, "I had to dress . . ."

The man laughed louder.

"My lady," Keiver said, rising slightly late, and flourishing what would now—thanks to Zakalwe—look like a rather awkward bow. "Forfend we should have disturbed your maidenly slumber . . ."

Keiver heard the other man stifle a guffaw as he kicked a log further into the fire. The princess Neinte giggled. Keiver felt his face heat up, and decided to laugh.

Neinte—still very young, but already beautiful in a delicate, fragile way—wrapped her arms round her drawn-up legs, and stared into the fire.

He looked from her to Keiver, in the silence that followed (except that the deputy vice-regent-in-waiting said, "Yes, well."), and thought—as the logs crackled and the scarlet flames danced—how like statues the two young people suddenly looked.

Just once, he thought, I'd like to know whose side I'm really on in something like this. Here I am, in this absurd fortress, packed with riches, crammed with concentrated nobility—such as it was, he thought, watching Keiver's vacant-looking eyes—facing out the hordes beyond (all claw and tackle, brute force and brute intelligence) trying to protect these delicate, simpering products of a millennia's privilege, and never knowing whether I'm doing the tactically or the strategically right thing.

The Minds did not assume such distinctions; to them, there was no cut-off between the two. Tactics cohered into strategy, strategy disintegrated into tactics, in the sliding scale of their dialectical moral algebra. It was all more than they ever expected the mammal brain to cope with.

He recalled what Sma had said to him, long long ago back in that new beginning (itself the product of so much guilt and pain); that they dealt in the intrinsically untoward, where rules were forged as you went along and were never the same twice anyway, where just by the nature of things nothing could be known, or predicted, or even judged with any real certainty. It all sounded very sophisticated and abstract and challenging to work with, but in the end it came down to people and problems.

This girl was what it came down to, here, this time; barely more than a child, and trapped in the great stone castle with the rest of the cream or scum (depending on how you looked at it), to live or die, depending on how well I advise, and on how capable these clowns are of taking that advice.

He looked at the girl's flame-lit face, and felt something more than distant desire (for she was attractive), or fatherly protectiveness (for she was so young, and he, despite his appearance, so old). Call it . . . he didn't know what. A realization; an awareness of the tragedy the whole episode represented; the breakup of the rule, the dissolution of power and privilege and the whole elaborate, top-heavy system this child represented.

The muck and dirt, the king with fleas. For theft, mutilation; for the wrong thoughts, death. An infant mortality rate as astronomical as the lifeexpectancy was minute, and the whole grisly, working package wrapped in a skein of wealth and advantage designed to maintain the dark dominion of the knowing over the ignorant (and the worst of it was the pattern; the repetition; the twisted variations of the same depraved theme in so many different places).

So this girl, called a princess. Would she die? The war was going against them, he knew, and the same symbolic grammar that presented her with the prospect of power if things went well, also dictated her use, her expendability, if all failed about them. Rank demanded its tribute; the obsequious bow or the mean stab, according to the outcome of this struggle.

He saw her suddenly old, in the flickering firelight. He saw her shut in some slimed dungeon, waiting, hoping, scabbed with lice and ragged in sackcloth, head shaved, eyes dark and hollow in the raw skin, and finally marched out one snow-filled day, to be nailed to a wall with arrows or bullets, or face the cold ax blade.

Or maybe that too was too romantic. Maybe there would be some desperate flight to asylum, a lonely and bitter exile spent growing old and worn, barren and senile, forever remembering the ever more golden old times, composing futile petitions, hoping for a return, but growing slowly, inevitably, into something like the pampered uselessness her upbringing had always conditioned her for, but without any of the compensations she had been bred to expect from her station.

With a feeling of sickness, he saw that she meant nothing. She was just another irrelevant part of another history, heading—with or without the Culture's carefully evaluated nudges in what they saw as the right direction—for what would probably be better times and an easier life for most. But not her, he suspected, not right at this moment.

Born twenty years earlier, she might have expected a good marriage, a productive estate, access to the court, and lusty sons, talented daughters . . . twenty years from now, perhaps an astutely mercantile husband, or even—in the unlikely event this particular genderist society was heading that way so soon—a life of her own; academic, in business, doing good works; whatever.

But, probably, death.

High in a turret of a great castle rising on a black crag above snowy plains, besieged and grand, crammed full of an empire's treasure, and he sitting by a log fire was a sad and lovely princess. . . . I used to dream about such things, he thought. I used to long for them, ache for them. They seemed the very stuff of life, its essence. So why does all this taste of ashes?

I should have stayed on that beach, Sma. Perhaps after all I am getting too old for this.

He made himself look away from the girl. Sma said he tended to get too involved, and she was not totally wrong. He'd done what they'd asked; he'd be paid, and at the end of all this, after all, there was his own attempt to claim absolution for a past crime. *Livueta, say you will forgive me.*

"Oh!" The princess Neinte had just noticed the wreckage of the bloodwood chair.

"Yes," Keiver stirred uncomfortably. "That, ah . . . that was, umm, me, I'm afraid. Was it yours? Your family's?"

"Oh, no! But I knew it; it belonged to my uncle; the archduke. It used to be in his hunting lodge. It had a great big animal's head above it. I was always frightened to sit in it because I dreamt the head would fall from the wall and one of the tusks would stick right into my head and I'd die!" She looked at both men in turn and giggled nervously. "Wasn't I silly?"

"Ha!" said Keiver.

(While he watched them both and shivered. And tried to smile.)

"Well," Keiver laughed. "You must promise not to tell your uncle that I broke his little seat, or I shall never be invited to one of his hunts again!" Keiver laughed louder. "Why, I might even end up with *my* head fixed on one of his walls!"

The girl squealed and put a hand on her mouth.

(He looked away, shivering again, then threw a piece of wood onto the fire, and did not notice then or afterward that it was a piece of the bloodwood chair he had added to the flames, and not a log at all.)

3

S ma suspected a lot of ship crews were crazy. For that matter, she suspected a fair few of the ships themselves weren't totally together in the sanity department, either. There were only twenty people on the very fast picket *Xenophobe*, and Sma had noticed that—as a general rule—the smaller the crew, the weirder the behavior. So she was already prepared for the ship's staff being pretty off the wall even before the module entered the ship's hangar.

"Ah-choo!" the young crewman sneezed, covering his nose with one hand while extending the other to Sma as she stepped from the module. Sma jerked her hand back, looking at the young man's red nose and streaming eyes. "Ais Disgarb, Ms. Sma," the fellow said, blinking and sniffing, and looking hurt, "Belcome aboard."

Sma put her hand out again cautiously. The crewman's hand was extremely hot. "Thank you," Sma said.

"Skaffen-Amtiskaw," the drone said from behind her.

"Heddo," the young man waved at the drone. He took a small piece of cloth from one sleeve and dabbed at his leaky eyes and nose.

"Are you entirely all right?" Sma said.

"Dot really," he said. "God a cold. Blease," he indicated to one side, "cob with be."

"A cold," Sma nodded, falling into step alongside the fellow; he was dressed in a jellaba, as though he'd just got out of bed.

"Yes," the young man said, leading the way through the *Xenophobe*'s collection of smallcraft, satellites and assorted paraphernalia toward the rear of the hangar. He sneezed again, sniffed. "Sobthig ob a fad on the shib ad the bowbid." (Here Sma, immediately behind the man as they walked between two closely parked modules, turned quickly back to look at Skaffen-Amtiskaw and mouthed the word. *"What?"* at it, but the machine wobbled, shrugging. ME NEITHER it printed on its aura field, in letters of gray on a rosy background.) "Be all tought it'd be abusing to relax our ibude systebs and cadge colds," the young crewman explained, showing her and the drone into an elevator at one end of the hangar.

"All of you?" Sma said, as the door closed and the elevator rolled and rose. "The whole crew?"

"Yes, dough dot all ad the sabe tibe. The peebil who've recobered say id's very pleasid abter it's ober."

"Yes," Sma said, glancing at the drone, which was keeping a standard pattern of formal blue on its aura field, apart from one large red dot on its side that probably only she could see; it was pulsing rapidly. When she noticed it she almost started laughing herself. She cleared her throat. "Yes, I suppose it would be."

The young man sneezed mightily.

"Due for a spot of R-and-R soon, are we?" Skaffen-Amtiskaw asked him. Sma nudged the machine with her elbow.

The young crewman looked puzzledly at the machine. "Jusd bidished sub, adjilly."

He glanced away to the elevator door as it started to open, Skaffen-Amtiskaw and Sma exchanged looks; Sma crossed her eyes.

They stepped into a wide social area, floored and walled with some dark red wood, polished to the point of gleaming; it supported a variety of richly upholstered couches and chairs, and a few low tables. The ceiling wasn't particularly high, but very attractive, composed of great flutes of gathered-up material rippling in from the walls and hung with many little lanterns. From the light level, it looked to be early morning, ship time. A group of people round one of the tables broke up and came toward her.

"Biz Sba," the young crewman said indicating Sma, his voice seeming to get thicker all the time. The other people—about fifty-fifty men and woman—smiled, introduced themselves. She nodded, exchanged a few words; the drone said hello.

One of the people in the group held a little bundle of brown and yellow fur, cradled against one shoulder rather as one might hold a baby. "Here," the man said, presenting the tiny furry creature to Sma. She took it reluctantly. It was warm, had four limbs arranged conventionally, smelled attractive and wasn't any sort of animal she'd ever seen before; it had large ears on a large head, and as he held it, it opened its huge eyes and looked at her. "That's the ship," the man who'd handed her the animal said.

"Hello," the tiny being squeaked.

Sma looked it up and down. "You're the *Xenophobe*?"

"Its representative. The bit you can talk to. You can call me Xeny." It smiled; it had little round teeth. "I know most ships just use a drone, but," it glanced at Skaffen-Amtiskaw, "they can be a bit boring, don't you think?"

Sma smiled, and sensed Skaffen-Amtiskaw's aura flicker out of the corner of her eye. "Well, sometimes," she agreed.

"Oh yes," the little creature said, nodding. "I'm *much* cuter." It wriggled in her hands, looking happy. "If you like," it giggled, "I'll show you to your cabin, yes?"

"Yes; good idea," nodded Sma, and put the thing over her shoulder. The crewpeople called out to say they'd see her later as she, the ship's bizarre remote drone and Skaffen-Amtiskaw headed for the accommodation section.

"Ooh, you're nice and warm," the little brown and yellow creature mumbled sleepily, snuggling into Sma's neck as they headed down a deeply carpeted corridor for Sma's quarters. It stirred and she found herself patting its back. "Left here," it said, at a junction, then, "That's us just breaking orbit now, by the way."

"Good," Sma said.

"Can I cuddle up with you when you sleep?"

Sma stopped, detached the creature from her shoulder with one hand and stared it in the face. "What?"

"Just for chumminess' sake," the little thing said, yawning wide and blinking. "I'm not being rude; it's a good bonding procedure."

Sma was aware of Skaffen-Amtiskaw glowing red just behind her. She brought the yellow and brown device closer to her face. "Listen, *Xenophobe*—"

"Xeny."

"Xeny; you are a million-tonne starship; a Torturer class Rapid Offensive Unit. Even—"

"But I'm demilitarized!"

"Even without your principal armament, I bet you could waste planets if you wanted to—"

"Aw, come on; any silly GCU can do *that*!"

"So what is all this shit for?" She shook the furry little remote drone, quite hard. Its teeth chattered.

"It's for a laugh!" it cried. "Sma; don't you appreciate a joke?"

"I don't know. Do you appreciate being drop-kicked back to the accommodation area?"

"Ooo! What's your problem, lady? Have you got something against small furry animals, or what? Look, Ms. Sma; I know very well I'm a ship, and I do everything I'm asked to do—including taking you to this frankly rather fuzzily specified destination—and do it very efficiently, too. If there was the slightest sniff of any real action, and I had to start acting like a warship, this construct in your hands would go lifeless and limp immediately, and I'd battle as ferociously and decisively as I've been trained to. Meanwhile, like my human colleagues, I amuse myself harmlessly. If you really hate my current appearance, all right; I'll change it; I'll be an ordinary drone, or just a disembodied voice, or talk to you through Skaffen-Amtiskaw here, or through your personal terminal. The last thing I want to do is *offend* a guest."

Sma pursed her lips. She patted the thing on its head, and sighed. "Fair enough."

"I can keep this shape?"

"By all means."

"Oh goody!" It squirmed with pleasure, then opened its big eyes wide and looked hopefully at her. "Cuddle?"

"Cuddle." Sma cuddled it, patted its back.

She turned to see Skaffen-Amtiskaw lying dramatically on its back in midair, its aura field flashing the lurid orange that was used to signal Sick Drone in Extreme Distress.

Sma nodded goodbye to the little brown and yellow animal as it waddled away down the corridor which led back to the social area (it waved back with one chubby little paw), then closed the cabin door and made sure the room's internal monitoring was off.

She turned to Skaffen-Amtiskaw. "*How* long are we on this ship for?"

"Thirty days?" Skaffen-Amtiskaw suggested.

Sma gritted her teeth and looked round the fairly cozy-looking but—compared to the echoing spaces of the old power station mansion—rather small cabin. "Thirty days with a crew of viral masochists and a ship that thinks it's a cuddly toy." She shook her head, sat into the bed field. "Subjectively, drone, this could be a long trip." She collapsed back into the bed, muttering.

Skaffen-Amtiskaw decided right now would probably still not be the best time to tell the woman about Zakalwe being missing.

"I'll just go and take a look round, if you don't mind," it said, drifting toward the door over the neat line of bags that was Sma's luggage.

"Yeah, on you go," Sma waved one arm lazily, then shucked off the jacket and let it fall to the deck.

The drone had almost made it to the door when Sma sat bolt upright, a frown on her face, and said, "Wait a minute; what did the ship mean about '. . . rather fuzzily specified destination'? Doesn't it know where the hell we're going?"

Oh-oh, thought the drone.

It spun in the air. "Ah," it said.

Sma's eyes narrowed. "We are just going to get Zakalwe, aren't we?"

"Yes. Of course."

"We're not doing anything else?"

"Absolutely not. We find Zakalwe; we brief him; we take him to Voerenhutz. Simple as that. We might be asked to hang around for a bit, overseeing, but that isn't definite yet.''

''Yes, yes, I expected that, but . . . where exactly *is* Zakalwe?''

''Where *exactly*?'' The drone said. ''Well, I mean; you know, that's . . .''

''All right,'' Sma said, exasperated. ''Approximately, then.''

''No problem,'' Skaffen-Amtiskaw said, backing off toward the door.

''No problem?'' Sma said, puzzled.

''Yes; no problem. We know that. Where he is.''

''Good,'' Sma nodded. ''Well?''

''Well what?''

''Well,'' Sma said loudly, ''where *is* he?''

''Crastalier.''

''Cras . . . ?''

''Crastalier. That's where we're heading.''

Sma shook her head, yawned. ''Never heard of it.'' She flopped back in the bed field, stretching. ''Crastalier.'' Her yawn deepened; she put a hand to her mouth. ''You only had to say that the first time, goddammit.''

''Sorry,'' the drone said.

''Mmm. Never mind.'' Sma put out one hand, waved it through the bedside beam that controlled the cabin lights, so that they dimmed. She yawned again. ''Think I'll catch some sleep. Take my boots off, will you?''

Gently but quickly, the drone slipped Sma's boots off, gathered her jacket and hung it in a walk-in cupboard, swept the bags in there too, then—as Sma turned over in the bed field, eyes fluttering closed—the drone slipped out of the room.

It hovered in the air outside, looking at its reflection in the polished wood on the far side of the corridor.

''That,'' it said to itself, ''was close.'' Then it went for a wander.

Sma had arrived on the *Xenophobe* just after breakfast, by ship time. When she awoke, it was early afternoon. She was completing her toilet, while the drone sorted her clothes into type and color order and hung or folded them in the cupboard, when the door chimed. Sma wandered out of the little bathroom area, wearing a pair of shorts, her mouth full of toothpaste. She tried saying Open, but the toothpaste apparently stopped the room monitor from recognizing the word. She walked over and pressed the door-open instead.

Sma's eyes flicked wide; she yelped, spluttered, jumped back from the door, a scream gathering in her throat.

The instant after her eyes had widened, before the signal to jump back from the door had traveled all the way to her leg muscles, there was an impression of almost invisibly sudden movement in the cabin, belatedly followed by a bang and a sizzling sound.

There, stationed between her and the door, were all three of the drone's knife missiles, hovering roughly level with her eyes, sternum and groin; she was looking at them through a haze of field the machine had also thrown in front of her. Then it clicked off.

The knife missiles swung lazily away through the air and clicked back into Skaffen-Amtiskaw's casing. "Don't *do* that to me," the machine muttered, returning to sorting out Sma's socks.

Sma wiped her mouth and stared at the three meter tall, brown and yellow colored furry monster cowering in the corridor outside the door.

"Ship . . . Xeny, what the *hell* are you doing?"

"I'm sorry," the huge creature said, its voice only a little deeper than when it had been baby-sized. "I thought if you didn't relate to a small furry animal, perhaps a bigger version . . ."

"Shee-it." Sma said, shaking her head. "Come in," she called, heading back for the bathroom area. "Or did you just want to show me how much you've grown?" She rinsed out the paste and spat.

Xeny squeezed through the door, stooped, and sidled into a corner. "Sorry about that, Skaffen-Amtiskaw."

"No problem," the other machine replied.

"Ah, no, Ms. Sma," Xeny called. "I actually wanted to talk to you about . . ."

Skaffen-Amtiskaw went still, just for a second. There was, in fact, a fairly lengthy, detailed and slightly heated exchange between the drone and the ship's Mind during that time, but Sma was only aware of Xeny pausing as it spoke.

". . . about having a fancy-dress party, this evening, in your honor," the ship improvised.

Sma smiled from the bathroom area, "That's a lovely idea, ship. Thank you, Xeny. Yes; why not?"

"Good; I just thought I'd check with you, first. Any ideas about costumes?"

Sma laughed. "Yeah; I'll go as you; make me one of those suits you're wearing."

"Ha. Yes. Good idea. Actually, that might be rather a common choice, but we'll make it two people can't go as the same thing. Right. I'll talk to you later." Xeny lumbered from the room and the door slid shut. Sma appeared out from the bathroom area, slightly surprised at this sudden departure, but just shrugged.

"Short but eventful visit," she observed, rummaging through the socks Skaffen-Amtiskaw had just carefully arranged in chromatic order. "That machine's weird."

"What do you expect?" Skaffen-Amtiskaw said. "It's a starship."

—You might (the ship Mind communicated to Skaffen-Amtiskaw) have told me you were keeping the size of our target destination from her.

—I am hoping (the drone replied) that our people already out there will find the guy we're looking for and give us an exact position, in which case Sma will never need to know there was ever any problem.

—Indeed, but why not just be honest with her in the first place?

—Ha! You don't know Sma!

—Oh. Do I take it she's temperamental?

—What do you expect? She's a human!

The ship prepared a feast, and put as many human-brain-chemistry-altering chemicals into the various dishes and drinks as was normally regarded proper without attaching a specific sanity warning to each bowl, plate, jug or glass. It told the crew about the party, and rearranged the social area, setting up a variety of mirrors and reverser fields (with a total guest list of only twenty-two—not including itself—making the place look suitably crowded was one of the major obstacles it faced in trying to encourage the feel of a serious, thorough-going whoopee).

Sma breakfasted, was shown round the ship—though there was little to see; the ship was almost an engine—and spent most of the rest of the day reviewing her knowledge of the Voerenhutz cluster's history and politics.

The ship sent formal invitations to each of the crew, and specified a strict rule of No Shop Talk. It hoped that this, plus the narcotic wealth of the consumables, would keep everybody off the subject of where exactly they were heading for. It had toyed with the idea of just telling people there was a problem here and asking them not to talk about it, but suspected there were at least two of the crew who would take such a proscription as a challenge to their integrity requiring them to raise the issue at the first possible opportunity. It was on occasions like this that the *Xenophobe* tended to consider changing its status to that of an unstaffed ship, but it knew it would miss the humans if it did decide to ask them to leave; they were fun to have around, usually.

The ship played loud music, showed exciting screen holos, and set up a fabulous surrounding holo landscape of lush green and blue, filled with floating bushes and hovering trees where strange, eight-winged birds capered and beyond which a glowing white layer of mist plied by tall, feathery cloudships extended to neck-stretchingly tall cliffs of pastel-shaded rock, set about with further small clouds, draped with blue and sparkling gold waterfalls, and topped by fabulous cities of spires and slender bridges. Ship-slaved soligrams of famous historical figures wandered about the party, adding to the illusion of numbers, and were only too happy to engage the disguised revelers in conversation. More treats and surprises were promised for later.

Sma went as Xeny, Skaffen-Amtiskaw as a model of the *Xenophobe*, and the ship itself produced yet another remote drone; an aquatic one, still brown and yellow, but looking like a rather fat and large-eyed fish, and floating in a field-held meter-diameter sphere of water which drifted through the party-space like some odd balloon.

"Ais Disgarve, who you've met before," the ship drone said, voice sounding rather bubbly as it introduced Sma to the young man who'd greeted her in the hangar the day before. "And Jetart Hrine."

Sma smiled, nodded at Disgarve—making a mental note to stop thinking of him as Disgarb—and the young woman at his side.

"Hello again. How do you do?"

"Heddo," said Disgarve, dressed as some sort of ancient cold-climate explorer, all swathed in furs.

"Hi," Jetart Hrine said. She was quite short and round, very young looking, and her skin was so black it was almost blue. She wore some ancient—and surprisingly brightly colored—military uniform, and sported a smoothbore projectile rifle slung over one shoulder. She sipped from a glass and said. "I know there's no shop talk, Ms. Sma, but frankly Ais and I have been wondering why our dest—"

"Aah!" the ship drone said, its water sphere suddenly collapsing. Water crashed all around the feet of Sma, Hrine and Disgarve, all of whom jumped back a little. The fish-drone fell to the redwood deck and flapped around. "Water!" it croaked. Sma picked it up by the tail.

"What happened?" she asked it.

"Field malfunction. Water! Quickly!"

Sma looked at Disgarve and Hrine, both of whom seemed rather bemused. Skaffen-Amtiskaw, in its starship disguise, wound quickly through the party-goers toward them. "Water!" the ship drone repeated, wriggling.

A frown gathered on Sma's brow, inside the brown and yellow suit. She looked at the woman dressed as a soldier. "What were you about to say, Ms. Hrine?"

"I was—oof!"

A one-in-five-hundred-and-twelfth scale model of the very fast picket *Xenophobe* thumped into the woman, making her stagger backward, dropping her glass.

"Hey!" Disgarve said, pushing the offending Skaffen-Amtiskaw away. Hrine looked annoyed, and rubbed her shoulder.

"Sorry; clumsy me!" Skaffen-Amtiskaw said, loudly.

"Water! Water!" yelped the ship drone, struggling in Sma's furry paw.

"Shut up!" Sma told it. She went close to Jetart Hrine, putting her own body between the woman and Skaffen-

Amtiskaw. "Ms. Hrine; complete your question, would you?"

"I just wanted to know why . . ."

The floor shook, the entire landscape around them trembled; light flashed from high above, and as they looked up, they saw the fabulous gleaming cities of the cliff tops far above disappear in vast blooms of light, which slowly faded, leaving falling clouds of debris, crashing towers and disintegrating bridges. The mighty cliffs split asunder and kilometers-high tsunami of seething lava and boiling gray-black clouds of smoke and ash burst out, exploding over the quivering landscape below, where the cloudships were sinking and the eight-winged birds were spinning so fast their wings were coming off, sending them spinning into the blue-green shrubbery in squawking explosions of feathers and leaves.

Jetart Hrine stared in disbelief. Sma grabbed the woman's collar with one paw and shook her. "It's trying to distract you!" she yelled. She turned to the fish-drone in her other paw. "Cut it out!" she screamed at it. She shook the woman again, while Disgarve tried to pry her paw away from the woman. Sma shook his hand off. "What were you trying to *say*?"

"Why don't we know where we're going?" Hrine shouted into Sma's face, over the noise of the earth splitting open in a gout of flame. A huge black shape reared from the chasm, red-eyed.

"We're going to Crastalier!" Sma yelled. A vast silver human baby appeared in the sky, shining, beatific and be-rayed, spun about with glowing figures.

"So what?" Hrine bellowed, as lightning zapped from mega-baby to earth-beast and thunder assaulted the ears. "Crastalier's an Open Cluster; there must be half a million stars in it!"

Sma froze.

The holos went back to the way they had been before the cataclysms. The music resumed, but it was quieter now, and very soothing. The ship's crew stood around, looking mystified. There was much shrugging.

The piscine ship-drone and Skaffen-Amtiskaw exchanged looks. The ship drone, still held in Sma's paw, suddenly became the holo of a fish skeleton. Skaffen-Amtiskaw projected the model of the *Xenophobe* tumbling disintegrating and trailing smoke to the deck. They both flashed back to their previous disguises as Sma turned slowly and looked at them both.

"An . . . Open . . . Cluster?" she said, and took off the brown and yellow head of the fancy-dress suit.

Sma's mouth was in the shape of a smile. It was not an expression Skaffen-Amtiskaw had learned to view with anything other than extreme trepidation.

—Oh shit.

—I think we are in the presence of one annoyed human female, Skaffen-Amtiskaw.

—You don't say. Any ideas?

—None whatsoever. You can field this; my fish-like ass is out of here.

—Ship! You can't do this to me!

—Can and am. This is your prototype. Talk to me later. Bye.

The fish-drone went limp in Sma's paw. She let it drop to the water-slicked floor.

The drone dispensed with the warship disguise; it floated in front of her, fields on clear. It dipped its front a little, held it there. "Sma," it said quietly. "I'm sorry. I didn't lie but I did deceive."

"My cabin," Sma said calmly, after a brief pause. "Excuse us," she said to Disgarve and Hrine, and walked away, followed by the drone.

She floated on the bed in the lotus position, naked but for the shorts, the Xeny suit discarded on the floor. She was glanding *calm* and she looked more sad than furious. Skaffen-Amtiskaw—expecting a fight—was feeling awful, faced with such measured disappointment.

"I thought if I told you, you wouldn't come."

"Drone; this is my job."

"I know, but you were so reluctant to leave . . ."

"After three years, with no warning, what do you expect? But how long did I actually hold out? Even knowing about the stand-in? Come on, drone; you told me what the situation was and I accepted. There was no need to keep quiet about Zakalwe giving us the slip."

"I'm sorry," the drone said, very quietly. "This is inadequate, I know, but I really am sorry. Please say you might be able to forgive me one day."

"Oh, don't take the contrition bit too far. Just tell me things in future."

"All right."

Sma let her head drop for a moment, then brought it back up. "You can start by telling me how Zakalwe got away. What did we have trailing him?"

"A knife missile."

"A *knife* missile?" Sma looked suitably amazed. She rubbed her chin with one hand.

"Quite a late model, too," the drone said. "Nanoguns, monofilament warps, effector; point seven value brain."

"And Zakalwe got *away* from this beast?" Sma was almost laughing.

"Not just away; he wasted it."

"Shee-it," Sma breathed. "I didn't think Zakalwe was that smart. *Was* he smart, or just incredibly lucky? What happened? How did he do it?"

"Well, it's *very* secret," the drone said. "So please don't tell anybody at all."

"My honor," Sma said ironically, palm on chest.

"Well," the drone said, making a sighing noise. "It took him a year to set up but, on the place where we dropped him—after his last job for us—the local humanoids shared their planet with large seagoing mammals of about equivalent intelligence; quite a viable symbiotic relationship, with much cross-cultural contact. Zakalwe—using the exchange we'd given him as payment for his work—bought a company which made medical and signaling lasers. His trap involved a hospital facility the humanoids were setting up on the coast of an ocean to treat these seagoing mammals. One of the pieces of medical equipment being tested was a very large Nuclear Magnetic Resonance Scanner."

"A what?"

"Fourth most primitive way of looking inside your average water-based living being."

"Go on."

"The process involves the use of extremely strong magnetic fields. Zakalwe was supposedly testing a laser attached to the machine—on a holiday, when there was nobody else around—when he somehow got the knife missile to enter the scanning machine, and then turned on the power.''

''I thought knife missiles weren't magnetic.''

''They're not, but there was just enough metal in it to set up crippling eddy currents if it tried to move too fast.''

''But it could still move.''

''Not fast enough to get out of the way of the laser Zakalwe had set up at one end of the scanner. It was only supposed to illuminate, to help produce holos of the mammals, but Zakalwe had in fact installed a military strength device; it grilled the knife missile.''

''Wow.'' Sma nodded, staring down at the floor. ''The man never ceases to amaze.'' She looked at the drone. ''Zakalwe must have wanted away from us awful bad.''

''It looks that way,'' agreed the drone.

''So maybe there's no way he'll want to work for us again. Maybe he never wants even to hear from us again.''

''I'm afraid that must be a possibility.''

''Even if we can find him.''

''Quite.''

''And all wc know is that he's somewhere in an Open Cluster called Crastalier?'' Sma's voice sounded tinged with disbelief.

''It's a bit more focused than that,'' Skaffen-Amtiskaw said. ''There are maybe ten or twelve systems he could be in by now, if he left immediately after stiffing the knife missile, and took the fastest ships available. Thankfully, the tech level in the meta-civilization isn't *that* high.'' The drone hesitated, then said, ''To be honest, we might have been able to catch up with him, if we'd gone in fast and strong immediately . . . But I think the controlling Minds were so impressed with Zakalwe's trick they thought he deserved to get away. We kept a very general watch on the volume, but it's only in the last ten days the search has become serious. We're bringing in ships and people from wherever we can now; I'm sure we'll find him.''

''Ten or twelve systems, drone?'' Sma said shaking her head.

''Twenty-plus planets; maybe three hundred sizeable space habitats . . . not including ships, of course.''

Sma closed her eyes. her head shook. ''I don't believe this.''

Skaffen-Amtiskaw thought the better of saying anything.

The woman's eyes opened. "Want to pass on a suggestion or two?"

"Certainly."

"Forget the habitats. And forget any planets that aren't fairly standard; check out . . . deserts, temperate zones; forests but not jungles . . . and no cities." She shrugged, rubbed her mouth with her hand. "If he's still trying hard to stay hidden, we'll never find him. If he only wanted to get away to live his own life without being watched, we have a chance. Oh, and look for wars, of course. Especially wars that aren't too big . . . and *interesting* wars, know what I mean?"

"Right. Transmitted." Normally the drone would have poured scorn on this bit of amateur psychological sleuthing, but this time it decided to bite its metaphorical tongue, and relayed Sma's remarks to the unresponding ship for transmission to the search fleet ahead of them.

Sma took a deep breath, shoulders rising and falling. "Party still going on?"

"Yes," Skaffen-Amtiskaw said, surprised.

Sma jumped off the bed and stepped into the Xeny suit. "Well; let's not be party poopers."

She fastened the suit, scooped up the brown and yellow head and walked for the door.

"Sma," the drone said, following. "I thought you'd be mad."

"Maybe I will be, once the *calm* wears off," she admitted, opening the door and putting the suit head on. "But just right now, I really can't be bothered."

They went down the corridor. She looked back at the clear-fielded machine behind her; "Come on, drone; it's meant to be fancy-dress. But try something a little more imaginative than a warship this time."

"Hmm," the machine said. "Any suggestions?"

"I don't know," Sma sighed. "What would suit you? I mean, what is the perfect role-model for a cowardly lying patronizing hypocritical bastard with no trust in or respect for another person?"

There was silence from behind as they approached the noise and light of the party. So she turned round and, instead of the drone, saw a classically proportioned, handsome, but somehow anonymous-looking young man following her down the corridor, his gaze just moving up from her behind to her eyes.

Sma laughed. "Yes; very good." She walked a few more steps. "On second thoughts, I think I preferred the warship."

XI

He never wrote things in the sand. He resented even leaving footprints. He saw it as a one-way commerce; he did the beachcombing, and the sea provided the materials. The sand was the middleman, displaying the goods as though it was a long, soggy shop counter. He liked the simplicity of this arrangement.

Sometimes he watched the ships passing, far out to sea. Now and again he'd wish that he was on one of the tiny dark shapes, on his way to some bright and strange place, or on his way—imagining harder—to a quiet home port, to twinkling lights, amiable laughter, friends and welcome. But usually he ignored the slow specks, and got on with his walking and gathering, and kept his eyes on the gray-brown wash of the beach's slope. The horizon was clear and far and empty, the wind sang low in the dunes, and the seabirds wheeled and cried, comfortingly random and argumentative in the cold skies above.

The brash, noisy home-cars came sometimes, from the interior. The home-cars were loaded with shining metal and flashing lights, they had multicolored windows and highly ornamental grilles, they fluttered with flags and dripped with enthusiastically imagined but sloppily executed paint jobs, and they groaned and flexed, overloaded, as they came coughing and spluttering and belching fumes down the sandy track from the parktown. Adults leaned out of windows or stood one-legged on running boards; children ran alongside, or clung to the ladders and straps that covered their sides, or sat squealing and shouting on the roof.

They came to see the strange man who lived in a funny wooden shack in the dunes. They were fascinated, if also slightly repelled, by the strangeness of living in something that was dug into the ground, something that did not—could not—move. They would stare at the line where the wood and tarpaper met the sand, and shake their heads, walking right round the small, skewed hut, as if looking for the wheels. They talked among themselves, trying to imagine what it must be like to have the same view and the same sort of weather all the time. They opened the rickety door and sniffed the dark, smoky, man-scented air inside the hut, and shut the door quickly, declaring that it must be unhealthy to live in the same place, joined to the earth. Insects. Rot. Stale air.

He ignored them. He could understand their language, but he pretended not to. He knew that the ever-changing population of the parktown inland called him the tree-man, because they liked to imagine he had put down roots like his wheelless shack had. He was usually out when they came to the shack, anyway. They lost interest in it fairly quickly, he found; they went to the shoreline to shriek when they got their feet wet, and throw stones at the waves, and build little cars in the sand; then they climbed back into their home-cars, and went sputtering and creaking back inland, lights flashing, horns honking, leaving him alone again.

He found dead seabirds all the time, and the washed-up carcasses of sea mammals every few days. Beachweed and seaflowers lay strewn like party streamers over the sands, and—when they dried—rippled in the wind and slowly unraveled, finally disintegrating to be blown out to sea or far inland in bright clouds of color and decay.

Once he found a dead sailor, lying washed and bloated by the ocean, extremities nibbled, one leg moving to the slow foamy beat of the sea. He stood and looked at the man for a while, then emptied his canvas bag of its flotsam booty, tore it flat, and gently covered the man's head and upper torso with it. The tide was ebbing, so he did not drag the body further up the beach. He walked to the parktown, for once not pushing his little wooden cart of tide treasure before him, and told the sheriff there.

The day he found the little chair he ignored it, but it was still there when he walked back past that stretch of beach on his return. He went on, and the next day combed in the other direction toward a different flat horizon, and thought the gale the following night would have removed it, but found it there again, the next day, and so took it, and in his shack repaired it with twine and a new leg made from a washed-up branch, and put it by the door of the shack, but never sat in it.

A woman came to the shack, every five or six days. He'd met her in parktown, soon after he'd arrived, on the third or fourth day of a drinking binge. He paid her in the mornings, always more than he thought she expected, because he knew she was frightened by the strange, unmoving shack.

She'd talk to him about her old loves and old hopes and new hopes and he half listened, knowing she thought he didn't really understand what she was saying. When he talked it was in another language, and the story was even less believeable. The woman would lie close to him, her head on his smooth and unscarred chest, while he talked into the dark air above the bed, his voice not echoing in the wood-flimsy space of the shack, and he'd tell her, in words she would never understand, about the magic land where everyone was a wizard and nobody ever had terrible choices to make, and guilt was almost unknown, and poverty and degradation were things you had to teach children about to let them understand how fortunate they were, and where no hearts broke.

He told her about a man, a warrior, who'd worked for the wizard doing things they could or would not bring themselves to do, and who eventually could work for them no more, because in the course of some driven, personal campaign to rid himself of a burden he would not admit to—and even the wizards had not discovered—he found, in the end, that he had only added to that weight, and his ability to bear was not without limit after all.

And he told her, sometimes, about another time and another place, far away in space and far away in time and even further away in history, where four children had played together in a huge and wonderful garden, but seen their idyll destroyed with gunfire, and of the boy who became a youth and then a man, but who forever after carried more than love for a girl in his heart. Years later, he would tell her, a small but terrible war was waged in this faraway place, and the garden itself laid waste. (And, eventually, the man did lose the girl from his heart.) Finally, when he had almost talked himself to sleep, and the night was at its darkest, and the girl was long since gone to the land of dreams, sometimes he would whisper to her about a great warship, a great metal warship, becalmed in stone but still dreadful and awful and potent, and about the two sisters who were the balance of that warship's fate, and about their own fates, and about the Chair, and the Chairmaker.

Then he would sleep, and when he woke, each time, the girl and the money would be gone.

He would turn back to the dark tarpaper walls then, and seek sleep, but not find it, and so rise and dress and go out, and comb the horizon-wide beach again, under the blue skies or the black skies, beneath the wheeling seabirds screaming their meaningless songs to the sea and the brine-charged breeze.

The weather varied, and because he'd never bothered to find out, he never knew what season it was, but the weather swung between warm and bright and cold and dull, and sometimes sleet came, chilling him, and winds blew around the dark hut, keening through the gaps in the planks and the tarpaper, and stirring the slack disturbances of sand on the floor inside the shack like abraded memories.

Sand would build up inside the hut, blown in from one direction or another, and he would scoop it carefully, throw it out the door to the wind like an offering, and wait for the next storm.

He always suspected there was a pattern to these slow sandy inundations, but he could not bring himself to try to work out what that pattern was. Anyway, every few days he had to trundle his little wooden cart into the parktown, and sell his sea-begotten wares, and collect money, and so food, and so the girl that came to the shack every five days or six.

The parktown changed every time he went there, streets being created or evaporating as the home-cars arrived or departed; it all depended where people chose to park. There were some fairly static landmarks, like the sheriff's compound and the fuel stockade and the smithy wagon and the area where the light-engineering caravans set up shop, but even those changed slowly, and all about them was in constant flux, so that the geography of the parktown was never the same on two visits. He drew a secret satisfaction from this inchoate permanence, and did not hate going there as much as he pretended.

The track there was rutted and soft, and never got any shorter; he always hoped the random shiftings of the parktown might slowly draw its bustle and light closer to him, but it never happened, and he would console himself with the thought that if the parktown came closer then so would the people, and their bumbling inquisitiveness.

There was a girl in the parktown, the daughter of one of the dealers he traded with, who seemed to care for him more than the others; she made him drinks and brought him sweetmeats from her father's caravan, and seldom said anything, but slipped the food to him, and smiled shyly and walked quickly off again, her pet seabird—flightless, half of each wing cut off—waddling after her, squawking.

He said nothing to her that he didn't have to say, and always averted his eyes from her slim brown shape. He did not know what the courting laws were in this place, and while accepting the drink and food always seemed the easiest course, he did not want to intrude any more than he had to in the lives of these people. He told himself she and her family would move away soon, and accepted the offerings she brought him with a nod but no smile or word, and did not always finish what he was given. He noticed there was a young man who always seemed to be around whenever the girl served him, and he caught the boy's eyes a few times, and knew that the youth wanted the girl, and looked away each time.

The young man came after him one day when he was on his way back to the shack within the dunes. The youth walked in front of him and tried to make him talk; hit him on the shoulder, shouting into his face. He feigned incomprehension. The young man drew lines in the sand in front of him which he duly plodded over with his cart and stood looking, blinking at the youth, both hands still on the handles of the cart, while the boy shouted louder and drew another line on the sand between them.

Eventually, he got fed up with the whole performance,

and the next time the young man prodded his shoulder he took his arm and twisted it and forced the youth to the sand and held him there for a while, twisting the arm in its socket just enough—he hoped—to avoid breaking anything but with sufficient force to disable the fellow for a minute or two while he took up his cart again and trundled it slowly away over the dunes.

It seemed to work.

Two nights later—the night after the regular woman had come and he'd told her about the terrible battleship and the two sisters and the man who was not yet forgiven—the girl came knocking at his door. The pet seabird with the clipped wings jumped and squawked outside while the girl cried and told him she loved him and there'd been an argument with her father, and he tried to push her away, but she slipped in underneath his arm and lay weeping on his bed.

He looked out into the starless night and stared into the eyes of the crippled, silent bird. Then he went over to the bed, dragged the girl from it and forced her out of the door, slamming it and bolting it.

Her cries, and those of the bird, came through the gaps in the planks for a while, like the seeping sand. He stuck his fingers in his ears and pulled the grimy covers over his head.

Her family, the sheriff, and perhaps twenty other people from the parktown, came for him the next night.

The girl had been found that evening, battered and raped and dead on the path from his shack. He stood in the doorway of the hut, looking out into the torch-lit crowd, met the eyes of the young man who had wanted the girl, and knew.

There was nothing he could do, because the guilt in one pair of eyes was outshone by the vengeance in too many others, and so he slammed the door and ran, across the shack and straight through the rickety planks on the far side and out into the dunes and the night.

He fought five of them that night and nearly killed two, until he found the young man and one of his friends searching unenthusiastically for him back near the track.

He clubbed the friend unconscious, took the young man by the throat. He gathered up both their knives, and held one blade to the throat of the youth as he marched him back to the shack.

He set fire to the shack.

When the light had attracted a dozen or so of the men, he stood up on the tallest dune above the hollow, holding the youth with one hand.

The parktown people gazed up at the stranger, lit by flames. He let the boy fall to the sand, threw him both knives.

The boy picked up the knives; charged.

He moved, let the boy go past, disarmed him. He gathered both knives; threw them hilt down in the sand in front of the boy. The youth struck out again, knife in each hand. Again—hardly seeming to move—he let the youth crash past, and slipped the knives from his grasp. He tripped the youth, and while he was still lying spread on the dune's top, threw the knives, sending them both thudding into the sand a centimeter on either side of his head. The youth screamed, plucked both blades out and threw them.

His head hardly moved as they hissed by his ears. The people watching in the flame-lit hollow moved their heads, following the trajectory the knives had to take, to the dunes behind them. But when they looked back again, wondering, both blades were in the stranger's hands, plucked from the air. He tossed them to the boy again.

The youth caught them, screamed, fumbled blood-handed to get them the right way round, and rushed again at the stranger, who dropped him, whacked the knives from his hands, and for a long moment held one of the young man's elbows poised over his knee, arm raised, ready to break . . . then shoved the boy away. He picked up the knives again, placed them in the open palms of the youth.

He listened to the boy sobbing into the dark sand, while the people watched.

He got ready to run again, glancing behind him.

The crippled seabird hopped and fluttered, clipped wings beating on air and sand, to the top of the dune. It cocked one flame-bright eye at the stranger.

The people in the hollow seemed frozen by the dancing flames.

The bird waddled to the prone, sobbing figure of the boy on the sand, and screamed. It flapped, shrieked, and stabbed at the boy's eyes.

The boy tried to fend it off, but the bird leapt into the air and whooped and beat and feathers flew and when the boy broke one of its wings and it fell to the sand, facing away from him, it jetted liquid shit at him.

The boy's face fell back to the sand. His body shook with sobs.

The stranger watched the eyes of the people in the hollow, while his shack caved in and the orange sparks swirled up into the still night sky.

Eventually the sheriff and the girl's father came and took the boy away, and a moon later the girl's family left, and two moons later the tightly bound body of the young man was lowered into a freshly picked hole in the nearest outcrop of rock, and covered with stones.

The people in the parktown would not talk to him, though one trader still took his flotsam. The brash and noisy home-cars stopped coming down the sandy track. He had not thought he would miss them. He pitched a small tent near the blackened remains of the shack.

The woman stopped coming to him; he never saw her again. He told himself he was getting so little for his haul that he could not have paid her and eaten as well.

The worst thing, he found, was that there was nobody to talk to.

He saw the seated figure on the beach, way in the distance, five moons or so after the night he'd burned his shack. He hesitated, then went on.

Twenty meters from the woman, he stopped and carefully inspected a length of fishing net on the tideline, the floats still attached and gleaming like earthbound suns in the low morning light.

He glanced at the woman. She was sitting, legs crossed, arms folded across her lap, staring out to sea. Her simple gown was the color of the sky.

He went up to the woman and put his new canvas bag down at her side. She did not move.

He sat beside her, arranged his limbs similarly, and stared out to sea, like her.

After a hundred or so waves had approached and broken and slipped away again, he cleared his throat.

"A few times," he said, "I had the feeling I was being watched."

Sma said nothing for a while. The seabirds pivoted inside the spaces of the air, calling in a language he still did not understand.

"Oh, people have always felt that," Sma said, at last.

He smoothed away a wormcast in the sand. "I don't belong to you, Diziet."

"No," she said, turning to him. "You're right. You don't belong to us. All we can do is ask."

"What?"

"That you come back. We have a job for you."

"What is it?"

"Oh . . ." Sma smoothed her gown over her knees. "Helping to drag a bunch of aristos into the next millenium, from the inside."

"Why?"

"It's important."

"Isn't everything?"

"And we can pay you properly this time."

"You paid me off very handsomely the last time. Lots of money and a new body. What more can a chap ask for?" He gestured at the canvas bag at her side, and at himself, clothed in salt-stained rags. "Don't let this fool you. I haven't lost the loot. I'm a rich man; very rich, here." He watched the waves roll up toward them, then break and foam and fall away again. "I just wanted the simple life, for a while." He gave a sort of half-laugh, and realized it was the first time he'd even started to laugh since he'd come here.

"I know," Sma said. "But this is different. Like I said; we can pay you properly, now."

He looked at her. "Enough. No more being cryptic. What do you mean?"

She turned her gaze to him. He had to work hard at not looking away.

"We've found Livueta," she said.

He stared into her eyes for a time, and then blinked and looked away. He cleared his throat, looking back out to the glittering sea, and had to sniff and wipe his eyes. Sma watched as the man moved one hand slowly to his chest, not realizing he was doing it, and rubbed at the skin there, just over his heart.

"Mm-hmm. You're sure?"

"Yes, we're sure."

He looked out over the waves after that, and suddenly felt that they were no longer bringing things to him, no longer messengers from the distant storms offering their bounty, but instead had become a pathway; a route, another distant sort of opportunity, beckoning.

That simple? he thought to himself. A word—a single name—from Sma and I'm all ready to go, take off, and take up their arms again? Because of *her*?

He let a few more waves roll up and down. The seabirds wailed. Then he sighed. "All right," he said. He pushed one hand up through his tangled, matted hair. "Tell me about it."

4

"The fact remains," Skaffen-Amtiskaw insisted, "that the last time we went through this rigmarole, Zakalwe fucked up. They froze his ass in that Winter Palace."

"All right," Sma said. "But it wasn't like him. Okay, so one time he gets it wrong . . . we don't know why. So maybe now he's had time to get over it, he'll actually want a chance to show he can still do the business. Maybe he can't wait for us to find him."

"Good grief," sighed the drone. "Wishful thinking from Sma the Cynical. Maybe you're starting to lose your touch too."

"Oh shut up."

She watched the planet swing toward them on the module screen.

Twenty-nine days had passed on the *Xenophobe*.

As an ice breaker, the fancy-dress party had been a crushing success. Sma had woken up in a cushion-filled alcove of the rec area, birth-naked and in a tangle of assorted equally nude limbs and torsos. She had extricated one arm carefully from under the voluptuous sleeping form of Jetart Hrine, stood shakily, and gazed round the softly breathing bodies, appraising the men in particular, and then—treading very carefully, nearly overbalancing several times on the plump cushions, her muscles all complaining and trembly—tiptoed her way between the slumbering crew to the welcome solidity of the redwood floor. The rest of the area had already been tidied. The ship must have sorted out everybody's clothes, for they lay in neat piles on a couple of large tables, just outside the alcove.

Sma massaged her slightly tingling genitals, grimacing. Bending over, they looked quite pink and raw; things looked slippery, and she decided she needed a bath.

The drone met her at the entrance to the corridor. Its red glowing field looked at least partially like a comment. "Good night's sleep?" it inquired.

"Don't start that again."

The drone floated at her shoulder as she headed for the elevator.

"You've made friends with the crew, then."

She nodded. "Very good friends with all of them, by the feel of it. Where's the ship's pool?"

"Floor above the hangar," the machine said, following her into the elevator.

"Record anything exciting last night?" Sma asked, leaning back against the elevator wall as they dropped.

"Sma," exclaimed the drone. "I would not be so ungallant!"

"Hmm." She raised one eyebrow. The elevator stopped, door opening. "What *memories*, though," the drone said, breathily. "Your appetite and stamina are a credit to your species. I think."

Sma dived into the smaller whirlpool, and, on surfacing, spat a jet of water at the machine, which dodged and backed into the elevator. "I'll just leave you to it, then. Judging from last night, even an innocent offensive-model drone isn't safe from you once you get the bit between your teeth. So to speak."

Sma splashed at it. "Get out of here, you prurient pisspot."

"And sweet-talking won't work ei . . ." the drone said, as the elevator door closed.

She would not have been surprised if the atmosphere in

the ship had been a little embarrassed for a day or two there-
after, but the crew seemed quite cool about it all, and she
decided that, basically, they were good sports. Happily, the
fad for having colds passed quickly. She settled down to
studying Voerenhutz, trying to guess where in the interlinked
civilizations they were heading for Zakalwe might be . . . and
enjoying herself, though—in the case of the latter activity—
not on anything like the same scale or with quite the same
frenetic abandon as she obviously had on her first night
aboard.

Ten days out, the *Just Testing* sent news that Gainly had
been delivered of twins; mother and pups doing well. Sma
prepared a signal that her stand-in was to give the hralz a big
kiss, from her, then hesitated, realizing that the machine that
was impersonating her would doubtless already have done so.
She felt bad, and in the end just sent a formal acknowledgment.

She kept up on recent developments in Voerenhutz; the
latest Contact forecasts were getting gloomier all the time.
The brush-fire conflicts on a dozen planets each threatened
to ignite a full-scale war, and—while getting a direct answer
was proving difficult—she formed the impression that even if
they found and convinced Zakalwe almost as soon as they
landed, and hauled his ass out on the *Xenophobe* with the
ship pushing its design limits, the chances of getting him to
Voerenhutz in time to make any difference were at best fifty-
fifty.

"Holy shit," the drone said one day, as she sat in her
cabin, reviewing cautiously optimistic reports on the peace
conference back home (for so she had started to think of it,
she admitted to herself).

"What?" She turned to the machine.

It looked at her. "They just changed the course schedule
for the *What Are the Civilian Applications*?"

Sma waited.

"That's a Continent class GSV," the drone said. "Sub-
class Prompt, one of the limiteds."

"You said it was a General; now it's a Limited; make up
your mind."

"No, I mean it's a limited edition; the go-faster model;
even nippier than this beast, once it gets going," the drone
said. It floated closer to her, fields set a weird mixture of

olive and purple, which she seemed to remember indicated Awe. She'd certainly never seen *that* expression on Skaffen-Amtiskaw before. "It's heading for Crastalier," it told her.

"For us? For Zakalwe?" she frowned.

"Nobody'll say, but it looks like it to me. A whole General Systems Vehicle, just for us. Wow!"

"Wow," Sma mimicked sourly, and pressed the screen for the view forward of the *Xenophobe*, still charging through the star systems for Crastalier. In their false representation on the screen, the stars ahead blazed blue-white, and—at the right magnification—the overall structure of the Open Cluster was easily visible.

She shook her head, went back to the peace conference reports. "Zakalwe, you asshole," she muttered to herself, "you'd better fucking show up soon."

Five days later, and still five days away, the General Contact Unit *Very Little Gravitas Indeed* signaled from the depths of the Open Cluster Crastalier that it thought it had picked up Zakalwe's trail.

The blue-white globe filled the screen; the module dipped its nose, plunging into the atmosphere.

"I just get the feeling this is going to be a complete debacle," the drone said.

"Yes," Sma said, "but you're not in charge."

"I'm serious," the machine told her. "Zakalwe's lost it. He doesn't want to be found, he won't be talked round, and even if by some miracle he can be, he can't do the same thing with Beychae. The man's washed up."

Sma had a sudden, strange flash of memory then, back to the horizon-wide beach, and the man who'd sat at her side for a while, watching the wide ocean roll its waves up and down the glistening slope of sand.

She shook herself out of it. "He's still together enough to junk a knife missile," she told the machine, watching the hazy, cloud-shadowed ocean scroll beneath the dropping module. They were approaching the cloud tops.

"That was for him. For us, it'll be another Winter Palace job; I can feel it."

She shook her head, apparently hypnotized by the view of cloud and curving ocean. "I don't know what happened

there. He got into that siege and just wouldn't break out. We
warned him; we *told* him, in the end, but he just wouldn't
. . . couldn't do it. I don't know what happened to him, I
really don't; he just wasn't himself.''

"Well, he lost his head on Fohls. Maybe he lost more
than that. Perhaps he lost it all on Fohls. Maybe we didn't
quite save him in time.''

"We got to him in time," Sma said, remembering Fohls
as well now, as they plunged into a bulging cloud top and the
screen went gray. She didn't bother to adjust the wavelength,
apparently content to look at the glowing, featureless interior
of the cumulus.

"It was still traumatic," the drone said.

"I'm sure, but . . ." she shrugged. The view of ocean
and clouds burst clear onto the screen again, and the module
angled steeper, powering down toward the waves. The sea
flashed up toward them; Sma turned the screen off. She looked
bashfully at Skaffen-Amtiskaw. "I never like watching that,"
she confessed. The drone said nothing. Inside the module,
all was peace and quiet. After a moment, she asked, "We in
yet?''

"Doing our submarine impression," the drone said
crisply. "Landfall in fifteen minutes.''

She turned the screen back on, got it to adjust for a sonic
display, and watched the rolling sea floor speed by beneath.
The module was maneuvering hard, swinging and diving and
zooming all the time, avoiding sea creatures as it followed
the slowly rising slope of continental shelf toward the land.
The view on the screen was disconcerting; she switched it off
again, turned to the drone.

"He'll be all right, and he'll come with us; we still know
where that woman is.''

"Livueta the Contemptuous?" sneered the drone. "Short
shrift she gave him last time. She'd have blown his head off
if I hadn't been there. Why the hell should Zakalwe want to
meet her again?''

"I don't know," Sma frowned. "He won't say, and Contact hasn't got round to doing the full procedure on the place
we think he came from. I think it must involve something
from his past . . . something he did, once, before we ever
heard of him. I don't know. I think he loves her, or did, and
still thinks he does . . . or just wants . . .''

"What? Wants what? Go on; you tell me."

"Forgiveness?"

"Sma, given all the things Zakalwe's done, just since we've known him, they'd have to invent a personal deity for him alone, to even start *forgiving* him."

Sma turned away to look at the blank screen again. She shook her head and said quietly, "It doesn't work that way, Skaffen-Amtiskaw."

Or any other way, the drone thought to itself, but didn't say anything.

The module surfaced in a deserted dock in the middle of the city, among the flotsam and jetsam. It roughed the texture of its outermost fields, so that the oily scum on the surface of the water stuck to it.

Sma watched its top hatch close, and stepped off the back of the drone, onto the pitted concrete of the dock. The module was ninety percent submerged; it looked like some flat-bottomed boat turned turtle. She straightened the rather vulgar culottes which were, regrettably, the height of fashion here just now, and looked up and around at the crumbling empty warehouses which all but enclosed the quiet dock. The city—she was oddly gratified to find—grumbled beyond.

"What was that you were saying about not looking in cities?" Skaffen-Amtiskaw inquired.

"Don't be crass," she said, then clapped her hands and rubbed them. Looking down at the drone, she grinned. "Anyway: time to start thinking like a suitcase, old chum. Make with a handle."

"I hope you realize I find this every bit as demeaning as you think I must," Skaffen-Amtiskaw said, with quiet dignity, then extended a soligram handle from one side, and flipped over. Sma gripped the handle and strained at it.

"An *empty* suitcase, asshole," she grunted.

"Oh, pardon me, I'm sure," Skaffen-Amtiskaw muttered, and went light.

Sma opened a wallet full of money displaced only hours earlier from a city-center bank by the good ship *Xenophobe*, and paid the cab driver. She watched a line of troop carriers thunder past, heading down the boulevard, then sat on a bench which formed part of a stone wall bordering a narrow strip of trees and grass, and looked out over the broad sidewalk and the boulevard beyond, to the large and impressive stone building on the far side. She placed the drone beside her. Traffic roared past; people hurried to and fro in front of her.

At least, she thought, they're fairly standard. She had never liked being altered to impersonate the natives. Anyway; they had inter-system travel here, and were fairly used to seeing people who looked different, even alien on occasion. As usual, of course, she was very tall in comparison, but she could live with a few stares.

"He's still in there?" she said quietly, looking at the armed guards outside the Foreign Ministry.

"Discussing some sort of weird trust setup with the top brass," the drone whispered. "Want to eavesdrop?"

"Hmm. No."

They had a bug in the appropriate conference chamber; literally a fly on the wall.

"Wa!" the drone yelped. "I don't believe this man!"

Sma glanced at the drone, despite herself. She frowned. "What's he said?"

"Not that!" the drone gasped. "The *Very Little Gravitas Indeed* just worked out what the maniac's been up to here."

The GCU was still in orbit, providing backup for the *Xenophobe*; its Contact procedures and equipment had provided and were providing most of the information about the place; its bug was monitoring the conference chamber. Meanwhile, it was scanning computers and information banks over the entire planet.

"Well?" Sma said, watching another troop carrier rumble past on the boulevard.

"The man's insane. Power mad!" the drone muttered, seemingly to itself. "Forget Voerenhutz; we have to get him out of here for the sake of *these* people."

Sma elbowed the suitcase-drone. "*What*, dammit?"

"Okay; here, Zakalwe's a goddamn magnate, right? Mega-powerful; interests everywhere; initial stake what he brought with him from the place he junked the knife missile; the loot we gave him last time, plus profits. And what is the core of his business empire, here? Genetechnology."

Sma thought for a moment. "Oh-oh," she said, sitting back on the bench, crossing her arms.

"Whatever you're imagining, it's worse. Sma; there are five rather elderly autocrats on this planet, in competing hegemonies. *They are all getting healthier.* They are all getting, in fact, younger. That oughtn't to be possible for another twenty, thirty years."

Sma said nothing. There was a funny feeling in her belly.

"Zakalwe's corporation," the drone said quickly, "is receiving crazy money from each of those five people. It *was* on the take from a sixth geezer, but he died about one-twenty days ago; assassinated. The Ethnarch Kerian. He controlled the other half of this continent. It's his demise that has led to all this military activity. Also, with the exception of the Ethnarch Kerian, these suddenly rejuvenated autocrats were showing signs of becoming uncharacteristically *benign*, from about the time they started getting so suspiciously frisky."

Sma closed her eyes for a moment, opened them. "Is it working?" she said, through a dry mouth.

"Like hell; they're all under threat from coups; their own military, as a rule. Worse than that, Kerian's death lit a slow fuse. This whole place is going super-critical! And we are talking tootsies on the event horizon; these meatbrained loonies have thermonukes. He's crazy!" the drone suddenly screeched. Sma hissed to quiet it, even though she knew the drone would be sound-fielding its words so that only she could hear. The drone spluttered on: "He must have cracked the gene-coding in his own cells; the steady-state retro-aging that *we gave him*; he's been selling it! For money and favors, trying to get these monomaniac dictators to behave like nice people. Sma! He's trying to set up his own contact section! And he's fucking it! Completely!"

She whacked the machine with one fist. "Calm down, dammit."

"Sma," the drone said, voice almost languid, "I am calm. I'm just trying to communicate to you the enormity of the planetary cock-up Zakalwe has managed to concoct here. The *Very Little Gravitas Indeed* has blown a fuse; even as we talk, Contact Minds in an ever-expanding sphere centered right here are clearing their intellectual decks and trying to work out what the hell to do to tidy this stunningly ghastly mess. If that GSV hadn't been on its way here anyway, they'd have

diverted it because of this. An asteroid belt-sized pile of shit
is about to hit a fan exactly the size of this planet, thanks to
Zakalwe's ludicrous good-guy schemes, and Contact is going
to have to try and field all of it," It hesitated. "Yeah; I just
got the word." It sounded relieved. "You have a day to haul
Zakalwe's loop-eyed ass out of here, otherwise we snatch
him; emergency displace, no holds barred."

Sma took a very deep breath. "Apart from that . . . everything all right?"

"This, Ms. Sma, is no time for levity," the drone said,
soberly. Then; "Shit!"

"What now?"

"Meeting's over, but Zakalwe the Insane isn't taking his
car; he's heading for the elevator down to the tube system.
Destination . . . naval base. There's a submarine waiting for
him."

Sma stood. "Submarine, eh?" She smoothed the culottes. "Back to the docks, agree?"

"Agreed."

She hefted the drone, started walking, looking for a cab.
"I've asked the *Very Little Gravitas Indeed* to fake a radio
message," Skaffen-Amtiskaw told her. "A cab should pull
up here momentarily."

"And they say there's never one around when you need
one."

"You're worrying me, Sma. You're taking all this far too
calmly."

"Oh, I'll panic later." Sma took a deep breath and let it
out slowly. "Could that be the cab?"

"I believe it is."

"What's 'To the docks'?"

The drone told her, and she said it. The cab sped off
through the largely military traffic.

Six hours later they were still following the submarine, as it
whined and whirred and gurgled its way through the layers
of ocean, heading for the equatorial sea.

"Sixty klicks an hour," fumed the drone. "Sixty klicks
an hour!"

"To them it's fast; don't be so unsympathetic to your fellow machines." Sma watched the screen as the vessel a ki-

lometer in front of them burrowed its way through the ocean. The abyssal plain was kilometers below.

"It isn't one of us, Sma," the drone said wearily. "It's just a submarine; the smartest thing inside it is the human captain. I rest my case."

"Any idea where it's heading yet?"

"No. The captain's orders are to take Zakalwe wherever he wants to go, and after giving him this general heading, Zakalwe's kept quiet. There's a whole heap of islands and atolls he could be making for, or—several days' travel away at this crawl—thousands of kilometers of coastline, on another continent."

"Check out the islands, and that coastline. There must be a reason he's heading this way."

"It's *being* checked out!" the drone snapped.

Sma looked at it. Skaffen-Amtiskaw flashed a delicate shade of purple, intimating contrition. "Sma; this . . . man . . . totally blew it the last time; we're five or six million down on that last job, all because he wouldn't break out of the Winter Palace and balance things out. I could show you scenes of the terror there that would blanch your hair. Now he's come very close indeed to instigating a global catastrophe here. Since the guy suffered what happened to him on Fohls—since he started trying to be a good guy in his own right—he's been a disaster. If we do get him, and can get him to Voerenhutz, I just worry what sort of chaos he'll engender there. The man's bad news. Never mind outing Beychae; offing Zakalwe would be doing everybody a favor."

Sma looked into the center of the drone's sensory band. "One;" she said, "don't talk about human lives as though they're just collateral." She breathed deeply. "Two; remember the massacre, in the courtyard of that inn?" she asked calmly. "The guys through the walls, and your knife missile let off the leash?"

"One; sorry to have offended your mammalian sensibilities. Two; Sma, will you ever let me forget it?"

"Remember what I said would happen if you ever tried anything like that again?"

"Sma," the drone said tiredly, "if you are seriously trying to imply that I might kill Zakalwe, all I can say is; don't be ridiculous."

"Just remember." She watched the slowly scrolling screen. "We have our orders."

"Agreed on courses of action, Sma. We don't have orders, remember?"

Sma nodded. "We have our agreed on courses of action. We lift Mr. Zakalwe and take him to Voerenhutz. If at any stage you disagree, you can always butt out. I'll be given another offensive drone."

Skaffen-Amtiskaw was silent for a second, then said, "Sma, that is probably the most hurtful thing you have ever said to me—which is saying a lot—but I'll ignore it, I think, because we are both under a lot of stress at the moment. Let my actions speak. As you say; we lift the planetfucker and drop him in Voerenhutz. Though, if this voyage goes on too much longer, it'll all be taken out of our hands—or fields, as the case may be—and Zakalwe will wake up on *Xenophobe* or the GCU, wondering what happened. All we can do is wait and see."

The drone paused then. "Looks like it could be those equatorial islands we're heading for," it told her. "Zakalwe owns half of them."

Sma nodded silently, watching the distant submarine creep through the ocean. She scratched at her lower abdomen after a while, and turned to the drone. "You sure you didn't record anything from that, umm, sort of orgy, first night on the *Xenophobe*?"

"Positive."

She frowned back at the screen. "Huh. Pity."

The submarine spent nine hours underwater, then surfaced near an atoll; an inflatable went ashore. Sma and the drone watched the single figure walk up the golden, sunlit beach toward a complex of low buildings; an exclusive hotel for the ruling class of the country he'd left.

"What's Zakalwe doing?" Sma said, after he'd been ashore for ten minutes or so. The submarine had dived again as soon as it recovered its inflatable, and taken a course back to the port it had departed from.

"He's saying goodbye to a girl," sighed the drone.

"Is that *it*?"

"That would appear to be the only thing to draw him here."

"Shit! Couldn't he have taken a plane?"

"Hmm. No; no airstrip, but anyway, this is a fairly sensitive demilitarized zone; no unexpected flights of any sort allowed, and the next seaplane isn't for a couple of days. The sub was actually the fastest way of . . ."

The drone fell silent.

"Skaffen-Amtiskaw?" Sma said.

"Well," the drone said slowly, "the doxy just smashed a lot of ornaments and a couple of pieces of very valuable furniture, and then ran off and buried herself in her bed, weeping . . . but apart from that, Zakalwe just sat down in the middle of the lounge with a large drink and said (and I quote), 'Okay; if that's you, Sma, come and talk to me.' "

Sma looked at the view on the screen. It showed the small atoll, the central island lying green and squashed looking between the vibrant blues and greens of ocean and sky.

"You know," she said, "I think I would like to kill Zakalwe."

"There's a queue. Surface?"

"Surface. Let's go see the asshole."

Light. Some light. Not very much. Air foul and everywhere pain. He wanted to scream and writhe, but could find no breath and make nothing move. A dark destroying shadow welled up inside him, exterminating thought, and he lost consciousness.

Light. Some light. Not very much. He knew there was pain, too, but somehow it did not seem so important. He was looking at it differently now. That was all you had to do; just think about it differently. He wondered where that idea had come from, and seemed to remember he'd been taught how to do this.

Everything was metaphor; all things were something other than themselves. The pain, for example, was an ocean, and he was adrift on it. His body was a city and his mind a citadel. All communications between the two seemed to have been cut, but within the keep that was his mind he still had power. The part of his consciousness that was telling him the pain did not hurt, and that all things were like other things, was like . . . like . . . he found it hard to think of a comparison. A magic mirror, maybe.

Still thinking about that, the light faded, and he slipped away again, into the darkness.

Light. Some light (he'd been here before, hadn't he?). Not very much. He seemed to have left the keep that was his mind, and now he was in a storm-struck leaking boat, images dancing before him.

The light grew slowly in strength until it was almost painful. He felt suddenly terrified, because it seemed to him that he really was on a tiny creaking leaking boat, tossed scudding across a seething black ocean, in the teeth of a howling gale, but now there was light, and it appeared to come from somewhere above him, but when he tried to look at his hand, or the tiny boat, he still couldn't see anything. The light shone into his eyes, but it failed to illuminate anything else. The idea terrified him; the tiny boat was swamped by a wave and he was submerged again in the ocean of pain, burning through every pore of his body. Somewhere, thankfully, somebody threw a switch, and he slipped underneath to darkness, silence and . . . no pain.

Light. Some light. He remembered this. The light showed a small boat assaulted by waves on a broad dark ocean. Beyond, unreachable for now, there was a great citadel on a small island. And there was sound. Sound . . . That was new. Been here before, but not with sound. He tried to listen, very hard, but could not make out the words. Still, he formed the impression that maybe somebody was asking questions.

Somebody was asking questions . . . Who . . . ? He waited for a reply, from outside or from within himself, but nothing came from anywhere; he felt lost and abandoned, and the worst of it was that he felt abandoned by himself.

He decided to ask himself some questions. What was the citadel? That was his mind. The citadel was supposed to come with a city attached, which was his body, but it looked like something else had taken over the city, and there was just the castle, just the keep left. What was the boat, and the ocean? The ocean was pain. He was in the boat now, but before that he'd been in the ocean, up to his neck, waves breaking over him. The boat was . . . some learned technique which was protecting him from the pain, not letting him forget it was there, but keeping its debilitating effects away from him, letting him think.

So far so good, he thought. Now, what is the light?

He might have to come back to that one. Same with: What is the sound?

He tried another question: Where is this happening?

He searched his sodden clothes but found nothing in any of the pockets. He looked for a name tag that he felt ought to be sewn on to his collar, but it seemed to have been ripped off. He searched the small boat, but still found no answers. So he tried to imagine being in the distant keep over the towering waves, and visualized himself walking into a cavernous storeroom of jumble and nonsense and memories buried deep in the castle . . . but could see nothing in detail. His eyes closed and he wept with frustration, while the small boat juddered and tipped underneath him.

When he opened his eyes, he was holding a little clip of paper with the word FOHLS printed on it. He was so surprised he let the slip of paper go; the wind whipped it away into the dark sky over the black waves. But he had remembered. Fohls was the answer. The planet of Fohls.

He felt relieved, and a little proud. He'd discovered something.

What was he doing here?

Funeral. He seemed to remember something about a funeral. Surely it had not been his own.

Was he dead? He thought about this question for a while. He supposed it was possible. Maybe there was an afterlife, after all. Well, if there was life after death, that would teach him. Was this sea of pain a divine punishment? Was the light a god? He dipped his hand over the side of the boat, into the pain; it filled him, and he withdrew. Cruel god if that really was the case. What about all the stuff I did for the Culture? he wanted to ask. Doesn't that cancel some of the bad out? Or were those smug self-satisfied bastards wrong all along? *God*, he'd love to be able to go back and tell them. Imagine the look on Sma's face!

But he didn't think he was dead. It hadn't been his funeral. He could remember the flat-topped tower by the cliffs looking out over the sea, and helping to carry some old warrior's body there. Yes, somebody had died and they were being ceremonially disposed of.

Something was nagging at him.

Suddenly he clutched at the boat's rotten timbers and stared out over the heaving ocean.

There was a ship. Every now and again he could see a ship, far in the distance. Barely more than a dot, and mostly the waves were in the way, but it was a ship. A hole seemed to open somewhere inside him; his guts fell through it.

He thought he recognized the ship.

Then the boat split apart, and he dropped through it, through the water underneath, then splashed out of the underside of the water, into air again, and saw the ocean beneath him, and a tiny speck on its surface, which he was falling toward. It was another small boat; he crashed through it, through more water, through more air, through the wreckage of a boat, through another layer of water and another level of air . . .

Hey—one part of his mind thought, as he fell—this is like how Sma described the Reality.

. . . splashed through more waves, through the water, out into air, heading for more waves . . .

This wasn't going to stop. He remembered that the Reality Sma had described was expanding all the time; you could fall through forever; really forever, not until the end of the universe; literally forever.

That won't do, he thought to himself. He'd have to face the ship.

He landed in a little creaking, leaking boat.

The ship was much closer now. The ship was huge and dark and bristled with guns and it was heading straight for him, bow wave a huge white V of foam bisected by its stem.

Shit, he wasn't going to be able to get away from it. The cruel curves of the bows raced slicing toward him. He closed his eyes.

Once upon a time there was . . . a ship. A great ship. A ship for destroying things with; other ships, people, cities . . . It was very big and it was designed to kill people and to keep people inside it from being killed.

He tried not to remember what the great ship was called. Instead he saw the ship somehow installed near the middle of a city, and felt confused, and could not work out how it got there. The ship started to look like a castle, for some reason, and that did, and did not, make sense. He began to feel frightened. The ship's name was like some huge sea creature, bumping into the hull of his boat; like a battering ram thudding into the walls of the castle keep. He tried to block it out, knowing it was just a name but not wanting to hear it because it always made him feel bad.

He put his hands over his ears. That worked for a moment. But then the ship, set in stone, near the center of the battered city, fired its great guns, gouting black and flashing yellow-white, and he knew what was coming, and tried to scream to cover the noise, but when it arrived it was the name of the ship that the guns had spoken, and it shattered the boat, demolished the castle, and resounded through the bones and spaces of his skull, like the laughter of an insane god, forever.

The light went out then, and he sank gratefully away from the awful, accusing sound.

Light. *Staberinde* said a calm voice from somewhere inside. *Staberinde. It's only a word.*

The Staberinde. The ship. He turned away from the light, back into the darkness.

Light. Sounds, too; a voice. What was I thinking about, earlier? (He recalled something about a name, but ignored that.) Funeral. Pains. And the ship. There was a ship. Or there had been. Maybe still is, for all . . . but there was something about a funeral. The funeral is why you are here. That was what confused you before. You thought you were dead, in fact you were only living. He remembered something about boats and oceans and castles and cities, but could not actually see them anymore.

Now, from somewhere, comes touch, touch coming in from out there. Not pain but touch. Two different things . . .

The touch, again. It feels like the touch of a hand; a hand touching his face, causing more pain, but still a touch, and distinguishably a hand. His face felt terrible. He must look terrible.

Where am I again? Crash. Funeral. Fohls.

Crash. Of course; my name is . . .

Too hard.

What do I do, then?

That's easier. You are a paid agent of the most advanced—well, certainly the most *energetic*—humanoid civilization in the . . . Reality? (No.) Universe? (No.) Galaxy? Yes, galaxy . . . and you were representing them at a . . . a . . . funeral, and you were coming back on some stupid *aircraft* to be picked up and taken away from all this, when something happened on board the aircraft and it went . . . and he'd seen flames and . . . and there had been that old jungle floating right . . . then nothing and pain, and nothing but pain. Then drifting and floating in and out of it.

The hand touched his face again. And this time there was something to see. He thought it looked like a cloud, or like a moon through a cloud, itself unseen but shining through.

Possibly the two were connected, he thought. Yes; here it comes again, and yes, there we are; sensation, feeling; the hand on the face again. Throat, swallowing, water or some liquid. You are being given something to drink. From the way it goes down there seems to be . . . yes, upright, we are upright, not on our back. The hands, own hands, they are . . . an open feeling, feeling very open, very vulnerable, naked.

Thinking about his body was bringing the pain back again. He decided to give up on that. Try something else.

Try the crash again. Back from the funeral and the desert coming right up . . . no, mountains. Or was it jungle? He couldn't remember. Where are we? Jungle, no . . . desert, no . . . what then? Don't know.

Asleep, he thought suddenly; you were asleep in the aircraft in the night, and had just enough time to wake up in the darkness and see flames and begin to realize before light detonated inside your head. After that, pain. But you didn't see any sort of terrain floating/rushing up to meet you, because it was very dark.

The next time he came round, everything had changed. He felt vulnerable and exposed. As his eyes opened and he tried to remember how to see, he slowly made out dusty streaks of light in a brown gloom, and saw earthenware pots near a mud or earth wall, and a small fireplace in the center of the room, and spears leaning against a wall, and other blades. Straining his neck to bring his head up, he could see something else; the rough wooden frame he was tied to.

The wooden frame was in the shape of a square; two diagonals made an X inside the square. He was naked, his hands and feet lashed one to each corner of the frame, which was propped against a wall at about forty-five degrees. A thick hide strap secured his waist to the center of the X, and all over his body were markings of blood and paint.

He relaxed his neck. "Oh shit," he heard himself croak. He didn't like the look of this.

Where the hell *was* the Culture? They ought to be rescuing him; that was their job. He did their dirty work, they looked after him. This was the deal. So where the hell were they?

The pain came back, like an old friend by now, from almost everywhere. Straining his neck like that had hurt. Sore head (maybe concussion); broken nose, cracked or broken ribs, one broken arm, two broken legs. Maybe internal injuries; his insides felt pretty sore too; the worst, in fact. He felt bloated and full of decay.

Shit, he thought, I might actually be dying.

He shifted his head, grimacing, (pain poured in as if some protecting shell on his skin had been cracked by the movement) and looked at the ropes lashing him to the wooden frame. Traction was no way to treat a fracture, he told himself, and laughed very briefly, because with the first contraction of his stomach muscles his ribs pulsed suddenly, as though they were at red heat.

He could hear things; distant noises of people shouting now and again, and children yelling, and some sort of animal baying.

He closed his eyes, but heard nothing more distinct. He opened them again. The wall was earth, and he was probably underground, for there were thick sawn-off roots sticking into the space around him. The light was composed of two nearly vertical shafts, slightly angled beams of direct sunlight, so . . . near midday, near the equator. Underground, he thought, and felt sick. Nice and hard to find. He wondered if the plane had been on course when it crashed, and how far from the crash site he'd been carried. No point in worrying about it.

What else could he see? Crude benches. A coarse cushion, dented. It looked like somebody had sat there, facing him. He assumed it was the owner of the hand he had felt, if there had been one. There was no fire in a circle of stones set underneath one of the holes in the roof. Spears leaned against the wall, and other weaponish things were strewn about the place. They were not battle-weapons; ceremonial, or maybe torture. He caught a whiff of something awful, just then, and knew it was gangrene, and knew it must be him.

He began to slip over the edge again, uncertain whether he was falling asleep or really going unconscious, but hoping for one or the other, willing either, because all this was more than he could handle just now. Then the girl came in. She had a jug in her hand, and set it down before looking at him. He tried to speak, but couldn't. Maybe he hadn't really spoken earlier when he'd thought he said, ''Shit,'' He looked at the girl and attempted a smile.

She went out again.

He felt somehow heartened, seeing the girl. A man would have been bad news, he thought. A girl meant things might not be so bad after all. Maybe.

The girl came back, with a bowl of water. She washed him, rubbing away the the blood and the paint. There was some pain. Predictably nothing happened when she washed his genitals; he'd have liked to show signs of life, just for form's sake.

He tried to speak, but failed. The girl let him sip some water from a shallow bowl, and he croaked at her, but nothing distinguishable. She left again.

The next time she came back with some men. They wore many strange clothes, like feathers and skins and bones and wooden tiles of armour laced with gut. They were painted too, and they brought pots and small sticks with them, and used them to paint him again.

They finished and stood back. He wanted to tell them he didn't suit red, but nothing came out. He felt himself falling away, out into the darkness.

When he came to again, he was moving.

The entire frame he was strapped to had been lifted and carted out of the gloom. He faced the sky. Blinding light filled his eyes, dust filled his nose and mouth, and shouts and screams filled his mind. He felt himself shiver like a fever victim, tearing pain from each shattered limb. He tried to shout, and to raise his head to see, but all there was was noise and dust. His insides felt worse; skin taut over his belly.

Then he was upright again, and the village was beneath him. It was small, there were some tents, some wicker and clay dwellings and some holes into the ground. Semiarid; an indeterminate scrub—stamped down inside the perimeter of the village—vanished quickly beyond it, into a yellow-glowing mist. The sun was just visible, low down. He couldn't work out if it was dawn or dusk.

What he really saw were the people. They were all in front of him; he was up on a mound, the frame tied to two large stakes, and the people were beneath him, all on their knees, heads bowed. There were tiny children, their heads forced down by nearby adults, there were old people held up from collapsing completely by those around them, and every age in between.

Then in front of him walked three people, the girl and two of the men. The men, one on either side of the girl, lowered their heads, knelt down quickly and arose again, and made a sign. The girl did not move, and her gaze was fixed on a point between his eyes. She was dressed in a bright red gown now; he could not remember what she had worn before.

One of the men held a large earthenware pot. The other had a long, curved, broad-bladed sword.

"Hey," he croaked. He couldn't manage anything else. The pain was getting very bad now; being upright didn't do his broken limbs any good at all.

The chanting people seemed to swing about his head; the sunlight dipped and veered, and the three people in front of him became many, multiplying and wavering, unsteady in the waste of mist and dust before him.

Where the hell was Culture?

There was a terrible roaring noise in his head, and the diffuse glow in the midst which was the sun was starting to pulse. The sword glittered to one side; the earthenware pot gleamed on the other. The girl stood directly in front of him, and put her hand into his hair, grasping it.

The roaring noise was filling his ears, and he could not

tell if he was shouting and screaming or not. The man to his right raised the sword.

The girl pulled his hair, yanking his head out; he screamed, above the roaring noise, as his broken bones grated. He stared at the dust at the hem of the girl's robe.

"You bastards!" he thought, not sure, even then, exactly who he meant.

He managed to scream one syllable. "El—!"

Then the blade slammed into his neck.

The name died. Everything had ended but it still went on.

There was no pain. The roaring noise was actually quieter. He was looking down at the village and the crouching people. The view swung; he could still feel the pull of the roots of his hair straining at the skin on his scalp. He was swung round.

The slack, headless body dribbled blood down its chest.

That was me! he thought. Me!

He was swung round again; the man with the sword was wiping blood from the blade with a rag. The man with the earthenware pot was trying not to look into his staring eyes, and holding the pot out toward him, the lid in his other hand. So *that's* what it's for, he thought, feeling somehow stunned into an eerie calmness. Then the roaring noise seemed to gather and start to fade at once. The view was going red. He wondered how much longer this could go on. How long did a brain survive without oxygen?

Now I really am two, he thought, remembering, eyes closing.

And he thought of his heart, stopped now, and only then realized, and wanted to cry but could not, for he had finally lost her. Another name formed in his mind. Dar . . .

The roar split the skies. He felt the girl's grip loosen. The expression on the face of the youth holding the pot was almost comically fearful. People looked up from the crowd; the roar became a scream, a blast of air swept dust into the air and made the girl holding him stagger; a dark shape swung quickly through the air above the village.

A little late . . . he heard himself think, slipping away.

There was more noise for a second or two—screams, maybe—and something whacked into his head, and he was rolling away, dust in his mouth and eyes . . . but he was starting to lose interest in all that stuff, and was happy to let the darkness wash over him. Maybe he was picked up again, later.

But that seemed to happen to somebody else.

When the terrible noise came, and the great, carved black rock landed in the middle of the village—just after the sky's offering had been separated from his body and so joined to the air—everybody ran into the thinning mist, to get away from the screaming light. They gathered, whimpering, at the water hole.

After only fifty heartbeats, the dark shape appeared above the village again, rising hazily into the thinner mists near the sky. It did not roar this time, but moved quickly off with a noise like the wind, and shrank to nothing.

The shaman sent his apprentice back to see how things stood; the quaking youth disappeared into the mist. He returned safely, and the shaman led the still terrified people back to the village.

The body of the sky-offering still hung limply on the wooden frame at the summit of the mound. His head had disappeared.

After much chanting and grinding entrails, spotting shapes in the mists and three trances, the priest and his apprentice decided it was a good omen, and yet a warning at the same time. They sacrificed a meat-animal belonging to the family of the girl who had dropped the sky-offering's head, and put the beast's head in the earthenware pot instead.

5

"**D**izzy! How the devil are you?" He took her hand and helped her up onto the wooden pier from the roof of the just-surfaced module. He put his arms round her. "Good to see you again!" he laughed. Sma patted his waist, finding herself unwilling to hug him back. He didn't seem to notice.

He let her go, looked down to see the drone rising up from the module. "And Skaffen-Amtiskaw! They still letting you out without a guard?"

"Hello, Zakalwe," the drone said.

He put his arm round Sma's waist. "Come on up to the shack; we'll have lunch."

"All right," she said.

They walked along the small wooden pier to a stone path laid across the sand, and on into the shade under the trees. The trees were blue or purple; huge puff heads of dark color standing out against the pale blue sky, and tugged at by a warm, intermittent breeze. They sweated delicate perfumes from the tops of their silver-white trunks. The drone lifted to above tree height a couple of times, when other people passed on the path.

The man and woman walked through the sunlit avenues between the trees until they came to where a wide pool of water trembled reflections of twenty or so white huts; a small, sleek seaplane floated at a wooden jetty. They entered the cluster of buildings and climbed some steps to a balcony that looked over the pool and the narrow channel that led from it to the lagoon on the far side of the island.

The sun was sifted through the tree-heads; shadows moved to and fro along the veranda and over the small table and the two hammocks.

He motioned Sma to sit on the first hammock; a female servant appeared and he ordered lunch for two. When the servant had gone, Skaffen-Amtiskaw floated down and sat on the parapet of the veranda's wall, overlooking the pool. Sma levered herself into the hammock carefully.

"It true you own this island, Zakalwe?"

"Um . . ." he looked round, apparently uncertain, then nodded his head. "Oh yes; so I do." He kicked off his sandals and slumped into the other hammock, letting it sway. He picked up a bottle from the floor, and with each sway of the hammock poured a little more from the bottle into two glasses on the small table. He increased the swing when he had finished to be able to hand her drink to her.

"Thank you."

He sipped at his drink and closed his eyes. She watched the glass on his chest where his hands held it, and watched the liquid swill this way, that way, lethargic and eye-brown. She moved her gaze to his face and saw he had not changed; hair a bit darker than she remembered; swept away from his broad, tanned forehead and tied in a ponytail behind. Fit-looking as ever. No older-looking, of course, because they'd stabilized his age as part of his payment for the last job.

His eyes opened slowly, heavy-lidded, and he looked back at her, smiling slowly. The eyes look older, she thought. But she could have been wrong.

"So," she said, "we playing games here, Zakalwe?"

"What do you mean, Dizzy?"

"I've been sent to get you back again. They want you to do another job. You must have guessed that, so tell me now whether I'm wasting my time here or not. I'm in no mood to try and argue you . . ."

"Dizzy!" he exclaimed, sounding hurt, pivoting his legs off the hammock and onto the floor, then smiling persuasively. "Don't be like that; of course you're not wasting your time. I've already packed."

He beamed at her like a happy child, his tanned face open and smiling. She looked at him with relief and disbelief.

"So what was all the runaround for?"

"What runaround?" he said innocently, sitting back in the hammock again. "I had to come here to say goodbye to a close friend, that was all. But I'm ready to go. What's the scam?"

Sma stared, open-mouthed. Then she turned to the drone. "Do we just go now?"

"No point," Skaffen-Amtiskaw said. "The course the GSV's on, you can have two hours here, then go back to the *Xenophobe*; it can match with the *What* in about thirty hours." It swiveled to look at the man. "But we need a definite word. There's a teratonne of GSV with twenty-eight million people on board charging in this direction; if it's to wait here it has to slow down first, so it needs to know for sure. You really are coming? This afternoon?"

"Drone, I just *told* you. I'll do it." He leaned toward Sma. "What is the job again?"

"Voerenhutz," she told him. "Tsoldrin Beychae."

He beamed, teeth gleaming. "Old Tsoldrin still above ground? Well, it'll be good to see him again."

"You have to talk him back into his working clothes again."

He waved one hand airily. "Easy," he said, drinking.

Sma watched him drink. She shook her head.

"Don't you want to know why, Cheradenine?" she asked.

He started to make a gesture with one hand that meant the same as a shrug, then thought better of it. "Umm; sure. Why, Diziet?" he sighed.

"Voerenhutz is coalescing into two groups; the people gaining the upper hand at the moment want to pursue aggressive terraforming policies . . ."

"That's sort of . . ." he burped, "redecorating a planet, right?"

Sma closed her eyes briefly. "Yes. Sort of. Whatever you choose to call it, it's ecologically insensitive, to put it mildly. These people—they call themselves the Humanists—also want a sliding scale of sentient rights which will have the effect of letting them take over whatever even intelligently inhabited worlds they're militarily able to. There are a dozen brush-fire wars going on right now. Any one of them could spark the big one, and to an extent the Humanists encourage these wars because they appear to prove their case that the Cluster is too crowded and needs to find new planetary habitats.''

''They also,'' Skaffen-Amtiskaw said, ''refuse to acknowledge machine sentience fully; they exploit proto-conscious computers and claim only human subjective experience has any intrinsic value; carbon fascists.''

''I see,'' he nodded, and looked very serious. ''And you want old Beychae to get into harness with these Humanist guys, right?''

''Cheradenine!'' Sma scolded, as Skaffen-Amtiskaw's fields went frosty.

He looked hurt. ''But they're called the Humanists!''

''That's just their name, Zakalwe.''

''Names are important,'' he said, apparently serious.

''It's still just what they call themselves; it doesn't make them the good guys.''

''Okay.'' He grinned at Sma. ''Sorry.'' He tried to look more business-like. ''You want him pulling in the other direction, like last time.''

''Yes,'' Sma said.

''Fine. Sounds almost easy. No soldiering?''

''No soldiering.''

''I'll do it.'' He nodded.

''Do I hear the sound of a barrel-bottom being scraped?'' Skaffen-Amtiskaw muttered.

''Just send the signal,'' Sma told it.

''Okay,'' said the drone. ''Signal sent.'' It made a good impression of glowering at the man with its fields. ''But you'd better not change your mind.''

''Only the thought of having to spend any time in your company, Skaffen-Amtiskaw, could possibly disinduce me from accompanying the delightful Ms. Sma here to Voerenhutz.'' He glanced concernedly at the woman. ''You are coming, I hope.''

Sma nodded. She sipped at her drink, while the servant laid some small dishes on the table between the hammocks.

''Just like that, Zakalwe?'' she said, once the servant had gone again.

''Just like what, Diziet?'' He smiled over his glass.

"You're leaving. After, what . . . five years? Building up your empire, sorting out your scheme to make the world a safer place, using our technology, trying to use our methods . . . you're prepared just to walk away from it all, for however long it takes? Dammit, even before you knew it was Voerenhutz you'd said yes; could have been on the other side of the galaxy, for all you knew; could have been the Clouds. You might have been saying yes to a four-year trip."

He shrugged. "I like long voyages."

Sma looked into the man's face for a while. He looked unworried, full of life. Pep and vim were the words that came to mind. She felt vaguely disgusted.

He shrugged, eating some fruit from one of the little dishes. "Besides, I have a trust arrangement set up. It'll all be looked after until I come back."

"If there's anything to come back to," Skaffen-Amtiskaw observed.

"Of course there will be," he said, spitting a pip over the edge of the veranda wall. "These people like to talk about war, but they aren't suicidal."

"Oh, that's all right then," the drone said, turning away.

The man just smiled at it. He nodded at Sma's untouched plate. "You not hungry, Diziet?"

"Lost my appetite," she said.

He swung out of the hammock, brushing his hands together. "Come on," he said, "let's go for a swim."

She watched him trying to catch fish in a small rock pool; paddling around in his long trunks. She had swum in her briefs.

He bent down, engrossed, his earnest face peering into the water, his face reflected there. He seemed to speak to it.

"You still look very good, you know. I hope you feel suitably flattered."

She went on drying herself. "I'm too old for flattery, Zakalwe."

"Rubbish." He laughed, and the water rippled under his mouth. He frowned hard and dipped his hands under, slowly.

She watched the concentration on his face as his arms slid deeper under the water, mirroring themselves.

He smiled again, his eyes narrowing as his hands steadied; his arms were in deep now, and he licked his lips.

He lunged forward, yelled excitedly, then cupped his hands out of the water and came over to her where she sat against some rocks. He was grinning hugely. He held his hands out for her to see. She looked in and saw a small fish, brilliant shimmering blue and green and red and gold, a gaudy splash of rippling light squirming inside the man's cupped hands. She frowned as he leaned back against the rock again.

"Now just you put that back where you found it, Cheradenine, and the way you found it."

His face fell and she was about to say something else, kinder, when he grinned again and threw the fish back into the pool.

"As if I'd do anything else." He came and sat beside her on the rock.

She looked out to sea. The drone was further up the beach, ten meters behind them. She carefully smoothed the tiny dark hairs on her forearms until they were lying flat. "Why did you try all that stuff, Zakalwe?"

"Giving the elixir of youth to our glorious leaders?" He shrugged. "Seemed like a good idea at the time," he confessed, lightly. "I don't know; I thought it might be possible. I thought interfering was maybe a lot easier than you lot made it out to be. I thought one man with a strong plan, not interested in his own aggrandizement . . ." He shrugged, glanced at her. "It might all work out yet. You never know."

"Zakalwe, it isn't going to work out. You're leaving us an incredible mess here."

"Ah," he nodded. "You are coming in, then. Thought you might."

"In some fashion, I think we'll have to."

"Best of luck."

"Luck . . ." Sma began, but then thought the better of it. She ran her fingers through her damp hair.

"How much trouble am I in, Diziet?"

"For this?"

"Yes, and the knife missile. You heard about that?"

"I heard." She shook her head. "I don't think you're in any more trouble than you're ever in, Cheradenine, just by being you."

He smiled. "I hate the Culture's . . . tolerance."

"So," she said, slipping her blouse over her head, "what are your terms?"

"Pay as well, eh?" He laughed. "Minus the rejuve . . . the same as the last time. Plus ten percent more negotiables."

"Exactly the same?" She looked at him sadly, her wet bedraggled hair hanging down from her shaking head.

He nodded. "Exactly."

"You're a fool, Zakalwe."

"I keep trying."

"It won't be any different."

"You can't know that."

"I can guess."

"And I can hope. Look, Dizzy, it's my business, and if you want me to come with you then you've got to agree to it, all right?"

"All right."

He looked wary. "You still know where she is?"

Sma nodded. "Yes, we know."

"So it's agreed?"

She shrugged and looked out to sea. "Oh; it's agreed. I just think you're wrong. I don't think you should go to her again." She looked him in the eye. "That's my advice."

He stood up and dusted some sand off his legs.

"I'll remember."

They walked back to the huts and the still sea pool in the center of the island. She sat on a wall, waiting while he made his final goodbyes. She listened for crying, or the sound of breakages, but in vain.

The wind blew her hair gently, and to her surprise, despite it all, she felt warm and well; the scent from the tall trees stretched around her, and their shifting shadows made the ground seem to move in time with the breeze so that air and trees and light and earth swayed and rippled like the bright-dark water in the island's central pool. She closed her eyes and sounds came to her like faithful pets, nuzzling her ear; sounds of the brushing tree-heads, like tired lovers dancing; sounds of the ocean, swirling over rocks, softly stroking the golden sands; sounds of what she did not know.

Perhaps soon she would be back in the house below the gray-white dam.

What an asshole you are, Zakalwe, she thought. I could

have stayed home; they could have sent the stand-in . . . dammit, they could probably have just sent the drone, and you'd still have come . . .

He appeared looking bright and fresh and carrying a jacket. A different servant carried some bags. "Okay; let's go," he said.

They walked to the pier while the drone tracked them, overhead.

"By the way," she said. "Why ten percent more money?"

He shrugged as they walked onto the wooden pier. "Inflation."

Sma frowned. "What's that?"

2:

AN
OUTING

IX

When you sleep beside a head full of images, there is an osmosis, a certain sharing in the night. So he thought. He thought a lot then; more than he ever had, perhaps. Or maybe he was just more aware of the process, and the identity of thought and passing time. Sometimes he felt as though every instant he spent with her was a precious capsule of sensation to be lovingly wrapped and carefully placed somewhere inviolable, away from harm.

But he only fully realized that later; it wasn't something he was fully aware of at the time. At the time, it seemed to him that the only thing he was fully aware of, was her.

He lay, often, looking at her sleeping face in the new light that fell in through the open walls of the strange house, and he stared at her skin and hair with his mouth open, transfixed by the quick stillness of her, struck dumb with the physical fact of her existence as though she was some careless star-thing that slept on quite unaware of its incandescent power; the casualness and ease with which she slept there amazed him; he couldn't believe that such beauty could survive without some superhumanly intense conscious effort.

On such mornings he would lie and look at her and listen

to the sounds that the house made in the breeze. He liked the house; it seemed . . . fit. Normally, he'd have hated it.

Here and now, though, he could appreciate it, and happily see it as a symbol; open and closed, weak and strong, outside and inside. When he'd first seen it, he'd thought it would blow away in the first serious gale, but it seemed these houses rarely collapsed; in the very rare storms, people would retreat to the center of the structures, and huddle round the central fire, letting the various layers and thicknesses of covering shake and sway on their posts, gradually sapping the force of the wind, and providing a core of shelter.

Still—as he'd pointed out to her when he first saw it from the lonely ocean road—it would be easy to torch and simple to rob, stuck out here in the middle of nowhere. (She'd looked at him as though he were mad, but then kissed him.)

That vulnerability intrigued and troubled him. There was a likeness to her there; to her as a poet and as a woman. It was similar, he suspected, to one of her images; the symbols and metaphors she used in the poems he loved to hear her read out loud but could never quite understand (too many cultural allusions, and this baffling language he had not yet fully understood, and still sometimes made her laugh with). Their physical relationship seemed to him at once more whole and complete, and more defyingly complex than anything similar he had known. The paradox of love physically incarnate and the most personal attack being the same thing tied knots in him, sometimes sickened him, as in the midst of this joy he fought to understand the statements and promises that might be being implied.

Sex was an infringement, an attack, an invasion; there was no other way he could see it; every act, however magical and intensely enjoyed, and however willingly conducted, seemed to carry a harmonic of rapacity. He took her, and however much she gained in provoked pleasure and in his own increasing love, she was still the one that suffered the act, had it played out upon her and inside her. He was aware of the absurdity of trying too hard to develop the comparison between sex and war; he had been laughed out of several embarrassing situations trying to do so ("Zakalwe," she would say, when he tried to explain some of this, and she would put her cool slim fingers behind his neck, and stare out from the rambunctious black tangle of her hair, "You have serious problems." She would smile), but the feelings, the acts, the structure of the two were to him so close, so self-evidently akin, that such a reaction only forced him deeper into his confusion.

But he tried not to let it bother him; at any time he could simply look at her and wrap his adoration for her around himself like a coat on a cold day, and see her life and body, moods and expressions and speech and movements as a whole enthralling field of study that he could submerge himself in like a scholar finding his life's work.

(This was more like it, some small, remindful voice inside him said. This is more like the way it's supposed to be; with this, you can leave all that other stuff behind, the guilt and the secrecy and the lies; the ship and the chair and the other man . . . But he tried not listen to that voice.)

They'd met in a port bar. He'd just arrived and thought he'd make sure their alcohol was as good as people had said. It was. She was in the next dark booth, trying to get rid of a man.

"You're saying nothing lasts forever," he heard the fellow whine. (Well, pretty trite, he thought.)

"No," he heard her say. "I'm saying with very few exceptions nothing lasts forever, and among those exceptions, no work or thought of man is numbered."

She went on talking after this, but he homed in on that. That was better, he thought. I liked that. She sounds interesting. Wonder what she looks like?

He stuck his head round the corner of the booth and looked in at them. The man was in tears; the woman was . . . well, lots of hair . . . *very* striking face; sharp and almost aggressive. Tidy body.

"Sorry," he told them. "But I just wanted to point out that 'Nothing lasts forever' can be a positive statement . . . well, in some languages . . ." Having said it, it did occur to him that in this language it wasn't; they had different words for different sorts of nothing. He smiled, ducked back into his own booth, suddenly embarrassed. He stared accusatorily at the drink in front of him. Then he shrugged, and pressed the bell to attract a waiter.

Shouts from the next booth. A clatter and a little shriek.

He looked round to see the man storming off through the bar, heading for the door.

The girl appeared at his elbow. She was dripping.

He looked up into her face; it was damp; she wiped it with a handkerchief.

"Thank you for your contribution," she said icily. "I was bringing things to a conclusion quite smoothly there until you stepped in."

"I'm very sorry," he said, not at all.

She took her handkerchief and wrung it out over his glass, dribbling. "Hmm," he said, "too kind." He nodded at the dark spots on her gray coat. "Your drink or his?"

"Both," she said, folding the handkerchief and starting to turn away.

"Please; let me buy you a replacement."

She hesitated. The waiter arrived at the same moment. *Good omen,* he thought. "Ah," he said to the man. "I'll have another . . . whatever it is I've been drinking, and for this lady . . ."

She looked at his glass. "The same," she said. She sat down across the table.

"Think of it as . . . reparations," he said, digging the word out of the implanted vocabulary he'd been given for his visit.

She looked puzzled. " 'Reparations' . . . that's one I'd forgotten; something to do with war, isn't it?"

"Yep," he said, smothering a belch with one hand. "Sort of like . . . damages?"

She shook her head. "Wonderfully obscure vocabulary, but totally bizarre grammar."

"I'm from out of town," he said breezily. This was true. He'd never been within a hundred light-years of the place.

"Shias Engin," she nodded. "I write poems."

"You're a poet?" he said, delighted. "I've always been fascinated by poets. I tried writing poems, once."

"Yes," she sighed and looked wary. "I suspect everyone does. And you are . . . ?"

"Cheradenine Zakalwe; I fight wars."

She smiled. "I thought there hadn't been a war for three hundred years; aren't you getting a little out of practice?"

"Yeah; boring, isn't it?"

She sat back in the seat, took off her coat. "From just how far out of town have you come, Mr. Zakalwe?"

"Aw heck, you've guessed," he looked downcast. "Yeah; I'm an alien. Oh. Thank you." The drinks arrived; he passed one to her.

"You do look funny," she said, inspecting him.

" 'Funny?' " he said indignantly.

She shrugged. "Different." She drank. "But not all that different." She leaned forward on the table. "Why do you look so similar to us? I know all the outworlders aren't humanoid, but a lot are. How come?"

"Well," he said, hand at his mouth again, "It's like this; the . . ." he belched. ". . . the dust clouds and stuff in the galaxy are . . . its food, and its food keeps speaking back to it. That's why there are so many humanoid species; nebulae's last meals repeating on them."

She grinned. "That simple, is it?"

He shook his head. "Na; not at all. Very complicated. But," he held up one finger. "I think I know the real reason."

"Which is?"

"Alcohol in the dust clouds. Goddamn stuff is everywhere. Any lousy species ever invents the telescope and the spectroscope and starts looking in between the stars, what do they find?" He knocked the glass on the table. "Loads of stuff; but much of it alcohol." He drank from the glass. "Humanoids are the galaxy's way of trying to get rid of all that alcohol."

"It's all starting to make sense now," she agreed, nodding her head and looking serious. She looked inquisitively at him. "So, why are you here? Not come to start a war, I hope."

"No, I'm on leave; come to get away from them. That's why I chose this place."

"How long you here for?"

"Till I get bored."

She smiled at him. "And how long do you think that will take?"

"Well," he smiled back, "I don't know." He put his glass down. She drained hers. He reached out for the button to call the waiter, but her finger was already there.

"My turn," she said. "Same again?"

"No," he said. "Something quite different, this time, I feel."

When he tried to tabulate his love, list all the things about her that drew him to her, he found himself starting at the larger facts—her beauty, her attitude to life, her creativity—but as he thought over the day that had just passed, or just watched her, he found individual gestures, single words, certain steps, a single movement of her eyes or a hand starting to claim equal attention. He would give up then, and console himself with something she'd said; that you could not love what you fully understood. Love, she maintained, was a process; not a state. Held still, it withered. He wasn't too sure about all that; he seemed to have found a calm clear serenity in himself he hadn't even known was there, thanks to her.

The fact of her talent—maybe her genius—played a role, too. It added to the extent of his disbelief, this ability to be more than the thing he loved, and to present to the outside world an entirely different aspect. She was what he knew here and now, complete and rich and measureless, and yet when both of them were dead (and he found he could think about his own death again now, without fear), a world at least—many cultures, perhaps—would know her as something utterly dissimilar, a poet; a fabricator of sets of meanings that to him were just words on a page or titles that she sometimes mentioned.

One day, she said, she would write a poem about him, but not yet. He thought what she wanted was for him to tell her the story of his life, but he had already told her he could never do that. He didn't need to confess to her; there was no need. She had already unburdened him, even if he did not know quite how. Memories are interpretations, not truth, she insisted, and rational thought was just another instinctive power.

He felt the slowly healing polarization of his mind, matching his to hers, the alignment of all his prejudices and conceits to the lodestone of the image she represented for him.

She helped him, and without knowing it. She mended him, reaching back to something so buried he'd thought it inaccessible forever, and drawing its sting. So perhaps it was also that which stunned him; the effect this one person was having on memories so terrible to him that he had long ago resigned himself to them only growing more potent with age. But she just ringed them off, cut them out, parceled them up and threw them away, and she didn't even realize she was doing it, had no idea of the extent of her influence.

He held her in his arms.

"How old are you?" she'd asked, near dawn on that first night.

"Older and younger than you."

"Cryptic crap; answer the question."

He grimaced into the darkness. "Well . . . how long do you people live?"

"I don't know. Eighty, ninety years?"

He had to remember the length of the year, here. Close enough. "Then I'm . . . about two hundred and twenty; a hundred and ten; and thirty."

She whistled, moved her head on his shoulder. "A choice."

"Sort of. I was born two hundred and twenty years ago, I have lived for a hundred and ten of them, and physically I'm about thirty."

The laughter was deep in her throat. He felt her breasts sweep across his chest as she swung on top of him. "I'm fucking a hundred-and-ten-year-old?" she sounded amused.

He laid his hands on the small of her back, smooth and cool. "Yeah; great, isn't it? All the benefits of experience without the con—"

She came down kissing him.

He put his head to her shoulder, drew her tighter. She stirred in her sleep, moved too, her arms around him, drawing him to her. He smelled the skin of her shoulder, breathing in the air that had been on her flesh, was scented by her, perfumed by no perfume, carrying her own smell only. He closed his eyes, to concentrate on this sensation. He opened them, drew in her sleeping look again, moved his head to hers, his tongue out flickering under her nose to feel the flow of breath, anxious to touch the thread of her life. The tip of his tongue, and the tiny hollow between her lips and her nose, vexed and caved, as if designed.

Her lips parted, closed again; her lips rubbed against each other, side to side, and her nose wrinkled. He watched these things with a secret delight, as fascinated as a child playing boo with an adult who kept disappearing round the side of a cot.

She slept on. He rested his head again.

That first morning, in the gray dawn, he had lain there while she inspected his body minutely.

"So many scars, Zakalwe," she said, shaking her head, tracing lines across his chest.

"I keep getting into scraps," he admitted. "I could have all these heal completely, but . . . they're good for . . . remembering."

She put her chin on her chest. "Come on; admit you just like showing them off to the girls."

"There is that, too."

"This one looks nasty, if your heart's in the same place as ours . . . given that everything else seems to be." She ran her finger round a little puckered mark near one nipple. She felt him tense, and looked up. There was a look in the man's eyes that made her shiver. Suddenly he seemed all the years he'd claimed, and more. She drew herself up, ran her hand through her hair. "That one still a bit fresh, huh?"

"That's . . ." he made the effort of trying to smile, and ran his own finger over the tiny dimpled crease on his flesh. ". . . that's one of the oldest, funnily enough." The look faded from his eyes.

"This one?" she said brightly, touching one side of his head.

"Bullet."

"In a big battle?"

"Well, sort of. In a car, to be precise. A woman."

"Oh no!" she clapped a hand to her mouth, mimicking horror.

"It was very embarrassing."

"Well, we won't go into that one . . . what about this?"

"Laser . . . very strong light," he explained, when she looked puzzled. "Much longer ago."

"This one?"

"Ahm . . . combination of things; insects, in the end."

"*Insects?*" She quivered.

(And he was back there; in the drowned volcano. A long time ago, now, but still there, still within him . . . and still safer to think about than that crater over his heart, where another, even more ancient memory dwelt. He remembered the caldera, and saw again the pool of stagnant water, the stone at its center and the surrounding walls of the poisoned lake. He felt once more the long slow scrape his body had made, and the intimacy of insects . . . But that remorseless concentricity didn't matter anymore; here was here and now was now.)

"You don't want to know," he grinned.

"I think I'll take your word for that," she agreed, nodding slowly, the long black hair swinging heavily. "I know; I'll kiss them all better."

"Could be a long job," he told her as she swiveled and moved to his feet.

"You in a hurry?" she asked him, kissing a toe.

"Not at all," he smiled, lying back. "Take all the time you want. Take forever."

He felt her move, and looked down. Her knuckles rubbed her eyes, her hair spilled, she patted her nose and cheeks and smiled at him. He looked at her smile. He had seen a few smiles he might have killed for, but never one he'd have died for. What else could he do but smile back?

"Why do you always wake before me?"

"I don't know," he sighed. So did the house, as the breeze moved its equivocal walls. "I like watching you sleep."

"Why?" She rolled and lay on her back, turning her head to him, the hair rolling bounteously to him. He laid his head on that dark fragrant field, remembering the smell of her shoulder, stupidly wondering if she smelled different awake than asleep.

He nuzzled her shoulder and she laughed a little, shrugging that shoulder and pressing her head against his. He kissed her neck and answered before he forgot the question completely.

"When you're awake you move, and I miss things."

"What things?" He felt her kissing his head.

"Everything you do. When you're asleep you hardly move, and I can take it all in. There's enough time."

"Strange." Her voice was slow.

"You smell the same awake as you do asleep, did you know that?" He propped up his head and looked into her face, grinning.

"You . . ." she started, then looked down. Her smile looked very sad when she looked back up. "I love hearing that sort of nonsense," she said.

He heard the unsaid part. "You mean; you love hearing that sort of nonsense now, but won't at some indeterminate point in the future." (He hated the awful triteness of it, but she had her own scars.)

"I suppose," she said, holding one of his hands.

"You think too much about the future."

"Maybe we cancel out each other's obsessions, then."

He laughed. "I suppose I walked into that one."

She touched his face, studied his eyes. "I really shouldn't fall in love with you, Zakalwe."

"Why not?"

"Lots of reasons. All the past and all the future; because you are who you are, and I am who I am. Just everything."

"Details," he said, waving one hand.

She laughed, shaking her head and burying it in her own hair. She surfaced and gazed up at him.

"I just worry it won't last."

"Nothing lasts, remember?"

"I remember," she nodded slowly.

"You think this won't last?"

"Right now . . . it feels . . . I don't know. But if we ever want to hurt each other . . ."

"Then let's not do that," he said.

She lowered her eyelids, bent her head to him, and he put out his hand and cradled her head.

"Maybe it is that simple," she said. "Perhaps I like to dwell on what might happen so as never to be surprised." She brought her face up to his. "Does that worry you?" she said, her head shaking, an expression very like pain around her eyes.

"What?" He leaned forward to kiss her, smiling, but she

moved her head to indicate she did not want to, and he drew
back while she said:

"That I . . . can't believe enough not have doubts."

"No. I don't worry about that." He did kiss her.

"Strange that taste buds have no taste," she murmured
into his neck. They laughed together.

Sometimes, at night, lying there in the dark when she was
asleep or silent, he thought he saw the real ghost of Cheradenine Zakalwe come walking through the curtain walls, dark
and hard and holding some huge deadly gun, loaded and set;
the figure would look at him, and the air around him seemed
to drip with . . . worse than hate; derision. At such moments,
he was conscious of himself lying there with her, lying as
lovestruck and besotted as any youth, lying there wrapping
his arms around a beautiful girl, talented and young, for whom
there was nothing he wouldn't do, and he knew perfectly and
completely that to what he had been—to what he had become
or always was—that sort of unequivocal, selfless, retreating
devotion was an act of shame, something that had to be wiped
out. And the real Zakalwe would raise his gun, look him in
the eye through the sights and fire, calmly and unhesitatingly.

But then he would laugh and turn to her, kiss her or be
kissed, and there was no threat and no danger under this sun
or any other that could take him from her then.

"Don't forget we've got to go up to that krih today. This
morning, in fact."

"Oh yes," he said. He rolled onto his back, she sat up
and stretched her arms out, yawning, forcing her eyes wide
and glaring up at the fabric roof. Her eyes relaxed, her mouth
closed, she looked at him, rested her elbow on the head of
the bed, and combed his hair with her fingers. "It probably
isn't stuck though."

"Mmm, maybe not," he agreed.

"It might not be there when we look today."

"Indeed."

"If it is still there we'll go up, though."

He nodded, reached up, took her hand, clasped.

She smiled, quickly kissed him and then sprang out of
the bed and walked to the far level. She opened the waving
translucent drapes and unslung a pair of field glasses from a
hook on a frame-pole. He lay and watched her as she brought
the glasses to her eyes, surveyed the hillside above.

"Still there," she said. Her voice was far away. He closed his eyes.

"We'll go up today. Maybe in the afternoon."

"We should." Far away.

"All right."

Probably the stupid animal hadn't got stuck at all; more than likely it had dozed off into an absentminded hibernation. They did that, so he heard; they just stopped eating and looked ahead and stared with their big dumb eyes at something, and closed them sleepily and went into a coma, purely by accident. The first rain, or a bird landing on it would probably wake it. Perhaps it was stuck though; the krih had thick coats and they got entangled with the bushes and tree branches sometimes, and couldn't move. They would go up today; the view was pleasant, and anyway he could do with some exercise that wasn't mostly horizontal. They would lie on the grass and talk, and look out to the sea sparkling in the haze, and maybe they would have to free the animal, or wake it up, and she would look after it with a look he knew not to disturb, and in the evening she would write, and that would be another poem.

As a nameless lover, he had appeared in many of her recent works, though as usual she would throw the bulk of them away. She said she would write a poem specifically about him, one day, maybe when he had told her more about his life.

The house whispered, moved in its parts, waving and flowing, spreading light and dimming it; the varying thicknesses and strengths of drape and curtain that formed the walls and divisions of the place rustled against each other secretly, like half-heard conversations.

Far away, she put her hand to her hair, pulled one side absently as she moved papers on the desk around with one finger. He watched. Her finger stirred through what she'd written yesterday, toying with the parchments; circling them around slowly; slowly flexing and turning, watched by her, watched by him.

The glasses hung from her other hand, straps down, forgotten, and he wandered a long slow gaze over her as she stood against the light; feet, legs, behind, belly, chest, breasts, shoulders, neck; face and head and hair.

The finger moved on the desktop where she would write

a short poem about him in the evening, one he would copy
secretly in case she wasn't happy with it and threw it out,
and as his desire grew and her calm face saw no finger move,
one of them was just a passing thing, just a leaf pressed
between the pages of the other's diary, and what they had
talked themselves into, they could be silent out of.

"I must do some work today," she said to herself.

There was a pause.

"Hey?" he said.

"Hmm?" Her voice was far away.

"Let's waste a little time, hmm?"

"A nice euphemism, sir," she mused, distantly.

He smiled. "Come and help me think of better ones."

She smiled, and they both looked at each other.

There was a long pause.

6

S waying slightly, scratching his head, he put the gun stock-down on the floor of the smallbay, held the weapon by its barrel, and squinted one-eyed into the muzzle, muttering.

"Zakalwe," Diziet Sma said, "we diverted twenty-eight million people and a trillion tons of spaceship two months off course to get you to Voerenhutz on time; I'd appreciate it if you'd wait until the job is done before you blow your brains out."

He turned round to see Sma and the drone entering the rear of the smallbay; a traveltube capsule flicked away behind them.

"Eh?" he said, then waved. "Oh, hi." He wore a white shirt—sleeves rolled up—black pantaloons, and nothing on his feet. He picked the plasma rifle up, shook it, banged it on the side with his free hand, and sighted down the length of the smallbay. He steadied, squeezed the trigger.

Light flared briefly, the gun leapt back at him, and there was an echoing snap of noise. He looked down to the far end of the bay, two hundred meters away, where a glittering black cube perhaps fifteen meters to a side sat under the overhead lights. He peered at the distant black object, pointed the gun at it again, and inspected the magnified view on one of the gun's screens. "Weird," he muttered, and scratched his head.

There was a small tray floating at his side; it held an ornate metal jug and a crystal goblet. He took a drink from the goblet, staring intently at the gun.

"Zakalwe," Sma said. "What, exactly, are you doing?"

"Target practice," he said. He drank from the goblet again. "You want a drink, Sma? I'll order another glass . . ."

"No thanks." Sma looked down to the far end of the bay, at the strange and gleaming black cube. "And what is *that*?"

"Ice," Skaffen-Amtiskaw said.

"Yeah," he nodded, putting the goblet down to adjust something on the plasma rifle. "Ice."

"Dyed black ice," the drone said.

"Ice," Sma said, nodding, but none the wiser. "Why ice?"

"Because," he said, sounding annoyed, "this . . . this *ship* with the incredibly silly name and its twenty-eight trillion people and its hyper-zillion billion squintillion tonnage hasn't got any decent *rubbish*, that's why." He flicked a couple of switches on the side of the rifle, aimed again. "Trillion fucking tons and it hasn't got any goddamn garbage; apart from its brain, I suppose." He squeezed the trigger again. His shoulder and arm were pushed back once more, while the light flickered from the weapon's muzzle and sound stuttered. He stared at the view in the sight-screen. "This is ridiculous!" he said.

"But why are you shooting at ice?" Sma insisted.

"Sma," he cried, "are you deaf? Because this parsimonious pile of junk claims it hasn't got any rubbish on board it can let me shoot at." He shook his head, opened an inspection panel on the side of the weapon.

"Why not shoot at target holos like everybody else?" Sma asked.

"Holos are all very well, Diziet, but . . ." He turned and presented her with the gun. "Here; hold this a minute, will you? Thanks." He fiddled with something inside the inspection panel while Sma held the gun in both hands. The plasma rifle was a meter and a quarter long, and very heavy. "Holos are all right for calibration and that sort of crap, but for . . . for getting the *feel* of a weapon, you have to really . . . really *waste* something, you know?" He glanced at her. "You have to feel the kick, and see the debris. Real debris. Not this holographic shit; the real stuff.''

Sma and the drone exchanged looks.

"You hold this . . . cannon," Sma said to the machine. Skaffen-Amtiskaw's fields were glowing pink with amusement. It took the weight of the gun from her while the man continued to tinker with the weapon's insides.

"I don't think a General Systems Vehicle thinks in terms of junk, Zakalwe," Sma said, sniffing dubiously at the contents of the ornately-worked metal jug. She wrinkled her nose. "Just matter that's currently in use and matter that's available to be recycled and turned into something else to be used. No such thing as rubbish."

"Yeah," he muttered. "That's the crap it came out with as well."

"Gave you ice instead, eh?" the drone said.

"Had to settle for it." He nodded, clicking the armoured inspection panel back into place and lifting the gun out of the drone's grip. "Should take a hit all right, but now I can't get the damn gun to work."

"Zakalwe," the drone sighed. "It would hardly be surprising if it isn't working. That thing belongs in a museum. It's eleven hundred years old. We make pistols that are more powerful, nowadays."

He sighted carefully, breathed smoothly . . . then smacked his lips, put the gun down and took a drink from the goblet. He looked back at the drone. "But this thing's *beautiful*," he told the machine, taking up the gun and flourishing it. He slapped the weapon's darkly cluttered side. "I mean, take a good look at it; it *looks* powerful!" He gave an admiring growl, then took up his stance again and shot.

This firing fared no better than the others. He sighed and shook his head, staring at the weapon. "It's not working," he said plaintively. "It just isn't working. I'm getting recoil, but it just isn't working."

"May I?" Skaffen-Amtiskaw said. It floated toward the gun. The man looked suspiciously at the drone. Then he turned the gun over to it.

The plasma rifle flashed from every available screen, things clicked and beeped, the inspection panels flicked open and shut, and then the drone gave the gun back to the man. "It's in perfect working order," it said.

"Huh." He held the weapon in one hand, up and out from his body, then slapped the back of the stock with his other hand, whirling the big rifle round so that it spun like a rotor in front of his face and chest. He didn't take his eyes off the drone while he did this. He was still looking at the machine when he twisted his wrist, brought the gun to a stop—already aimed straight at the distant black cube of ice—and fired it, all in one smooth action. Again, the gun seemed to fire, but the ice sat undisturbed.

"The hell it's working," he said.

"How exactly did your conversation with the ship go, when you asked for your 'rubbish'?" the drone inquired.

"I don't remember," he said loudly. "I told it what a complete cretin it was for not having some junk to shoot at, and it said when people wanted to shoot at real shit they usually used ice. So I said, all right then, you scumbag rocket . . . or something like that; give me some ice!" He held out his hands expressively. "That was all." He dropped the gun.

The drone caught it. "Try asking it to clear the bay for firing practice," it suggested. "Specifically, ask it to clear a space in its trapdoor coverage."

He accepted the gun from the drone, looking disdainful. "All right," he said slowly. He looked about to say something else, talking into midair, then looked uncertain. He scratched his head, glanced at the drone and appeared to be about to talk to it, then looked away again. Finally he jabbed a finger at Skaffen-Amtiskaw. "You . . . you ask for . . . all that. It'll sound better coming from another machine."

"Very well. It's done," the drone said. "You only had to ask."

"Hmm," he said. He switched his suspicious look from the drone to the distant black cube. He lifted the gun and aimed at the icy mass.

He fired.

The gun rammed back against his shoulder, and a blinding flash of light threw his shadow behind him. The sound was like a grenade going off. A pencil-thin white line seared the length of the smallbay and joined the gun to the fifteen meter cube of ice, which shattered into a million fragments in a floor-thumping detonation of light and steam and a furiously blossoming cloud of black vapor.

Sma stood, her hands clasped behind her back, and

watched debris fountain fifty meters to the top of the bay, where it ricocheted off the roof. More black shrapnel flew the same distance to crash into the bay's side walls . . . and tumbling, glittering black shards slithered across the floor toward them. Most skidded to a stop on the ridged surface of the bay, though a few small pieces—blown a long way through the air before thumping onto the deck—did actually slide past the two humans and the watching drone, and clunk into the rear wall of the bay. Skaffen-Amtiskaw picked up a fist-size piece from near Sma's feet. The sound of the explosion echoed clangingly back off the walls a few times, gradually fading.

Sma felt her ears relax. "Happy, Zakalwe?" she asked.

He blinked, then switched the gun off and turned to Sma. "Seems to be working all right now," he shouted.

Sma nodded. "Mm-hmm."

He motioned with his head. "Let's go get a drink." He took up the goblet, and drank as he walked toward the traveltube port.

"A drink?" Sma said, falling into step with the man and nodding at the glass he was drinking from. "Why; what's that?"

"Nearly finished, that's what this is," he told her, loudly. He poured a last half-glass from the metal jug into the goblet.

"Ice?" the drone offered, holding up the dripping black lump.

"No thanks."

Something flickered in the traveltube, and a capsule was suddenly there, door rolling open. "What's this . . . trapdoor coverage, anyway?" he asked the machine.

"General Systems Vehicle internal explosion protection," the drone explained, letting the humans board the capsule first. "Snaps anything significantly more powerful than a fart straight into hyperspace; blast, radiation; the lot."

"Shit," he said, disgusted. "You mean you can let nukes off in these fuckers and they don't even *notice*?"

The drone wobbled. "*They* notice; probably nobody else does."

The man stood swaying in the capsule, watching the door roll back into place, shaking his head sorrily. "You people just have no idea of fair play, do you?"

• • •

The last time he had been on a GSV had been ten years earlier, after he'd almost died on Fohls.

"Cheradenine? . . . Cheradenine?"

He heard the voice, but wasn't sure the woman was really talking to him. It was a beautiful voice. He wanted to reply to it. But he couldn't work out how to. It was very dark.

"Cheradenine?"

A very patient voice. Concerned, somehow, but a hopeful voice; a cheerful, even loving voice. He tried to remember his mother.

"Cheradenine?" the voice said again. Trying to get him to wake up. But he *was* awake. He tried moving his lips.

"Cheradenine . . . can you hear me?"

He moved his lips, exhaled at the same time, and thought he might have produced a noise. He tried to open his eyes. The darkness wavered.

"Cheradenine . . . ?" There was a hand at his face, gently stroking his cheek. *Shias!* he thought for a second, then swept that memory away to where he kept all the others.

"H . . ." he managed. Just the start of a sound.

"Cheradenine . . ." the voice said, close to his ear now. "It's Diziet here. Diziet Sma. Remember me?"

"Diz . . ." he succeeded in saying, after a couple of failures.

"Cheradenine?"

"Yeah . . ." he heard himself breathe.

"Try to open your eyes, will you?"

"Try'n . . ." he said. Then light came, as though it had had nothing to do with him trying to open his eyes. Things took a while to gel, but eventually he saw a restful green ceiling, illuminated from the sides by a fan-shaped glow of concealed lighting, and Diziet Sma's face looking down at him.

"Well done, Cheradenine." She smiled at him. "How are you feeling?"

He thought about this. "Weird," he said. He was thinking hard now, trying to remember how he'd got here. Was this some sort of hospital? How *had* he got here?

"Where is this?" he said. Might as well try the direct approach. He tried shifting his hands, but without success. Sma glanced somewhere over his head as he did so.

"The GSV *Congenital Optimist*. You're all right . . .
you're going to be all right."

"If I'm all right, why can't I move my hands or fee . . .
shit."

Suddenly he was tied to the wooden frame again; the girl
was in front of him. He opened his eyes and saw her; Sma.
A misty, uncertain light glowed all around. He wrenched at
his bonds, but there was no sign of give, no hope . . . he felt
the tug on his hair, then the thudding cut of the blade, and
saw the girl in the red robe looking at him from somewhere
over his de-bodied head.

Everything revolved. He closed his eyes.

The moment passed. He swallowed. He took a breath and
opened his eyes again; at least these things seemed to be
working. Sma looked down, relieved. "You just remembered?"

"Yeah. I just remembered."

"You going to be okay?" She sounded serious, but still
reassuring.

"I'll be all right," he said. Then; "It's just a scratch."

She laughed, looked away for a bit, and when she looked
to him again, she was biting her lip.

"Hey," he said. "Narrow one, this time, huh?" he
smiled.

Sma nodded. "You could say that. Another few seconds
and you'd have suffered brain damage; another few minutes
and you'd have been dead. If only you'd had a homing implant; we could have picked you up days . . ."

"Oh now, Sma," he said gently. "You know I can't be
bothered with all that stuff."

"Yeah, I know," she said. "Well, whatever; you're going
to have to stay like this for a while." Sma smoothed hair
from his forehead. "It'll take about two hundred days or so
to grow a new body. They want me to ask you; do you want
to sleep through the whole thing, or do you want to stay
awake as normal . . . or anything in between? It's up to you.
Makes no difference to the process."

"Hmm." He thought about this. "I suppose I get to do
lots of improving things, like listen to music and watch films
or whatever, and read?"

"If you want," Sma shrugged. "You can go the whole
hog and spool fantasy head-tapes if you want."

"Drink?"

"Drink?"

"Yeah; can I get drunk?"

"I don't know," Sma said, looking above and to one side. A voice muttered something.

"Who's that?" he asked.

"Stod Perice." A young man nodded, coming into view, upside down. "Medic. Hello there, Mr. Zakalwe. I'll be looking after you, however you decide to spend the time."

"D'you dream when you're under, if you do it that way?" he asked the medic.

"Depends how deep you want to go. We can send you so far down you think no more than a second's passed during those two hundred days, or you can lucid dream every second of them. Whatever you want."

"What do most people do?"

"Switch right off; wake up with a new body after no appreciable time."

"Thought so. Can I get drunk while I'm hooked up to whatever the hell it is I'm hooked up to?"

Stod Perice grinned. "I'm sure we could arrange it. If you want, we could give you drug-glands; ideal opportunity, just . . ."

"No thanks." He closed his eyes briefly and tried to shake his head. "Occasional inebriety will be quite sufficient."

Stod Perice nodded. "Well, I think we can rig you for that."

"Great. Sma?" he looked at her. She raised her eyebrows. "I'll stay awake," he told her.

Sma smiled slowly. "I had a feeling you might."

"You sticking around?"

"Could do," the woman said. "Would you like me to?"

"I'd appreciate it."

"And I'd like to." She nodded thoughtfully. "Okay. I'll watch you put on weight."

"Thanks. And thanks for not bringing that goddamn drone. I can imagine the jokes."

". . . Yes," Sma said, hesitantly, so that he said:

"Sma? What is it?"

"Well . . ." The woman looked uncomfortable.

"Tell me."

"Skaffen-Amtiskaw," she said, awkwardly. "It sent you

a present." She fished a small package from her pocket, flourished it, embarrassed. "I . . . I don't know what it is, but . . ."

"Well *I* can't open it. Come on, Sma."

Sma opened the package. She looked at the contents. Stod Perice leaned over, and then turned quickly away, holding one hand at his mouth, coughing.

Sma pursed her lips. "I may ask for a new escort drone."

He closed his eyes. "What is it?"

"It's a hat."

He laughed at that. Sma did too, eventually (though she threw things at the drone, later). Stod Perice accepted the hat as an onward gift.

It was only later, in the dim red of the hospital section light, while Sma danced slowly with some new conquest, and Stod Perice was dining out with friends and telling them the story of the hat, and life went on throughout the rest of the great ship, that he remembered how, a few years earlier, and very far away, Shias Engin had traced the wounds on his body (cool slim fingers on the puckered new-looking flesh, the smell of her skin and the tingling sweep of her hair).

And in two hundred days he would have a new body. And (*And this? . . . I'm sorry. Still fresh, that one?*) . . . the wound over his heart would be gone forever, and the heart beneath his chest would not be the same one.

And he realized he had lost her.

Not Shias Engin, whom he'd loved, or thought he had, and certainly lost . . . but her; the other one, the real one, the one who'd lived within him through a century of icy sleep.

He had thought he would not lose her until the day he died.

Now he knew differently, and felt broken by the knowledge and the loss.

He whispered her name to the quiet red night.

Overhead, the ever-watchful medical monitoring unit saw some fluid seep from the bodiless human's tear ducts, and wondered dumbly at it.

"How old is old Tsoldrin, now?"

"Eighty, relative," the drone said.

"You think he'll want to come out of retirement? Just because I ask him to?" He looked skeptical.

"You're all we could think of," Sma told him.

"Can't you just let the old guy grow old in peace?"

"There's a little more at stake than the happy retirement of one aging politico, Zakalwe."

"What? The universe? Life as we know it?"

"Yes; tens, maybe hundreds of millions of times over."

"Very philosophical."

"And you didn't let the Ethnarch Kerian grow old in peace, did you?"

"Damn right," he said, and wandered a little further into the armory. "That old pisshead deserved to die a million times."

The converted minibay engineering space housed a dazzling array of Culture and other weaponry. Zakalwe, Sma thought, was like a kid in a toy store. He was selecting gear and loading it onto a pallet which Skaffen-Amtiskaw was guiding after the man, down the aisles of racks and drawers and shelves all stuffed and packed with projectile weapons, line guns, laser rifles, plasma projectors, multitudinous grenades, effectors, plane charges, passive and reactive armor, sensory and guard devices, full combat suits, missile packs, and at least a dozen other distinctly different types of device Sma didn't recognize.

"You'll never be able to carry this lot, Zakalwe."

"This is just the shortlist," he told her. He took a stocky, boxy-looking gun with no appreciable barrel from a shelf. He held it out to the drone. "What's this?"

"CREWS; assault rifle," Skaffen-Amtiskaw said. "Seven fourteen-ton batteries; seven-element single shot to forty-four point eight kilorounds a second (minimum firing time eight point seven five seconds), maximum single burst; seven times two-fifty kilograms; frequency from mid-visible to high X-ray."

He hefted it. "Not very well balanced."

"That's its stowed configuration. Slide the whole top back."

"Hmm." He pretended to aim the readied gun. "Now, what's to stop you putting your supporting hand over here, where the beams are going?"

"Common sense?" suggested the drone.

"Uh-huh. I'll stick with my obsolete plasma rifle." He put the gun back. "Anyway, Sma; you should be pleased old men do want to come out of retirement for you. Dammit, I should be devoting myself to gardening or something, not storming off to the galactic backwoods doing your dirty work."

"Oh, yeah," Sma said. "And a big struggle I had too, convincing you to quit your 'gardening' and come back to us. Shit, Zakalwe; your bags were packed."

"I must have telepathically already realized the urgency of the situation." He heaved a massive black gun from a rack, swung it with both hands, grunting with the effort. "Holy shit. Do you fire this mother or just use it as a battering ram?"

"Idiran hand cannon," Skaffen-Amtiskaw sighed. "Don't wave it around like that; it's very old and quite rare."

"No fucking wonder." He struggled to lift the gun back into its rack, then continued down the aisle. "Come to think of it, Sma, I'm so old my whole life ought to be on triple time or something; I'm probably grossly undercharging you for this whole sorry escapade."

"Well, if you're going to look at it that way, we should be charging you for . . . patent infringement? Giving those old guys their youth back using our technology."

"Don't knock it. You don't know what it's like getting that old that early."

"Yeah, but it applies to everybody; you were giving it only to the most evil, power-mad bastards on the planet."

"They were top-down societies! What do you expect? Anyway; if I'd given it to everybody . . . think of the population explosion!"

"Zakalwe, I thought about that when I was about fifteen; they teach you that sort of stuff in early school, in the Culture. It was all thought through long ago; it's part of our history, part of our upbringing. That's why what you did would look insane to a schoolkid. *You* are like a schoolkid, to us. You don't even want to get old. Nothing more immature than that."

"Whoo!" he said, stopping suddenly and taking something from an open shelf. "What's *this*?"

"Beyond your ken," Skaffen-Amtiskaw said.

"What a beauty!" He gripped the stunningly complicated weapon and twirled it. "What *is* this?" he breathed.

"Micro Armaments System, Rifle," the drone narrated. "It's . . . oh, look, Zakalwe; it has ten separate weapon systems, not including the semi-sentient guard facility, the reactive shield components, the IFF-set quick-reaction swing-packs or the AG unit, and before you ask, the controls are all on the wrong side because that's the left-hand bias version, and the balance—like the weight and the independently variable inertia—are fully adjustable. It also takes about half a year's training just to learn how to use it *safely*, let alone competently, so you can't have one."

"I don't *want* one," he said, stroking the weapon. "But what a *device*! He put it back with the rest. He glanced at Sma. "Dizzy; I know the way you people think; I respect it, I guess . . . but your life isn't my life. I live in unsafe ways in dangerous places; always have done, always will do. I'll die soon enough anyway, so why should I suffer the additional burden of getting old, even slowly?"

"Don't try and hide behind necessity, Zakalwe. You could have changed your life; you don't have to live the way you do; you could have joined the Culture, become one of us; at least lived the way we do, but—"

"Sma!" he exclaimed, turning to her. "That's for you; it isn't for me. You think I'm wrong to have my age stabilized; even the chance of immortality is . . . wrong, to you. Okay; I can see that. In your society, the way you live your lives, of course it is. You have your three-fifty, four hundred years, and know you'll get right to the end of them; die with your boots off. For me . . . that won't work. I don't have that certainty. I enjoy the perspective from the edge, Sma; I like to feel that updraft on my face. So sooner or later I'll die; violently, probably. Maybe even foolishly, because that's often the way of it; you avoid nukes and determined assassins . . . and then choke on a fish bone . . . but who cares? So; your stasis is your society, and mine . . . is my age. But we are both assured of death."

Sma looked at the floor, hands clasped behind her back. "All right," she said. "But don't forget who gave you that perspective from the edge."

He smiled sadly. "Yes; you saved me. But you've also lied to me; sent—no, listen—sent me on damn fool missions

where I was on the opposite side from the one I thought I
was on, had me fight for incompetent aristos I'd gladly have
strangled, in wars where I didn't know you were backing both
sides, filled my balls full of alien seed I was supposed to
inject into some poor damn female . . . nearly got me killed
. . . *very* nearly got me killed a dozen times or more . . ."

"You've never forgotten me for that hat, have you?"
Skaffen-Amtiskaw said, with fake bitterness.

"Oh, Cheradenine," Sma said. "Don't pretend it hasn't
been fun, too."

"Sma, believe me; it has not all been 'fun.' " He leaned
against a cabinet full of ancient projectile weapons. "And,
worse than all that," he insisted, "is when you turn the goddamn maps upside down."

"What?" Sma said, puzzled.

"Turning the maps upside down," he repeated. "Have
you any *idea* how annoying and inconvenient it is when you
get to a place and find that they map the place the other way
up compared to the maps you've got? Because of something
stupid like some people think a magnetic needle is pointing
up to heaven, when other people think it's just heavier and
pointing *down*? Or because it's done according to the galactic
plane or something? I mean, this might sound trivial, but it's
very upsetting."

"Zakalwe, I had no idea. Let me offer you my apologies
and those of the entire Special Circumstances Section; no,
all of Contact; no: the entire Culture; no: all intelligent species."

"Sma, you remorseless bitch, I'm trying to be serious."

"No, I don't think you are. Maps . . ."

"But it's true! They turn them the wrong way up!"

"Then there must," Diziet Sma said, "be a reason for
it."

"What?" he demanded.

"Psychology," Sma and the drone said at the same time.

"Two suits?" Sma said later, when he was making his final
equipment selection. They were still in the armory mini-bay,
but Skaffen-Amtiskaw had gone off to do something more
interesting than watch a kid shop for toys.

He heard the accusatory tone in Sma's voice, and looked up. "Yes; two suits. So what?"

"Those can be used to imprison somebody, Zakalwe; I know that. They're not just for protection."

"Sma; if I'm lifting this guy out of a hostile environment, with no immediate help from you guys because you have to stand off and be seen to be pure—fake though that might be— I have to have the tools to do the job. Serious FYT suits are numbered among those tools."

"*One,*" Sma said.

"Sma, don't you trust me?"

"One," Sma repeated.

"Goddamn it! All right!" He dragged the suit away from the pile of equipment.

"Cheradenine," Sma said, suddenly conciliatory. "Remember; we need Beychae's . . . commitment, not just his presence. That's why we couldn't impersonate him; that's why we couldn't tamper with his mind . . ."

"Sma, you're sending *me* to tamper with his mind."

"All right," Sma said, suddenly nervous-looking. She clapped her hands once softly, looked a little embarrassed. "By the way, Cheradenine, ah . . . what exactly are your plans? I know better than to ask for a mission profile or anything formal, but how *do* you mean to get to Beychae?"

He sighed. "I'm going to make him want to come to me."

"How?"

"Just one word."

"A *word*?"

"A name."

"What, yours?"

"No; mine was supposed to be kept a secret when I was advisor to Beychae, but it must have leaked out by now. Too dangerous. I'll use another name."

"Ah hah." Sma looked expectantly at him, but he went back to choosing between the various bits of equipment he'd picked out.

"Beychae's in this university, right?" he said, not turning to look at Sma.

"Yes; in the archives, almost permanently. But there are a lot of archives and he moves around a lot, and there are always guards."

"Okay," he told her. "If you want to do something useful, try finding something that the university might want."

Sma shrugged. "It's a capitalist society. How about money?"

"I'll be doing that myself . . ." he paused, looked suspicious. "I will be allowed plenty of discretion in that area, won't I?"

"Unlimited expenses," Sma nodded.

He smiled. "Wonderful." He paused. "What source? A ton of platinum? Sack of diamonds? My own bank?"

"Well, more or less your own bank, yes," Sma said. "We've been building up something called the Vanguard Foundation since the last war; commercial empire, comparatively ethical, expanding quietly. That's where your unlimited expenses will come from."

"Well, with my unlimited expenses I'll probably try offering this university lots of money; but it would be better if there was some actual *thing* we could tempt them with."

"All right," she said, nodding. Then her brow wrinkled. She indicated the combat suit. "*What* did you call that thing?"

He looked puzzled, then said, "Oh; it's an FYT suit."

"Yes; a serious FYT suit; that's what you said. But I thought I knew all the nomenclature; I've never heard that acronym before. What does it stand for?"

"It stands for a serious fuck-you-too suit." He grinned.

Sma made a clicking noise with her tongue. "Should have known better than to ask, shouldn't I?"

Two days later, they stood in the hangar of the *Xenophobe*. The very fast picket had left the GSV a day earlier, slung at the Voerenhutz cluster. It had accelerated hard, and now it was braking hard. He was packing the gear he would need into a capsule that would take him down to the surface of the planet where Tsoldrin Beychae was; the initial stage of his in-system journey would be on a fast three-person module; it would loiter in the atmosphere of a nearby gas-giant planet. The *Xenophobe* itself would wait in interstellar space, ready to provide support if needed.

"Are you *positive* you don't want Skaffen-Amtiskaw to come with you?"

"Absolutely positive; keep that airborne asshole to yourself."

"Some other drone?"

"No."

"A knife missile?"

"Diziet; *no*! I don't want Skaffen-Amtiskaw or anything else that thinks it can think for itself."

"Hey; just refer to me as though I'm not here," Skaffen-Amtiskaw said.

"Wishful thinking, drone."

"Better than none at all, so above par for you," the machine said.

He looked at the drone. "You *sure* they didn't issue a factory recall on your batch number?"

"Myself," said the drone, sniffily, "I have never been able to see what virtue there could be in something that was eighty percent water."

"Anyway," Sma said. "You know all the relevant stuff, yes?"

"Yes," he said tiredly. The man's tanned, smoothly muscled body rippled as he bent, securing the plasma rifle in the capsule. He wore a pair of briefs. Sma—hair still tousled from bed, for this was early morning by ship time—wore a jellaba.

"You know the people to contact?" she fretted. "And who's in charge and on what side . . ."

"And what to do if my credit facilities are suddenly withdrawn? Yes; everything."

"If—when you get him out—you head for . . ."

"The enchanting, sunny system of Impren," he said tiredly, in a singsong voice, "Where there are lots of friendly natives in a variety of ecologically sound space Habitats. Which are neutral."

"Zakalwe," Sma said suddenly, taking his face in both hands and kissing him. "I hope this all works out."

"Me too, funnily enough," he said. He kissed Sma back; she pulled away eventually. He shook his head, running his gaze down and up the woman's body, grinning. "Ah . . . one day, Diziet."

She shook her head and smiled insincerely. "Not unless I'm unconscious or dead, Cheradenine."

"Oh. I can still hope, then?"

Sma slapped his backside. "On your way, Zakalwe."

He stepped into the armored combat suit. It closed around him. He flipped the helmet back.

He looked suddenly serious. "You just make sure you know where—"

"We know where she is," Sma said quickly.

He looked at the floor of the hangar for a moment, then smiled back into Sma's eyes.

"Good." He clapped his gloves together. "Great; I'll be off. See you later, with any luck." He stepped into the capsule.

"Take care, Cheradenine," Sma said.

"Yes; look after your disgusting cloven butt," Skaffen-Amtiskaw said.

"Depend on it," he said, and blew both of them a kiss.

From General Systems Vehicle to very fast picket to small module to the lobbed capsule to the suit that stood in the cold desert dust with a man encased inside it.

He looked out through the open faceplate, and wiped a little sweat from his brow. It was dusk over the plateau. A few meters away, by the light of two moons and a fading sun, he could see the rimrock, frost-whitened. Beyond was the great gash in the desert which provided the setting for the ancient, half-empty city where Tsoldrin Beychae now lived.

Clouds drifted, and the dust collected.

"Well," he sighed, to no one in particular, and looked up into yet another alien sky. "Here we are again."

VIII

The man stood on a tiny spur of clay and watched the roots of the huge tree as they were uncovered and washed bare by a gurgling wash of dun-colored water. Rain swarmed through the air; the broad brown swell of rushing water tearing at the roots of the tree leapt with thrashing spray. The rain alone had brought visibility down to a couple of hundred meters and had long since soaked the man in the uniform to the skin. The uniform was meant to be gray, but the rain and the mud had turned it dark brown. It had been a fine, well-fitting uniform, but the rain and the mud had reduced it to a flopping rag.

The tree tipped and fell, crashing back into the brown torrent and spraying mud over the man, who stepped back, and lifted his face to the dull gray sky, to let the incessant rain wash the mud from his skin. The great tree blocked the thundering stream of brown slurry and forced some of it over the clay spur, forcing the man further back, along a crude stone wall to a high lintel of ancient concrete, which stretched, cracked and uneven, up to a small ugly cottage squatting near the crown of the concrete hill. He stayed, watching the long brown bruise of the swollen river as it flowed over and ate into the little isthmus of clay; then the spur collapsed, the tree lost its anchorage on that side of the river, and was turned round and turned over and transported bodily on the back of the tumbling waters, heading into the sodden valley and the low hills beyond. The man looked at the crumbling bank on the other side of the flood, where the great tree's roots protruded from the earth like ripped cables, then he turned and walked heavily up toward the little cottage.

He walked around it. The vast square concrete plinth, nearly a half kilometer to a side, was still surrounded by water; brown waves washed its edges on every side. The towering hulks of ancient metal structures, long since fallen into disrepair, loomed through the haze of rain, squatting on the pitted and cracked surface of the concrete like forgotten pieces in some enormous game. The cottage—already made ridiculous by the expanse of concrete around it—looked somehow even more grotesque than the abandoned machines, just because of their proximity.

The man looked all about as he walked round the building, but saw nothing that he wanted to see. He went into the cottage.

The assassin flinched as he threw open the door. The chair she was tied to—a small wooden thing—was balanced precariously against a thick set of drawers, and when she jerked, its legs rasped on the stone floor and sent chair and girl sliding to the ground with a whack. She hit her head on the flagstones and cried out.

He sighed. He walked over, boots squelching with each step, and dragged the chair upright, kicking a piece of broken mirror away as he did so. The woman was hanging slackly, but he knew she was faking. He maneuvered the chair into the center of the small room. He watched the woman carefully as he did this, and kept out of the way of her head; earlier when he'd been tying her up she'd butted him in the face, very nearly breaking his nose.

He looked at her bonds. The rope that bound her hands behind the back of the chair was frayed; she had been trying to cut through the bindings using the broken hand mirror from the top of the set of drawers.

He left her hanging inertly in the middle of the room, where he could see her, then went over to the small bed cut into one thick wall of the cottage, and fell heavily into it. It was dirty, but he was exhausted and too wet to care.

He listened to the rain hammering on the roof, and listened to the wind whining through the door and the shuttered windows, and listened to the steady plopping of drops coming through the leaking roof and dropping onto the flagstones. He listened for the noise of helicopters, but there were no helicopters. He had no radio and he wasn't sure they knew where to look anyway. They would be searching as well as the weather allowed, but they'd be looking for his staff car, and it was gone; washed away by the brown avalanche of river. Probably, it would take days.

He closed his eyes, and started to fall asleep almost immediately, but it was as though the consciousness of defeat would not let him escape, and found him even there, filling his nearly sleeping mind with images of inundation and defeat, and harried him out of his rest, back into the continuing pain and dejection of wakefulness. He rubbed his eyes, but the scummy water on his hands ground grains of sand and earth into his eyes. He cleaned one finger as best he could on the filthy rags on the bed, and rubbed some spit into his eyes, because he thought if he allowed himself to cry, he might not be able to stop.

He looked at the woman. She was pretending to come round. He wished he had the strength and the inclination to go over and hit her, but he was too tired, and too conscious that he would be taking out on her the defeat of an entire army. Belting any one individual—let alone a helpless, cross-eyed woman—would be so pathetically petty a way of trying to find recompense for a downfall of that magnitude that even if he did live, he would be ashamed forever that he had done such a thing.

She moaned dramatically. A thin strand of snot detached itself from her nose and fell onto the heavy coat she wore.

He looked away, disgusted.

He heard her sniff, loudly. When he looked back, her eyes were open, and she was staring malevolently at him. She was only slightly cross-eyed, but the imperfection annoyed him more than it should have. Given a bath and a decent set of clothes, he thought, the woman might almost have looked pretty. But right now she was buried inside a greasy green greatcoat smudged all over with mud, and her dirty face was almost completely hidden; partially by the collar of the heavy coat, and partially by her long, filthy hair, which was attached to the green greatcoat in various places by glistening blobs of mud. She moved oddly in the chair, as though scratching her back against the chair. He could not decide whether she was testing the ropes that bound her, or was just troubled by fleas.

He doubted she had been sent to kill him; almost certainly she was what she was dressed as; an auxiliary. Probably she had been left behind in a retreat and had wandered about too frightened or proud or stupid to surrender until she had seen the staff car in difficulties in the storm-washed hollow. Her attempt at killing him had been brave but laughable. By sheer luck she'd killed his driver with one shot; a second had struck him a glancing blow on the side of the head, making him groggy while she threw the empty gun away and leapt into the car with her knife. The driverless car had slid down a greasy grass slope into the brown torrent of the river.

Such a stupid act. Sometimes, heroics revolted him; they seemed like an insult to the soldier who weighed the risks of the situation and made calm, cunning decisions based on experience and imagination; the sort of unshowy soldiering that didn't win medals but wars.

Still dazed from the bullet-graze, he had fallen into the car's rear footwell as it pitched and yawed, caught in the swollen force of the river. The woman had nearly buried him in the voluminous thick coat. Stuck like that, head still ringing from the shot that had grazed his skull, he'd been unable to get a good swing at her. For those absurd, confined, frustrating minutes, the struggle with the girl had seemed like a microcosm of the plain-wide muddle his army was now embroiled in; he had the strength to knock her out cold, but the cramped battleground and the hiding weight of her enveloping coat had muffled him and imprisoned him until it was too late.

The car had hit the concrete island and tipped right over, throwing them both out onto the corroded gray surface. The woman had given a little scream; she'd raised the knife that had been caught in the folds of the green greatcoat all that time, but he had finally got his clear punch, and connected satisfyingly with her chin.

She'd thumped back to the concrete; he'd turned round to

see the car scraping off the slipway, torn away by the surging brown tide. Still on its side, it had sunk almost immediately.

He'd turned back, and felt tempted to kick the unconscious woman. He'd kicked the knife instead, sending it whirling away into the river, following the drowned staff car.

"You won't win," the woman said, spitting. "You can't win, against us." She shook the little chair, angrily.

"What?" he said, shaken from his reverie.

"We'll win," she said, giving a furious shake that rattled the chair's legs on the stone floor.

Why did I tie the silly fool to a chair, of all things? he thought. "You could well be right," he told her, tiredly. "Things are looking . . . damp at the moment. Make you feel any better?"

"You're going to die," the woman said, staring.

"Nothing more certain than that," he agreed, gazing at the leaking roof above the rag bed.

"We are invincible. We will never give up."

"Well, you've proved fairly vincible before." He sighed, remembering the history of this place.

"We were betrayed!" the woman shouted. "Our armies never were defeated; we were—"

"Stabbed in the back; I know."

"Yes! But our spirit will never die. We—"

"Aw, shut up!" He said, swinging his legs off the narrow bed and facing the woman. "I've heard that shit before. 'We was robbed.' 'The folks back home let us down.' 'The media were against us.' Shit . . ." He ran a hand through his wet hair. "Only the very young or the very stupid think wars are waged just by the military. As soon as news travels faster than a despatch rider or a bird's leg the whole . . . nation . . . whatever . . . is fighting. That's your spirit; your will. Not the grunt on the ground. If you lose, you lose. Don't whine about it. You'd have lost this time too if it hadn't been for this fucking rain." He held up a hand as the woman drew breath. "And no, I don't believe God is on your side."

"Heretic!"

"Thank you."

"I hope your children die! Slowly!"

"Hmm," he said, "I'm not sure I qualify, but if I do it'd

be a long spit.'' He collapsed back on the bed, then looked aghast, and levered himself back up again. ''Shit; they really must get to you people young; that's a terrible thing for any-body to say, let alone a woman.''

''Our women are more manly than your *men*,'' the woman sneered.

''And still you breed. Choice must be limited, I sup-pose.''

''May your children suffer and die horribly!'' the woman shrieked.

''Well, if that's really the way you feel,'' he sighed, lying back again, ''then there's nothing worse I can wish on you than to be exactly the fuckhead you so obviously are.''

''Barbarian! Infidel!''

''You'll run out of expletives soon; I'd advise saving some for later. Not that keeping forces in reserve has ever been precisely you guys' strong point, has it?''

''We will crush you!''

''Hey; I'm crushed, I'm crushed.'' He waved one hand languidly. ''Now back off.''

The woman howled and shook the small chair.

Maybe, he thought, I ought to be thankful for the chance to be away from the responsibilities of command, the minute-to-minute changes in conditions that the fools couldn't deal with themselves and that bogged you down as surely as the mud; the continual flood of reports of units immobilized, washed away, deserting, cut off, retreating from vital posi-tions, yelling for help, for relief, for reinforcements, more trucks, more tanks, more rafts, more food, more radios . . . past a certain point there was nothing he could do; he could only acknowledge, reply, turn-down, delay, order to make a stand; nothing, nothing. The reports kept on coming in, building up like a one-color, paper mosaic of a million pieces, the picture of an army, bit-by-bit disintegrating, softened by the rain just like a sheet of paper, made soggy and tearable and gradually coming apart.

That was what he was escaping by being marooned here . . . yet he was not secretly thankful, he was not actually glad; he was furious and angry at being away, at leaving it all in the hands of others, of being away from the center, from knowing what was happening. He fretted like a mother for a young son just marched off to war, driven to tears or pointless screams for the powerlessness of it, the heedless unstoppable momentum. (It struck him then that the whole process didn't really require any enemy forces at all. The battle was him and the army under his command, against the elements. A third party was superfluous.)

First the rains, then their unheard-of severity, then the landslide that had cut them off from the rest of the command convoy, then this bedraggled idiot of a would-be assassin . . .

He swung back upright again, held his head in his hands.

Had he tried to do too much? He had had ten hours' sleep in the last week; had that clouded his mind, impaired his judgment? Or had he slept too much; might that little extra bit of wakefulness have made all the difference?

"I hope you die!" the woman's voice squawked.

He looked at her, frowning, wondering why she had interrupted his thoughts, wishing she'd shut up. Maybe he should gag her.

"You're retreating," he pointed out. "A minute ago you were telling me I *would* die." He slumped back on the bed.

"Bastard!" she screamed.

He looked at her, suddenly thinking that he was as much a prisoner where he lay as she was where she sat. Snot gathered under her nose again. He looked away.

He heard her snort back, then spit. He would have smiled if he'd had the strength. She showed contempt with a spit; what was her one dribble compared to the deluge that was drowning a fighting machine he had worked two years to bring together and train?

And why, *why* had he tied her to a chair of all things? Did he try to make chance and fate redundant by scheming against himself? A chair; a girl tied to the chair . . . about the same age, maybe a little older . . . but the same slim figure, with a lying greatcoat that tried to pretend she was bigger, but failed. About the same age, about the same shape . . .

He shook his head, forcing his thoughts away from that battle, that failure.

She saw him look at her and shake his head.

"Don't you laugh at me!" she screamed, shaking backward and forward in the chair, furious at his scorn.

"Shut up, shut up," he said wearily. He knew it wasn't convincing, but he could not sound any more authoritative.

She shut up, remarkably.

The rains, and her; sometimes he wished he did believe in Fate. Maybe it did sometimes help to believe in Gods. Sometimes—like now, when things fell against him and every turn he took brought him up against another vicious twist of the knife, another hammering on the bruises he'd already collected—it would be comforting to think that it was all designed, all preordained, all already written, and you just turned the pages of some great and inviolable book . . . Maybe you never did get a chance to write your own story (and so his own name, even that attempt at terms, mocked him).

He didn't know what to think; was there as petty and suffocating a destiny as some people seemed to think?

He didn't want to be here; he wanted to be back where the busy to-and-fro of report and command stifled all other traffic in the mind.

"You're losing; you've lost this battle, haven't you?"

He considered saying nothing, but on reflection she would take this as a sign he was weak, and so continue.

"What a penetrating insight," he sighed. "You remind me of some of the people who planned this war. Cross-eyed, stupid and static."

"I'm not cross-eyed!" she screamed, and instantly started crying, her head forced down by the weight of huge sobs that shook her body and waved the folds of the coat, making the chair creak.

Her dirty long hair hid her face, falling from her head over the wide lapels of the greatcoat; her arms were almost level with the ground, so far forward had she slumped in her crying. He wanted the strength to go over and cuddle her, or bash her brains out; anything to stop her making that unnecessary noise.

"All right, all right, you haven't got cross-eyes, I'm sorry."

He lay back with one arm thrown across his eyes, hoping he sounded convincing, but sure he sounded as insincere as he was.

"I don't want your sympathy!"

"Sorry again; I retract the retraction."

"Well . . . I haven't . . . It's just a . . . a slight defect, and it didn't stop the army board from taking me."

(They were also, he recalled, taking children and pensioners, but he didn't say that to the woman.) She was trying to wipe her face on the lapels of the greatcoat.

She sniffed heavily, and when she brought her head back and her hair swung away, he saw there was a large dew-drop on the tip of her nose. He got up without thinking—the tiredness shrieking in indignation—and tore a portion of the thin curtain over the bed-alcove off as he went over to her.

She saw him coming with the ragged scrap and screamed with all her might; she emptied her lungs with the effort of announcing to the rainy world outside that she was about to be murdered. She was rocking the chair, and he had to jump at it and land with one boot on one of the cross-members between the legs to stop it from tipping over.

He put the rag over her face.

She stopped struggling. She went limp, not fighting or squirming but knowing it was utterly pointless to go on doing anything.

"Good," he said, relieved. "Now, blow."

She blew.

He withdrew the rag, folded it over, put it back over her face and told her to blow again. She blew again. He folded it over again and wiped her nose, hard. She squealed; it was sore. He sighed again and threw the rag away.

He didn't lie down again because it only made him sleepy and thoughtful, and he didn't want to sleep because he felt he might never wake up, and he didn't want to think because it wasn't getting him anywhere.

He turned away and stood at the door, which was as close anywhere as it could be and still half open. Rain spattered in.

He thought of the others; the other commanders. Damn; the only other one he trusted was Rogtam-Bar, and he was too junior to take charge. He hated being put into positions like this, coming in on an already established command structure, usually corrupt, usually nepotistic, and having to take so much on himself that any absence, any hesitation, even any rest, gave the clueless froth-heads around him a chance to fuck things up even further. But then, he told himself, what general was ever totally happy with the command he took over?

Anyway, he hadn't left them enough: a few crazy plans that would almost certainly never come off; his attempts to use the weapons that were not obvious. Too much of it was still inside his own head. That one private place, where he knew even the Culture did not look, though through their own warped fastidiousness, not through inability . . .

He forgot all about the woman. It was as if she didn't exist when he wasn't looking at her, and her voice and her attempt to cut herself free were the results of some absurd supernatural manifestation.

He opened the cottage door wide. You couldn't see anything in the rain. The individual drops became streaks with the slowness of the eye; they merged and reemerged as ciphers for the shapes you carried inside you; they lasted less than a heartbeat in your sight and they went on forever.

He saw a chair, and a ship that was not a ship; he saw a man with two shadows, and he saw that which cannot be seen; a concept; the adaptive, self-seeking urge to survive, to bend everything that can be reached to that end, and to remove and to add and to smash and to create so that one particular collection of cells can go on, can move onward and decide, and keeping moving, and keeping deciding, knowing that—if nothing else—at least it lives.

And it had two shadows, it was two things; it was the need and it was the method. The need was obvious; to defeat what opposed its life. The method was that taking and bending of materials and people to one purpose, the outlook that everything could be used in the fight; that nothing could be excluded, that everything was a weapon, and the ability to handle those weapons, to find them and choose which one to aim and fire; that talent, that ability, that use of weapons.

A chair, and a ship that was not a ship, a man with two shadows, and . . .

"What are you going to do with me?" The woman's voice was quivering. He looked round at her.

"I don't know; what do you think?"

She looked at him with her eyes widening, horrified. She seemed to be gathering her breath for another scream. He didn't understand it; he'd asked her a perfectly normal, pertinent question and she acted as if he'd said he was going to kill her.

"Please don't. Oh please don't, oh please please don't," she sobbed again, dryly. Then her back seemed to break, and her imploring face bowed almost to her knees as she drooped again.

"Do *what*?" He was mystified.

She didn't appear to hear him; she just hung there, her slack body jerked by her sobs.

It was at moments like this he stopped understanding people; he just had no comprehension of what was going on in their minds; they were denied, unfathomable. He shook his head and started walking round the room. It was smelly and damp, and it carried this atmosphere as though this was no innovation. This had always been a hole. Probably some illiterate had lived here, custodian of the derelict machines from another, more fabulous age, long-shattered by the conspicuous love of war these people exhibited; a mean life in an ugly place.

When would they come? Would they find him? Would they think he was dead? Had they heard his message on the radio, after the landslide had cut them off from the rest of the command convoy?

Had he worked the damn thing right?

Maybe he hadn't. Maybe he would be left behind; they might think a search was useless. He hardly cared. It would be no additional pain to be captured; he'd drowned in that already, in his mind. He could almost welcome it, if he set his mind to it; he knew he could. All he needed was the strength to be bothered.

"If you're going to kill me, please will you do it quickly?"

He was getting annoyed at these constant interruptions.

"Well, I wasn't going to kill you, but keep on whining like this and I may change my mind."

"I hate you." It seemed to be all she could think of.

"And I hate you too."

She started crying again, loudly.

He looked out into the rain again, and saw the Staberinde.

Defeat, defeat, the rain whispered; tanks foundering in the mud, the men giving up under the torrential rain, everything coming to bits.

And a stupid woman, and a runny nose . . . He could laugh at it, at the sharing of time and place between the grand and the petty, the magnificently vast and the shoddily absurd, like horrified nobility having to share a carriage with drunk and dirty peasants being sick over them and copulating under them; the finery and fleas.

Laugh, that was the only answer, the only reply that couldn't be bettered or itself laughed down; the lowest of the low of common denominators.

"Do you know who I am?" he said, turning suddenly. The thought had just occurred to him that maybe she didn't realize who he was, and he wouldn't have been in the least surprised to find out that she had tried to kill him just because he was in a big car, and not because she had recognized the commander-in-chief of the entire army. He wouldn't be at all surprised to find that; he almost expected it.

She looked up. "What?"

"Do you know who I am? Do you know my name or rank?"

"No," she spat. "Should I?"

"No, no," he laughed, and turned away.

He looked briefly out at the gray wall of rain, as though it was an old friend, then turned, went back to the bed and fell onto it again.

The government wouldn't like it either. Oh, the things he'd promised them, the riches, the lands, the gains of wealth, prestige and power. They'd have him shot if the Culture didn't pull him out; they'd see him dead for this defeat. It would have been their victory but it would be his defeat. Standard complaint.

He tried to tell himself that, mostly, he'd won. He knew he had, but it was only the moments of defeat, the instants of paralysis that made him really think, and try to join up the weave of his life into a whole. That was when his thoughts returned to the battleship Staberinde and what it represented; that was when he thought about the Chairmaker, and the reverberating guilt behind that banal description . . .

It was a better sort of defeat this time, it was more impersonal. He was the commander of the army, he was responsible to the government, and they could remove him; in the final reckoning, then, he was not responsible; they were. And there was nothing personal in the conflict. He'd never met the leaders of the enemy; they were strangers to him; only their military habits and their patterns of favored troop movements and types of buildup were familiar. The

cleanness of that schism seemed to soften the rain of blows.
A little.

He envied people who could be born, be raised, mature
with those around them, have friends, and then settle down
in one place with one set of acquaintances, live ordinary and
unspectacular, unrisky lives and grow old and be replaced,
their children coming to see them . . . and die old and senile,
content with all that had gone before.

He could never have believed he would ever feel like
this, that he would so ache to be like that, to have despairs
just so deep, joys just so great; to never strain the fabric of
life or fate, but to be minor, unimportant, uninfluential.

It seemed utterly sweet, infinitely desirable, now and forever, because once in that situation, once you were there . . .
would you ever feel the awful need to do as he had done, and
try for those heights? He doubted it. He turned back to look
at the woman in the chair.

But it was pointless, it was stupid; he thought about
thoughtless things. If I were a seabird . . . but how could *you*
be a seabird? If you were a seabird your brain would be tiny
and stupid and you would love half-rotted fish guts and
tweaking the eyes out of little grazing animals; you would
know no poetry and you could never appreciate flying as fully
as the human on the ground yearning to be you.

If you wanted to be a seabird you deserved to be one.

"Ah! The camp leader and the camp follower. You haven't
quite got it right though, sir, you're supposed to tie her in the
bed . . ."

He jumped; spun round, hand going to the holster at his
waist.

Kirive Socroft Rogtam-Bar kicked the door shut and stood
shaking rain from a large shiny cape in the doorway, smiling
ironically and looking annoyingly fresh and handsome considering he'd had no sleep for days.

"Bar!" He almost ran to him, they clapped their arms
about each other and laughed.

"The very same. General Zakalwe; hello there. I wondered if you would like to join me in a stolen vehicle. I have
an Amph outside . . ."

"What!" He threw open the door again and looked out
onto the waters. There was a large and battered amphibious
truck fifty meters away, near one of the towering machines.

"That's one of their trucks," he laughed.

Rogtam-Bar nodded unhappily. "Yes, I'm afraid so. They seem to want it back, too."

"They do?" He laughed again.

"Yes. By the way, I'm afraid the government has fallen. Forced out of office."

"What? Because of this?"

"That's the impression I got, I must say. I think they were so busy blaming you for losing their idiotic war that they didn't realize people connected them with it as well. Wide asleep as usual." Rogtam-Bar smiled. "Oh; and that manic idea of yours; the commando squad placing the sink-charges on the Maclin reservoir? It worked. Sent all that water into the dam and made the thing overflow; didn't actually break, according to the intelligence reports, but it . . . overtopped, is that the expression? Anyway; an awful lot of water went down the valley and swept away most of the Fifth Army's High Command . . . not to mention quite a bit of the Fifth itself, judging from the bods and tents seen floating past our lines over the last few hours . . . And there we all were, thinking you were crazy for dragging that hydrologist around with the general staff for the past week." Rogtam-Bar clapped his gloved hands. "Whatever. Things must be serious; there's talk of peace, I'm afraid." He looked the General up and down. "But you'll have to present a prettier picture than that, I suspect, if you're to start talking terms with our pals on the other side. You been mud wrestling, General?"

"Only with my conscience."

"Really? Who won?"

"Well, it was one of those rare occasions when violence really doesn't solve anything."

"I know the scenario well; usually crops up when one is trying to decide whether to open the next bottle, or not." Bar nodded at the door. "After you." He produced a large umbrella from within his cloak, opened it and held it out. "General; allow me!" Then he looked into the center of the room. "And what about your friend?"

"Oh." He looked back at the woman, who had turned herself around and was staring, horrified, at them. "Yes, my captive audience." He shrugged. "I've seen stranger mascots; let's take her, too."

"Never question the high command," Bar said. He

handed over the umbrella. "You take this. I'll take her." He looked reassuringly at the woman, tipped his cap. "Only literally, ma'am."

The woman let out a piercing shriek.

Rogtam-Bar winced. "Does she do that a lot?" he asked.

"Yes; and watch her head when you pick her up; near busted my nose."

"When it's such an attractive shape already. See you in the Amph, sir."

"Right you are," he said, maneuvering the umbrella through the doorway, and walking down the concrete slope, whistling.

"Bastard infidel!" the woman in the chair screamed, as Rogtam-Bar approached her and the chair from behind, cautiously.

"You're in luck," he told her. "I don't normally stop for hitchers."

He picked up the chair with the woman in it and took them both down to the vehicle, where he dumped them in the back.

She screamed the whole way.

"Was she this noisy all the time?" Rogtam-Bar asked, as he reversed the machine back out into the flood.

"Mostly."

"I'm surprised you could hear yourself think."

He looked out into the pouring rain, smiling ruefully.

In the ensuing peace, he was demoted, and stripped of several medals. He left later that year, and the Culture didn't seem in the least displeased with how he'd done.

7

The city was built inside a canyon two kilometers deep and ten across; the canyon wound through the desert for eight hundred kilometers, a jagged gash in the crust of the planet. The city took up only thirty of those kilometers.

He stood on the rimrock, looking inward, and was confronted by a staggered confusion of buildings and houses and streets and steps and storm drains and railway lines, all gray and misty in filmy layers under a foggy-red setting sun.

Like slow waters from a broken dam, nebulous rollers of cloud swung down the canyon; they foundered persistently among the juts and cracks of the architecture, and seeped away like tired thoughts.

In a very few places, the topmost buildings had overreached the rimrock and spilled onto the desert, but the rest of the city gave the impression that it lacked the energy or the momentum to proceed that far, and so had kept within the canyon, sheltered from the winds and kept temperate by the canyon's own natural microclimate.

The city, speckled with dim lights, seemed strangely silent and motionless. He listened hard, and finally caught what sounded like the high howl of some animal, from deep inside some misty suburb. Searching the skies, he could see the far specks of circling birds, wheeling in the still and coldly heavy air. Gliding in the deep distance over the cluttered terraces, stepped streets and zigzagging roads, they were the source of a far, hoarse crying.

Further down, he saw some silent trains, thin lines of light, slowly crossing between tunnels. Water showed as black lines, in aqueducts and canals. Roads ran everywhere, and vehicles crawled along them, lights like sparks as they scuttled like the tiny prey of the wheeling birds.

It was a cold autumn evening, and the air was bitter. He'd taken off the combat suit and left it in the capsule, which had buried itself in a sandy hollow. Now he wore the baggy clothes that were popular here again; they had been in fashion when he'd worked here last time, and he felt oddly pleased that he'd been away long enough for the style to cycle round again. He was not superstitious, but the coincidence amused him.

He squatted down and touched the rimrock. He lifted a handful of pebbles and topweeds, then let them sift through his fingers. He sighed and got to his feet, pulling on gloves, putting on a hat.

The city was called Solotol, and Tsoldrin Beychae was here.

He dusted a little sand from his coat—an old raincoat from far away, and of purely sentimental value—placed a pair of very dark glasses on his nose, picked up a modest case, and went down into the city.

"Good afternoon, sir. How may I help you?"

"I'd like your two top floors, please."

The clerk looked confused, then leaned forward. "I'm sorry, sir?"

"The two top floors of the hotel; I'd like them." He smiled. "I haven't made a reservation; sorry."

"Aah . . ." the clerk said. He appeared a little worried as he looked at his reflection in the dark glasses. "The two . . . ?"

"Not a room, not a suite, not a floor, but two floors, and not any two floors; the two top floors. If you have any guests presently occupying any of the rooms in the top two floors,

I suggest you ask them politely to accept a room on another floor; I'll pay their bills up till now.''

"I see . . ." the hotel clerk said. He seemed unsure whether to take all this seriously or not. "And . . . how long was sir thinking of staying?''

"Indefinitely. I'll pay for a month, in advance. My lawyers will cable the funds by lunchtime tomorrow." He opened the case and took out a wad of paper money, placing it on the desk. "I'll pay for one night in cash, if you like."

"I see," the clerk said, eyes fixed on the money. "Well, if sir would like to fill in this form . . ."

"Thank you. Also, I'll want an elevator for my personal use, and access to the roof. I expect a pass key will be the best solution."

"Aah. Indeed. I see. Excuse me just a moment, sir." The clerk went off to get the manager.

He negotiated a bulk discount for the two floors, then agreed a fee for the use of the lift and the roof that brought the deal back to what it had been in the first place. He just liked haggling.

"And sir's name?"

"I'm called Staberinde," he said.

He chose a suite on the top floor, on a corner which looked out into the great depth of canyon city. He unlocked all the cupboards and closets and doors, window shutters, balcony covers and drug cabinets, and left everything open. He tested the bath in the suite; the water ran hot. He took a couple of small chairs out of the bedroom, and another set of four from the lounge, and put then in another suite alongside. He turned all the lights on, looking at everything.

He looked at patterns of coverings and curtains and hangings and carpets, at the murals and paintings on the walls, and at the design of the furniture. He rang for some food to be delivered, and when it came, on a small trolley, he pushed the trolley in front of him from room to room, eating on the move while he wandered through the quiet spaces of the hotel, gazing all about, and occasionally looking at a tiny sensor which was supposed to tell him if there were any surveillance devices around. There weren't.

He paused at a window, looking out, and rubbed absently

at a small puckered mark on his chest that was not there anymore.

"Zakalwe?" said a tiny voice from his breast. He looked down, took a thing like a bead out of a shirt pocket. He clipped it to one ear, taking off his dark glasses and putting them in the pocket instead.

"Hello."

"It's me; Diziet. You all right?"

"Yeah. I found a place to stay."

"Great. Listen; we've found something. It's *perfect*!"

"What?" he said, smiling at the excitement in Sma's voice. He pressed a button to close the curtains.

"Three thousand years ago here there was a guy who became a famous poet; wrote on wax tablets set in wooden frames. He did a group of one hundred short poems he always maintained were the best things he ever wrote. But he couldn't get them published, and he decided to become a sculptor instead; he melted the wax from ninety-eight of the tablets—keeping numbers one and one hundred—to carve a wax model, made a sand mold around it, and cast a bronze figure which still exists.

"Sma, is this leading anywhere?" he said, pressing another button to open the curtains again. He rather liked the way they swished.

"Wait! When we first found Voerenhutz and did the standard total scan of each planet, we naturally took a holo of the bronze statue; found some traces of the original casting sand *and the wax* in a cranny.

"And it wasn't the right wax!

"It didn't match the two surviving tablets! So the GCU waited till it had finished the total scan and then did some detective work. The guy who did the bronze, and who had done the poems, later became a monk, and ended up an abbot of a monastery. There was one building added while he was head man; legend has it he used to go there and contemplate the vanished ninety-eight poems. The building has a double wall." Sma's voice rose triumphantly; "Guess what's in the cavity!"

"Walled-in disobedient monks?"

"The poems! The waxes!" Sma yelled. Then her voice dropped a little. "Well, most of them. The monastery was abandoned a couple of hundred years ago, and it looks like

some shepherd lit a fire against a wall some time and melted
three or four of them . . . but the rest are *there*!''

"Is that good?"

"Zakalwe; they're one of the great lost literary treasures
of the planet! The university of Jarnsaromol, where your pal
Beychae's hanging out, has most of the guy's parchment
manuscripts, the other two tablets *and* the famous bronze.
They'd give *anything* to get their hands on those tablets! Don't
you see? It's perfect."

"Sounds all right, I suppose."

"Damn you, Zakalwe! Is that all you can say?"

"Dizzy, luck this good never lasts long; it'll average out."

"Don't be so pessimistic, Zakalwe."

"Okay, I won't," he sighed, closing the curtains again.

There was a noise of exasperation from Diziet Sma.
"Well; I just thought I'd tell you. We'll be going soon. Sleep
well."

The channel beeped closed. He smiled ruefully. He left
the little terminal where it was, like an earring.

He gave orders he was not to be disturbed, and as the
night deepened, he turned all the heating up full and opened
all the windows. He spent some time testing the balconies
and drainage pipes around the outer walls; he climbed nearly
to the ground and all the way round the facade as he tested
ledges and pipes and sills and cornices for their strength. He
saw lights in less than a dozen other guest rooms. When he
was satisfied he knew the outside of the hotel, he returned to
his floor.

He leaned on the balcony, a smoky bowl cradled in his
hand. Occasionally he lifted the bowl to his face and inhaled
deeply; the rest of the time he looked out over the sparkling
city, whistling.

Watching the light-speckled view, he thought while most
cities looked like canvases, spread flat and thin, Solotol was
like a half-open book; a rippling sculptured V sinking deep
into the planet's geological past. Above, the clouds over the
canyon and the desert glowed with orange-red light, reflecting
the channeled flare of the city.

He imagined that from the other side of the city, the hotel
must look rather strange, with its topmost floor fully lit, the
others practically black.

He supposed he had forgotten how different the setting of

the canyon made the city, compared to others. Still, this too is similar, he thought. All is similar.

He had been to so many different places and seen so much the same and so much utterly different that he was amazed by both phenomena . . . but it was true; this city was not so different from many others he'd known.

Everywhere they found themselves, the galaxy bubbled with life and its basic foods kept on speaking back to it, just like he'd told Shias Engin (and, thinking of her, felt again the texture of her skin and the sound of her voice). Still, he suspected if the Culture had really wanted to, it could have found far more spectacularly different and exotic places for him to visit. Their excuse was that he was a limited creature, adapted to certain sorts of planets and societies and types of warfare. A martial niche, Sma had called it.

He smiled a little grimly, and took another deep breath from the drug bowl.

The man walked past empty arcades and deserted flights of steps. He wore an old raincoat of a style unknown but still somehow old-fashioned looking; he wore very dark glasses. His walk was economical. He appeared to have no mannerisms.

He entered the courtyard of a large hotel which contrived to look expensive and slightly run-down at the same time. Dully-dressed gardeners, raking leaves from the surface of an old swimming pool, stared at the man as though he had no right to be there.

Men were painting the interior of the porch outside the lobby, and he had to work his way round them to get in. The painters were using specially inferior paint made to very old recipes; it was guaranteed to fade and crack and peel in a most authentic manner within a year or two.

The foyer was rich with decoration. The man pulled a thick purple rope near one corner of the reception desk. The clerk appeared, smiling.

"Good morning, Mr. Staberinde. A pleasant walk?"

"Yes, thank you. Have breakfast sent up, will you?"

"Immediately, sir."

"Solotol is a city of arches and bridges, where steps and pavements wind past tall buildings and lance out over steep

rivers and gullies on slender suspension bridges and fragile stone arches. Roadways flow along the banks of water
courses, looping and twisting over and under them; railways splay out in a tangle of lines and levels, swirling
through a network of tunnels and caverns where underground reservoirs and roads converge, and from a speeding train passengers can look out to see galaxies of lights
reflecting on stretches of dark water crossed by the slants
of underground funiculars and the piers and ways of sub-
terranean roads.''

He was sitting in the bed, dark glasses on the other pillow,
eating breakfast and watching the hotel's own introductory
tape on the suite screen. He switched the sound down when
the antique telephone beeped.

''Hello?''

''Zakalwe?'' It was Sma's voice.

''Good grief; you still here?''

''We're about to break orbit.''

''Well, don't wait on my account.'' He felt inside a shirt
pocket and fished out the terminal bead. ''Why the phone?
This transceiver packed up?''

''No; just making sure there are no problems patching
into the phone system.''

''Fine. That all?''

''No. We've located Beychae more exactly; still in Jarnsaromol University, but he's in library annex four. That's a
hundred meters under the city; the university's safest safe
store. Quite secure at the best of times, and they have extra
guards, though no real military.''

''But where does he live; where does he sleep?''

''The curator's apartments; they're attached to the library.''

''He ever come to the surface?''

''Not that we can find out.''

He whistled. ''Well, that might or might not be a problem.''

''How are things at your end?''

''Fine,'' he said, biting into a sweetmeat. ''Just waiting
for the offices to open; I've left a message with the lawyers
to phone me. Then I start causing a fuss.''

''All right. There shouldn't be any problems there; the

necessary instructions have been issued, and you should get anything you want. Any problems, get in touch and we'll fire off an indignant cable.''

"Yeah, Sma, I've been thinking; just how big is this Culture commercial empire, this Vanguard Corporation?''

"Vanguard *Foundation*. It's big enough.''

"Yeah, but how big? How far can I go?''

"Well, don't buy anything bigger than a country. Look, Cheradenine; be as extravagant as you want in creating your fuss. Just get Beychae for us. Quickly.''

"Yeah, yeah; okay.''

"We're heading off now, but we'll keep in touch. Remember; we're here to help if you need it.''

"Yeah. Bye.'' He put the phone down and turned the screen sound up again.

"Caves, natural and artificial, are scattered through the rock of the canyon walls in almost as great a profusion as the buildings on the sloping surface. Many of the city's old hydroelectric sources are there, hollowed out into rock and humming; and a few small factories and workshops still survive, hidden away beneath the cliffs and shale, with only their stubby chimneys on the desert surface to show their position. This upward river of warm fumes counterpoints the network of sewage and drainage pipes, which also show on the surface on occasion, and presents a complex pattern of tracery through the fabric of the city.''

The phone beeped.
"Hello?''
"Mr. . . . Staberinde?''
"Yes.''
"Ah, yes; good morning. My name is Kiaplor, of . . .''
"Ah; the lawyers.''
"Yes. Thank you for your message. I have here a cable granting you full access to the income and securities of the Vanguard Foundation.''

"I know. Are you quite happy with this, Mr. Kiaplor?''

"Umm . . . I . . . yes; the cable makes the position quite clear . . . though it is an unprecedented degree of individual discretion, given the size of the account. Not that the Vanguard Foundation has ever behaved exactly conventionally at any time.''

"Good. The first thing I'd like is to have funds sufficient to cover a month's hire of two floors of the Excelsior transferred to the hotel's account, immediately. Then I want to start buying a few things.''

"Ah . . . yes. Such as?''

He dabbed at his lips with a napkin. ''Well, for a start, a street.''

"A street?''

''Yes. Nothing too ostentatious, and it doesn't have to be very long, but I want a whole street, somewhere near the city center. Do you think you can look for a suitable one, immediately?''

''Ah . . . well, yes, we can certainly start looking. I . . .''

"Good. I'll call at your offices in two hours; I'd like to be in a position to come to a decision then.''

''Two . . . ? Umm . . . well, ah . . .''

''Speed is essential, Mr. Kiaplor. Put your best people on it.''

"Yes. Very well.''

''Good. I'll see you in a couple of hours.''

''Yes. Right. Good-bye.''

He turned the screen sound back up again.

''Very little new building has been done for hundreds of years; Solotol is a monument, an institution; a museum. The factories, like the people, are mostly gone. Three universities lend areas of the city some life, during part of the year, but the general air is said by many people to be archaic, even stultified, though some people enjoy the feel of living in what is, in effect, the past. Solotol has no sky-lighting; the trains still run on metal rails, and the ground vehicles must remain on the ground, because flying within the city or immediately above it is banned. A sad old place, in many ways; large sections of the city are uninhabited or only occupied for part of the year. The city is still a capital in name, but it does not represent the culture to which it belongs; it is an exhibit, and while many come to visit it, few choose to stay.''

He shook his head, put his dark glasses on, and turned the screen off.

• • •

When the wind was in the right direction he blasted huge netted balls of paper money into the air from an old firework mortar mounted in a high roof garden; the notes drifted down like early snowflakes. He'd had the street decorated with bunting, streamers and balloons and filled with tables and chairs and bars serving free drink; covered ways extended the length of it and music played; there were brightly colored canopies over the important areas, such as the bandstands and the bars, but they were not needed; the day was bright, and unseasonably warm. He looked out of one of the highest windows in one of the tallest buildings in the street, and smiled at the sight of all the folk.

So little happened in the city during the off season that the carnival had attracted instant attention. He had hired people to serve the drugs and food and drink he had laid on; he had banned cars and unhappy faces, and people who didn't smile when they tried to get into the street were made to wear funny masks until they had livened up a bit. He breathed in deeply from where he leaned on the high window, and his lungs soaked up the heady fumes of a very busy bar just below; the drug smoke made it just this far up and hung in a cloud. He smiled, found it very heartening; it was all perfect.

People walked around and talked together or in groups, exchanging their smoky bowls, laughing and smiling. They listened to the band and watched people dancing. They gave a great cheer each time the mortar fired. Many of them laughed at the leaflets full of political jokes that were given out with every bowl of drugs or food and every mask and novelty; they laughed too at the big, guady banners that were strung across the fronts of the dilapidated old buildings and across the street itself. The banners were either absurd or humorous, too. PACIFISTS AGAINST WALLS! and, EXPERTS? WHAT DO THEY KNOW? were two of the more translatable examples.

There were games and trials of wit or strength, there were free flowers and party hats and a much frequented compliments stall were one paid a little money, or gave a paper hat or whatever, and was told what a nice, pleasant, good, unshowy, quiet-tempered, undemonstrative, restrained, sincere, respectful, handsome, cheerful, good-willed person one was.

He looked down on all of this, shades pushed up onto the tied-back hair above his forehead. Down there, submerged in it, he knew he would feel somehow apart from it all. But from his high vantage point he could look down and see the people as a mass with different faces; they were far enough away to present a single theme, close enough to introduce their own harmonious variations. They enjoyed themselves, were made to laugh or to giggle, encouraged to get drugged and silly, captivated by the music, slightly deranged by the atmosphere.

He watched two people in particular.

They were a man and a woman, walking slowly through the street, looking all around. The man was tall and had dark hair cut short and kept artificially unkempt and curly; he was smartly dressed and carried a small dark beret in one hand; a mask dangled from the other.

The woman was almost as tall, and slimmer. She was dressed like the man, in unfussy dark gray-black, with a mandala of pleated white at her neck. Her hair was black, shoulder-length, and quite straight. She walked as though there were many admiring people watching her.

They walked side by side, without touching each other; they spoke now and again, merely tipping their heads in the direction of their companion and looking to the other side, perhaps at what they were talking about, as they spoke.

He thought he remembered their photographs from one of the briefings on the GSV. He moved his head a little to one side, to make sure the earring terminal had a good shot of them, then told the tiny machine to record the view.

A few moments later, the two people disappeared beneath the banners at the far end of the street; they'd walked through the carnival without taking part in anything.

The street party went on; a small shower came and drove people under the awnings and covers and into some of the small houses, but it was short, and more people were coming all the time; small children ran with bright streamers of paper, winding colored trails round posts and people and stalls and tables. Puff-bombs exploded in smoky balls of colored incense, and laughing, choking people staggered about, thumping each others' backs and shouting at the laughing children who threw the things.

He drew away from the window, losing interest. He sat

in the room for a little, squatting on an old chest in the dust, hand rubbing his chin, thoughtful, only raising his eyes when an upward landslide of balloons jostled up past the casement. He brought the dark glasses down. From inside, the balloons looked just the same.

He walked down the narrow stairs, his boots clacking on the old wood; he took the old raincoat up from the rail at the bottom, and let himself out of the rear door into another street.

The driver pulled the car away and he sat in the back as they rolled past the rows of old buildings. They came to the end of the street and turned into the steep road that ran at right-angles to it and the street the party was in. They slid past a long dark car with the man and the woman in it.

He looked round. The dark car followed them.

He told the driver to exceed the speed limit. They sped, and the car following them kept pace. He hung on and watched the city slithering past. They raced through some of the old government areas; the grand buildings were gray, and heavily decorated with wall founts and water channels; elaborate patterns of water ran down their walls in vertical waves, dropping like theater curtains. There were some weeds, but less than he would have expected. He couldn't remember if they let the water-walls ice up, turned them off, or added anti-freeze. Scaffolding hung from many of the buildings. Workmen scratched and scraped at the worn stones, and turned to watch the two big cars go tearing through the squares and plazas.

He clung on to a grab handle in the rear of the car, and sorted through a large collection of keys.

They stopped in an old narrow street, down near the banks of the great river itself. He got out smartly and hurried into a small entrance under a tall building. The following car roared into the street as he closed but did not lock the door. He went down some steps, unlocking several rusting sets of gates. When he got down to the bottom of the building he found the funicular car waiting on the platform. He opened the door, got in and pulled the lever.

There was a slight jerk as the car started off up the incline, but it ran smoothly enough. He watched through the back windows as the man and then the woman came out onto the platform. He smiled as they looked up and saw the car dis-

appearing into the tunnel. The little coach struggled up the
smooth slope into the daylight.

At the point where the uphill and the downhill coach
passed each other, he got out onto the outer platform of the
car and stepped over onto the downhill coach. It ran on, propelled by the extra weight of water that it carried in its tanks,
picked up from the stream at the high terminal of the old
line. He waited a bit, then jumped out of that car about a
quarter of the way down, onto the steps at the side of the
track. He climbed up a long metal ladder, into another building.

He was sweating slightly by the time he got to the top.
He took off the old raincoat and walked back to the hotel
with it over his arm.

The room was very white and modern-looking, with large
windows. The furniture was integrated with the plasticized
walls, and light came from bulges in the one-piece roof. A
man stood watching the first snow of winter as it fell softly
over the gray city; it was late afternoon, and getting dark
quickly. On a white couch a woman lay facedown, her elbows
spread out, but her hands together under her side-turned face.
Her eyes were closed and her pale, oiled body was massaged
with apparent roughness by a powerfully built man with gray
hair and facial scars.

The man at the window watched the falling snow in two
ways. First as a mass, with his eyes on one static point, so
that the snowflakes became a mere swirl and the currents of
air and gusts of light wind that moved them became manifest
in patterns of circling, spiraling, falling. Then, by looking at
the snow as individual flakes, selecting one high in the indeterminate galaxy of gray on gray, he saw one path, one
separate way down through all the quiet hurry of the fall.

He watched them as they hit the black sill outside, where
they grew steadily but imperceptibly to form a soft white
ledge. Others struck the window itself, sticking there briefly,
then falling away, blown off.

The woman seemed asleep. She smiled slightly, and the
exact geography of her face was altered by the forces that the
gray-haired man exerted on her back, shoulders and flanks.
Her oiled flesh moved this way and that, and the gliding fin-

gers seemed to provide force without causing friction, ribbing and creasing the skin like the smooth action of the sea on underwater grass. Her buttocks were covered by a black towel, her hair was loose and spilling over part of her face, and her pale breasts were long ovals squashed beneath her trim body.

"What is to be done, then?"

"We need to know more."

"That is always true. Back to the problem."

"We could have him deported."

"For what?"

"We need to give no reason, though we could invent one easily enough."

"That might start the war before we are ready for it."

"Shush now; we must not talk of this 'war' thing. We are officially on the best of terms with all our Federation members; there is no need for worry. Everything is under control."

"Said an official spokesperson . . . Do you think we should get rid of him?"

"It may be the wisest course. One might feel better with him out of the way . . . I have a horrible feeling he must be here for a purpose. He has been given full use of the Vanguard Foundation's monies, and that . . . willfully mysterious organization has opposed us every step along the road for thirty years. The identity and location of its owners and executives have been one of the Cluster's best-kept secrets; unparalleled reserve. Now—suddenly—this man appears, spending with a quite vulgar profligacy and maintaining a high, if still coquettishly shy, profile . . . just when it might prove extremely awkward."

"Perhaps he *is* the Vanguard Foundation."

"Nonsense. If it's anything appreciable at all, it's some interfering aliens, or a do-good machine, either running on some dead magnate's conscience will—or even running with a transcription of a human personality—or it's a rogue machine, accidentally conscious with no one to oversee it. I think every other possibility has been discounted over the years. This man Staberinde is a puppet; he spends money with the desperation of an indulged child worried such generosity will not last. He's like a peasant winning a lottery. Revolting. But he must—I repeat—be here for a purpose."

"If we kill him, and he turns out to have been important, then we might start a war, and too early."

"Perhaps, but I feel we must do what is not expected. To prove our humanity, to exploit our intrinsic advantage over the machines, if for no other reason."

"Indeed, but isn't it possible he could be of use to us?"

"Yes."

The man at the window smiled at his reflection in the glass and tapped out a little rhythm on the inside sill.

The woman on the couch kept her eyes closed, her body moving to the steady beat of the hands that plied her waist and flanks.

"But wait. There were links between Beychae and the Vanguard Foundation. If this is so . . ."

"If this is so . . . then perhaps we can persuade Beychae to our side, using this person, this Staberinde." The man put his finger to the glass and traced the path of a snowflake, drifting down the other side. His eyes crossed as he watched it.

"We could . . ."

"What?"

"Adopt the Dehewwoff system."

"The . . . ? Need to know more."

"The Dehewwoff system of punishing by disease; graded capital punishment; the more serious the crime the more serious the disease the culprit is infected with. For minor crimes a mere fever, loss of livelihood and medical expenses; for more damaging misdeeds a bout of something lasting perhaps months, with pain and a long convalescence, bills and no sympathy, sometimes marks to show later on. For really ghastly crimes, infection with diseases rarely survived; near certain death but possible divine intervention and miracle cure. Of course, the lower one's class, the more virulent one's punishment, to allow for the hardier constitutions of the toilers. Combinations, and recurring strains, provide sophistications to the basic idea."

"Back to the problem."

"And I *hate* those dark glasses."

"I repeat; back to the problem."

". . . we need to know more."

"So they all say."

"And I think we should speak to him."

"Yes. *Then* we kill him."

"Restraint. We speak to him. We shall find him again and ask him what he wants and perhaps who he is. We shall keep quiet and be thoughtful and we shall not kill him unless he needs to be killed."

"We nearly spoke to him."

"No sulking. It was preposterous. We are not here to chase cars and run after idiot recluses. We plan. We think. We shall send a note to the gentleman's hotel . . ."

"The Excelsior. Really, one would have hoped such a respected establishment might not have been so easily seduced by mere money."

"Indeed; and then we shall go to him, or have him come to us."

"Well, we certainly ought *not* to go to him. And as for him coming to us, he may refuse. Regret that . . . Due to an unforeseen . . . A previous commitment prevents . . . Feel it would be unwise at this juncture, perhaps another . . . Can you imagine how humiliating that would be?"

"Oh, all right. We'll kill him."

"All right we'll *try* to kill him. If he survives we shall talk to him. If he survives he will want to talk to us. Commendable plan. Must agree. No question, left no choice; mere formality."

The woman fell silent. The gray-haired man heaved at her hips with his great hands, and strange patterns of sweat broke from the unscarred areas of his face; the hands swirled and swept over the woman's rump, and she bit her bottom lip just a little as her body moved in a sweet impersonation, flat beat on a white plain.

Snow was falling.

VII

"You know," he told the rock, "I've got this really
nasty feeling that I'm dying . . . but then all my feelings are pretty nasty at the moment, come to think of it. What
do you think?"

The rock didn't say anything.

He had decided that the rock was the center of the universe, and he could prove it, but the rock just didn't want to
accept its obviously important place in the overall scheme of
things, at least not yet anyway, so he was left talking to himself. Or he could talk to the birds and the insects.

Everything wavered again. Things like waves, like clouds
of carrion birds, closed in on him, centering, zeroing, trap-
ping his mind and picking it off like a rotten fruit under a
machine gun.

He tried to crawl away unobtrusively; he could see what
was coming next; his life was going to flash before him. What
an appalling thought.

Mercifully, only bits of it came back to him, as if the
images mirrored his smashed body, and he remembered
things like sitting in a bar on a little planet, his dark glasses
making strange patterns with the darkened window; he remembered a place where the wind was so bad they used to

judge its severity by the number of trucks that got blown over each night; he remembered a tank battle in the great mono-culture fields like seas of grass, all madness and submerged desperation and commanders standing on the tanks and the areas of burning crop, slowly spreading, burning through the night, spreading darkness ringed by fire . . . the cultivated grassland was the reason for and prize of that war, and was destroyed by it; he remembered a hose playing under searchlit water, its silent coils writhing; he remembered the never-ending whiteness and the attritional tectonics of the crashing tabular bergs, the bitter end of a century's slow sleep.

And a garden. He remembered the garden. And a chair.

"Scream!" he screamed, and started flapping his arms about, trying to work up enough of a run to get into the air and away from . . . from . . . he hardly knew. He hardly moved, either; his arms flapped a little and scraped a few more guano pellets away, but the ring of patient birds clus-tered around him, waiting for him to die, just looked on, unfooled, at this display of inadequately avian behavior.

"Oh all right," he mumbled, and collapsed back, clutch-ing his chest and staring into the bland blue sky. What was so terrible about a chair, anyway? He started crawling again.

He hauled himself around the little puddle, scraping his way through the dark pellets the birds had left, then at a certain point set off toward the waters of the lake. He got only so far, then stopped, turned back, and went on round the puddle again, scraping aside the black bird-shit pellets, apologizing to the little insects he disturbed as he did so. When he got back to the place where he'd been earlier, he stopped and took stock.

The warm breeze brought the smell of sulphur from the lake to him.

. . . And he was back in the garden again, remembering the smell of flowers.

Once there had been a great house which stood in an estate bordered on three sides by a broad river, midway between the mountains and the sea. The grounds were full of old woods and well-grazed pasture land; there were rolling hills full of shy, wild animals, and winding paths and winding streams crossed by little bridges; there were follies and pergolas and ha-has, ornamental lakes and quiet, rustic summerhouses.

Over the years and the generations, many children were born and brought up in the great house, and played in the wonderful gardens that surrounded it, but there were four in particular whose story became important for people who had never seen the house, or heard of the family's name. Two of the children were sisters, called Darckense and Livueta; one of the boys was their elder brother, called Cheradenine, and they all shared the family name; Zakalwe. The last child was not related to them, but came from a family that had long been allied to theirs; he was called Elethiomel.

Cheradenine was the older boy; he could just remember the fuss when Elethiomel's mother came to the great house, large with child, in tears, and surrounded by fussing servants and huge guards and weeping maids. For a few days the attention of the whole house seemed to be centered on the woman with the child in her womb, and—though his sisters played happily on, glad of the lessened watchfulness of their nannies and guards—he already resented the unborn infant.

The troop of royal cavalry came to the house a week later, and he remembered his father out on the broad steps leading down into the courtyard, talking calmly, his own men running quietly through the house, taking up positions at every window. Cheradenine ran to find his mother; as he ran through the corridors, he put one hand out in front of him, as though holding reins, and with his other hand slapped one hip, making a one-two-three, one-two-three clopping noise, pretending he was a cavalryman. He discovered his mother with the woman who had the child inside her; the woman was crying and he was told to go away.

The boy was born that night, to the sound of screams.

Cheradenine noticed that the atmosphere in the house changed greatly after that, and everyone was at once even more busy than before but less worried.

For a few years he could torment the younger boy, but then Elethiomel, who grew faster than he did, started to retaliate, and an uneasy truce developed between the two boys. Tutors taught them, and Cheradenine gradually came to realize that Elethiomel was their favorite, always learning things more quickly than he did, always being praised for his abilities developing so early, always being called advanced and bright and clever. Cheradenine tried hard to match him, and gleaned a little recognition for not just giving up, but it never seemed that he was really appreciated. Their martial instructors were more evenly divided on their merits; Cheradenine was better at wrestling and strike-fighting; Elethiomel the more accomplished with gun and blade (under proper supervision; the boy could get carried away sometimes), though Cheradenine was perhaps his equal with a knife.

The two sisters loved them both, regardless, and they played through the long summers and the brief, cold winters, and—apart from the first year, after Elethiomel was born—spent a little of each spring and autumn in the big city, far down the river, where the parents of Darckense, Livueta and Cheradenine kept a tall town house. None of the children liked the place, though; its garden was so small and the public parks so crowded. Elethiomel's mother was always quieter when they went to the city, and cried more often, and went away for a few days every so often, all excited before she went, then sobbing when she returned.

They were in the city once, one fall, and the four children were keeping out of the way of the short-tempered adults when a messenger came to the house.

They couldn't help but hear the screams, and so abandoned their toy war and ran out of the nursery onto the landing to peer through the railings down into the great hall, where the messenger stood, head down, and Elethiomel's mother screamed and shrieked. Cheradenine, Livueta and Darckense's mother and father both held onto her, talking calmly. Finally, their father motioned the messenger away, and the hysterical woman slumped silent to the floor, a piece of paper crumpled in her hand.

Father looked up then, and saw the children, but looked at Elethiomel, not at Cheradenine. They were all sent to bed soon after.

When they returned to the house in the country a few days later, Elethiomel's mother was crying all the time, and did not come down for meals.

"Your father was a murderer. They put him to death because he killed lots of people." Cheradenine sat with his legs dangling over the edge of the stone bulwark. It was a beautiful day in the garden and the trees sighed in the wind. The sisters were laughing and giggling in the background, collecting flowers from the beds in the center of the stone boat. The stone ship sat in the west lake, joined to the garden by a short stone causeway. They had played pirates for a while, and then started investigating the flower beds on the upper of the boat's two decks. Cheradenine had a collection of pebbles by his side, and was throwing them, one at a time, down into the calm water, producing ripples that looked like an archery target as he tried always to hit the same place.

"He didn't do any of those things," Elethiomel said, kicking the stone bulwark, looking down. "He was a good man."

"If he was good, why did the king have him killed?"

"I don't know. People must have told tales about him. Told lies."

"But the king's clever," Cheradenine said triumphantly, throwing another pebble into the spreading circles of waves. "Cleverer than anybody. That's why he's king. He'd *know* if they were telling lies."

"I don't care," Elethiomel insisted. "My father wasn't a bad man."

"He was, and your mother must have been *extremely* naughty too, or they wouldn't have made her stay in her room all this time."

"She hasn't been bad!" Elethiomel looked up at the other boy, and felt something build up inside his head, behind his nose and eyes. "She's ill. She can't leave her room!"

"That's what she says," Cheradenine said.

"Look! *Millions* of flowers! Look; we're going to make perfume! Do you want to help?" The two sisters ran up behind them, arms full of flowers. "Elly . . ." Darckense tried to take Elethiomel's arm.

He pushed her away.

"Oh, Elly . . . Sheri, please don't," Livueta said.

"She hasn't been bad!" he shouted at the other boy's back.

"Yes she ha-as," Cheradenine said, in a singsong voice, and flicked another pebble into the lake.

"She *hasn't*!" Elethiomel screamed, and ran forward, pushing the other boy hard in the back.

Cheradenine yelled and fell off the carved bulwark; his head struck the stonework as he fell. The two girls screamed.

Elethiomel leaned over the parapet and saw Cheradenine splash into the center of his many-layered circle of waves. He disappeared, came back up again, and floated facedown.

Darckense screamed.

"Oh, Elly, no!" Livueta dropped all her flowers and ran toward the steps. Darckense kept on screaming and squatted down on her haunches, back against the stone bulwark, crushing her flowers to her chest. "Darkle! Run to the house!" Livueta cried from the staircase.

Elethiomel watched the figure in the water move weakly, producing bubbles, as Livueta's steps sounded slapping on the deck underneath.

A few seconds before the girl jumped into the shallow water to haul her brother out, and while Darckense screamed on, Elethiomel swept the remaining pebbles off the parapet, sending them pattering and plopping into the water around the boy.

No, that wasn't it. It had to be something worse than that, didn't it? He was sure he remembered something about a chair (he remembered something about a boat too, but that didn't seem to be quite it either). He tried to think of all the nastiest things that could happen in a chair, dismissed them one by one as they hadn't happened to him or to anybody he knew—at least as far as he could remember—and finally concluded that his fixation on the idea of a chair was a random thing; it just so happened to be a chair and that was all there was to it.

Then there were the names; names that he'd used; pretend names that didn't really belong to him. Imagine calling himself after a *ship*! What a silly person, what a naughty boy; that was what he was trying to *forget*. He didn't know, he didn't understand how he could have been so stupid; now it all seemed so clear, so obvious. He wanted to forget about the ship; he wanted to bury the thing, so he shouldn't go calling himself after it.

Now he realized, *now* he understood, now when it was too late to do anything about it.

Ah, he made himself want to be sick.

A chair, a ship, a . . . something else; he forgot.

The boys learned metalwork, the girls pottery.

"But we're not peasants, or . . . or . . ."

"Artisans," Elethiomel provided.

"You will not argue, and you shall learn something of what it is to work with materials," Cheradenine's father told the two boys.

"But it's common!"

"So is learning how to write, and to work with numbers. Proficiency in those skills will not make you clerks any more than working with iron will make you blacksmiths."

"But . . ."

"You will do as you are told. If it is more in accord with the martial ambitions you both lay claim to, you may attempt to construct blades and armor in the course of your lessons."

The boys looked at each other.

"You might also care to tell your language tutor that I instructed you to ask him whether it is acceptable for young men of breeding to begin almost every sentence with the unfortunate word, 'But.' That is all."

"Thank you, sir."

"Thank you, sir."

Outside, they agreed that metalwork might not be so bad after all. "But we've got to tell Big-nose about saying 'But.' We'll get lines!"

"No we won't. Your old man said that we *might* care to tell Big-nose; that's not the same as actually *telling* us to tell him."

"Ha. Yeah."

Livueta wanted to take up metalwork too, but her father would not allow her to; it was not seemly. She persevered. He would not relent. She sulked. They compromised, on carpentry.

The boys make knives and swords, Darckense pots, and Livueta the furniture for a summerhouse, deep in the estate. It was in that summerhouse where Cheradenine discovered . . .

•   •   •

No no no, he didn't want to think about that, thank you. He knew what was coming.

Dammit, he'd rather think about the other bad time, the day with the gun they'd taken from the armory . . .

Na; he didn't want to think at all. He tried to stop thinking about it all by bashing his head up and down, staring at the mad blue sky and hitting his head up-down, up-down off the pale scaly rocks beneath his head where the guano pellets had been swept away, but it hurt too much and the rocks just gave and he didn't have the strength seriously to threaten a determined speckfly anyway, so he stopped.

Where was he?

Ah yes, the crater, the drowned volcano . . . we're in a crater; an old crater in an old volcano, long dead and filled with water. And in the middle of the crater there was a little island and he was *on* the little island, and he was looking *off* the little island at the crater walls and he was a *man* wasn't he children, and he was a *nice* man and he was *dying* on the little island and . . .

"Scream?" he said.

Doubtfully, the sky looked down.

It was blue.

It had been Elethiomel's idea to take the gun. The armory was unlocked but guarded at the moment; the adults seemed busy and worried all the time, and there was talk of sending the children away. The summer had passed and still they hadn't gone to the city. They were getting bored.

"We could run away."

They were scuffling through the fallen leaves on a path through the estate. Elethiomel talked quietly. They couldn't even walk out here now without guards. The man kept thirty paces ahead and twenty behind. How could you play properly with all these guards around? Back nearer the house they were allowed out without guards, but that was even more boring.

"Don't be silly," Livueta said.

"It's not silly," Darckense said. "We could go to the city. It would be something to do."

"Yes." Cheradenine said. "You're right. It would be."

"Why do you want to go to the city?" Livueta said. "It might be . . . dangerous there."

"Well it's boring here," Darckense said.

"Yeah, it is," Cheradenine agreed.

"We could take a boat and sail away," Cheradenine said.

"We wouldn't even really have to sail, or row," Elethiomel said. "All we'd have to do is push the boat out and we'd end up in the city eventually anyway."

"I wouldn't go," Livueta said, kicking at a pile of leaves.

"Oh, Livvy," Darckense said. "Now you're being boring. Come on. We've got to do things together."

"I wouldn't go," Livueta repeated.

Elethiomel pressed his lips together. He kicked hard at a huge pile of leaves, sending them up into the air like an explosion. A couple of the guards turned round quickly, then relaxed, looking away again. "We've got to do something," he said, looking at the guards ahead, admiring the big automatic rifles they were allowed to use. He'd never even been allowed to touch a proper big gun; just piddling little small-bore pistols and light carbines.

He caught one of the leaves as it fell past his face.

"Leaves . . ." he turned the leaf, this way and that, in front of his eyes. "Trees are stupid," he told the others.

"Of course they are," Livueta said. "They don't have nerves and brains, do they?"

"I don't mean that," he said, crumpling the leaf in his hands. "I mean they're such a stupid idea. All this waste every autumn. A tree that kept it leaves wouldn't have to grow new ones; it would grow bigger than all the rest; it would be the king of the trees."

"But the leaves are beautiful!" Darckense said.

Elethiomel shook his head, exchanging looks with Cheradenine. "Girls!" he laughed, sneering.

He forgot what the other word was for a crater; there was another word for a crater, for a big volcanic crater, there was definitely another word for it, there was absolutely and positively another word for it, I just put it down for a minute here and now some bastard's swiped it, the bastard . . . if I could just find it, I . . . I just put it down here a minute ago . . .

Where was the volcano?

The volcano was on a big island on an inland sea, some-where.

He looked around at the distant heights of the crater walls, trying to remember where this somewhere was. As he moved, his shoulder hurt, where one of the robbers had stabbed him. He'd attempted to protect the wound by shooing the clouds of flies away, but he was fairly sure they'd already laid their eggs.

(Not too near the heart; at least he still carried her there, and it would take a while for the corruption to spread that far. He'd be dead by then, before they found their way to his heart and her.)

But why not? Go ahead; be my guests, little maggots, eat away, sup your fill; quite probably I'll be dead anyway by the time you hatch, and will save you the pain and torment of my attempts to scratch you out. . . . Dear little maggots, *sweet* little maggots. (Sweet little me; I'm the one that's being eaten.)

He paused and thought about the pool, the little puddle that he orbited around, like a captured rock. It was at the bottom of a small depression, and it seemed to him that he kept on trying to get out away from the stinking water and the slime and the flies that crowded around it and the bird shit he kept crawling through . . . He didn't manage it; he always seemed to end up back here for some reason, but he *thought* about it a lot.

The pool was shallow, muddy, rocky and smelly; it was foul and horrid and bloated past its normal limits with the sickness and the blood that he had spilled out into it; he wanted to leave, to get well away from it. Then he would send it a heavy-bomber raid.

He started to crawl again, hauling himself round the pool, disturbing pellets and insects, and heading off toward the lake at one point, then coming back, back to the same point as before, and stopping, gazing transfixed at the pool and the rock.

What had he been doing?

Helping the locals, as usual. Honest counsel; advisor, keeping the loonies at bay and people sweet; later leading a small army. But they'd assumed he'd betray them, and that he'd use the army he'd trained as his own power base. So, on the eve of their victory, the very hour they'd finally stormed the Sanctum, they'd struck at him, too.

They'd taken him to the furnace room, stripped him naked; he'd escaped, but soldiers had been pounding down the stairs and he'd had to run. He'd been forced into the river, when they cornered him again. The dive almost knocked him out. Currents took him and he spun, lazily . . . he woke up in the morning, under a winch housing on a big river barge; he had no idea how he'd got there. There was a rope trailing astern, and he could only guess he'd climbed up that. His head still hurt.

He took some clothes which were drying on a line behind the wheelhouse, but he was seen; he dived overboard with them, swam to the shore. He'd still been hounded, and all the time he was forced further away from the city and Sanctum, where the Culture might look for him. He spent hours trying to work out how to contact them.

He'd been on a stolen moment, skirting the edge of a water-filled volcanic crater when the robbers struck; they'd beaten him and raped him and cut the tendons in his legs and tossed him into the stinking, yellow-tinged waters of the crater lake, then thrown boulders at him as he tried to swim away, using only his arms, legs floating uselessly behind him.

He knew one of the rocks would hit him sooner or later, so he tried to coax up some of that wonderful Culture training, quickly hyperventilated, and then dived. He only had to wait a couple of seconds. A big rock splashed into the water, in the line of bubbles he'd left when he dived; he embraced the rock like a lover as it wobbled down toward him, and let it take him deep into the darkness of the lake, switching off the way he'd been taught to, but not really caring very much if it didn't work, and he never woke up again.

He'd thought *ten minutes* when he dived. He woke up in crushing darkness; remembered, and dragged his arms out from under the rock. He kicked for the light but nothing happened. He used his arms. The surface came down to meet him, eventually. Air had never tasted so sweet.

The walls of the crater lake were sheer; the tiny rock island was the only place to swim to. Screeching birds lifted from the island as he thrashed his way ashore.

At least, he thought, as he dragged himself onto the rock

through the guano, it wasn't the priests that found me. Then I'd *really* have been in trouble.

The bends set in a few minutes later, like slow acid seeping into every joint, and he wished the priests had got him.

Still—he told himself, talking to keep his mind away from the pain—they would come for him; the Culture would come down with a beautiful big ship and they would take him up and make it all better.

He was sure they would. He'd be looked after and made better and he'd be safe, very safe and well looked after and free from pain, back in their paradise, and it would be like . . . like being a child again; like being in the garden again. Except—some rogue part of his mind reminded him—bad things happened in gardens too, sometimes.

Darckense got the armory guard to help her with a door that was stuck, along the corridor, just round the corner. Cheradenine slipped in and took the autorifle Elethiomel had described. He got back out, covering the gun in a cape, and heard Darckense thanking the guard profusely. They all met up in the rear hall cloakroom, where they whispered excitedly in the comforting smell of wet cloth and floor polish, and took turns holding the gun. It was very heavy.

"There's only one magazine!"

"I couldn't see the others."

"God you're blind, Zak. Have to do, I suppose."

"Ugh; it's oily," Darckense said.

"That stops rust," Cheradenine explained.

"Where are we supposed to let it off?" Livueta asked.

"We'll hide it here and then get out after dinner," Elethiomel said, taking the weapon from Darckense. "It's Big-nose for studies and he always sleeps right through anyway. Mother and father will be entertaining that colonel; we can get out of the house and into the woods and fire—not 'let off,' actually—fire the gun there."

"We'll probably get killed," Livueta said. "The guards will think we're terrorists."

Elethiomel shook his head patiently. "Livvy, you are stupid." He pointed the gun at her. "It's got a silencer; what do you think this bit is?"

"Huh," Livueta said, pushing the point away from her. "Has it got a safety catch?"

Elethiomel looked uncertain for just a moment. "Of course," he said, loudly, then flinched a little and glanced at the closed door to the hall. "Of course," he whispered. "Come on; we'll hide it here and come back for it when we've got away from Big-nose."

"You can't hide it here," Livueta said.

"Bet I can."

"It smells too much," Livueta said. "The oil smells; you'd smell it as soon as you walked in here. What if father decides to go for a walk?"

Elethiomel looked worried. Livueta moved past him, opened a small high window.

"How about hiding it on the stone boat?" Cheradenine suggested. "Nobody ever goes there at this time of year."

Elethiomel thought about this. He grabbed the cloak Cheradenine had wrapped the gun in originally and covered the weapon again. "All right. You take it."

Still not far enough back, or not far enough forward . . . he wasn't sure. The right place; that was what he was looking for. The right place. Place was all important, place meant everything. Take this rock . . .

"Take you, rock," he said. He squinted at it.

Ah yes, here we have the nasty big flat rock, sitting doing nothing, just amoral and dull, and it sits like an island in the polluted pool. The pool is a tiny lake on the little island, and the island is in a drowned crater. The crater is a volcanic crater, the volcano forms part of an island in a big inland sea. The inland sea is like a giant lake on a continent and the continent is like an island sitting in the seas of the planet. The planet is like an island in the sea of space within its system, and the system floats within the cluster, which is like an island in the sea of the galaxy, which is like an island in the archipelago of its local group, which is an island within the universe; the universe is like an island floating in a sea of space in the continua, and they float like islands in the Reality, and . . .

But down through the Continua, the Universe, the Local Group, the Galaxy, the Cluster, the System, the Planet, the

Continent, the Island, the Lake, the Island . . . the rock remained. AND THAT MEANT THE ROCK, THE CRAPPY AWFUL ROCK HERE WAS THE CENTER OF THE UNIVERSE, THE CONTINUA, *THE WHOLE REALITY*!

The word was caldera. The lake was in a drowned caldera. He raised his head, looked out over the still, yellowish water toward the crater cliffs, and seemed to see a boat made of stone.

"Scream," he said.

"Piss off," he heard the sky say, unconvinced.

The sky was full of cloud and it was getting dark early; their language tutor took longer than usual to fall asleep behind his high desk, and they almost decided to abandon the whole plan until tomorrow, but couldn't bear to. They crept out of the classroom, then walked as normally as they could, down to the rear hall, where they picked up their boots and jackets.

"See," Livueta whispered. "It smells a bit of gun-oil anyway."

"I can't smell any," Elethiomel lied.

The banqueting rooms—where a visiting colonel and his staff were being wined and dined that evening—faced the parks to the front of the house; the lake with the stone boat was at the rear.

"Just going to walk round the lake, Sergeant," Cheradenine told the guard who stopped them on the gravel path toward the stone boat. The sergeant nodded, told them to walk quickly; it would soon be dark.

They sneaked onto the boat, found the rifle where Cheradenine had hidden it, under a stone bench on the upper deck.

As he lifted it from the flagstone deck, Elethiomel knocked the gun against the side of the bench.

There was a snapping noise, and the magazine fell off; then there was a noise like a spring, and bullets clicked and clattered over the stones.

"Idiot!" Cheradenine said.

"Shut up!"

"Oh no," Livueta said, bending down and scooping up some of the rounds.

"Let's go back," Darckense whispered. "I'm frightened."

"Don't worry," Cheradenine said, patting her hand. "Come on; look for the bullets."

It seemed to take ages to find them and clean them and press them back into the magazine. Even then, they thought there were probably a few missing. By the time they'd finished and got the magazine slotted back into place, it was almost night.

"It's far too dark," Livueta said. They were all crouched down at the balustrade, looking out over the lake to the house. Elethiomel held the gun.

"No!" he said. "We can still see."

"No, we can't, not properly," Cheradenine told him.

"Let's leave it till tomorrow," Livueta said.

"They'll notice we're gone soon," Cheradenine whispered. "We haven't got the time!"

"No!" Elethiomel said, looking out to where the guard walked slowly past the end of the causeway. Livueta looked too; it was the sergeant who'd talked to them.

"You're being an idiot!" Cheradenine said, and put one hand out, taking hold of the gun. Elethiomel pulled away.

"It's mine; leave it!"

"It is *not* yours!" Cheradenine hissed. "It's ours; it belongs to our family, not yours!" He got both hands on the gun. Elethiomel pulled back again.

"Stop it!" Darckense said, her voice tiny.

"Don't be so . . ." Livueta started to say.

She looked over the edge of the parapet, to where she thought she'd heard a noise.

"Give it *here*!"

"Let it go!"

"Please stop; please stop. Let's go back in, please . . ."

Livueta didn't hear them. She was staring, wide-eyed, dry-mouthed, over the stone parapet. A black-covered man picked up the rifle the guard sergeant had dropped. The guard sergeant himself lay on the gravel. Something glittered in the black-dressed man's hand, reflecting the lights of the house. The man pushed the slack form of the sergeant off the gravel, into the lake.

Her breath caught in her throat. Livueta ducked down. She

flapped her hands at the two boys. "St . . ." she said. They still struggled.

"St . . ."

"Mine!"

"Let *go*!"

"Stop!" she hissed, and struck them both on the head. They both stared at her. "Somebody just killed that sergeant; just out there."

"What?" Both boys looked over the parapet. Elethiomel still held the gun.

Darckense squatted down and started to cry.

"Where?"

"There; that's his body! There in the water!"

"Sure," Elethiomel said in a whispered drawl. "And who . . ."

The three of them saw one shadowy figure move toward the house, keeping in the shade of the bushes bordering the path. A dozen or so men—just patches of darkness on the gravel—moved along the side of the lake, where there was a narrow strip of grass.

"Terrorists!" Elethiomel said excitedly, as the three all ducked back behind the balustrade, where Darckense wept quietly.

"Tell the house," Livueta said. "Fire the gun."

"Take the silencer off first," Cheradenine said.

Elethiomel struggled with the end of the barrel. "It's stuck!"

"Let me try!" All three tried.

"Fire it anyway," Cheradenine said.

"Yeah!" Elethiomel whispered. He shook the gun, hefted it. "Yeah!" he said. He knelt, put the gun on the stone bulwark, sighted.

"Be careful," Livueta said.

Elethiomel aimed at the dark men, crossing the path toward the house. He pulled the trigger.

The gun seemed to explode. The whole deck of the stone boat lit up. The noise was tremendous; Elethiomel was thrown back, gun still firing, blaster tracer into the night sky. He crashed into the bench. Darckense shrieked at the top of her lungs. She leapt up; firing sounded from near the house.

"Darkle; get down!" Livueta screamed. Lines of light flickered and cracked above the stone boat.

Darckense stood screaming, then started to run for the stairs. Elethiomel shook his head, looked up as the girl ran past him. Livueta grabbed at her and missed. Cheradenine tried to tackle her.

The lines of light lowered, detonating chips of rock off the stones all around them in tiny clouds of dust, at the same time as Darckense, still screaming, stumbled to the stairs.

The bullet entered Darckense through the hip: the other three heard—quite distinctly—the noise that it made, above the gunfire and the girl's scream.

He was hit too, though he didn't know by what at the time.

The attack on the house was beaten off. Darckense lived. She almost died, from loss of blood, and shock; but she lived. The best surgeons in the land fought to rebuild her pelvis, shattered into a dozen major pieces and a hundred splinters by the impact of the round.

Bits of bone had traveled her body; they found fragments in her legs, in one arm, in her internal organs, even a piece in her chin. The army surgeons were fairly used to dealing with that sort of injury, and they had the time (because the war hadn't yet started then) and the incentive (for her father was a very important man) to put her back together as best they could. Still, she would walk awkwardly until she stopped growing, at least.

One of the bone shards traveled further than her own body; it entered his. Just above the heart.

The army surgeons said it would be too dangerous to operate. In time, they said, his body would reject the fragment of bone.

But it never did.

He started to crawl round the pool again.

Caldera! That was the word, the name.

(Such signals were important, and he'd found the one he'd been looking for.)

Victory, he said to himself, as he hauled himself round, scattering a last few of the bird droppings out of his way, and apologizing to the insects. Everything was going to be just fine, he decided. He knew that, now, and knew that in the end you always won, and that even when you lost, you never knew, and there was only one fight, and he was at the center of the whole ridiculous thing anyway, and Caldera was the word, and Zakalwe was the word, and Staberinde was the word, and—

They came for him; they came down with a big beautiful ship, and they took him up and away and they made him all better again . . .

"They never learn," the sky sighed, quite distinctly.

"Fuck you," he said.

It was years later that Cheradenine—returned from the military academy and looking for Darckense, and sent in that direction by a monosyllabic gardener—walked up the soft carpet of leaves to the door of the little summerhouse.

He heard a scream from inside. Darckense.

He dashed up the steps, drawing his pistol, and kicked the door open.

Darckense's startled face twisted over her shoulder, regarding him. Her hands were still clasped round Elethiomel's neck. Elethiomel sat, trousers round his ankles, hands on Darckense's naked hips under her bunched-up dress, and looked calmly at him.

Elethiomel was sitting on the little chair that Livueta had made in her carpentry class, long ago.

"Hi there, old chap," he said to the young man holding the pistol.

Cheradenine looked into Elethiomel's eyes for a moment, then turned away, holstering the pistol and buttoning the holster and walking out, closing the door behind him.

Behind him he heard Darckense crying, and Elethiomel laughing.

The island in the center of the caldera became quiet again. Some birds flew back to it.

The island had changed, thanks to the man. Scraped in a circle all round the central depression of the islet, drawn in a pathway of black bird droppings cleared away from the pale rock, and with the appropriate tail of just the right length leading off to one side (its other end pointing at the rock, which was the central dot), the island seemed to have a letter or simple pictogram printed on it, white on black.

It was the local signal for "Help me!" and you would only have seen it from an aircraft, or from space.

A few years after the scene in the summerhouse, one night while the forests burned and the distant artillery thundered, a young army major jumped up onto one of the tanks under his command, and ordered the driver to take the machine through the woods, following a path which wound between the old trees.

They left behind the shell of the recaptured mansion and the glowing red fires which lit its once grand interior (the fires reflected on the waters of an ornamental lake, by the wreckage of a demolished boat made of stone).

The tank ripped through the woods, demolishing small trees and little bridges over streams.

He saw the clearing with the summerhouse through the trees; it was lit by a flickering white light, as though by God.

They got to the clearing; a star-shell had fallen into the trees above, its parachute entangled in the branches. It sizzled and sputtered and shed a pure, sharp, extreme light all over the clearing.

Inside the summerhouse, the little wooden chair was quite visible. The tank's gun was pointing straight at the small building.

"Sir?" the tank commander said, peering worriedly from the hatch beneath.

Major Zakalwe looked down at him.

"Fire," he said.

8

The first snow of the year settled over the upper slopes of the cleft city; it floated out of the gray-brown sky and fitted itself over the streets and the buildings like a sheet thrown over a corpse.

He dined alone at a large table. The screen he had wheeled into the middle of the brightly lit room flickered with the images of released prisoners from some other planet. The balcony doors were lying open, and through them drifted small examples of the falling snow. The rich carpet of the room was frosted white where the snow had settled, and stained dark farther in where the heat of the room had melted the crystals back into water again. Outside, the city was a mass of half-unseen gray shapes. Ordered lights ran in !ines and curls, dimmed by distance and passing flurries.

Darkness came like a black flag waved over the canyon, drawing back the grayness from the shores of the city, then pushing forward the individual specks of street and building lights as though in recompense.

The silent screen and silent snow conspired; light flung a path into the silent chaos of the fall beyond the window. He got up and closed the doors, the shutters and the curtains.

•   •   •

The next day was bright and clear, and the city could be seen sharply as far as the canyon's broad curve would allow; buildings and lines of roads and aqueducts stood out as though freshly drawn, gleaming like new paint, while cold, keen sunlight rubbed a shine into the dullest gray stone. The snow lay over the top half of the city; below, where the temperature stayed more level, the snow had fallen as rain. There too the precise new day was displayed; he looked down from the car and studied the sight. Every detail delighted him; he counted arches and cars and traced the lines of water and road and flue and track through all their convolutions and hidings; he inspected every flash of reflected sunlight, squinted at every dot of wheeling bird and noted every broken window, through the very dark glasses.

The car was the longest and sleekest of all those he'd bought or hired; it was an eight seater with a huge inefficient rotary engine driving both rear axles, and he had its collapsible slatted hood down. He sat in the back and enjoyed the feel of the cold air on his face.

The terminal earring beeped. "Zakalwe?"

"Yes, Diziet?" he said. Talking quietly, he didn't think the driver would hear him over the wind-roar. He raised the screen between them anyway.

"Hello. Good. Very slight time delay from here, but not much. How's it going?"

"Nothing yet. I'm called Staberinde and I'm causing a fuss. I own Staberinde Airlines, there's a Staberinde Street, a Staberinde Store, a Staberinde Railway, Staberinde Local Broadcasts . . . there's even a cruise liner called the *Staberinde*. I've spent money like hydrogen, established within a week a business empire most people would take a lifetime to set up, and I'm instantly one of the most talked-about people on the planet, maybe in the Cluster . . ."

"Yes. But, Cher . . ."

"Had to take a service tunnel and leave the hotel by an annex this morning; the courtyard's crammed with press." He glanced over his shoulder. "I'm amazed we really seem to have shaken the hounds off."

"Yes, Che . . ."

"Dammit, I'm probably putting the war off all by myself

just by being this crazy; people would rather see what I'm going to squander my money on next than fight.''

"Zakalwe; Zakalwe," Sma said. "Fine; great. But what is all this supposed to *do*?''

He sighed, looked out at the derelict buildings speeding by to one side, not far under the rimrock. "It's supposed to get the name Staberinde into the media, so that even a recluse studying ancient documents will get to hear the name.''

". . . And?''

". . . And there was something we did in the war, Beychae and I; a particular stratagem. We called it the Staberinde strategy. But only between ourselves. *Strictly* between ourselves; it only meant anything to Beychae because I explained about its . . . origin. If he hears that word he *must* wonder what's going on.''

"Sounds like a great theory, Cheradenine, but it hasn't actually *worked*, has it?''

"No.'' He sighed, then frowned. "There is media input to this place he's in, isn't there? You're sure he's not just a prisoner?''

"There is network access, but not directly. They've got it well screened; even we can't see exactly what's going on. And we are certain he's not a prisoner.''

He thought for a moment. "How's the prewar situation?''

"Well, the full-scale still looks inevitable, but the likely lead time's increased by a couple of days, to eight-to-ten, after a viable trigger event. So . . . so far, so good, to be optimistic.''

"Hmm.'' He rubbed his chin, watching the frozen waters of an aqueduct slide past, fifty meters beneath the turnpike. "Well,'' he said. "I'm on my way now to the university; breakfast with the dean. I'm setting up the Staberinde Scholarship and the Staberinde Fellowship and the Staberinde . . . Chair,'' he grimaced. "And maybe even the Staberinde College. Perhaps I should mention these stupendously important wax tablets to the man as well.''

"Yes, good idea,'' Sma said, after a short pause.

"Okay. I don't suppose they have any bearing on what Beychae's got his nose buried in, have they?''

"No,'' Sma said. "But they'd certainly be stored in the same place he's working; I guess you could reasonably ask to inspect their security arrangements down there, or just want to see where they'd be kept.''

"All right. I'll mention the tablets.''

"Check the guy hasn't got a weak heart, first.''

"Yeah, Diziet.''

"One other thing. That couple you asked us about; the ones that came to your street party.''

"Yeah.''

"They're Governance; that's the term they use for major local stockholders who tell the corporate chiefs . . .''

"Yes, Diziet, I remember the term.''

"Well, these two are Solotol's and what they say goes; the chief execs will almost certainly do exactly as they suggest as far as Beychae is concerned, and that means the official government will, too. They are also, of course, effectively above the law. Don't mess with them, Cheradenine.''

"Me?'' he said innocently, smiling to the cold, dry wind.

"Yes, you. That's all from this end. Have a nice breakfast.''

"Bye,'' he said. The city slid past; the car's tires made hissing, tearing noises on the dark-surfaced turnpike. He turned up the heating in the footwell.

This was a quiet part of the under-cliff road. The driver slowed for a sign and some flashing lights ahead, then almost skidded at the sudden diversion sign and emergency road markings that turned them off the road, over a ramp and down onto a long concrete channel with sheer walls.

They came to a steep rise with only sky visible beyond; the red lines indicating the diversion led over the summit. The driver slowed, then shrugged and gunned the engine. The hump of concrete raised the nose of the big car, hiding what was on the far side.

When the driver saw what was over the concrete summit, he shouted in fear and tried to turn and brake. The big car tipped forward, onto the ice, and started to slide.

He had been jolted by the turn and then annoyed that the view had been taken away. He looked round at the driver and wondered what was going on.

Somebody had diverted them off the turnpike and onto a storm drain. The turnpike was heated and didn't ice up; the storm drain was a sheet of ice. They had entered near the top, through one small sluice out of several dozen spread in a semicircle; the broad drain led down into the depths of the city, crossed by bridges, for over a kilometer.

The car had partially turned as the driver came over the top of the sluice baffle; the vehicle was sliding down sideways, its wheels spinning and engine roaring, lumbering on and on down the steepened expanse of the drain and rapidly picking up speed.

The driver tried to brake again, then attempted to go into reverse, and finally tried to steer toward the slab-high sides of the drain, but the car was slithering down faster all the time, and the ice provided no purchase. The car's wheels shook and the whole body shuddered as it hit ridges in the ice. The air whistled and the side-on tires whined.

He was staring at the sides of the drain, whirling by at a ridiculous speed. The vehicle was still slowly turning as it skidded; the driver screamed as they headed for a massive bridge support; the rear of the car banged and the whole vehicle leapt as it battered into the concrete. Bits of metal flew into the air and crashed into the ice behind, then started skidding down after them. The car was spinning faster now, in the other direction.

Bridges, tributary drains, viaducts, overhanging buildings, aqueducts and huge pipes spanning the drain all flashed by the revolving car, hurtling past in the bright light, some shocked white faces gasping from parapets or open windows.

He looked forward and saw the driver opening his door.

"Hey!" he shouted, reaching forward to grab the man.

The car thundered over the uneven ice. The driver jumped.

He flung himself into the front, just missing the driver's ankles. He landed down at the pedals, grasped at the levers and controls and tugged himself into the driver's seat. The vehicle was turning faster, jolting and screaming as it hit ridges and raised metal grilles set in the slope; he glimpsed one wheel and various bits of bodywork bouncing away behind him. Another teeth-chattering contact with a bridge support ripped an entire axle free; it flew into the air and exploded against an iron leg supporting a building, dislodging bricks and glass and scattering metal like shrapnel.

He grabbed the steering wheel; it flopped about uselessly. He had the idea of keeping the car pointing forward if he could, until the gradually increasing temperature further down

the canyon provided a wet rather than icy slope, but if there
was no steering he might as well jump off too.

The wheel thumped and burned his hands as it turned;
the tires squealed wildly; he was thrown forward and his nose
hit the wheel. That felt like a dry patch, he thought. He looked
ahead, down the slope, where the ice was becoming patchy,
hugging the shadows of buildings where the shade fell across
the spillway.

The car was almost straight. He grabbed at the wheel
again and tramped the brake. It didn't seem to do anything.
He pedaled reverse instead. Now the gearbox screamed too;
his face wrinkled at the appalling noise, his feet juddered on
the quivering pedal. The wheel came alive again, for longer,
and he was thrown forward once more; this time he kept a
hold of the wheel, and ignored the blood streaming from his
nose.

Everything was roaring now. The wind and the tires and
the body of the car; his ears popped and throbbed with the
rapidly increasing air pressure. He looked ahead and saw the
concrete was green with weeds.

"Shit!" he yelled to himself. There was another lip ahead;
he wasn't near the bottom yet; there was another length of
slope to come.

He recalled the driver mentioning tools inside the front
passenger bench; he hauled the seat up and grabbed the biggest piece of metal he could see, then kicked the door open
and jumped.

He slammed into the concrete, almost losing his grip on
the metal tool. The car started to slew in front of him, leaving
a last patch of ice and hitting the section of the slope covered
by weed; curved fountains of spray leapt from its remaining
wheels. He rolled over, onto his back, spray hissing up into
his face as he slithered down the steep, weeded slope; he
held the metal tool in both hands, clamped it between his
chest and upper arm; forced it down into the concrete under
the water and weeds.

The metal thrummed in his hands.

The spillway lip swept up toward him. He pressed harder;
the tool bit into the rough concrete, shaking his whole body,
jarring his teeth and his vision; a tight wad of ripped-up weed
grew under his arm like some mutant hair.

The car hit the lip first; it somersaulted into the air and

started tumbling, disappearing. He hit the lip and almost lost his hold on the tool again. He rose and slowed, but not enough. Then he was over. The dark glasses sailed off his face; he resisted the urge to grab at them.

The spillway continued for another half kilometer; the car smashed upside down into the concrete slope, scattering debris which continued skidding down toward the river at the bottom of the canyon's great V; the gearbox and remaining axle parted company with the chassis and bounced into some pipes straddling the drain, fracturing them. Water poured out.

He went back to treating the metal tool as though it was an ice-ax, and slowly reduced his speed.

He passed under the fractured pipes, which were gushing warm water.

What, not sewage? he thought brightly. Today was looking up.

He looked, perplexed, at the metal tool still vibrating in his grip, and wondered exactly what it was; probably something to do with the tires or starting the engine, he decided, looking around.

He negotiated one final spillway lip and slid gently into the shallows of the broad river Lotol itself. Bits of the car had already arrived.

He stood up and squelched ashore. He checked there was nothing else coming down the spillway that might strike him, and sat. He was shaking; he dabbed at his bloody nose. He felt bruised from the battering in the car. There were some people staring at him over the top of a nearby promenade. He waved at them.

He stood up, wondering how you got out of this concrete canyon. He looked up the spillway, but could see only a short way; a final lip of concrete blocked the rest of the view.

He wondered what had happened to the driver.

The concrete lip he was looking at formed a dark bump against the skyline. The bump hung for a few seconds, then came down on the thin coating of water that floated down the slope, staining it red. What was left of the driver skidded past him and bumped into the river, edging past the chassis of the shattered car and setting off downstream, swirling pinkly in the water, revolving.

He shook his head. He brought his hand up to his nose,

waggled the tip experimentally, and gasped with pain. This made the fifteenth time he'd broken his nose.

He grimaced into the mirror, snorting back a mixture of blood and warm water. The black porcelain basin swirled with gently steaming suds, pink-flecked. He touched his nose with great delicacy and frowned into the mirror.

"I miss breakfast, lose a perfectly proficient driver and my best car, I break my nose yet again *and* get an old raincoat of immense sentimental value dirtier than it's ever been in its life before, and all you can say is 'That's funny'?"

"Sorry, Cheradenine. I just mean, that's weird. I don't know why they'd do something like that. You are certain it was deliberate? Oof."

"What was that?"

"Nothing. You are certain it wasn't just an accident."

"Positive. I called for a spare car, and the police, then went back to where it happened. No diversion; all gone. But there were traces of industrial solvent where they'd removed the false red road markings from the top of the storm drain."

"Ah. Ah; yeah . . ." Sma's voice sounded odd.

He took the transceiver bead off his earlobe and looked hard at it. "Sma . . ."

"Whoo. Yeah, well, as I said; if it was those two Governance bods, the police won't do anything. But I can't understand them behaving like that."

He let the washbowl drain and dabbed tenderly at his nose with a fluffy hotel towel. He put the terminal earring back on his ear. "Maybe they just object to the fact I'm using Vanguard money. Maybe they think I'm Mr. Vanguard or something." He waited for a reply. "Sma? I said maybe they . . ."

"Ow. Yes. Sorry. Yes; I heard you. You might be right."

"Anyway, there's more."

"God. What?"

He picked up an ornately decorated plastic screen-card, which—against a background of what looked like a fairly wild party—slowly flashed a message on and off. "An invitation. To me. I'll read it out: 'Mr. Staberinde; congratulations on your narrow escape. Do please come to a fancy-dress party this evening; a car will pick you up at rim-set. Costume pro-

vided.' No address.'' He put the card back behind the washbowl taps. ''According to the concierge that arrived at about
the same time I called the police after my car went tobog-
ganing.''

''Fancy-dress party, eh?'' Sma giggled. ''Better watch
your ass, Zakalwe.'' There was more giggling, not all of it
Sma's.

''Sma,'' he said frostily. ''If I've called at an awkward
time . . .''

Sma cleared her throat, sounded suddenly businesslike.
''Not at all. Sounds like it was the same lot. You going?''

''I think so, but not in their costume, whatever that turns
out to be.''

''All right. We'll track you. Are you absolutely positive
you don't want a knife missile or . . .''

''I don't want to get into that argument again, Diziet,''
he said, dabbing his face dry and sniffing hard again, inspecting himself in the mirror. ''What I was thinking about was
this; if these people did react like this just because of Vanguard, maybe we can persuade them there's an opportunity
for them here.''

''What sort of opportunity?''

He went through to the bedroom, collapsed on the bed,
staring up at the painted ceiling. ''Beychae was connected
with Vanguard at first, yes?''

''Honorary President-Director. Gave it credibility while
we were starting up. He was only involved for a year or two.''

''But there is that link.'' He swung his legs off the bed
and sat up, staring out of the window at the snow-bright city.
''And one of the theories we believe these guys have is that
Vanguard is run by some sort of namby-pamby machine that's
developed consciousness and conscience . . .''

''Or just by some old recluse with philanthropic inten-
tions,'' Sma agreed.

''So; say this mythical machine or person had existed, but
then somebody else got hold of the reins; disabled the machine, killed the philanthropist. And then started spending
their ill-gotten gains.''

''Hmm,'' Sma said. ''Mmm. Mmm.'' She coughed again.
''Yes . . . ah. Well, they'd be acting a lot like you've been, I
suppose.''

"So do I," he said, going to the window; he picked up a pair of dark glasses from a small table, put them on.

Something beeped near the bed. "Hold on." He turned, crossed to the bedside and picked up the same small device he'd scanned the two top floors with when he'd first arrived. He looked at the display, smiled, and left the room. Walking down the corridor, still holding the machine, he said, "Sorry; somebody bouncing a laser off the window in the room I was in, trying to eavesdrop."

He entered a suite facing uphill and sat on the bed. "Anyway; could you make it look like there'd been some sort of . . . event in the Vanguard Foundation, a few days before I arrived here? Some sort of cataclysmic change but the signs are only appearing now? I don't know what, especially as it all has to be back-dated, but something that the markets, say, only just get hold of now; something buried in the trading figures . . . would that be possible?"

"I . . ." Sma said, hesitantly. "I don't know. Ship?"

"Hello," the *Xenophobe* said.

"Can we do what Zakalwe just asked?"

"I'll listen to what it was," the ship said. Then, "Yes; best get one of the GCUs to handle it, but it can be done."

"Great," he said, lying back on the bed. "Also, as of now—and again, back-dating where we can interfere with computer records—Vanguard becomes an unethical corporation. Sell the R&D department investigating ultra-strong materials for space habitats and that sort of stuff; have it pick up stock in companies promoting terraforming. Close a few factories; start a few lock-outs; halt all charitable works; skim the pension fund."

"Zakalwe! We're supposed to be the good guys!"

"I know, but if I can get our Governance pals to think I've taken over Vanguard, and I think the way they do . . ." He paused. "Sma; do I have to spell it out?"

"Ah . . . ouch. What? Oh . . . no; you think they might try and get you to convince Beychae that Vanguard's still doing what *we* want it to do, and so get him to declare for it?"

"Exactly." He clasped his hands under his neck, adjusting his ponytail. This bed had mirrors on the ceiling above, not a painting. He studied the distant reflection of his nose.

"Long . . . um, shot, Zakalwe," Sma said.

"I think we have to try it."

"It means wrecking a commercial reputation it's taken decades to establish."

"That more important than stopping the war, Diziet?"

"Of course not, but . . . ah . . . of course not, but we can't be certain it'll work."

"Well, I say we do it now. It has a better chance than offering the university those goddamn tablets."

"You've never liked that plan, have you, Zakalwe?" Sma sounded annoyed.

"This one's better, Sma. I can feel it. Get it done now, so they've heard about it by the time I get to the party tonight."

"Okay, but that thing about the tablets . . ."

"Sma; I've rearranged the meeting with the dean for the day after tomorrow, okay? I can mention the goddamn tablets then. But make sure all this Vanguard stuff goes through now, all right?"

"I . . . oh . . . ah . . . yeah, right. I suppose so . . . so . . . oh, wow. Look, Zakalwe, something's just come up; was there anything else?"

"No," he said loudly.

"Aww . . . *great*. Umm . . . right, Zakalwe; bye."

The transceiver beeped. He tore it off his ear and threw it across the room.

"Rampant bitch," he breathed. He looked at the ceiling.

He lifted the bedside telephone. "Yeah; can I speak to . . . Treyvo? Yes please." He waited, dug between two molars with a fingernail. "Yeah; night clerk Treyvo? My very good friend . . . listen, I'd like a little company, you know? Indeed . . . well, there's a largish tip if . . . that's right . . . and, Treyvo; if she comes with a press pass secreted anywhere, you're a dead man."

The suit was vulnerable to a shortish list of comparatively heavy battlefield weaponry, and not much else. He watched the capsule vibrate its way back under the surface of the desert as the suit clasped itself around him. He got back into the car and drove back down to the hotel, just in time to meet the limousine sent by his hosts for that evening.

The Cluster's media had been cleared from the hotel courtyard that afternoon, on his instructions, so there was no undignified dive through their lights and mikes and questions. He stood, dark glasses in place, on the steps of the hotel as the great dark car—significantly more impressive than the one he'd almost been killed in that morning, he was somewhat disappointed to note—drew smoothly to a halt. A huge man, gray-haired, with a pale, heavily scarred face, unfolded himself from the driver's compartment and held open a rear door, bowing slowly.

"Thank you," he said to the big man as he stepped into the vehicle. The fellow bowed again, and closed the door. He sat back in plushly luxurious upholstery that couldn't make up its mind whether it was a seat or a bed. The car's windows dimmed in response to the lights of the media people as the vehicle exited from the hotel courtyard. He gave what he hoped was a regal wave, all the same.

The evening city lights streamed past; the car thundered quietly. He inspected a package in the seat/bed beside him; it was paper-wrapped, and tied up with colorful ribbons. "MR. STABERINDE" said a handwritten note. He brought the suit helmet over, pulled carefully on a ribbon, opening the package. There were clothes inside. He lifted them out and looked at them.

He found a switch on an arm that let him talk to the gray-haired driver. "I take it this is my fancy-dress costume. What is it exactly?"

The driver looked down, took something from a jacket pocket, and manipulated it. "Hello," said an artificial voice. "My name is Mollen. I cannot talk, so I use this machine instead." He glanced up at the road, then down again at whatever machine he was using. "What do you want to ask me?"

He didn't like the way the big guy took his eyes off the road each time he wanted to say something, so he just said, "never mind." He sat back and watched the lights go past, taking the suit helmet off again.

They drew into the courtyard of a large, dark house down near a river in a side-canyon. "Please follow me, Mr. Staberinde," Mollen said through his machine.

"Certainly." He lifted the suit helmet and followed the taller man up the steps and into a large foyer. He was carrying the costume he'd found in the car. Animal heads glared from the walls of the tall entrance hall. Mollen closed the doors and led him to an elevator which hummed and rattled its way down for a couple of floors; he heard the noise and could detect the drug-smoke odor of the party even before the doors were opened.

He handed the bundle of clothes to Mollen, keeping only a thin cloak. "Thanks; I won't be needing the rest."

They went out into the party, which was noisy and crowded and full of bizarre costumes. The men and women all looked sleek and well-fed; he breathed in the drug smoke that wreathed the motley figures about him; Mollen led the way through the crowd. People fell silent as they passed, and a babble of conversation started up in his wake. He heard the word "Staberinde" several times.

They went through doors guarded by men even bigger than Mollen, down a flight of softly carpeted stairs, and into a large room walled with glass on one side. Boats bobbed on black water in an underground dock on the far side of the glass, which reflected a smaller but more bizarre party. He peeked under the dark glasses, but the view was no brighter.

As on the floor above, people walked around with either drug bowls or, for the especially daring, drink glasses. Everybody was either badly injured or actually mutilated.

Men and women turned to look at the new arrival as he followed Mollen in. Some men and women had arms broken and twisted, the bones tearing through the skin, showing whitely under the plain light; some had huge gashes cut into their bodies, some had whole areas of their flesh flayed and seared, some had had breasts or arms amputated, or eyes put out, often with the removed article or articles dangling from other parts of their bodies. The woman from the street party came toward him, a hand-wide flap of her belly hanging down over her glistening skirt, her belly muscles rippling inside like dull red glistening cords.

"Mr. Staberinde; you've come as a space man," she said. There was an over-elaborate modulation to her voice he found instantly annoying.

"Well, I've sort of compromised," he said, swirling the cape and fastening it across his shoulders.

The woman held out her hand. "Well; welcome, anyway."

"Thank you," he said, taking her hand and kissing it. He half expected the suit sensory fields to pick up a whiff of some deadly poison on the woman's delicate hand, and signal danger, but the alarm remained quiet. He grinned as she took her hand away.

"What do you find funny, Mr. Staberinde?"

"This!" he laughed, nodding at the people around them.

"Good," she said, laughing a little (her belly quivered). "We did hope our party might amuse you. Allow me to introduce our good friend who is making all this possible."

She took his arm and guided him through the grisly multitude to a man sitting on a stool next to a tall, dull gray machine. He was small and smiling and kept wiping his nose with a large handkerchief which he stuffed raggedly into his otherwise immaculate suit.

"Doctor, this is the man we told you of, Mr. Staberinde."

"Sincere greetings and things," said the little doctor, his face collapsing into a moist and toothy smile. "Welcome to our Injured Party." He waved round the room at the wounded people, and waved his hands enthusiastically. "Would you like an injury? The process is quite painless, and causes no inconvenience; repairs are speedy and there aren't any scars. What can I tempt you with? Lacerations? Compound fracture? Castration? How about a multiple trepanning? You'd be the only one here."

He folded his arms and laughed. "You're too kind. Thank you, but no."

"Oh don't, please," the little man said, looking wounded. "Don't spoil the party; everybody else is taking part; do you really want to feel so left out? There is no risk of pain or permanent damage of any sort. I have carried out this sort of operation all over the civilized universe, and have never had any complaints except from people who get too attached to their injuries and resist repair. My machine and I have performed novelty injuries and wounds in every center of civilization in the Cluster; you may not have this chance again, you know; we leave tomorrow, and I'm all booked up for the next two years standard. Are you absolutely sure you don't want to participate?"

"More than absolutely."

"Leave Mr. Staberinde alone, Doctor," the woman said.

"If he does not want to join us then we must respect his wishes. Must we not, Mr. Staberinde?" The woman took his arm in hers. He looked at her injury, wondering what sort of transparent shielding kept everything intact. Her breasts were frosted with small, tear-shaped gems, and kept high by tiny field projectors on their undersides.

"Yes, of course."

"Good. Would you wait a moment, please? Please share this." She pushed her drink into his hand and stooped forward to talk to the doctor.

He turned to look at the people in the room. Strips of flesh hung from beautiful faces, grafted breasts swung from tanned backs, slender arms hung like bloated necklaces; chips of bone peeped from torn skin, veins and arteries and muscles and glands squirmed and sparkled in the plain light.

He lifted the glass the woman had given him and wafted some of its fumes into the fields around the helmet neck; an alarm sounded and a small screen on the suit's wrist revealed the specific poison in the glass. He smiled, pushed the glass through the suit's neck-field and knocked the contents back, then coughed a little as the half-alcohol concoction went down his throat. He smacked his lips.

"Oh, you've finished it," the woman came back to him. She was patting her smooth belly, now whole again, and motioned him toward another area of the room. She donned a small, glittering waistcoat as they walked through the mutilated throng.

"Yes." He handed her the glass.

They went through a door into an old workshop; lathes and punches and drills stood around under layers of dust and flaking paint and metal. Three chairs stood under a hanging light, a small cabinet beside them. The woman shut the door and waved him into one of the low seats. He sat down, placing the suit helmet on the floor at his side.

"Why didn't you come in the costume we sent you?" She altered the lock on the door, then turned to him, suddenly smiling. She adjusted the glittering waistcoat.

"It didn't suit me."

"You think that does?" she nodded at the black suit as she sat down, crossing her legs. She tapped the cabinet. It opened out with chinking glasses and already smoking drug bowls.

"I find it reassuring."

She leaned over, offering him a glass of gleaming liquid, which he accepted. He settled into the chair again.

She sat back too, cradling a bowl in both hands and closing her eyes as she leaned over it, breathing in deeply. She flapped a little of the smoke under the lapels of the waistcoat, so that as she spoke the heavy fumes curled back out between the material and her breasts, and twisted slowly into her face.

"We are so glad you could come, whatever your attire. Tell me; how are you finding the Excelsior? Does it meet with your requirements?"

He smiled thinly. "It'll do."

The door opened. The man he'd seen with the woman at the street party and when they had chased him in their car was outside. He stood back for Mollen to enter before him. Then he strode to the remaining seat and placed himself in it. Mollen stood near the door.

"What have you been saying?" the man asked, waving away the woman's hand with a glass in it.

"He's about to tell us who he is," the woman said; they both looked at him. "Aren't you, Mr. . . . Staberinde?"

"No I'm not. You tell me who you are."

"I think you know who we are, Mr. Staberinde," the man said. "We *thought* we knew who you were, up until a few hours ago. Now we're not so sure."

"Me, I'm just a tourist." He sipped at the drink, looking at them over the top of the glass. He inspected his drink. Minute specks of gold floated in its glittering depths.

"For a tourist, you've bought an awful lot of souvenirs that you'll never be able to take home with you," the woman said. "Streets, railways, bridges, canals, apartment blocks, stores, tunnels." She waved her hand in the air to indicate that the list went on. "And that's just in Solotol."

"I get carried away."

"Were you trying to attract attention?"

He smiled. "Yes, I suppose I was."

"We heard you suffered an unpleasant experience this morning, Mr. Staberinde," the woman said. She wriggled down deeper into the chair, drawing up her legs. "Something to do with a storm drain."

"That's right. My car was diverted down a spillway, from the top."

"You weren't hurt?" She sounded sleepy.

"Not seriously; I stayed in the car until . . ."

"No, please." The hand waved up from the indistinct mass of the chair, tiredly. "I have no head for details."

He said nothing; he pursed his lips.

"I understand your driver was not so lucky," the man said.

"Well, he's dead." He leaned forward in his seat. "Actually, I thought you people might have arranged the whole thing."

"Yes," said the woman from the mass of the chair, her voice floating up like the smoke, "Actually we did."

"I find frankness so appealing, don't you?" The man looked admiringly at the knees, breasts and head of the woman, the only parts of her still showing above the furry arms of the seat. He smiled. "Of course, Mr. Staberinde, my companion jests. We would never do such a terrible thing. But we might be able to lend you some assistance in finding the real culprits."

"Really?"

The man nodded. "We think now we might like to help you, you see?"

"Oh, sure."

The man laughed. "Who exactly are you, Mr. Staberinde?"

"I told you; I'm a tourist." He sniffed the bowl. "I wandered into a little money recently, and I always wanted to visit Solotol—in style—and that's what I've been doing."

"How did you get control of the Vanguard Foundation, Mr. Staberinde?"

"I thought direct questions like that were impolite."

"They are," the man smiled. "I beg your pardon. May I guess your profession, Mr. Staberinde? I mean before you became a gentleman of leisure, of course."

He shrugged. "If you like."

"Computers," the man said.

He had started to raise his glass to his lips, just so he could hesitate, as he now did. "No comment," he said, not meeting the man's eyes.

"So," the man said. "The Vanguard Foundation is under new management, is it?"

"Damn right. Better management."

The man nodded. "So I heard, just this afternoon." He sat forward in his chair and rubbed his hands together. "Mr. Staberinde; I don't want to pry into your commercial operations and future plans, but I wonder if you'd give us even a vague idea in what direction you see the Vanguard Foundation going, over the next few years. Purely as a matter of interest, for now."

"That's easy," he grinned. "More profits. Vanguard could have been the biggest corp of the lot if it had been aggressive with its marketing. Instead it's been run like a charity; relied on coming up with some new technological gizmo to restore its position each time it falls behind. But from now on it fights like the other big boys, and it backs winners." (The man nodded wisely.) "The Vanguard Foundation's been too . . . meek until now." He shrugged. "Maybe that's just what happens when you leave something to be run by machines. But that's over. From now on the machines do what I tell them to, and the Vanguard Foundation becomes a competitor; a predator, yeah?" He laughed, not too harshly, he hoped, conscious he might overdo this.

The man smiled slowly but broadly. "You . . . believe in keeping machines in their place, yes?"

"Yeah." He nodded vigorously. "Yeah, I do."

"Hmm. Mr. Staberinde, have you heard of Tsoldrin Beychae?"

"Sure. Hasn't everybody?"

The man raised his eyebrows liquidly. "And you think . . . ?"

"Could have been a great politician, I suppose."

"Most people say he *was* a great politician," the woman said from the chair's depth.

He shook his head, looking into his drug bowl. "He was on the wrong side. It was a shame, but . . . to be great you have to be on the winning side. Part of greatness is knowing that. He didn't. Same as my old man."

"Ah . . ." said the woman.

"Your father, Mr. Staberinde?" the man said.

"Yeah," he admitted. "He and Beychae . . . well, it's a long story, but . . . they knew each other, long ago."

"We have time for the story," the man said easily.

"No," he said. He stood up, putting down the bowl and glass, and taking up the suit helmet. "Look; thanks for the invitation and all, but I think I'll head back now; I'm a little tired, and I took a bit of a battering in that car, you know?''

"Yes," the man said, standing too. "We're really sorry about that."

"Oh, thanks."

"Perhaps we can offer something in compensation?''

"Oh yeah? Like what?" He fiddled with the suit helmet. "I got lots of money."

"How would you like to talk to Tsoldrin Beychae?''

He looked up, frowning. "I don't know; should I? Is he here?" He gestured out toward the party. The woman giggled.

"No." The man laughed. "Not here. But in the city. Would you like to talk to him? Fascinating fellow, and no longer actively on the wrong side, as it were. Devoted to a life of study, these days. But still fascinating, as I say."

He shrugged. "Well . . . maybe. I'll think about it. It crossed my mind to leave, after the craziness this morning."

"Oh, I beg you to reconsider that, Mr. Staberinde. Please; sleep on it. You might do a great deal of good, for all of us, if you would talk to the chap. Who knows; you might even help make him great." He held out one hand toward the door. "But I can tell you want to go. Let me see you to the car." They walked to the door. Mollen stood back. "Oh. This is Mollen. Say hello, Mollen." The gray-haired man touched a small box at his side.

"Hello," it said.

"Mollen can't speak, you see. Hasn't said a word in all the time we've known him."

"Yes," said the woman. She was completely submerged in the chair now. "We decided he needed to clear his throat; so we took out his tongue." She either giggled or belched.

"We've met." He nodded to the big man, whose face contorted strangely under the scars.

The party in the boathouse cellar went on. He almost collided with a woman who had her eyes on the back of her head. Some of the revelers were exchanging limbs now. People sported four arms, or none (begging for drinks to be brought to their mouths), or an extra leg, or had arms or legs of the wrong sex. One woman was parading around with a man in tow who wore a sickly stupid grin; the woman kept lifting her skirt and displaying a complete set of male sexual equipment.

He hoped they all forgot who had what at the end of the evening.

They passed through the tame party, where fireworks were showering everybody with cool sparks; they were all laughing at that and—he could think of no other word—cavorting.

He was wished farewell. It was the same car that took him back, though it had a different driver. He watched the lights and the city's calm expanses of snow, and thought about people at parties and people at war; he saw the party they had just left, and he saw the gray-green trenches with mud-caked men waiting nervously; he saw people dressed in shiny black, whipping each other and being tied up . . . and he saw people shackled to bed frames or chairs, shrieking, while the uniformed men applied their particular skills.

He sometimes had to be reminded, he realized, that he still possessed the capacity to despise.

The car powered its way through the silent streets. He took the dark glasses off. The empty city swept past.

VI

nce—between the time he'd taken the Chosen across the badlands and the time he'd ended up broken like an insect in the flooded caldera, scratching signs in the dirt—he had taken some leave, and for a while had entertained the idea of giving up his work for the Culture, and doing something else instead. It had always seemed to him that the ideal man was either a soldier or a poet, and so, having spent most of his years being one of those—to him—polar opposites, he determined to attempt to turn his life around and become the other.

He lived in a small village, in a small, rural country on a small, undeveloped, unhurried planet. He stayed with an old couple in a cottage in the trees in the dales beneath the high tors. He rose early and went for long walks.

The countryside looked new and green and fresh; it was summer, and the field and woods, the path sides and riverbanks were full of unnameable flowers of every color. The tall trees flexed in the warm summer winds, leaves bright and fluttering like flags, and water ran off the moors and hills and across the bunched stones of sparkling streams like some clarified concentrate of the air itself. He sweated to the crests of the gnarled hills, climbed the outcrop rocks at their sum-

mits, and ran whooping and laughing across the broader tops,
under the brief shadows of the small high clouds.

On the moors, in the hills, he saw animals. Tiny ones that
darted invisibly into thickets from almost underfoot, larger
ones that leapt and stopped, looked back, then leapt away
again, disappearing into burrows or between rocks; larger
ones still that ran flowing off across the ground in herds,
watching him, and then became almost invisible when they
stopped to graze. Birds mobbed him when he walked too near
their nests; others called out from nearby, one-wing fluttering, trying to distract him, when he approached theirs. He
was careful not to step on their nests.

He always took a small notebook with him on his walks,
and made a point of writing down anything interesting. He
tried to describe the feel of the grasses in his fingers, the way
the trees sounded, the visual diversity of the flowers, the way
the animals and birds moved and reacted, the color of the
rocks and the sky. He kept a proper journal in a larger book,
back in his room at the old couple's cottage. He wrote his
notes up in that each evening, as though filling out a report
for some higher authority.

In another large journal book, he wrote his notes out
again, along with further notes on the notes, and then started
to cross words out of the completed, annotated notes, carefully removing word after word until he had something that
looked like a poem. This was how he imaged poetry to be
made.

He had brought some books of poetry with him, and when
the weather was wet, which was only rarely, he stayed in and
tried to read them. Usually, though, they sent him to sleep.
The books he had brought *about* poetry and poets confused
him even more, and he had to continually reread passage after
passage to retain each word, and even then still felt none the
wiser.

He went into the village tavern every few days, and played
skittle and pebble games with the locals. The mornings after
these evenings he regarded as recovery periods, and left his
notebook behind when he walked.

The rest of the time he tired himself out and kept fit;
climbing trees to see how high he could get before the
branches became too thin, climbing rock faces and old quar-
ries, balancing his way across fallen trees in steep gullies,

leaping from rock to rock across rivers, and sometimes stalking and then chasing the animals on the moor, knowing he could never catch up with them, but laughing as he sprinted after them.

The only other people he saw in the hills were farmers and shepherds. Sometimes he saw slaves working in the fields, and very rarely he met other people out walking. He didn't like to stop and talk to them.

The one other person he ever saw regularly was a man who flew a kite on the high hills. They only saw each other from a distance. At first it just happened that their paths never crossed, but later he made sure that they didn't meet; he would change direction if he saw the gaunt figure of the man walking toward him, climb up a different hill if he saw the little red kite flying above the summit he'd intended to head for. It had become a sort of tradition, a little private custom.

The days went on. He sat on a hill once, and saw a slave running through the fields beneath, through the strange slow patterns that the currents in the wind pushed through the golden-red pelt of the land. The slave's path left a trail like the wake behind a ship. She got as far as the river, where the landlord's mounted overseer ran her down. He watched the overseer beat the woman—saw the long stick rise and fall, tiny in the distance—but he couldn't hear anything because the wind was in the wrong direction. When the woman finally lay still on the riverbank, the overseer got down off his mount and knelt near her head; he saw something flash, but could not tell exactly what was going on. The overseer rode off; hobbled slaves came and took the woman away, later.

He made a note.

That evening, after dinner in the house of the old couple, once the wife had gone to bed, he told the old man what he had seen. The man nodded slowly, chewing on a mildly narcotic root, and spat juice into the fire. The overseer was known to be strict, the old man said; he took the tongue of any slave who tried to escape. He kept the tongues drying on a string stretched over the entrance to the slaves' compound at the lordship's farm.

He and the old man drank some fierce grain spirit from little cups, and then the old man told him a folk tale.

In the tale, a man walking through the wild wood was

tempted from the path by some beautiful flowers, and then saw a handsome young woman lying asleep in a clearing. He went to the maiden, and she woke. He sat down beside her and as they talked he realized that she smelled of flowers, a perfume more wonderful than anything he had ever experienced before, and so intense that he was made dizzy by the heady strength of it. After a while, surrounded by her flowery scent, enchanted by her softly lilting voice and shy demeanour, he asked to kiss her, and finally was allowed, and their kisses grew passionate, and they coupled.

But as they did so, even from the first moment that joined them, whenever the man looked out of one eye he saw the woman change. From one eye she looked as she had from the first, but looking through the other eye she was older, no longer just past her childhood. With each beat of their love she grew older (though only seen through one eye), through her maturity and late glow and the matron look, to spry then frail old age.

All the time the man could see her in all her youth by just closing one eye—and certainly could not stop himself from the act they had embarked upon—but always he was tempted to sneak a look through the other eye, and be shocked and amazed at the terrible transformation taking place beneath him.

In the last few movements of his knowledge, he closed his eyes, only opening both at the moment of fulfillment, when he saw—with both eyes, now—that he had taken to him a rotting corpse, already known by worms and grubs; the smell of flowers changed in that instant to an overpowering stench of corruption, but in such a way that he knew that it had always smelled like that, and as his loins gave themselves to the corpse, his belly threw out his last meal at the same time.

The wood spirit had his life by two strands, therefore, and with both hands took a firm grip of him, unraveled him from the weave of life, and dragged him away to the shadow world.

His soul was shattered into a million pieces there, and thrown over the world, to make up the souls of all pollen-flies, which bring new life and old death to flowers, at the same time.

He thanked the old man for telling him the story, and told him some tales he remembered from his own upbringing.

A few days later he was running after one of the small animals on the moor; it skidded on some dew-wet grass and tumbled end over end, finally falling, limbs spread, on some stones, winding itself. He gave a victorious, whooping cry and threw himself forward down the slope toward the animal as it wobbled to its feet; he jumped the last couple of meters, landing with both feet, just beside where the animal had fallen; it collected itself and sped off again, unharmed, and vanished down a hole. He laughed, breathing hard, sweating. He stood there, put his hands on his knees and bent at the waist, trying to get his breath back.

Something moved under his feet. He saw it, felt it.

There was a nest under him. He had landed right on it. The eggs, their speckled shells shattered, spread their fluids over his boot heels and into the twigs and moss.

He moved his foot, already sick in his heart. Something black wriggled underneath. It moved into the sunlight; a black head and neck; a black eye staring up at him, bright and hard as a jet pebble at the bottom of a brook. The bird struggled, making him jump back a little, as though he had landed with naked feet on something that stung; the bird flapped hopelessly out onto the moor grass, hopping on one foot, dragging one limp wing after it. It stopped, a little way off, sideways to him, and tipped its head, seeming to regard him.

He wiped his boots on the moss. All the eggs were smashed. The bird made a small keening noise. He turned away and began to walk off, then stopped, cursed, retraced his steps and stamped after the bird, catching it easily in a storm of squawks and feathers.

He twisted its neck and dropped the limp remains into the grass.

That evening he stopped writing his journal and never returned to it. The weather grew humid and oppressive and no rains fell. The man with the kite waved and called out to him one day, from the top of a hill; he hurried away, sweating.

It was ten or so days after the incident with the bird that he admitted to himself he would never be a poet.

He left a couple of days later and was never heard of again, even though the lord's marshal sent word to every town in the land, because the stranger was suspected of being

involved in what happened the night he left, when the overseer at the lord's farm was found trussed in his bed, his face
fixed in an expression of darkest horror, and his mouth and
throat stuffed with dried human tongues and pieces of blank
paper, on which he had choked to death.

9

He slept until after dawn, then went for a walk to think.
He left via the service tunnel from the main hotel to the
annex, and left his dark glasses in his pocket. The hotel had
cleaned the old raincoat; he put it on and some thick gloves
and wound a scarf round his neck.

He walked carefully along warmed streets and dripping
pavements, and held his head up to gaze at the sky. His breath
went before him. Little snowfalls slumped off buildings and
wires as the weak sunlight and a mild breeze raised the temperature. The gutters ran with clear water and soggy bergs of
bumping slush; pipes from buildings ran or dripped with the
melt and, when a vehicle passed, it did so with a wet hiss.
He crossed the road to the other side, where the sun was.

He climbed steps and crossed bridges; he walked gingerly
over icy parts where there was no heating, or it had failed.
He wished he'd put on better boots; these looked fine but
they didn't have enough grip. To avoid falling you had to walk
like an old man, hands splayed as though trying to grasp a
stick, bending at the waist when you wanted to walk straight-
backed. This annoyed him, but walking on without acknowl-
edging the changed conditions, and slipping on his backside,
appealed to him even less.

When he did slip, it was in front of some young people. He was walking carefully down some icy steps leading onto a broad suspension bridge over a railway junction. The youngsters were walking toward him, laughing and joking with each other. He divided his attention between the treacherous steps and the group. They looked very young, and their actions, gestures and pealing voices all seemed to bubble with energy, suddenly making him feel his age. There were four of them; the two young men trying to impress the girls, talking loudly. One of the girls in particular was tall and dark, and elegant in that unself-conscious manner of the recently matured. He kept his eyes on her, straightened his back, and just before his feet went out from under him, felt a slight swagger return to his walk.

He crashed down on the last step, and sat for a moment, then smiled thinly and got up just before the four young people drew level with him. (One of the young men was guffawing, making a show of covering his mufflered mouth with a gloved hand.)

He brushed some snow from the tails of the raincoat, and flicked some of it at the young man. They went by and on up the steps, laughing. He walked halfway across the bridge—grimacing at the pain seeping up from his backside—and heard a voice call; he turned around and took a snowball full in the face.

He caught a glimpse of them laughing as they sprinted away from the top of the steps, but he was too busy clearing the snow from his nostrils and stinging eyes to see properly. His nose throbbed fiercely, but hadn't rebroken. He walked on, passing an older couple walking arm in arm, who shook their heads and tutted and said something about damned students. He just nodded to them and wiped his face with a handkerchief.

He smiled as he left the bridge, up more steps to an esplanade cut under old office buildings. Once, he knew, he would have been embarrassed at what had happened, embarrassed at slipping, at being seen to slip, at being hit by the snowball after so gullibly turning round on cue, and at the elderly couple witnessing his embarrassment. Once he might have chased after the youngsters, to give them a fright at least, but not now.

He stopped at a small hot drinks stall set up on the esplanade and ordered a mug of soup. He leaned against the stall and pulled off one glove with his teeth; he held the steaming mug in his hand, feeling the warmth. He went to the railings, sat down on a bench and drank the soup slowly, in careful sips. The man in the soup stall wiped the counter and listened to the radio, smoking a ceramic cigarette on a chain round his neck.

His backside still ached dully from the slip. He smiled at the city through the steam rising from the mug. Served him right, he told himself.

When he got back to the hotel they'd left a message. Mr. Beychae would like to meet him. They would send a car after lunch, unless he objected.

"This is wonderful news, Cheradenine."

"Well, I suppose."

"You're not still being pessimistic, are you?"

"All I'm saying is, don't get your hopes up." He lay back on the bed looking at the ceiling paintings, talking to Sma via the earring transceiver. "I might just get to meet him, but I doubt I'll have any chance to get him out. Probably find he's gone senile and says, 'Hey, Zakalwe; still working for the Culture against these gas-heads?' In which case I want my ass hauled out, all right?"

"We'll get you out, don't worry about that."

"If and when I do get the guy, you still want me to head for the Impren Habitats?"

"Yes. You'll have to use the module; we can't risk bringing the *Xenophobe* in. If you do spring Beychae they'll be on maximum alert; we'd never get in and out without being noticed, and that could swing the whole Cluster against us for interfering."

"So how far's Impren by module?"

"Two days."

He sighed. "I suppose we can handle that."

"You all ready, in case you can do anything today?"

"Yeah. Capsule's buried in the desert and primed; module's hiding in the nearest gas-giant, waiting for the same signal. If they take the transceiver from me, how do I get in touch?"

"Well," Sma said. "Much as I'd like to say 'I told you

so,' and displace you a scout or knife missile, we can't; their surveillance might just be good enough to spot it. Best we can do is put a microsat in orbit and just passive-scan; watch, in other words. If it sees you in trouble, we'll signal the capsule and the module for you. The alternative is to use the phone, would you believe. There's the unlisted Vanguard numbers you already have . . . Zakalwe?''

"Hmm?"

"You do have those numbers?''

"Oh, yeah.''

"Or, we've a downlink tap on Solotol's emergency services; just dial three ones and scream 'Zakalwe!' at the operator; we'll hear.''

"I am filled with confidence,'' he breathed, shaking his head.

"Don't worry, Cheradenine.''

"Me, worry?''

The car came; he saw it from his window. He went down to meet Mollen. He'd liked to have worn the suit again, but doubted they'd let him into their high security areas wearing it. He took the old raincoat, and the dark glasses.

"Hello.''

"Hello there, Mollen.''

"A pleasant day.''

"Yes.''

"Where are we going?''

"I don't know.''

"But you're driving.''

"Yes.''

"Then you must know where we're going.''

"Please repeat that?''

"I said you must know where you're going if you're driving.''

"I'm sorry.''

He stood by the side of the car while Mollen held the door open.

"Well, at least tell me whether it's very far, I may want to tell people I won't be back for a while.''

The large man frowned, the scarred face creasing in strange directions, unusual patterns. He hesitated over which

button on the box to press. Mollen's tongue licked his lips as
he concentrated. So they had not literally taken his tongue
out, after all.

He assumed whatever was wrong with Mollen was to do
with his vocal chords. Why the man's superiors hadn't just
fitted him with an artificial or regrown set he couldn't de-
duce, unless they preferred their underlings to have a limited
set of replies. Certainly they'd have a hard time speaking ill
of you.

"Yes."

"Yes it's far away?"

"No."

"Make up your mind." He stood with his hand on the
open car door, indifferent to his unkindness to the gray-haired
man; he rather wanted to test his inbuilt vocabulary.

"I'm sorry."

"Is it quite close then, within the city?"

The scarred face frowned again. Mollen tutted with his
lips and pressed another set of buttons with an apologetic
look. "Yes."

"Within the city?"

"Perhaps."

"Thank you."

"Yes."

He got in. It was a different car to that he'd been in the
night before. Mollen got into the separate driver's compartment and belted himself in carefully; he pedaled a gear and
drew smoothly away. A couple of other cars followed immediately behind them, then stopped at the entrance to the
first street they took outside the hotel, blocking the cars of
the pursuing media people.

He was watching the small, high specks of wheeling birds
when the view started to disappear. At first he thought that
black screens were rising outside the windows behind and to
either side of him. Then he saw the bubbles; it was some
black liquid which was filling the space between the double
layers of glass in the back of the car. He pressed the button
to talk to Mollen. "Hey!" he shouted.

The black liquid was halfway up the screens, gradually
rising between him and Mollen as well as on the other three
sides.

"Yes?" Mollen said.

He grabbed a door handle. The door opened; a draft of cold air whistled in. The black liquid continued to fill the space between the panes of glass. "What is this?"

He saw Mollen carefully pressing a button on his voice synthesiser, before the liquid blocked the view forward.

"Do not be alarmed, Mr. Staberinde. This is just a precaution, to ensure that Mr. Beychae's privacy is respected," said an obviously prepared message.

"Hmm. Okay." He shrugged; he shut the door and was left in the dark until a small light came on. He sat back and did nothing. The unexpectedness of the blacking out was perhaps meant to frighten him, perhaps designed to see what he would do.

They drove on; the yellow light of the small bulb gave a stale, warm feel to the interior of the car, which although large was made to seem small by the absence of an exterior view; he turned up the ventilation, sat back again. He kept the dark glasses on.

They turned corners, zoomed and dived, boomed through tunnels and over bridges. He guessed he noticed the vehicle's motions more because of the lack of any outside reference.

They echoed through a tunnel for a long time, going downward in what felt like a straight line but could have been a wide spiral, then the car stopped. There was a moment of silence, then some indistinct noises from outside, perhaps including voices, before they moved forward again a short way. The transceiver jabbed delicately at his earlobe. He pushed the bead further into his ear. "X-ray radiation," the earring whispered.

He allowed himself a small smile. He waited for them to open the door and demand the transceiver . . . but the car only moved forward a little again.

The vehicle dropped. Its engine was silent; he presumed they were in a large elevator. They stopped, moved forward again, still silent, paused, then carried on forward and down. This time the spiral was obvious. There was still no noise from the vehicle's engine, so they were either being towed, or freewheeling.

The black liquid drained slowly from the windows as they drew to a halt. They were in a wide tunnel under long white strip lights. The tunnel extended back until it started to curve, forward until it ended before large metal doors.

Mollen was nowhere to be seen.

He tested the car door, opened it, stepped out.

The tunnel was warm, though the air seemed fresh enough. He took off the old raincoat. He looked at the metal doors. Set into them was a smaller door. There was no handle to pull, so he pushed it, but nothing happened. He went back to the car, found the horns, blew them.

The noise crashed into the tunnel, rang in his ears, echoing. He sat in the back of the car.

After a while, the woman came through the small door. She came to the car, looked in through the window.

"Hello."

"Good afternoon. Here I am."

"Yes. And still wearing your glasses." She smiled. "Please; come with me," she said, and walked quickly off. He collected the old raincoat and followed.

Behind the doors the tunnel went on, then they came to doors set into the side of the wall; a small elevator took them down still further. The woman wore a straight, all-covering gown in black with thin white stripes.

The lift stopped. They entered a small hallway like that of a private house, set about with pictures and potted plants and finished in streaky, smokily smooth stone. A thick carpet smothered their footsteps as they went down some steps and onto a large balcony set halfway up the wall of a large hall; everywhere else the hall was covered with books or tables, and they walked down a staircase with books below the wood under their feet, books above the wood over their heads.

She guided him round floor-standing bookstacks, and led him to a table with chairs around it. A machine stood on the tabletop with a small screen set into it and spools scattered about it.

"Wait here, please."

Beychae was in his bedroom, resting. The old man—bald, face deeply lined, dressed in robes which hid the modest paunch he'd developed since he'd devoted himself to study—blinked as she tapped at and opened the door. His eyes were still bright.

"Tsoldrin. I'm so sorry to disturb you. Come and see who I've brought to see you."

He came with her along the corridor, and stood at the door while the woman pointed to the man standing at the table with the tape-reading screen on it.

"Do you know him?"

Tsoldrin Beychae put on some glasses—he was old-fashioned enough to wear his age rather than try to disguise it—and peered at the man. The fellow was fairly young, long-legged, dark-haired—the hair swept back, held in a ponytail—and possessing a striking, even handsome face, darkened by the sort of beardgrowth that never disappears through surface shaving alone. The lips were disquieting, looked at exclusively; they appeared cruel and arrogant, and only when the eye took in the rest of the face as well did this impression seem too severe, and—reluctantly, perhaps—the observer had to allow that the dark glasses could not completely hide wide eyes and full brows, which—open and obvious—made the complete impression not disagreeable.

"I might have met him, I'm not sure," Beychae said slowly. He thought that perhaps he had met the man before; there was something worryingly familiar about that face, even behind the shades.

"He wants to meet you," the woman said. "I took the liberty of telling him it was mutual. He thinks you might have known his father."

"His father?" Beychae said. That might account for it; perhaps the fellow bore a resemblance to somebody he'd known, and that accounted for the odd, slightly disturbing feeling he was experiencing. "Well," he said, "let's see what he has to say for himself, shall we?"

"Why not?" the woman said. They walked out into the center of the library. Beychae drew himself up; he'd noticed that he was stooping more these days, but he was still vain enough to want to greet people straight-backed. The man turned round toward them. "Tsoldrin Beychae," the woman said; "Mr. Staberinde."

"An honor, sir," he said, looking at Beychae with a strange, intense expression, his face tight-looking, wary. He took the older man's hand in his.

The woman looked puzzled. The expression on Beychae's old, lined face was unreadable. He stood looking at the man, his hand limp in the other's grip.

"Mr. . . . Staberinde," Beychae said, flatly.

Beychae turned to the woman in the long black gown. "Thank you."

"My pleasure," she murmured, and backed away.

He could see Beychae knew. He turned and walked toward an aisle between the bookstacks, and watched Beychae follow him, eyes full of wonderment. He stood between the shelved books, and—as though it might have been an unconscious movement—tapped his ear as he spoke to Beychae. "I think you may have known my . . . ancestor. He went by a different name." He took off the dark glasses.

Beychae looked at him. His expression did not change. "I think I did," Beychae said, glancing round the space behind him. He indicated a table and chairs. "Please; let's sit down."

He replaced the glasses.

"So what brings you here, Mr. Staberinde?"

He sat down across the table from the older man. "Curiosity, as far as you're concerned. What brought me to Solotol was . . . just an urge to see it. I'm, ah . . . connected with the Vanguard Foundation; there have been some changes at the top there. I don't know if you've heard."

The old man shook his head. "No; I don't keep up with the news, down here."

"Yes." He made a show of looking around. "I guess . . ." he looked back into Beychae's eyes " . . . I guess it isn't the best place for communication, hmm?"

Beychae opened his mouth, then looked annoyed. He glanced behind him. "Perhaps not," he agreed. He stood up again. "Excuse me."

He watched the older man go. He forced himself to sit where he was.

He looked round the library. So many old books; they smelled. So many words set down, so many lives spent scribbling, so many eyes dimmed by reading. He wondered that people bothered as much as they did.

"Now?" he heard the woman say.

"Why not?"

He turned in the seat to watch Beychae and the woman emerge from the stacks. "Well, Mr. Beychae," the woman said. "It might be awkward . . ."

"Why? Have the elevators stopped working?"

"No, but . . ."

"Then what's to stop us? Let's go; I haven't seen the surface for too long."

"Ah. Well, all right . . . I'll make the arrangements." She smiled uncertainly, then walked away.

"Well, Z . . . Staberinde," Beychae sat down again, smiling apologetically for an instant. "We'll take a little trip to the surface, shall we?"

"Yeah; why not?" he said, carefully not looking too enthusiastic. "You keeping well, Mr. Beychae? I heard you retired."

They talked generally for a few minutes, then a young blonde woman walked out of the stacks, arms loaded with books. She blinked hard when she saw him, then came over behind Beychae, who looked up and smiled at her. "Ah; my dear, this is Mr. . . . Staberinde." Beychae smiled diffidently at him. "My assistant, Ms. Ubrel Shiol."

"Delighted," he nodded.

Shit, he thought.

Ms. Shiol put the books down on the table and put her hand on Beychae's shoulder. The old man put his own thin fingers on top of hers.

"I hear we might be taking a trip up to the city," the woman said. She looked down at the old man, smoothed her plain smock dress with her other hand. "This is very sudden."

"Yes," Beychae agreed. He smiled up at her. "You'll find that old men still retain the ability to surprise, on occasion."

"It'll be cold," the woman said, drawing away. "I'll fetch your warm clothes."

Beychae watched her go. "Wonderful girl," he said. "Don't know what I'd do without her."

"Indeed," he replied. *You may have to learn,* he thought.

The journey back up to the surface took an hour to arrange. Beychae seemed excited. Ubrel Shiol made him put on warm clothes, changed out of her smock into a one-piece, and put her hair up. They took the same car; Mollen drove. He, Beychae and Ms. Shiol sat on the broad rear bench; the woman in the black robe sat across from them.

They left the tunnel for the bright light of day; snow covered a broad yard with tall wire gates before them. Security men watched the car go past as the gates opened. The car set off down a side road for the nearest turnpike, then stopped at the junction.

"Is there a fair on anywhere?" Beychae asked. "I always enjoyed the noise and bustle of fairs."

He recalled there was some sort of traveling circus camped in a meadow down near the river Lotol. He suggested they went there. Mollen turned the car onto the broad, almost empty boulevard.

"Flowers," he said, suddenly.

They all looked at him.

He'd put his arm back on the seat, behind Beychae and Ubrel Shiol, and brushed Shiol's hair, dislodging a clasp Shiol had secured her hair with. He laughed, and retrieved the clasp from the shelf under the car's rear window. The maneuver had given him the chance to look back.

There was a large half-track vehicle following them.

"Flowers, Mr. Staberinde?" the woman in the black robe said.

"I'd like to buy some flowers," he said, smiling first at her, then at Shiol. He clapped his hands. "Why not? To the Flower Market, Mollen!" He sat back, smiling beatifically. Then he sat forward, all apologetic. "If that's all right," he said to the woman.

She smiled. "Of course. Mollen; you heard."

The car turned down another road.

In the Flower Market, among the packed and flurried stalls, he bought flowers and presented them to the woman and to Ubrel Shiol. "There's the fair!" he said, pointing over the river, where the tents and holograms of the fair sparkled and rotated.

As he'd hoped, they took the Flower Market Ferry. It was a tiny, one-vehicle platform. He looked back at the half-track waiting on the other side.

The far bank. They drove toward the fair; Beychae chattered, remembering fairs from his youth for Ubrel Shiol.

"Thank you for my flowers, Mr. Staberinde," the woman sitting across from him said, putting them to her face and breathing in their scent.

"My pleasure," he said, then leaned across Shiol to tap Beychae on the arm, to attract his attention to a piece of fairground equipment wheeling into the sky over some nearby roofs. The car drew to a stop at a light-controlled junction.

He reached across Shiol again, pulled down a zip before she realized what was happening, and extracted the gun he'd already felt there. He looked at it and started to laugh, as though the whole thing was a silly mistake, then turned it and fired at the glass screen behind Mollen's head.

The glass shattered. He was already kicking through it, launching himself from the seat and lancing forward with one leg. His foot crashed through the disintegrating glass and connected with Mollen's head.

The car leapt forward, then stalled. Mollen slumped.

The instant of stunned silence lasted just long enough for him to shout, "Capsule; *here!*"

The woman across from him moved; her hand dropped the flowers and went to her waist and a fold in the robe. He punched her in the jaw, sending her head cracking back against the still intact part of the glass screen behind her. He swiveled, crouched near the door, as the woman slid unconscious to the floor beside him and the flowers spilled across the footwell. He looked back at Beychae and Shiol. Both their mouths were open. "Change of plan," he said, taking off the dark glasses and throwing them onto the floor.

He dragged them both out. Shiol was screaming. He threw her against the rear of the car.

Beychae found his voice; "Zakalwe, what the hell do you . . ."

"She had *this*, Tsoldrin!" he yelled back, flourishing the gun.

Ubrel Shiol used the second or so that the gun wasn't pointing at her to stab a kick at his head. He dodged it, let the woman spin, then cracked her, open handed, across the neck. She crumpled. The flowers he had given her rolled under the car.

"Ubrel!" Beychae shrieked, falling to the woman's side. "Zakalwe! What have you done to . . ."

"Tsoldrin . . ." he began. The driver's door burst open and Mollen launched himself at him. They tumbled across the road into the gutter; the gun went spinning.

He found himself wedged against the curb, Mollen above

him, bunching his lapels in one hand, the other arm swinging up, the voice machine swinging out on a lanyard as the huge, scarred fist plunged downward.

He feinted, then flung himself in the other direction. He jumped up as Mollen's fist hit the curbstones.

"Hello," said Mollen's voice box as it clattered into the road surface.

He tried to steady, aiming a kick at Mollen's head, but he was off balance. Mollen caught his foot with his good hand. He wriggled out of the grip, but only by turning away.

"Pleased to meet you," the box said, swinging again as Mollen rose, shaking his head.

He aimed another kick at Mollen's head. "What do you require?" The machine said, as Mollen dodged the kick and threw himself forward. He dived, skidded across the concrete road surface, rolled and stood.

Mollen faced him; his neck was bloody. He staggered, then seemed to remember something, and dug inside his tunic.

"I am here to help you," said the voice box.

He flung himself forward, smashing a fist into Mollen's head as the big man turned, loosing a small gun from his tunic. He was too far away to grab it, so he pivoted and swung one foot, connecting with the gun in the man's fist and forcing his hand up. The gray-haired man staggered back, looking pained and rubbing his wrist.

"My name is Mollen. I cannot speak."

He'd hoped the kick might have dislodged the gun from Mollen's grip but it didn't. Then he realized that directly behind him were Beychae and the unconscious Shiol; he stood for a second while Mollen aimed the gun at him, waggling his body one way then the other, so that Mollen, shaking his head again, let his hand waver on the gun.

"Pleased to meet you."

He dived at Mollen's legs. Collided satisfactorily.

"No, thank you." They crashed into the curbside. "Excuse me . . ."

He brought his fist up, tried to whack the man across the head again.

"Could you tell me where this is?"

But Mollen rolled. His punch sailed through air. Mollen

shifted and almost head-butted him. He had to duck, hitting his head against the curbstones.

"Yes, please."

He splayed his fingers as his head rang with light, flung them out where he thought Mollen's eyes ought to be, and felt something connect liquidly. Mollen screamed.

"I cannot reply to that."

He bounced up using hands and feet, kicking out at Mollen as he did so.

"Thank you." His foot slammed into Mollen's head. "Would you repeat that, please?"

Mollen rolled slowly into the gutter and lay still. "What time is it? What time is it? What time is it?"

He stood up shakily on the sidewalk.

"My name is Mollen. Can I help you? You are not allowed in here. This is private property. Where do you think you are going? Stop or I shoot. Money is no object. We have powerful friends. Could you direct me to the nearest telephone? I'll fuck you harder all right, bitch; feel this."

He smashed Mollen's voice machine with one boot.

"Graap! No user-serviceable components ins—"

Another stamp silenced it.

He looked up at Beychae, who was crouched by the side of the car, Ubrel Shiol's head cradled in his lap.

"Zakalwe! You madman!" Beychae screeched.

He dusted himself down, looked back in the direction of the hotel. "Tsoldrin," he said calmly. "This is an emergency."

"What have you done?" Beychae—eyes wide, face aghast—screamed at him, glancing from Shiol's inert form to Mollen's, then taking a detour via the slumped feet of the woman lying unconscious in the car, flowers scattered around her feet, before returning to Shiol's already bruised neck.

He looked to the sky. He saw a speck. Relieved, he turned back to Beychae. "They were about to kill you," he told him. "I was sent to stop them. We have about . . ."

There was a noise beyond the buildings shielding the river and the Flower Market; a bang and a whoosh. They both looked to the sky; the enlarging speck that was the capsule blossomed with light on a stalk that led back behind the buildings toward the Flower Market. The capsule sailed through the resulting incandescent bloom, seemed to shake itself, then a lance of light darted from it back down the same line, as though in reply.

The sky above the Flower Market flared; the road underneath them bounced, and a terrific crack of sound burst over the roadway and rolled back from cliffs further up the slope city.

"We had about a minute," he said, breathless, "before we had to leave." The capsule swooped from the sky, a four-meter cylinder of darkness impacting on the road surface. Its hatches opened. He went to it and took out a very large gun. He touched a couple of controls. "Now we have no time."

"Zakalwe!" Beychae said, voice suddenly controlled. "Are you insane?"

A tearing, screaming noise came above the city, from up-canyon. They both looked up at a slim shape streaking toward them, bellying down through the air.

He spat into the gutter. He raised the plasma rifle, sighted at the fast approaching dot, and fired.

A bolt of light leapt from gun to sky; the aircraft burst smoke, and veered away on a helix of debris, crashing somewhere down-canyon in a scream that became thunder, echoes rolling back from all over the city.

He looked back at the old man.

"What was the question again?"

V

The black fabric of the tent roof was above him and yet he could see through it to the sky, which was the shaded blue of day, and bright, but black as well because he could see through that easy blueness, and beyond was a darkness more profound than that inside the tent, a darkness where the scattered suns burned, tiny firefly lights in the cold black empty deserts of the night.

A dark crop of stars reached out toward him, picked him up softly between vast fingers like some delicate ripe fruit. In that immense enfolding he felt deliriously sane, and understood then that in an instant—any instant, and with only the most minute of efforts—he might understand everything, but did not desire to. He felt as though some awesome galaxy-quaking machinery, always hidden under the surface of the universe, had somehow connected itself to him, and dusted him with its power.

He sat in a tent. His legs were crossed, his eyes were closed. He had sat like this for days now. He wore a loose-fitting robe, like the nomad people. His uniform lay neatly folded a meter behind him. His hair was short; stubble grew on his face, and there was a sheen of sweat on his skin. It seemed to him that sometimes he was outside of himself, looking back at his body, sitting there on the cushions under the dark fabric roof. His face grew darker because the black hairs grew through the skin, yet looked lighter because the film of sweat on it glistened in the lights of the lamps and the smoke-hole in the roof. This adversarial symbiosis, competition creating stasis, amused him. He would rejoin his body, or set off further afield, with a sense of rightness at the core of things.

The tent was dark inside, filled with a thick and heavy atmosphere at once stale and sweet; heavy with perfume, smoky with incense. All was sweet and rich and highly decorated; the hanging rugs were thick and picked out with many colors and precious metal thread; the carpet was piled like a field of golden grain, and the plump, scented cushions and languorously thick coverings made a fabulously patterned landscape under the dark flute of roof. Small censers smoked lazily; little night-heaters sat extinguished, dream-leaf holders and crystal chalices, jeweled boxes and clasped books were strewn across the undulating fabric landscape like glittering temples on the plains.

Lies. The tent was bare and he sat on a sack stuffed with straw.

The girl watched him move. It was a hypnotic movement, barely noticeable at first, but once you had seen it, once the eye grew accustomed to it, it became very obvious and quite fascinating. He moved from the waist, round and round, neither slowly nor quickly, his head describing a flattened circle. It reminded the girl of the way that, sometimes, rising smoke would begin to twist as it rose toward the hole in the roof of a tent. The man's eyes seemed to move in compensation for this subtle, ceaseless motion, shifting tinily behind the brown-pink lids.

The tent was just big enough for the girl to stand up in. It was pitched at a crossroads in the desert, where two tracks crossed the sea of sand. It would have been a town or even a city long since, but the nearest water was three days' ride away. The tent had been here for four days, and might be here another two or three, depending on how long the man stayed in the dream-leaf sleep. She took up a pitcher from a small tray and filled a cup with water. She went over to the man, and put the cup to his lips, holding one hand under his chin as she carefully tipped the cup.

The man drank, still moving. He turned his face away after he'd drunk half the water in the cup. She took a cloth and dabbed at his face, removing a little of the sweat.

Chosen, he said to himself. Chosen, Chosen, Chosen. A long way to a strange place. Taking the Chosen one through the scorching dust and the mad tribes of the badlands to the lush meadows and gleaming spires of the Perfumed Palace on the cliff. Now he reaped a little reward.

The tent sits between the trade routes, outside turned in for the season, and in the tent sits a man, a soldier, back from uncounted wars, scarred and seared and broken and healed and broken and healed and repaired and made good again . . . and for once he was unwary, guard down, committing his mind to a wild, affecting drug, and his body to the care and protection of a young girl.

The girl, whose name he did not know, brought water to his lips and a cool cloth to his brow. He remembered a fever, a hundred and more years ago, a thousand and more years away, and the hands of another girl, cool and tender, soothing and smoothing. He heard the lawn birds keen from the grounds outside the great house that lay in the estate cradled in the broad river's bend; an oxbow of calm in the livid landscape of his memories.

Torpor-heavy, the drug flowed through him, winding and unwinding, a current of random ordering. (He remembered a stone beach on the river's banks, where the ever-flowing water had swept silt, sand, gravel, pebbles, stones and boulders in a linear progression of size and weight, ordering— through its steady, liquid weight—the elemental stone in a curve, like something distributed on a graph.)

The girl watched and waited, calm that the stranger had taken to the drug like one of their own, and was himself calm under its influence. She hoped this was, as he seemed to be, an exceptional man, and not an ordinary one, for that would imply their nomad kind was not the uniquely strong race they believed they were.

She had feared the power of the drug would be too much for him, and that he would shatter like a red-glowing cooking pot dropped into water, the way she had heard other strangers had, vainly thinking the dream-leaf was just another dalliance in their self-indulgent lives. But he had not fought it. For one who was a soldier, used to fighting, he had displayed a rare insight in just giving in without a struggle, and accepting the prescriptions of the drug. She admired this in an outsider. She doubted the conquerors would be so pliably strong. Even some of their own young men—often the most impressive, in every other way—could not accept the crushing gifts the dream-leaf brought, and yelped and gibbered through an abbreviated nightmare, mewling for their mother's breast, pissing and shitting and crying and screaming their most shaming fears to the desert winds. The drug was rarely fatal, in the supervised quantities that had become ritual, but the after-effects could be; more than one young brave had chosen the blade in the belly to the disgrace of knowing a leaf had been stronger than he.

It was, she reflected, a pity that this man was not one of their own kind; he might have made a good husband, and sired many strong sons and cunning daughters. Many marriages were made in dream-leaf tents, and she had at first taken it as an insult that she had been asked to shepherd the stranger through his leaf-days, until she'd been convinced it was an honor, that he had done their people a great service, and she would be allowed her pick of the tribe's young novitiates, when their testing time came.

And, when he took the dream-leaf, he had insisted on the stage that they normally reserved for their elder soldiers and matriarchs; no child's dose for him. She watched him circle, flexing continually from the waist, as though he sought to stir something in his brain.

By the roads, by the crossed signs of those single lines, worn by trade, commerce and passing knowledge; thin trails in the dust, pale marks in the brown page of the desert. The tent stood in summer, when the white side was turned out and the black side in. In winter it was outside-in.

He imagined that he felt his brain revolve inside his skull.

In the white tent that was black, and both at once, by the crossroads on the desert, a white/black impermanence like a fallen leaf before the winds blow, trembling in the breeze beneath the poised wave that was the stone circumference of mountains, capped by snow and ice like foam frozen in the high thin air.

He swept away, leaving the tent, so that it fell away beneath him, became a speck beside the thin trails in the dust, and the mountains swam past, white capping ochre, and the trails and the tent disappeared, and the mountains shrank, and the glaciers and the starveling snows of summer became white claws on the rock, and the curved edge pressed in, compressing the view, so that the globe beneath became a colored boulder, stone, pebble, gravel, grain of sand, speck of silt-dust, then was lost in the sandstorm whirl of the great revolving lens that was the home of all of them, which itself became a fleck on a thin bubble surrounding emptiness, skeined to its lonely siblings by the fabric that was only a slimly different articulation of nothingness.

More specks. All vanished. Darkness reigned.

He was still there.

Beneath it all, he'd been told, was more. All you had to do, Sma said, was think in seven dimensions and see the whole universe as a line on the surface of a torus, starting at a point, becoming a circle as it was born, then expanding, moving up the inside of the torus, over the top, to the outside, then relapsing, falling back in, shrinking. Others had gone before it, others came after it (the greater/smaller spheres outside of/inside their own universe, seen in four dimensions). Different time scales lived outside and inside the torus; some universes expanding forever, others living less than a blink of an eye.

But it was too much. It all meant too much to matter. He had to concentrate on what he knew and what he was and what he had become, for the moment at least.

He found a sun, a planet, out of all that existence, and fell toward it, knowing this was the place, the font of all his dreams and memories.

He searched for meaning, found ashes. Where does it hurt? Well, just *here*, actually. A wrecked summerhouse, smashed and burned. No sign of a chair.

Sometimes, like now, the banality of it all quite took his breath away. He stopped and checked, for there were drugs that did that; took your breath away. He was still breathing. Probably his body was already set up to ensure that anyway, but the Culture—Chaos bless it twice—had set up a further program in him, to make certain. Cheating, as far as these people were concerned (he saw the girl in front of him, and watched her, through mostly-closed eyes, then closed again), but that was just too bad; he'd done something for them, little though they really knew it, and now they could do something for him.

But the throne, Sma had said once, is the ultimate symbol for many cultures. To sit, in splendor, is the highest articulation of power. The rest come to you; lower, often bowing, frequently backing off, sometimes prostrate (though that is always a bad sign, said the Culture's blessed statistics), and to sit, to be made less animal by that evolutionarily uncalled-for posture, signified the ability to use.

There were some small civilizations—barely more than tribes, Sma had said—where they slept sitting, in special sleep chairs, because they believed that to lie down was to die (did they not always find the dead lying down?).

Zakalwe (was that really his name? It suddenly sounded strange and alien in his remembrance), Zakalwe, Sma said, I visited a place (How had they come to this? What had made him mention anything about this? Had he been drunk? Guard down again? Probably trying to seduce Sma, but ended up under the table again.) Zakalwe I once visited a place where they killed people by putting them in a chair. Not torture—that was common enough; beds and chairs were very much the par when it came to getting people helpless and confined, to inflict pain upon them—but actually set it up to kill them while they sat. They—get this—they either gassed them or they passed very high electric currents through them. A pellet dropped into a container beneath the seat, like some obscene image of a commode, producing a fatal gas; or a cap over their head, and their hands dipped in some conducting fluid, to fry their brains.

You want to know the punch line? Yeah, Sma, give us the punch line. This same state had a law that forbade—and I quote—''cruel and unusual punishments!'' Can you believe that?

He circled around the planet, so far away.

Then fell toward it, through the air to the ground.

He found the shell of the mansion, like a forgotten skull; he found the wrecked summerhouse, like a shattered skull; he found the stone boat, like a deserted image of a skull. Fake. It was never floating.

He saw another boat; a ship; a hundred thousand tons of destruction, sitting in its own dry image of desuetude, its layers bristling outward. Primary, secondary, tertiary, anti-aircraft, small . . .

He circled, then tried to approach, zeroing in . . .

But there were too many layers, and they defeated him.

He was thrown out again, and had to circle the planet once more, and as he did so, saw the Chair, and saw the Chairmaker—not the one he'd thought of, before; the other Chairmaker, the real one, and one that he had to keep returning to, through all the memories—in all his ghastly glory.

But some things were too much.

Some things were too much to bear.

Damn people. Damn others. Damn there being other people.

Back to the girl. (Why did there have to be other people?)

Yes she still had little experience as a guider-through, but as a stranger the man had been given to her, because they thought she was the best of the untried. But she would show them. Perhaps, through this, they were already considering her for the Matriarchs.

She would lead them one day. She felt this in her bones. The same bones that ached when she saw a child fall; the same ache in her cupped child-bones that came when she saw someone fall hard to the ground, would be her guide through the politics and tribulations of the tribe. She would prevail. Like this man here in front of her, but different. She had that inner strength, too. She would lead her people; it was like a child inside her, growing, that certainty. She would stir her people against the conquerors; she would show their brief hegemony for what it was; a side track on the desert trail that was their destiny. The people beyond the plains, in their corrupt perfumed palace on the cliff, would fall beneath them. The power and thought of the women, and the power and bravery of their men—desert thorns—would crush the decadent petal-people of the cliffs. The sands would be theirs again. Temples would be carved in her name.

Lies. The girl was young and knew nothing of the tribe's thoughts or destiny. She was a scrap thrown to him, to ease his passage into what they imagined would be his death-dream. Her vanquished people's fate scarcely mattered to her; they had replaced that ancient heritage with thoughts of prestige and gadgets.

Let her dream. He relaxed into the calm frenzy of the drug.

There was a nexus where the vanishing point of memory met the time-light from another place, and he was not yet sure he had outrun it.

He tried to see the great house again, but it was obscured by smoke and star-shell. He looked to the great battleship, confined within its dry-land dock, but it would not grow any larger. It was a capital ship, no more, no less, and he could not access the depths of meaning that it really held for him.

All he'd done was take the Chosen across the wastes to the Palace. Why had they wanted the Chosen to get to the Court? It seemed absurd. The Culture did not believe in such supernatural, superstitious nonsense. But the Culture required him to make sure the Chosen got to the Court, despite all sorts of nastiness getting in his way.

To perpetuate a corrupt line. To carry on a reign of stupidness.

Well, they had their own reasons. You took the money and ran. Except there was no money, as such. What was a boy to do?

Believe. Though they scorned belief. Do. Act, though they were wary of action. He was their whipper boy, he realized. A borrowed hero. They thought little enough of heroes for this to be a boost to one's own self-belief.

Come with us, do these things, that you would like to do anyway, except more so, and we will give you what you could never really have anywhere or anytime else; real proof that you are doing the right thing; that not only are you having immense *fun*, it is also for the common good. So enjoy.

And he *did*, and he enjoyed, though he was not always sure it was for the right reasons. But that did not matter to them.

The Chosen to the Palace.

He stood back from his life and was not ashamed. All he'd ever done was because there was something to be done. You used those weapons, whatever they might happen to be. Given a goal, or having thought up a goal, you had to aim for it, no matter what stood in your way. Even the Culture recognized that. They couched it in terms of what could be done at a specific time and level of technological capability, but they recognized that all was relative, everything was in flux . . .

He tried, all of a sudden—hoping to take it by surprise—to sweep and crash back down to that place with the war-shelled mansion and the burned-out summerhouse and the foundering boat made of stone . . . but the memory would not bear the weight of it, and he was flung out again, swirled away, cast into the nothingness, consigned to the oblivion of the deliberately not-thought thoughts.

The tent stood at the focus of the desert trails. White without, black within, it seemed to image his crossroad imaginings.

Hey hey hey. It's only a dream.

Except it wasn't a dream, and he was in complete control, and if he opened his eyes he could see the girl sitting there in front of him, staring at him, wondering, and there was never any doubt about who was where and what was when, and in a way that was the worst thing about this drug; that it let you go anywhere, anytime—as not a few drugs did—but it still let you connect back to reality whenever you really wanted to.

Cruel, he thought.

The Culture might just have it right after all; being able to call up almost any drug or combinations of drugs seemed suddenly less indulgent and decadent than he'd imagined, before.

The girl, he saw, in one awful instant, would do great things. She would be famous and important, and the tribe around her would do great—and terrible—things, and it would all be for nothing, because whatever terrible train of events he had set in motion by taking the Chosen to the Palace, this tribe would not survive; they were the dead. Their mark upon the desert of life was already being obscured, sands blowing over, grain by grain by grain . . . He had already helped to scuff it out, no matter that they hadn't realized this yet. They would, after he was gone. The Culture would take him away from here, and put him down somewhere else, and this adventure would collapse with the rest into meaninglessness, and nothing very much would be left, as he went on to do roughly the same thing somewhere else.

Actually, he could happily have killed the Chosen, because the boy was a fool, and he had seldom been in the company of anybody quite so stupid. The youth was a cretin, and didn't even realize that he was.

He could think of no more disastrous combination.

He swept back toward the planet he had once abandoned.

Came in so far, was forced away. He tried again, but without any real self-belief.

Was rejected. Well, he'd expected no more.

The Chairmaker was not the person who made the chair, he thought, immediately lucid. It was and was not him. There are no Gods, we are told, so I must make my own salvation.

His eyes were already closed, but he closed them again.

He swayed in a circle, unknowing.

Lies; he wept and screamed, fell at the scornful feet of the girl.

Lies; he circled on.

Lies; he fell to the girl, hands out, grasping for a mother that was not there.

Lies.

Lies.

Lies; he circled on, tracing his own private symbol in the air between the crown of his head and the day-bright hole that was the tent's smoke hole.

He sank toward the planet again, but the girl in the black/white tent reached out and wiped his brow and, in that tiny movement, seemed to wipe his being away . . .

(Lies.)

. . . It was a long time later he found out he'd only taken the Chosen to the Palace because the brat was to be the last of the line. Not merely stupid, but also impotent, the Chosen fathered no strong sons and no cunning daughters (as the Culture had known all along), and the fractious desert tribes swept in a decade later led by a Matriarch who had guided most of the warriors under her command through the dream-leaf time, and had seen one stronger and stranger than all of them suffer its effects and come through unscathed but still unfulfilled, and known through that very experience that there was more to their desert existence than had been guessed at by the myths and elders of her nomad tribe.

3:

REMEMBRANCE

10

He loved the plasma rifle. He was an artist with it; he could paint pictures of destruction, compose symphonies of demolition, write elegies of annihilation, using that weapon.

He stood, thinking about it, while the wind moved dead leaves round his feet and the ancient stones faced into the wind.

They hadn't made it off the planet. The capsule had been attacked by . . . something. He couldn't tell from the damage whether it had been a beam weapon or some sort of warhead going off nearby. Whatever it had been, it had disabled them. Clamped to the outside of the capsule, he'd been lucky to be on the side that shielded him from whatever had hit it. Had he been on the other side, facing the beam or the warhead, he'd be dead.

They must have been hit by some crude effector weapon as well, because the plasma rifle seemed to have fused. It had been cradled between his suit and the capsule skin and couldn't have been affected by whatever wrecked the capsule itself, but the weapon had smoked and got hot, and when they'd finally landed—Beychae shaken but unhurt—and opened up the gun's inspection panels, it was to find a melted, still-warm mess inside.

Maybe if he'd taken just a little less time to convince Beychae; maybe if he'd just knocked the old guy out and left the talking for later. He'd taken too much time, given them too much time. Seconds counted. Dammit, milliseconds, nanoseconds counted. Too much time.

"They're going to kill you!" he'd shouted. "They want you on their side or they want you dead. The war's going to start soon, Tsoldrin; you support them or you'll have an accident. They won't *let* you stay neutral!"

"Insane," Beychae repeated, cradling Ubrel Shiol's head in his hands. Saliva trickled from the woman's mouth. "You're insane, Zakalwe; insane." He started to cry.

He went over to the old man, knelt on one knee, holding the gun he'd taken from Shiol. "Tsoldrin; what do you think she had this for?" He put his hand on the old man's shoulder. "Didn't you see the way she moved when she tried to kick me? Tsoldrin; librarians . . . research assistants . . . they just don't move like that." He reached out and patted the unconscious woman's collar flat and tidy again. "She was one of your jailers, Tsoldrin; she would probably have been your executioner." He reached under the car, pulled out the bouquet of flowers, and placed them gently under her blonde head, removing Beychae's hands.

"Tsoldrin," he said. "We have to go. She'll be all right." He arranged Shiol's arms in a less awkward position. She was already on her side, so she wouldn't choke. He reached carefully under Beychae's arms and slowly drew the old man up to his feet. Ubrel Shiol's eyes flickered open; she saw the two men in front of her; she muttered something, and one hand went to the back of her neck. She started to roll over, unbalanced in her grogginess; the hand that had gone to her neck came away clutching a tiny cylinder like a pen; he felt Beychae stiffen as the girl looked up and, as she fell forward, tried to point the little laser at Beychae's head.

Beychae looked into her dark, half-unfocused eyes, over the top of the pen laser, and felt a sort of appalled disconnectedness. The girl tried hard to steady herself, aiming at him. Not Zakalwe, he thought; at *me*. Me!

"Ubrel . . ." he began.

The girl fell back in a dead faint.

Beychae stared down at her body lying limp on the road. Then he heard somebody saying his name and tugging his arm.

"Tsoldrin . . . Tsoldrin . . . Come on, Tsoldrin."

"Zakalwe; she was aiming at *me*, not you!"

"I know, Tsoldrin."

"She was aiming at me!"

"I know. Come on; here's the capsule."

"At me . . ."

"I know, I know. Get in here."

He watched the gray clouds move overhead. He stood on the flat stone summit of a high hill, surrounded by other hilltops almost as high, all wooded. He looked resentfully around the forested slopes and the curious, truncated stone pillars and plinths that covered the platform peak. He felt a sense of vertigo, exposed to such wide horizons again after so long spent in the cleft city. He left the view, kicked his way through some wind-piled leaves, back to where Beychae sat and the plasma rifle rested against a great round stone. The capsule was a hundred meters away, down in the trees.

He picked up the plasma rifle for the fifth or sixth time and inspected it.

It made him want to cry; it was such a beautiful weapon. Every time he picked it up he half hoped that it would be all right, that the Culture had fitted it with some self-repair facility without telling him, that the damage would be no more . . .

The wind blew; the leaves scattered. He shook his head, exasperated. Beychae, sitting in his thickly padded trousers and long jacket, turned to look at him.

"Broken?" the old man asked.

"Broken," he said. His face took on an expression of annoyance; he gripped the weapon round the muzzle with both hands and swung it round his head, then let it go and sent it whirling away into the trees below; it disappeared in a flurry of dislodged leaves.

He sat down beside Beychae.

Plasma rifle gone, just a pistol left; only one suit; prob-

ably no way he could use the suit's AG without giving away
their position; capsule wrecked; module nowhere to be seen;
no word from the terminal earring or the suit itself . . . it
was a sorry mess. He checked the suit for whatever broadcast
signals it was picking up; the wrist screen displayed some
news headlines programme; nothing about Solotol was mentioned. A few of the Cluster's brushfire wars were.

Beychae looked at the small screen too. "Can you tell
from that whether they are looking for us?" he asked.

"Only if we see it on the news. Military stuff will be
tight-beamed; slim chance we'll pick up a transmission." He
looked at the clouds. "We'll probably find out more directly,
soon enough."

"Hmm," Beychae said. He frowned at the flagstones,
then said, "I think I might know where this place is, Zakalwe."

"Yeah?" he said, unenthusiastically. He put his elbows
on his knees, his chin in his hands, and looked out over the
wooded plains to the low hills on the horizon.

Beychae nodded. "I've been thinking about it. I believe
this is the Srometren Observatory, in Deshal Forest."

"How far is that from Solotol?"

"Oh; different continent. Good two thousand kilometers."

"Same latitude," he said glumly, looking up at the chill
gray skies.

"Approximately, if this is the place I think it is."

"Who's in charge here?" he asked. "Whose jurisdiction?
Same lot as in Solotol; the Humanists?"

"The same." Beychae said, and got up, brushing the seat
of his pants and looking around the flattened hilltop at the
curious stone instruments that covered its flagstones. "Srometren Observatory!" he said. "How ironic we should happen to come down here, on our way to the stars!"

"Probably not just chance," he said, picking up a twig
and brushing a few random shapes in the dust at his feet.
"This place famous?"

"Of course," Beychae said. "It was the center of astronomical research for the old Vrehid Empire for five hundred
years."

"On any tourist routes?"

"Certainly."

"Then it probably has a beacon nearby, to guide aircraft in. Capsule may have made for it when it knew it was crippled. Makes us easier to find." He gazed up at the sky. "For everybody, unfortunately." He shook his head, went back to scratching in the dust with the twig.

"What happens now?" Beychae said.

He shrugged. "We wait and see who turns up. I can't get any of the communication gear to work, so we don't know if the Culture knows all that's happened or not . . . for all I know the Module's still coming for us, or a whole Culture starship's on its way, or—probably more likely—your pals from Solotol . . ." He shrugged, threw down the twig and sat back against the stonework behind him, glancing skyward. "They might be watching us right now."

Beychae looked up too. "Through the clouds?"

"Through the clouds."

"Shouldn't you be hiding, then? Running off through the woods?"

"Maybe," he said.

Beychae stood looking down at the other man. "Where were you thinking of taking me, if we'd got away?"

"The Impren System. There are space Habitats there," he said. "They're neutral, or at least not as pro-war as this place."

"Do your . . . superiors really think war is so close, Zakalwe?"

"Yes," he sighed. He already had the suit's faceplate hinged up; now, with another look at the sky, he took the whole helmet off. He put one hand up over his forehead and through his drawn-back hair, then reached back and took the ponytail out of its little ring, shaking his long black hair down. "It might take ten days, might take a hundred, but it's coming." He smiled thinly at Beychae. "For the same reasons as last time."

"I thought we'd won the ecological argument against terraforming," said Beychae.

"We did, but times change; people change, generations change. We won the battles for the acknowledgment of machine sentience, but by all accounts the issue was fudged after that. Now people are saying, yes, they're sentient, but it's only human sentience that *counts*. Plus, people never need too much of an excuse to see other species as inferior."

Beychae was silent for a while, then said, "Zakalwe, has it ever occurred to you that in all these things the Culture may not be as disinterested as you imagine, and it claims?"

"No, it never occurred to me," he said, though Beychae got the impression the man hadn't really thought first before answering.

"They want other people to be like them, Cheradenine. They don't terraform, so they don't want others to either. There are arguments for it as well, you know; increasing species diversity often seems more important to people than preserving a wilderness, even without the provision of extra living space. The Culture believes profoundly in machine sentience, so it thinks everybody ought to, but I think it also believes every civilization should be run by its machines. Fewer people want that. The issue of cross-species tolerance is, I'll grant, of a different nature, but even there the Culture can sometimes appear to be insistent that deliberate inter-mixing is not just permissible but desirable; almost a duty. Again, who is to say that is correct?"

"So you should have a war to . . . what? Clear the air?" He inspected the suit helmet.

"No, Cheradenine, I'm just trying to suggest to you that the Culture may not be as objective as it thinks it is, and, that being the case, its estimation concerning the likelihood of war may be equally untrustworthy."

"There are small wars on a dozen planets right now, Tsoldrin. People are talking war in public; either about how to avoid it, or how it might be limited, or how it can't possibly happen . . . but it's coming; you can smell it. You should catch the newscasts, Tsoldrin. Then you'd know."

"Well then, perhaps war is inevitable," Beychae said, looking away over the wooden plains and hills beyond the observatory. "Maybe it's just . . . time."

"Crap," he said. Beychae looked at him, surprised. "There's a saying: 'War is a long cliff.' You can avoid the cliff completely, you can walk along the top for as long as you have the nerve, you can even choose to leap off, and if you only fall a short way before you hit a ledge you can always scramble back up again. Unless you're just plain invaded, there are always choices, and even then, there's usu-ally something you've missed—a choice you didn't make—

that could have avoided invasion in the first place. You people still have your choices. There's nothing inevitable about it.''

"Zakalwe," Beychae said. "You surprise me. I'd have thought you—''

"You'd have thought I'd be in favor of war?'' he said, standing, a sad small smile on his lips. He put one hand on the other man's shoulder. "You've had your nose buried in books for too long, Tsoldrin.'' He walked away past the stone instruments. Beychae looked down at the suit helmet, lying on the flagstones. He followed the other man.

"You're right, Zakalwe. I have been out of the flow of things for a long time. I probably don't know who half the people in power are these days, or exactly what the issues are, or the precise balance of the various alliances . . . so the Culture cannot be so . . . desperate they think I can alter whatever's going to happen. Can they?''

He turned round. He looked into Beychae's face. "Tsoldrin, the truth is I don't know. Don't think I haven't thought about this. It might be just that you, as a symbol, really would make all the difference, and maybe everybody is desperate to find an excuse not to have to fight; you could be that excuse if you come along, uncontaminated by recent events, as though from the dead, and provide a face-saving compromise.

"Or maybe the Culture secretly thinks a small short war is a good idea, or even knows there's nothing it can do to stop a full-scale one, but has to be seen to be doing something, no matter how long a shot it might be, so that people can't say later, 'Why didn't you try *this*?' '' He shrugged. "I never try to second-guess the Culture, Tsoldrin, let alone Contact, and certainly not Special Circumstances.''

"You just do their bidding.''

"And get well paid for it.''

"But you see yourself on the side of good, do you, Cheradenine?''

He smiled and sat on the stone plinth, legs swinging. "I have no idea whether they're the good guys or not, Tsoldrin. They certainly *seem* to be, but then who knows that seeming is being?'' He frowned, looked away. "I have never seen them be cruel, even when they might have claimed they had an excuse to be so. It can make them seem cold, sometimes.'' He shrugged again. "But there are folks that'll tell you it's the bad gods that always have the most beautiful faces and the softest voices. Shit," he said, and jumped off the stone table. He went to stand by the balustrade which marked one edge of the old observatory, looking to where the sky was starting to redden above the horizon. It would be dark in an hour. "They keep their promises and they pay top rates. They make good employers, Tsoldrin."

"That does not mean we ought to let them decide *our* fate."

"You'd rather let those decadent dickheads in Governance do it instead?"

"At least they're *involved*, Zakalwe; it isn't just a game to them."

"Oh, I think it is. I think that's exactly what it is to them. The difference is that unlike the Culture's Minds, they don't know enough to take games seriously." He took a deep breath and watched the wind stir the branches beneath them; leaves fell away. "Tsoldrin; don't say you're on their side."

"The sides were always strange," Beychae said. "We all said that all we wanted was the best for the Cluster, and I think we all meant it, mostly. We all still want that. But I don't know what the right thing to do is; I sometimes think I know too much, I've studied too much, learned too much, remembered too much. It all seems to average out, somehow; like dust that settles over . . . whatever machinery we carry inside us that leads us to act, and puts the same weight everywhere, so that always you can see good and bad on each side, and always there are arguments, precedents for every possible course of action . . . so of course one ends up doing nothing. Perhaps that's only right; perhaps that's what evolution requires, to leave the field free for younger, unencumbered minds, and those not afraid to act."

"Okay, so it's a balance. All societies are like that; the damping hand of the old and the firebrand youth together. It works out through generations, or through the setup of your institutions, and their change and even replacement; but Governance, the Humanists, combine the worst of both approaches. Ancient, vicious, discredited ideas backed with adolescent war-mania. It's a crock of shit, Tsoldrin, and you know it. You've earned the right to some leisure; nobody's arguing. But that won't stop you feeling guilty when—not if—the bad stuff comes. You have the power, Tsoldrin, whether you like it or not; just doing nothing is a statement, don't you understand that? What is all your studying worth, all your learning, all your knowledge, if it doesn't lead to wisdom? And what's wisdom but knowing what is right, and what is the right thing to do? You're almost a god to some of the people in this civilization, Tsoldrin; again, whether you like it or not. If you do nothing . . . they'll feel abandoned. They'll feel despair. And who can blame them?''

He made a resigned sort of gesture with his hands, putting them both down on the stone parapet, gazing out to the darkening sky. Beychae was silent.

He gave the old man a while longer to think, then looked round at the flat stone summit of the hill, at all the strange stone instruments. ''An observatory, eh?''

''Yes,'' Beychae said after a moment's hesitation. He touched one of the stone plinths with one hand. ''Believed to have been a burial site, four or five thousand years ago; then to have had some sort of astrological significance; later, they may have predicted eclipses with readings taken here. Finally, the Vrehids built this observatory to study the motions of the moons, planets and stars. There are water clocks, sundials, sextants, planet-dials . . . partial orreries . . . there are crude seismographs here, too, or at least earthquake direction indicators.''

''They have telescopes?''

''Very poor ones, and only for a decade or so before the Empire fell. The results they got from the telescopes caused a lot of problems; contradicted what they already knew, or thought they knew.''

''That figures. What's this?'' One of the plinths held a large, rusty metal bowl with a sharp central spindle.

''Compass, I think,'' Beychae said. ''It works by fields,'' he smiled.

''And this? Looks like a tree stump.'' It was a huge, rough, very slightly fluted cylinder perhaps a meter in height, and twice that across. He tapped the edge. ''Hmm; stone.''

''Ah!'' Tsoldrin said, joining him at the stone cylinder. ''Well, if it's what I think it is . . . it was originally just a tree stump, of course . . .'' He ran his hand over the stone surface, looked round the edge for something. ''But it was petrified, long ago. Look though; you can still see the rings in the wood.''

He leaned closer, looking at the gray stone surface by the fading afternoon light. The growth rings of the long dead tree were indeed visible. He leaned forward, taking off one of the suit gloves, and with his fingers stroked the surface of the stone. Some differential weathering of the wood-become-rock had made the rings tangible; his fingers felt the tiny ridges run beneath their surface like the fingerprint of some mighty stone god.

"So many years," he breathed, putting his hand back to the very sapling center of the stump, and running his hand out again. Beychae said nothing.

Every year a complete ring, signature of bad year and good by the spacing, and every ring complete, sealed, hermetic. Every year like part of a sentence, every ring a shackle, chained and chaining to the past; every ring a wall, a prison. A sentence locked in the wood, now locked in stone, frozen twice, sentenced twice, once for an imaginable time, then for an unimaginable time. His finger ran over the ring walls, dry paper over ridged rock.

"This is just the cover," Beychae said from the other side. He was squatting down, looking for something on the side of the great stone stump. "There ought to be . . . ah. Here we are. Don't expect we'll be able to actually lift it, of course . . ."

"Cover?" he said, putting the glove back on and walking round to where Beychae was. "Cover for what?"

"A sort of puzzle the Imperial Astronomers played when the viewing was patchy," Beychae said. "There; see that handhold?"

"Just a second," he said. "Want to stand back a little?"

Beychae stood back. "It's supposed to take four strong men, Zakalwe."

"This suit's more powerful than that, though balancing might be a little . . ." He found two handholds on the stone. "Suit command; strength normal max."

"You have to talk to the suit?" Beychae asked.

"Yeah," he said. He flexed, lifting one edge of the stone cover up; a tiny explosion of dust under the sole of one of the suit's boots announced a trapped pebble giving up the struggle. "This one you do; they have ones you just have to think about something, but . . ." he pulled on one edge of the cover, sticking one leg out to shift his center of gravity

as he did so. ". . . but I just never liked the idea of that."
He held the whole stone top of the petrified stump above his
head, then walked awkwardly, to the noise of crunching, pop-
ping gravel under his feet, to another stone table; he lowered,
shifted the stone cover sidways until it rested on the table,
and returned; he made the mistake of clapping his hands together, and produced what sounded like a gunshot. "Oops,"
he grinned. "Suit command; strength off."

Revealed by the removal of the stone cap was a shallow
cone. It seemed to have been carved from the petrified stump
itself. Looking closer, he could see that it was ridged, tree
ring by tree ring.

"Quite clever," he said, mildly disappointed.

"You're not looking at it properly, Cheradenine," Beychae told him. "Look closer."

He looked closer.

"I don't suppose you have anything very small and spherical, do you?" Beychae said, "Like a . . . ball bearing."

"A ball bearing?" he said, a pained expression on his
face.

"You don't have such things?"

"I think you'll find in most societies ball bearings don't
last much beyond room-temperature superconductivity, let
alone field technology. Unless you're into industrial archae-
ology and trying to keep some ancient machine running. No,
I don't have any ball . . ." he peered closer at the center of
the shallow rock cone. "Notches."

"Exactly." Beychae smiled.

He stood back, looking at the ridged cone as a whole.
"It's a maze!"

Maze. There had been a maze in the garden. They out-
grew it, became too familiar with it, eventually only used it
when other children they didn't like came for the day to the
great house; they could lose them in the maze for a few hours.

"Yes," Beychae nodded. "They would start out with
small colored beads or pebbles, and try to work their way to
the rim." He looked closer. "They say there might have been
a way to turn it into a game, by painting lines that divided
each ring into segments; little wooden bridges and blocking
pieces like walls could be used to facilitate one's own progress or prevent that of one's rivals." Beychae squinted closer
in the fading light. "Hmm. Paint must have faded."

He looked down at the hundreds of tiny ridges on the surface of the shallow cone—like a model of a huge volcano, he thought—and smiled. He sighed, looked at the screen set into the wrist of the suit, tried the emergency signal button again. No reply.

"Trying to contact the Culture?"

"Mmm," he said, gazing again at the petrified maze.

"What will happen to you if Governance find us?" Beychae asked.

"Oh," he shrugged, walking back to the balustrade they had stood at earlier. "Probably not much. Not very likely they'll just blow my brains out; they'll want to question me. Should give the Culture plenty of time to get me out; either negotiated or just snapped away. Don't worry about me." He smiled at Beychae. "Tell them I took you by force. I'll say I stunned you and stuffed you into the capsule. So don't worry; they'll probably let you go straight back to your studies."

"Well," Beychae said, rejoining the other man at the balustrade. "My studies were a delicate construction, Zakalwe; they maintained my carefully developed disinterest. They may not be so easy to resume, after your . . . exuberantly violent interruption."

"Ah." He tried not to smile. He looked down at the trees, then at the suit gloves, as though checking all the fingers were there. "Yeah. Look, Tsoldrin . . . I'm sorry . . . I mean about your friend, Ms. Shiol."

"As am I," Beychae said quietly. He smiled uncertainly. "I felt happy, Cheradenine. I hadn't felt like that for . . . well, long enough." They stood watching the sun sink behind the clouds. "You are certain she was one of theirs? I mean, absolutely?"

"Beyond any reasonable doubt, Tsoldrin." He thought he saw tears in the old man's eyes. He looked away. "Like I said; I'm sorry."

"I hope," Beychae said, "that is not the only way the old can be made happy . . . can be happy. Through deceit."

"Maybe it wasn't all deceit," he said. "And anyway, being old isn't what it used to be; I'm old," he reminded Beychae, who nodded, took out a handkerchief and sniffed.

"Of course; so you are. I forgot. Strange, isn't it? Whenever we see people after a long time we are always surprised how they've grown or aged. But when I see you, well, you haven't changed a bit, and instead I feel very old—unfairly, unjustifiably old—beside you, Cheradenine.''

"Actually I have changed, Tsoldrin." He grinned. "But no, I haven't got any older." He looked Beychae in the eye. "They'd give you this, too, if you asked them. The Culture would let you grow younger, then stabilize your age, or let you grow old again, but very slowly."

"Bribery, Zakalwe?" Beychae said, smiling.

"Hey, it was just a thought. And it'd be a payment, not a bribe. And they wouldn't force it on you. But it's academic, anyway." He paused, nodding to the sky. "Completely academic now. Here comes a plane."

Tsoldrin looked out to the red clouds of sunset. He couldn't see any aircraft.

"A Culture one?" Beychae asked cautiously.

He smiled. "In the circumstances, Tsoldrin, if you can see it, it isn't a Culture one." He turned and walked quickly, picking up the suit helmet and putting it on. Suddenly the dark figure became inhuman, behind the armored, sensor-studded faceplate of the suit. He took a large pistol from the suit holster. "Tsoldrin," his voice came booming from speakers set in the suit chest as he checked the settings on the gun. "If I were you I'd get back to the capsule, or just plain run away and hide." The figure turned to face Beychae, the helmet like the head of some gigantic, fearsome insect. "I'm fixing to give these assholes a fight, just for the sheer hell of it, and it might be best for you if you weren't nearby."

IV

The ship was over eighty kilometers long and it was called
the *Size Isn't Everything*. The last thing he'd been on for
any length of time had actually been bigger, but then that had
been a tabular iceberg big enough to hide two armies on, and
it didn't beat the General Systems Vehicle by much.

"How do these things hold *together*?" He stood on a
balcony, looking out over a sort of miniature valley composed
of accommodation units; each stepped terrace was smothered
in foliage, the space was crisscrossed by walkways and slender bridges, and a small stream ran through the bottom of the
V. People sat at tables in little courtyards, lounged on the
grass by the stream side or among the cushions and couches
of cafés and bars on the terraces. Hanging above the center
of the valley, beneath a ceiling of glowing blue, a travel-tube
snaked away into the distance on either side, following the
wavy line of the valley. Under the tube, a line of fake sunlight
burned, like some enormous strip light.

"Hmm?" Diziet Sma said, arriving at his elbow with two
drinks; she handed one to him.

"They're too big," he said. He turned to face the woman.
He'd seen the things they called *bays*, where they built smaller
spaceships (smaller in this case meant over three kilometers

long); vast unsupported hangars with thin walls. He'd been near the immense engines, which as far as he could gather were solid, and inaccessible (how?), and obviously extremely massive; he'd felt oddly threatened on discovering that there was no control room, no bridge, no flight deck anywhere in the vast vessel, just three Minds—fancy computers, apparently—controlling everything (what!?).

And now he was finding out where the people lived, but it was all too big, too much, too flimsy somehow, especially if the ship was supposed to accelerate as smartly as Sma claimed. He shook his head. "I don't understand; how does it hold together?"

Sma smiled. "Just think; fields, Cheradenine. It's all done with force fields." She put one hand out to his troubled face, patted one cheek. "Don't look so confused. And don't try to understand it all too quickly. Let it soak in. Just wander around; lose yourself in it for a few days. Come back whenever."

Later, he had wandered off. The huge ship was an enchanted ocean in which you could never drown, and he threw himself into it to try to understand if not it, then the people who had built it.

He walked for days, stopping at bars and restaurants whenever he felt thirsty, hungry or tired; mostly they were automatic and he was served by little floating trays, though a few were staffed by real people. They seemed less like servants and more like customers who'd taken a notion to help out for a while.

"Of course I don't have to do this," one middle-aged man said, carefully cleaning the table with a damp cloth. He put the cloth in a little pouch, sat down beside him. "But look; this table's clean."

He agreed that the table was clean.

"Usually," the man said, "I work on alien—no offense—alien religions; Directional Emphasis In Religious Observance; that's my specialty . . . like when temples or graves or prayers always have to face in a certain direction; that sort of thing? Well, I catalog, evaluate, compare; I come up with theories and argue with colleagues, here and elsewhere. But . . . the job's never finished; always new examples, and even

the old ones get reevaluated, and new people come along
with new ideas about what you thought was settled . . . but,"
he slapped the table, "when you clean a table you clean a
table. You feel you've done something. It's an achievement."

"But in the end, it's still just cleaning a table."

"And therefore does not really signify on the cosmic scale
of events?" the man suggested.

He smiled in response to the man's grin. "Well, yes."

"But then, what *does* signify? My other work? Is that
really important, either? I could try composing wonderful
musical works, or day-long entertainment epics, but what
would that do? Give people pleasure? My wiping this table
gives me pleasure. And people come to a clean table, which
gives *them* pleasure. And anyway," the man laughed, "people die; stars die; universes die. What is any achievement,
however great it was, once time itself is dead? Of course, if
all I did was wipe tables, then of course it would seem a
mean and despicable waste of my huge intellectual potential.
But because I choose to do it, it gives me pleasure. And,"
the man said with a smile, "it's a good way of meeting people. So; where are you from, anyway?"

He talked to people all the time; in bars and cafés, mostly.
The GSV's accommodation seemed to be divided into various
different types of layout; valleys (or ziggurats, if you wanted
to look at them like that) seemed to be the most common,
though there were different configurations.

He ate when he was hungry and drank when he was
thirsty, every time trying a different dish or drink from the
stunningly complicated menus, and when he wanted to
sleep—as the whole vessel gradually cycled into a red-tinged
dusk, the ceiling light-bars dimming—he just asked a drone,
and was directed to the nearest unoccupied room. The rooms
were all roughly the same size, and yet all slightly different;
some were very plain, some were highly decorated. The ba-
sics were always there; bed—sometimes a real, physical bed,
sometimes one of their weird field-beds—somewhere to wash
and defecate, cupboards, places for personal effects, a fake
window, a holo screen of some sort, and a linkup to the rest
of the communications net, both aboard and off-ship. The
first night away, he linked into one of their direct-link sensory

entertainments, lying on the bed with some sort of device activated under the pillow.

He did not actually sleep that night; instead he was a bold pirate prince who'd renounced his nobility to lead a brave crew against the slaver ships of a terrible empire among the spice and treasure isles; their quick little ships darted among the lumbering galleons, picking away the rigging with chain shot. They came ashore on moonless nights, attacking the great prison castles, releasing joyous captives; he personally fought the wicked governor's chief torturer, sword against sword; the man finally fell from a high tower. An alliance with a beautiful lady pirate begot a more personal liaison, and a daring rescue from a mountain monastery when she was captured . . .

He pulled away from it, after what had been weeks of compressed time. He knew (somewhere at the back of his mind) even as it happened that none of it was real, but that seemed like the least important property of the adventure. When he came out of it—surprised to discover that he had not actually ejaculated during some of the profoundly convincing erotic episodes—he discovered that only a night had passed, and it was morning, and he had, somehow, shared the strange story with others; it had been a game, apparently. People had left messages for him to get in touch, they had enjoyed playing the game with him so much. He felt oddly ashamed, and did not reply.

The rooms he slept in always contained places to sit; field extensions, moldable wall units, real couches, and—sometimes—ordinary chairs. Whenever the rooms held chairs, he moved them outside, into the corridor or onto the terrace.

It was all he could do to keep the memories at bay.

"Na," the woman said in the mainbay. "It doesn't really work that way." They stood on a half-constructed starship, on what would eventually be the middle of the engines, watching a huge field-unit swing through the air, out of the engineering space behind the bay proper and up toward the skeletal body of the General Contact Unit. Little lifter tugs maneuvered the field unit down toward them.

"You mean it makes no difference?"

"Not much," the woman said. She pressed on a little studded lanyard she held in one hand, spoke as though to her shoulder. "I'll take it." The field-unit put them in shadow as it hovered above them. Just another solid slab, as far as he could see. It was red; a different color from the black slickness of the starboard Main Engine Block Lower under their feet. She manipulated the lanyard, guiding the huge red block down; two other people standing twenty meters away watched the far end of the unit.

"The trouble is," the woman said, watching the vast red buildingbrick come slowly down, "that even when people do get sick and die young, they're always surprised when they get sick. How many healthy people do you think actually say to themselves, 'Hey, I'm healthy today!' unless they've just had a serious illness?" She shrugged, pressed the lanyard again as the field-unit lowered to a couple of centimeters off the engine surface. "Stop," she said quietly. "Inertia down five. Check." A line of light flashed on the surface of the engine block. She put one hand on the block, and pressed it again. It moved. "Down dead slow," she said. She pressed the block into place. "Sorzh; all right?" she asked. He didn't hear the reply, but the woman obviously did.

"Okay; positioned; all clear." She looked up as the lifter tugs sailed back toward the engineering space, then back at him. "All that's happened is that reality has caught up with the way people always did behave anyway. So, no, you don't feel any wonderful release from debilitating illnesses." She scratched one ear. "Except maybe when you think about it." She grinned. "I guess in school, when you're seeing how people used to live . . . how aliens still do live . . . then it hits home, and I suppose you never really lose that entirely, but you don't spend much time thinking about it."

They walked across the black expanse of thoroughly featureless material. ("Ah," the woman had said, when he'd mentioned this, "you take a look at it under a microscope; it's beautiful! What did you expect, anyway? Cranks? Gears? Tanks full of chemicals?")

"Can't machines build these faster?" he asked the woman, looking around the starship shell.

"Why, of course!" she laughed.

"Then why do you do it?"

"It's fun. You see one of these big mothers sail out those doors for the first time, heading for deep space, three hundred people on board, everything working, the Mind quite happy, and you think; I helped build that. The fact a machine could have done it faster doesn't alter the fact that it was you who actually did it.''

"Hmm," he said.

(Learn woodwork; metalwork; they will not make you a carpenter or a blacksmith any more than mastering writing will make you a clerk.)

"Well, you may 'hmm' as you wish," the woman said, approaching a translucent hologram of the half-completed ship, where a few other construction workers were standing, pointing inside the model and talking. "But have you ever been gliding, or swum underwater?"

"Yes," he agreed.

The woman shrugged. "Yet birds fly better than we do, and fish swim better. Do we stop gliding or swimming because of this?"

He smiled. "I suppose not."

"You suppose correctly," the woman said. "And why?" she looked at him, grinning. "Because it's fun." She looked at the holo model of the ship to one side. One of the other workers called to her, pointing at something in the model. She looked at him. "Excuse me, will you?"

He nodded, as he backed off. "Build well."

"Thank you. I trust we shall."

"Oh," he asked. "What's this ship to be called?"

"Its Mind wishes it to be called the *Sweet and Full of Grace*," the woman laughed. Then she was deep in discussion with the others.

He watched their many sports; tried a few. Most of them he just didn't understand. He swam quite a lot; they seemed to like pools and water complexes. Mostly they swam naked, which he found a little embarrassing. Later he discovered there were whole sections—villages? areas? districts? he wasn't sure how to think of them—where people never wore clothes, just body ornaments. He was surprised how quickly he got used to this behavior, but never fully joined in.

It took him a while to realize that all the drones he saw—even more various in their design than humans were in their physiology—didn't all belong to the ship. Hardly any did, in fact; they had their own artificial brains (he still tended to think of them as computers). They seemed to have their own personalities, too, though he remained skeptical.

"Let me put this thought experiment to you," the old drone said, as they played a card game which it had assured him was mostly luck. They sat—well, the drone floated—under an arcade of delicately pink stone, by the side of a small pool; the shouts of people playing a complicated ball game on the far side of the pool filtered through bushes and small trees to them.

"Forget," said the drone, "about how machine brains are actually put together; think about making a machine brain—an electronic computer—in the image of a human one. One might start with a few cells, as the human embryo does; these multiply, gradually establish connections. So one would continually add new components and make the relevant, even—if one was to follow the exact development of one single human through the various states—the *identical* connections.

"One would, of course, have to limit the speed of the messages transmitted down those connections to a tiny fraction of their normal electronic speed, but that would not be difficult, nor would having these neuronlike components act like their biological equivalents internally, firing their own messages according to the types of signal they received; all this could be done comparatively simply. By building up in this gradual way, you could mimic exactly the development of a human brain, *and* you could mimic its output; just as an embryo can experience sound and touch and even light inside the womb, so could you send similar signals to your developing electronic equivalent; you could impersonate the experience of birth, and use any degree of sensory stimulation to fool this device into thinking it was feeling, touching, tasting, smelling, hearing and seeing everything your real human was (or, of course, you might choose not actually to fool it, but always give it just as much genuine sensory input, and of the same quality, as the human personality was experiencing at any given point).

"Now; my question to you is this; where is the difference? The brain of each being works in exactly the same way as the other; they will respond to stimuli with a greater correspondence than one finds even between monozygotic twins;

but how can one still choose to call one a conscious entity, and the other merely a machine?

"Your brain is made up of matter, Mr. Zakalwe, organized into information-handling, processing and storage units by your genetic inheritance and by the biochemistry of first your mother's body and later your own, not to mention your experiences since some short time before your birth until now.

"An electronic computer is also made up of matter, but organized differently; what is there so magical about the workings of the huge, slow cells of the animal brain that they can claim themselves to be conscious, but would deny a quicker, more finely grained device of equivalent power—or even a machine hobbled so that it worked with precisely the same ponderousness—a similar distinction?

"Hmm?" the machine said, its aura field flashing the pink he was beginning to identify as drone amusement. "Unless, of course, you wish to invoke superstition? Do you believe in gods?"

He smiled. "I have never had that inclination," he said.

"Well then," the drone said. "What would you say? Is the machine in the human image conscious, sentient, or not?"

He studied his cards. "I'm thinking," he said, and laughed.

Sometimes he saw other aliens (obviously aliens, that is; he was sure that a few of the humans he saw each day were not Culture people, though without stopping to ask them it was impossible to tell; somebody dressed as a savage, or in some obviously non-Culture garb, was quite possibly just dressing up like that for a laugh, or going to a party . . . but there were some very obviously different species around as well).

"Yes, young man?" the alien said. It had eight limbs, a fairly distinct head with two quite small eyes, curiously flower-like mouth parts, and a large, almost spherical, lightly haired body, colored red and purple. Its own voice was composed of clicks from its mouth and almost subsonic vibrations from its body; a small amulet did the translating.

He asked if he could sit with the alien; it directed him to the seat across the table from it in the café where he had overheard it talking briefly to a passing human about Special Circumstances.

". . . It is in layers," the alien replied to his question.
"A tiny core of Special Circumstances, a shell of Contact,
and a vast chaotic ecosphere of everything else. Bit like a
. . . you come from a planet?"

He nodded. The creature glanced at its amulet for a translation of the gesture the man had used—it was not what the
Culture called nodding—then said, "Well, it is like a planet,
only the core is tiny; very tiny. And the ecosphere is more
disparate and less distinct than the wrapping of atmosphere
round a globe; a red giant star might even be a better comparison. But in the end, you will never know them, because
you will be like me, in Special Circumstances, and only ever
know them as the great, irresistible force behind you; people
like you and I are the edge; you will in time come to feel
like a tooth on the biggest saw in the galaxy, sir." The alien's
eyes closed; it waggled all its limbs very energetically, and
its mouth parts crackled. "Ha ha ha!" the amulet said,
primly.

"How did you know I was actually involved with Special
Circumstances?" he asked, sitting back.

"Ah! How much my vanity wishes me to claim I simply
guessed, so clever I am . . . but I heard there was a new
recruit coming aboard," the alien told him. "And that it was
a fairly human-basic male. You . . . smell right, if I may use
that turn of phrase. And you . . . have just been asking all
the right questions."

"And you're in SC too?"

"For ten standard years now."

"Think I should do it? Work for them?"

"Oh yes; I imagine it's better than what you left, no?"

He shrugged, remembering the blizzard and the ice. "I
suppose."

"You enjoy . . . fighting, yes?"

"Well . . . sometimes," he admitted. "I'm good at it, so
they say. Not that I'm necessarily convinced of that myself."

"No one wins all the time, sir," the creature said. "Not
through skill, anyway, and the Culture does not believe in
luck, or at the very least does not believe it is transferrable.
They must like your attitude, that's all. Hee hee."

The alien laughed quietly.

"To be good at soldiering," it said, "is a great curse, I
think sometimes. Working for these people at least relieves

one of some of the responsibility. I have never found cause to complain." The alien scratched its body, looked down, picked something from the hairs around where he would have guessed its belly might be, and ate it. "Of course, you must not expect to be told the truth all the time. You can insist that they do, always, and they will do so, but they may not be able to use you as often as they might like to; sometimes they need you not to know you are fighting on the wrong side. My advice would be to just do as they ask; much more exciting."

"Are you in it for the excitement?"

"Partly, and partly because of family honor; SC did something for my people once, and we could not let them steal our honor by accepting nothing in return. I work until that debt is paid off."

"How long's that?"

"Oh, for life," the creature said, sitting back in a gesture he felt reasonably justified in translating as surprise. "Until I die, of course. But who cares? As I say; it's fun. Here." It banged its drink bowl on the table to attract a passing tray. "Let's have another drink; see who gets drunk first."

"You have more legs." He grinned. "I think I might fall over more easily."

"Ah, but the more the legs, the bigger the tangle."

"Fair enough." He waited for a fresh glass.

To one side of them was a small terrace and the bar, to the other a gulf of airy space. The ship, the GSV, went on beyond its apparent boundaries. Its hull was pierced multitudinously by terraces, balconies, walkways, open windows, and open bay doors. Surrounding the vessel proper was an immense ellipsoid bubble of air, held inside dozens of different fields, which together made up the vehicle's real—though insubstantial—hull.

He took up the recharged glass when it arrived, and watched a puttering, piston-engined, paper-winged hang glider zip past the terrace; he waved at the pilot, then shook his head.

"To the Culture," he said, raising his glass to the alien. It matched his gesture. "To its total lack of respect for all things majestic."

"Agreed," the alien said, and together they drank.

•   •   •

The alien was called Chori, he found out later. It was only due to a chance remark that he discovered Chori was a female, which at the time seemed hilariously funny.

He woke up the next morning lying soaked as well as soused half underneath a small waterfall in one of the acc section valleys; Chori was suspended from a nearby railing by all eight leg-hooks, making a sporadic clattering noise that he decided was snoring.

The first night he spent with a woman, he thought she was dying; he thought he'd killed her. She seemed to climax at almost the same time as he did, but then—apparently—had a seizure; screaming, clutching at him. He had an awful, sickening idea that despite the seeming similarity of their physiology, his race and the mongrel species that was the Culture were somehow quite different, and for a few ghastly moments entertained the idea that his seed was like acid inside her. It felt like she was trying to break his back with her arms and legs. He tried to pull himself away from her, calling her name, trying to see what was wrong, what he had done, what he could do.

"What's wrong?" she gasped.

"What? With me; nothing! What's wrong with *you*?"

She made a sort of shrugging motion, looked puzzled. "I came; that's all; what's the . . . Oh." She put one hand to her mouth, eyes wide. "I forgot. I'm sorry. You're not . . . Oh dear." She giggled. "How embarrassing."

"What?"

"Well, we just . . . you know; it takes . . . it goes on . . . longer, you know?"

He didn't think he had quite believed what he had heard about the Culture's altered physiology until then. He hadn't accepted that they had changed themselves so. He had not believed that they really had chosen to extend such moments of pleasure, let alone breed into themselves all the multifarious drug glands that could enhance almost any experience (not least sex).

Yet—in a way—it made sense, he told himself. Their machines could do everything else much better than they could; no sense in breeding super-humans for strength or intelligence, when their drones and Minds were so much more matter- and energy-efficient at both. But pleasure . . . well, that was a different matter.

What else was the human form good for?

He supposed such single-mindedness was admirable, in a way.

He took the woman in his arms again. "Never mind," he said. "Quality not quantity. Let's try that again, shall we?"

She laughed and took his face in her hands. "Dedication; that's a good quality in a man."

(The cry in the summerhouse that had attracted; "Hello, old chap." Tanned hands on the pale hips . . .)

He was away five nights, just wandering. As far as he could tell, he never crossed his own trail, and never visited the same section twice. He ended up with different women on three of those nights, and politely turned down one young man.

"Any more at your ease, Cheradenine?" Sma asked him, stroking up the pool ahead of him. She turned on her back to look at him. He swam after her.

"Well, I have stopped offering to pay for things in bars."

"That's a start."

"It was a very easy habit to break."

"Par for the course. That all?"

"Well . . . also, your women are very friendly."

"So are the men," Sma arched one eyebrow.

"The life here seems . . . idyllic."

"Well, you have to like crowds, perhaps."

He looked round the almost deserted pool complex. "That's relative, I suspect."

(And thought: the garden; the garden. They have made their life in its image!)

"Why," Sma smiled. "Are you tempted to stay?"

"Not even slightly." He laughed. "I'd go crazy here, or slip forever into one of your shared dream-games. I need . . . more."

"But will you take it from us?" Sma said, stopping, treading water. "Do you want to work with us?"

"Everybody seems to think I should; they believe you're fighting the good fight. It's just that . . . I get suspicious when everybody agrees about something."

Sma laughed. "How much would it matter if we weren't fighting the good fight, Cheradenine? If all we were offering was pay and excitement?"

"I don't know," he admitted. "It would make it even harder. I'd just like . . . I'd like to believe, to finally *know*, to finally be able to prove that I was . . ." He shrugged, grinned. ". . . doing good."

Sma sighed. In the water, this meant that she bobbed up then sank down a little. "Who knows, Zakalwe? We don't know that; we think we're right; we even think we can prove it, but we can never be sure; there are always arguments against us. There *is* no certainty; least of all in Special Circumstances, where the rules are different."

"I thought the rules were meant to be the same for everybody."

"They are. But in Special Circumstances we deal in the moral equivalent of black holes, where the normal laws—the rules of right and wrong that people imagine apply everywhere else in the universe—break down; beyond those metaphysical event-horizons, there exist . . . special circumstances." She smiled. "That's us. That's our territory; our domain."

"To some people," he said, "that might sound like just a good excuse for bad behavior."

Sma shrugged. "And perhaps they would be right. Maybe that is all it is." She shook her head, pulled one hand through her long wet hair. "But if nothing else, at least we need an excuse; think how many people need none at all."

She swam off.

He watched her stroke powerfully away through the water for a moment. One of his hands went, without him really realizing it, to a small puckered scar on his chest, just over where his heart was, and rubbed it, while he frowned, staring at the glittering, unsteady surface of the water.

Then he swam after the woman.

He spent a couple of years on the *Size Isn't Everything*, and on a few of the planets, rocks, habitats and orbitals it stopped at. He was being trained, and learning to use some of the new abilities he had let them give him. When he eventually left the craft, to go on his first tour of duty for the Culture—a series of missions which culminated in him taking the Chosen to the Perfumed Palace on the cliff—it was on a ship just starting its second tour of duty; the General Contact Unit *Sweet and Full of Grace*.

He never saw Chori again, and heard that she'd been killed on active service some fifteen years later. He was told this news while they were regrowing his body on the GSV *Congenital Optimist*, after he'd been beheaded on—and then rescued from—a planet called Fohls.

11

H e crouched behind the parapet, at the far edge of the old observatory from the single approaching plane. Behind him, down a steep slope, were bushes and trees and a collection of roofless, overgrown buildings. He watched the aircraft come closer, checked for more coming from other directions, but couldn't find any. Inside the suit, watching the transmitted view, he frowned as the aircraft came closer, slowing all the time, its obese arrowhead shape silhouetted against the sunset as it approached.

He watched it drop slowly toward the observatory platform; a ramp hinged from the craft's belly; three legs flexed out. He took some effector readings from the machine, then shook his head, ducked and ran back down the slope.

Tsoldrin was sitting in one of the ruined buildings. He looked surprised when the suited figure entered through the creeper-choked doorway.

"Yes, Cheradenine?"

"It's a civilian craft," he said, pushing the faceplate up. He was grinning. "I don't think it's looking for us after all. Might still provide an escape route, though." He shrugged. "Worth a try." He gestured back up the slope. "You coming along?"

Tsoldrin Beychae looked through the dusk at the mat-black figure in the doorway. He had been sitting here wondering what he ought to do, and had not yet come up with any answers. Part of him just wanted to get back to the peace and quiet and certainty of the university library, where he could live happily, without fuss, ignore the world, and immerse himself in the old books, trying to understand ancient ideas and histories, hoping to make sense of them, one day, and perhaps explain his own ideas, try to point out the lessons of these elder histories, perhaps make people think again about their own times and ideologies. For a time—for a long time, there—it had seemed entirely and definitely the most worthwhile and productive thing he could do . . . but he was not sure of that any longer.

Perhaps, he thought, there were more important things to be done which he could have a hand in. Perhaps he ought to go with Zakalwe, as the man—and the Culture—wanted.

Could he just relapse back into his studies, after this?

Zakalwe coming back from the past, as rash and brash as ever; Ubrel—could she really have been?—just acting a part, making him feel very old and foolish, now, but angry as well; and the whole Cluster drifting rudderless toward the rocks, all over again.

Did he have any right not to try and do something, even if the Culture was wrong about his stature in the civilization? He didn't know. He could see that Zakalwe had tried to appeal to his vanity, but what if even half of what he said was true? Was it right to sit back and just let things happen, however much it might be the easiest, least stressful course? If there was a war, and he knew he'd done nothing, how would he feel afterward?

Damn you, Zakalwe, he thought. He stood up. "I'm still thinking," he said. "But let's see how far you can get."

"Good man." The suited figure's voice betrayed no obvious trace of emotion.

". . . *Extremely* sorry for the delay, gentlepeople; it really wasn't within our control; some sort of traffic control panic, but do let me apologize again on behalf of Heritage Tours. Well; here we are, a bit later than we expected (but isn't that a pretty sunset?); the *very* famous Srometren Observatory; at

least four and a half thousand years of history have been
played out beneath your feet here, gentlepeople. I'm going to
have to fairly rattle through it to tell it all to you in the time
we have here, so listen close . . .''

The aircraft hovered, AG field buzzing, just above the
western edge of the observatory platform. Its legs hung, dangling in midair, apparently extended merely as a precaution.
About forty people had disembarked from it down the belly
ramp, and now stood around one of the stone instrument
plinths while an eager young tour guide talked to them.

He watched through the stone balustrade, scanning the
group with the suit's built-in effector and watching the results
on the visor screen head up. Thirty plus of the people were
carrying what were in effect terminals; links to the planet's
communications net. The suit's computer covertly interro-
gated the terminals through the effector. Two of the terminals
were switched on; one receiving a sports broadcast, another
receiving music. The rest were on stand-by.

"Suit," he whispered (not that even Tsoldrin, right beside
him, could have heard him, let alone the people in the tourist
group). "I want to disable those terminals, quietly; to stop
them from transmitting."

"Two receiving terminals are transmitting location code,"
the suit said.

"Can I disable their transmit function without altering
their present location code function, or their present reception?"

"Yes."

"Right; the priority being preventing any further new signals, disable all the terminals."

"Disabling all thirty-four non-Culture personal commnet
terminals within range; confirm."

"Confirmed, dammit; do it . . ."

"Order carried out."

He watched the head up alter as the internal power states
of the terminals sank back to near zero. The tour guide was
leading the people across the stone plateau of the old observatory, toward where he and Beychae were, and away from
the hovering aircraft.

He shoved the suit faceplate up, looked round at the other
man. "Okay; let's go. Quietly."

He went first, through the undergrowth, between the

crowding trees; it was quite dark under the half-fallen foliage, and Beychae stumbled a couple of times, but they made relatively little noise as they trod the carpet of dead leaves round two sides of the observatory platform.

When they were under the aircraft, he scanned it with the suit effector.

"You beautiful little machine," he breathed, watching the results come up. The aircraft was automatic, and very stupid. A bird probably had a more complicated brain. "Suit; patch into the aircraft; assume control without letting anybody else know."

"Assuming covert control-jurisdiction of single aircraft within range; confirm."

"Confirmed. And stop asking me to confirm everything."

"Control-jurisdiction assumed. Lapsing confirmatory instruction protocols; confirm."

"Good grief. Confirmed!"

"Confirm protocol lapsed."

He considered just floating up, holding Beychae, into the craft, but even though the aircraft's own AG would probably mask the signal his suit gave off, it might not. He glanced up the steep slope, then turned to Beychae and whispered. "Give me your hand; we're going up." The old man did as he asked.

They went steadily up the slope, the suit kicking footholds in the earth. They stopped at the balustrade. The aircraft blocked out the evening sky above them, yellow light spilling from the belly entrance above the ramp, faintly illuminating the nearer stone instruments.

He checked on the tour group while Beychae got his breath back. The tourists were at the far side of the observatory; the guide was shining a flashlight at some ancient piece of stonework. He stood up. "Let's go," he told Beychae, who straightened. They stepped over the balustrade, walked to the ramp and up into the aircraft. He followed Beychae; he watched the rear view on the helmet screen, but couldn't tell whether anybody in the tour group had noticed them or not.

"Suit; close the ramp," he told the suit, as he and Beychae entered the single large space of the craft's interior. It was ornately luxurious, its walls slung with hangings and its deeply carpeted floor dotted with large chairs and couches; there was an autobar at one end, while the opposite wall was a single huge screen, presently displaying the last of the sunset.

The ramp chimed and hissed as it came up. "Suit; retract legs," he said, hinging the suit faceplate back. Happily, the suit was smart enough to realize he meant the aircraft's legs, not its own. It had occurred to him that somebody might just be able to leap onto one of the craft's legs from the observatory balustrade. "Suit; adjust aircraft altitude; up ten meters."

The light buzzing noise around them changed, then settled back to what it had been before. He watched Beychae take off his heavy jacket, then looked round the interior of the craft; the effector said there was nobody else aboard, but he wanted to make sure. "Let's see where this thing was headed next," he said, as Beychae sat down on a long couch, sighing and stretching. "Suit; the aircraft's next destination?"

"Gipline Space Terminal," the clipped voice told him.

"That sounds perfect. Take us there, suit, and make it look as legal and normal as possible."

"Under way," the suit said. "ETA forty minutes."

The craft's background noise altered, climbing in pitch; the floor moved just a little. The screen on the far side of the large cabin showed them moving out across the wooded hills, rising into the air.

He took a walk round the craft, confirming there was nobody else aboard, then sat by Beychae, who he thought looked very tired. It had been a long day, he supposed.

"You all right?"

"I'm glad to be sitting down, I'll say that." Beychae kicked off his boots.

"Let me get you a drink, Tsoldrin," he said, taking off the helmet and heading for the bar. "Suit," he said, suddenly struck by an idea. "You know one of the Culture's down-link numbers in Solotol."

"Yes."

"Connect with one via the aircraft."

He bent down, looking at the autobar. "And how does this work?"

"The autobar is voice acti—"

"Zakalwe!" Sma's voice cut across that of the suit, making him start. He straightened. "Where are . . . ?" the wom-

an's voice said, then paused. "Oh; you've got yourself an
aircraft, have you?"

"Yes," he said. He looked across to where Beychae was
watching him. "On our way to Gipline Port. So what happened? Where's that module? And Sma, I'm hurt; you haven't
called, you haven't written, sent flowers . . ."

"Is Beychae all right?" Sma said urgently.

"Tsoldrin's fine," he told her, smiling at the other man.
"Suit; get this autobar to fix us a couple of refreshing but
strong drinks."

"He's okay; good." The woman sighed. The autobar
made a clicking, gurgling noise. "We haven't called," Sma
said, "because if we had we'd have let them know where you
were; we lost the tight-link when the capsule got blasted.
Zakalwe, that was ridiculous; it was pure chaos after the capsule wasted the truck in the Flower Market and you downed
that fighter; you're lucky you made it as far as you did. Where
is the capsule, anyway?"

"Back at the observatory; Srometren," he said, looking
down as a hatch opened in the autobar. He took the tray with
the two drinks on it over to Beychae, sat down at his side.
"Sma; say hello to Tsoldrin Beychae," he said, handing the
other man his drink.

"Mr. Beychae?" Sma's voice said from the suit.

"Hello?" Beychae said.

"Pleased to talk to you Mr. Beychae. I do hope Mr. Zakalwe is treating you all right. Are you well?"

"Tired, but hale."

"I trust Mr. Zakalwe has found time to communicate to
you the seriousness of the political situation in the Cluster."

"He has," Beychae said. "I am . . . I am certainly considering doing what you ask, and for the moment have no
urge to return to Solotol."

"I see," Sma said. "I appreciate what you say. I'm sure
Mr. Zakalwe will do all he can to keep you safe and well
while you're deliberating, won't you, Cheradenine?"

"Of course, Diziet. Now; where's that module?"

"Stuck under the cloud tops of Soreraurth, where it was
before. Thanks to your nova-profile escapades down there,
everything's on maximum alert; we can't move anything without being seen, and if we're seen to be interfering, we might
start the war all by ourselves. Describe where that capsule is

again; we're going to have to passive-spot it from the micro-satellite and then blast it from up here, to remove the evidence. Shit, this is messy, Zakalwe.''

"Well, pardon me," he said. He drank again. "The capsule's under a large yellow-leafed deciduous tree between eighty and . . . one-thirty meters northeast of the observatory. Oh; and the plasma rifle's about . . . twenty to forty meters due west.''

"You lost it?" Sma sounded incredulous.

"Threw it away in a fit of pique," he admitted, yawning. "It got Effectorized.''

"Told you it belonged in a museum," another voice interrupted.

"Shut up, Skaffen-Amtiskaw," he said. "So, Sma, what now?''

"Gipline Space Terminal, I suppose," the woman replied. "We'll see if we can book you on something outgoing; for Impren, or nearby. At worst, you've got a civilian trip ahead of you of weeks at least; if we're lucky they'll stand down the alert and the module can sneak out and rendezvous. Either way though, the war may be a little closer, thanks to what happened in Solotol today. Just think about that, Zakalwe.'' The channel closed.

"She sounds unhappy with you, Cheradenine," Beychae said.

He shrugged. "No change there," he sighed.

"I'm really most terribly sorry, gentlepeople; this has never happened before; never. I really am sorry . . . I just can't understand it . . . I'll, um . . . I'll try . . .'' The young man hit buttons on his pocket terminal. "Hello? Hello! HELLO!'' He shook it, banged it with the heel of his hand. "This is just . . . just . . . this has never, never happened before; it really hasn't . . .'' He looked apologetically up at the people in the tour group, clustered round the single light. Most of the people were looking at him; a few were trying their own terminals with no more success than he, and a couple were watching the western sky as though the last red smudge there would give up the aircraft that had so mysteriously decided to leave of its own accord. "Hello? Hello? Anybody? Please reply.'' The young man sounded almost in tears. The very

last dreg of light left the sunset sky; moonglow lit up some
thinner patches of cloud. The flashlight flickered. "Anybody
at all; please reply! Oh, please!"

Skaffen-Amtiskaw got back in touch a few minutes later to
say that he and Beychae had cabins reserved on a clipper
called the *Osom Emananish*, heading for Breskial System,
just three light years from Impren; the hope was that the
module would get to them before that. It would probably have
to; their trail would almost certainly be picked up. "It might
be an idea for Mr. Beychae to alter his appearance," the
drone's smooth voice told them.

He looked up at the wall drapes. "I suppose we could try
and make some clothes out of stuff here," he said doubtfully.

"The aircraft baggage hold might prove a more fruitful
source of attire," the drone's voice purred, and told him how
to open the floor hatch.

He surfaced with two suitcases, wrenched them open.
"Clothes!" he said. He took some out; they looked sufficiently unisex.

"And you'll have to lose your suit and weaponry, too,"
the drone said.

"What?"

"You'll never get on board a ship with that stuff, Zakalwe, even with our help. You've to pack it all in something—one of those cases would be ideal—and leave it in the
port; we'll try and pick it up once the heat's off."

"But!"

Beychae himself suggested they shave his head, when they
were discussing how to disguise him. The last use the wonderfully sophisticated combat suit was put to was as a razor.
Then he took it off; they both changed into the rather loud
but thankfully loose-fitting clothes.

The craft landed; the Space Terminal was a wilderness of
concrete lined off like a game board by the lifts that took
craft down to and up from the handling facilities.

Tight beam established again, the earring terminal could
whisper to him, guide him and Beychae.

But he felt naked without the suit.

∙ ∙ ∙

They stepped from the aircraft into a hangar; pleasantly for-
gettable music tinkled. Nobody met them. They could hear a
distant alarm.

The earring terminal indicated which door to take. They
moved along a staff-only corridor, through two security doors
which swung open for them even before they got to them,
then—after a pause—came out into a huge crowded concourse
full of people, screens, kiosks and seats. Nobody noticed
them, because a moving walkway had just slammed to a stop,
toppling dozens of people on top of each other.

A security camera in the left luggage area swung up to
look at the ceiling for the minute it took them to deposit the
suitcase with the suit in it. The instant they'd gone, the camera resumed its slow sweeping.

More or less the same happened when they picked up
their tickets at the appropriate desk. Then, while they were
walking along another corridor, they saw a party of armed
security guards enter from the other end.

He just kept on walking. He sensed Beychae hesitate at
his side. He turned, smiled easily at the other man, and when
he turned back, the guards were stopped, the leading guard
holding one hand to his ear and looking at the floor; he nodded, turned and pointed to a side corridor; the guards set off
down it.

"We're not just being incredibly lucky, I take it?" Beychae muttered.

He shook his head. "Not unless you count it as incredibly
lucky that we've got a near military-standard electromagnetic
effector controlled by a hyper-fast starship Mind working this
entire port like an arcade game from a light-year or so off,
no."

They were passed through a VIP channel to the small shuttle
that would take them to the orbiting station. The final security
check was the only one the ship couldn't rig; a man with
practiced eyes and hands. He seemed happy they had nothing
dangerous on them. The earring jabbed his ear as they passed
down another corridor; more X-rays, and a strong magnetic
field, both manually controlled, double-checking.

The shuttle flight was relatively uneventful; in the station, they passed across one transit lounge—in something of a commotion, due to a man with a direct neural implant seemingly having a fit on the floor—straight into a final security check.

In the corridor between the lounge lock and the ship, he heard Sma's voice, tiny in his ear. "That's it, Zakalwe. Can't tight beam on the ship without being spotted. We'll only contact in a real emergency. Use the Solotol phone link if you want to talk, but remember it'll be monitored. Goodbye; good luck."

And then he and Beychae were through another air lock, and on the clipper *Osom Emananish*, which would take them into interstellar space.

He spent the hour or so before departure walking round the clipper, just checking it all out, so that he knew where everything was.

The speaker system, and most of the visible screens, announced their departure. The clipper drifted, then dawdled, then raced away from the station; it swung away past the sun and the gas-giant Soreraurth. Soreraurth was where the module was having to keep hidden, a hundred kilometers deep in the vast perpetual storm that was the mighty planet's atmosphere. An atmosphere that would be plundered, mined, stripped and altered by the Humanists, if they had their way. He watched the gas-giant fall astern, wondered who was really right and wrong, and felt an odd helplessness.

He was passing through the bustle of a small bar, on his way to check on Beychae, when he heard a voice behind him say, "Ah; sincere hellos, and things! Mr. Starabinde, isn't it?"

He turned slowly.

It was the small doctor from the scar party. The little man stood at the crowded bar, beckoning to him.

He walked over, squeezing between the chattering passengers.

"Doctor; good day."

The little man nodded, "Stapangarderslinaiterray; but call me Stap."

"With pleasure, and even relief." He smiled. "And please call me Sherad."

"Well! Small cluster, isn't it? May I buy you a drink?"

He flashed his toothy grin, which—caught in a small spotlight above the bar—glared quite startlingly.

"What an excellent idea."

They found a small table, wedged up against one bulk-head. The doctor wiped his nose, adjusted his immaculate suit.

"So, Sherad, what brings you along on this little jaunt?"

"Well, actually . . . Stap," he said quietly. "I'm traveling sort of . . . incognito, so I'd appreciate it if you didn't . . . broadcast my name, you know?"

"Absolutely!" Doctor Stap said, nodding fiercely. He glanced round conspiratorially, leaned closer. "My discretion is exemplary. Have had to 'travel quietly' . . ." his eyebrows waggled ". . . myself, on occasion. You just let me know if I can be of any help."

"You're very kind." He raised his glass.

They drank to a safe voyage.

"Are you going to the 'end of the line,' to Breskial?" Stap asked.

He nodded. "Yes; myself and a business associate."

Doctor Stap nodded, grinning. "Ah, a 'business associate.' Ah."

"No, doctor; not a 'business associate,' a business associate; a gentleman, and quite elderly, and in a different cabin . . . would that all three descriptions were their opposite, of course."

"Ha! Quite!" the doctor said.

"Another drink?"

"You don't think he knows anything?" Beychae asked.

"What's to know?" He shrugged. He glanced at the screen, on the door of Beychae's cramped cabin. "Nothing on the news?"

"Nothing," Beychae said. "They mentioned an all-ports security exercise, but nothing directly about you or me."

"Well, we probably aren't in any more danger because the doc's aboard than we were already."

"How much is that?"

"Too much. They're bound to work out what happened eventually; we'll never get to Breskial before they do."

"Then?"

"Then, unless I can think of something, the Culture either has to let us be taken back, or take this ship over, which is going to be tricky to explain, and bound to remove some of your credibility."

"*If* I decide to do as you ask, Cheradenine."

He looked at the other man, sitting alongside him on the narrow bed. "Yeah; if."

He prowled the ship. The clipper seemed cramped and crowded; he'd got too used to Culture vessels, he supposed. There were plans of the ship available on-screen, and he studied them, but they were really just for people to find their way about, and provided little useful information on how the ship might be taken over or disabled. Judging from watching the crew when they appeared, entry to crew-only areas was by voice and/or handprint match.

There was little flammable on board, nothing explosive, and most of the circuitry was optical rather than electronic. Doubtless the *Xenophobe* could make the clipper *Osom Emananish* dance and sing with the effector equivalent of one hand tied behind its back, from somewhere in the next stellar system, but without the combat suit or a weapon, he was going to have a tough job trying to do anything, if and when it came to it.

Meanwhile the clipper crawled through space; Beychae stayed in his cabin, catching up on the news via the screen, and sleeping.

"I seem to have swapped one subtle form of imprisonment for another, Cheradenine," he observed, the day after they left, as the other man brought him supper.

"Tsoldrin, don't go cabin crazy; if you want to go out, go out. It's a little safer this way, but . . . well, only a little."

"Well," Tsoldrin said, taking the tray and lifting the cover to inspect the contents. "For now it's easy enough to treat the news and current affairs casts as my research material, so I do not feel unduly confined." He set the cover aside. "But a couple of weeks might be asking rather too much, Cheradenine."

"Don't worry," he said, dejectedly. "I doubt it'll come to that."

•   •   •

"Ah; Sherad!" The small fussy shape of Doctor Stap sidled up to him a day later, while people were watching a magnified view of an impressive gas-giant in a nearby system slide past on the principal lounge main screen. The small doctor took his elbow. "I'm having a small private party, this evening, in the Starlight Lounge; one of my, um, *special* parties, you know? I wondered if you and your hermitlike business partner might like to participate?"

"They let you *aboard* with that thing?" he laughed.

"Shh, good sir," the doctor said, pulling the other man away from the press of people. "I have a long-standing arrangement with the shipping line; my machine is recognized as being of primary medical importance."

"Sounds expensive. You must have to charge a lot, doctor."

"There is, of course, a small consideration involved, but well within the means of most cultured people, and I can assure you of some very exclusive company, and complete discretion, as ever."

"Thank you for the offer, Doctor, but I'm afraid not."

"It really is the opportunity of a lifetime; you are most lucky to have the chance a second time."

"I'm sure. Perhaps if it occurs a third time. Excuse me." He patted Stap on the shoulder. "Oh; shall I see you for drinks this evening?"

The doctor shook his head. "I'll be setting up; preparing, I'm afraid, Sherad." He looked somehow plaintive. "It is a *great* opportunity," he said, toothily.

"Oh, I'm well aware of that, Doctor Stap."

"You're a wicked man."

"Thank you. It's taken years of diligent practice."

"I bet."

"Oh no; you're going to tell me you're not wicked at all; I can see it in your eyes. Yes; yes, it's there; purity! I recognize the symptoms. But," he put one hand on her forearm, "don't worry. It can be cured."

She pushed him away, but only with the softest of pressures. "You're terrible." The hand that had pushed him away lingered just for a moment on his chest. "You're bad."

"I confess. You have seen into my soul . . ." He looked round for a second, as the background noise of the ship altered. He smiled back at the lady. "But, ah, it gives me such succor to confess to one so close to a goddesslike beauty."

She laughed throatily, her slender neck exposed as she put her head back. "Do you *normally* get anywhere with this line?" she asked, shaking her head.

He looked hurt, shook his head sadly. "Oh, why are beautiful women so cynical these days?"

Then he saw her gaze shift to somewhere behind him.

He turned. "Yes, Officer?" he said to one of the two junior officers he found standing behind him. Both had guns in open holsters.

"Mr. . . . Sherad?" the young man said.

He watched the young officer's eyes and suddenly felt sick; the man knew. They'd been traced. Somebody somewhere had put the numbers together and come up with the right answer.

"Yes?" he said, grinning rather stupidly. "You guys wanna drink?" He laughed, looked round at the woman.

"No thank you, sir. Would you come with us please?"

"Whassa matter?" he said, sniffing, then draining his glass. He wiped his hands on the lapels of his jacket. "Captain need some help steering the ship, yeah?" he laughed, slid off his bar stool, turned to the woman, took her hand and kissed it. "My dear lady; I bid you farewell, until we meet again." He put both hands to his chest. "But always remember this; there is forever a piece of my heart that belongs to you."

She smiled uncertainly. He laughed loudly, turned and bumped into the bar stool. "Whoops!" he said.

"This way, Mr. Sherad," the first one said.

"Yeah; yeah; just wherever."

He'd hoped they'd take him into the crew-only section, but when they got into the small lift, they pressed for the lowest deck; stores, non-vacuum luggage, and the brig.

"I think I'm going to be sick," he said, as soon as the doors closed. He bent over, retched, forcing out the last few drinks.

One jumped out of the way, to keep his shiny boots clean; the other, he sensed, was bending down, putting one hand to his back.

He stopped throwing up, slammed one elbow up into the man's nose; he crashed back into the elevator's rear doors.

The second man hadn't quite recovered his balance. He straightened and punched him straight in the face. The second one folded, knees then backside hammering into the floor. The lift chimed, stopped between decks, its weight-limit alarm triggered by all the commotion. He thumped the topmost button and the lift started up.

He took the guns from the two unconscious officers; neural stunners. He shook his head. The elevator chimed again. The floor they'd left. He stepped forward, stuffing the two stun guns into his jacket as he braced his feet in the far corners of the small space, straddling the two men, and pressed his hands against the doors. He grunted with the effort of holding the doors closed, but eventually the elevator gave up the struggle. Still holding the doors with both hands, he twisted his body until he got his head to the topmost button, and pressed it with his forehead. The lift hummed upward again.

When the doors opened, three people stood outside, on the private lounge level. They looked at the two unconscious guards and the small watery pool of vomit. Then he zapped them with the stun guns, and they fell. He pulled one of the officers half out of the elevator so the lift couldn't close its doors, and used a stun gun on both men too.

The Starlight Lounge door was closed. He pressed the button, looking back down the corridor, where the lift doors pulsed gently against the fallen officer's body like some unsubtle lover. There was a distant chime, and a voice said, "Please clear the doors. Please clear the doors."

"Yes?" said the door to the Starlight Lounge.

"Stap; it's Sherad. I changed my mind."

"Excellent!" The door opened.

He went quickly inside, hit the shut button. The modest lounge was full of drug smoke, low light, and mutilated people. Music played, and all eyes—not all of them in their sockets—turned to him. The doctor's tall gray machine was over near the bar, where a couple of people were serving.

He got the doctor between him and the others, stuck the stun gun under the little man's chin. "Bad news, Stap. These things can be fatal at close range, and this one's on maximum. I need your machine. I'd prefer to have your co-operation, too, but I can get by without it. I'm *very* serious, and in a terrible hurry, so what's it to be?"

Stap made a gurgling noise.

"Three," he said, pressing the stun gun a little harder into the little doctor's neck. "Two . . ."

"All right! This way!"

He let him go, following Stap across the floor to the tall machine he used for his strange trade. He kept his hands together, stun pistols hidden up each sleeve; he nodded to a few people as they passed. He spotted a clear line of fire to somebody on the far side of the room, just for an instant. He zapped them; they fell spectacularly onto a laden table. While everybody was looking there, he and Stap—prodded once to keep going when the crash came from the distant table—got to the machine.

"Excuse me," he said to one of the bar girls. "Would you help the doctor?" He nodded behind the bar. "He wants to move the machine through there, don't you, Doc?"

They entered the small storeroom behind the bar. He thanked the girl outside, closed the door, locked it, and shifted a pile of containers in front of it. He smiled at the alarmed-looking doctor.

"See that wall behind you, Stap?"

The doctor's gaze flicked that way.

"We're going through it, Doc, with your machine."

"You can't! You . . ."

He put the stun gun against the man's forehead. Stap closed his eyes. A corner of handkerchief, protruding from a breast pocket, trembled.

"Stap; I think I know how that machine must work to do what it does. I want a cutting field; a slicer that'll take molecular bonds apart. If you won't do it, and right now, I'll put you out and try it myself, and if I get it wrong and fuse the fucker, you're going to have some very, very unhappy customers out there; they might even do what you've done to them, but without the old machine here, hmm?"

Stap swallowed. "Mm . . ." he began. One of his hands moved slowly toward his jacket. "Mmm . . . mmm . . . my t-t-tool k-kit."

He took the wallet of tools out, turned shakily to the machine and opened a panel.

The door behind them chimed. He found some sort of chromed bar utensil on a shelf, moved the containers in front of the door aside—Stap looked round, but saw the gun was still pointed at him, and turned back—and jammed the piece of metal into the gap between the sliding door and its housing. The door gave an outraged chirp, and a red light blinked urgently on the open/close button. He slid the containers back again.

"Hurry up, Stap," he said.

"I'm doing all I can!" the little doctor yelped. The machine made a deep buzzing noise. Blue light played around a cylindrical section about a meter from the floor.

He looked at the section, eyes narrowing.

"What are you hoping to do?" the doctor said, voice shaking.

"Just keep working, Doc; you have half a minute before I try doing it myself." He looked over the doctor's shoulder, saw him fiddling with a circular control mapped out in degrees.

All he could hope to do was get the machine going and then attack whatever parts of the ship he could. Disable it, somehow. All ships tended to be complicated, and, to a degree, the cruder a ship was, paradoxically the more complicated it was too. He just had to hope he could hit something vital without blowing the thing up.

"Nearly ready," the doctor said. He looked nervously backward, one shaking finger going toward a small red button.

"Okay, Doc," he told the trembling man, looking suspiciously at the blue light playing round the cylindrical section. He squatted down level with the doctor. "Go on," he nodded.

"Um . . ." The doctor swallowed. "It might be better if you stood back, over there."

"No. Let's just try it, eh?" He hit the little red button. A hemi-disc of blue light shot out over their heads from the cylindrical section of the machine and sliced through the containers he had stacked against the door; fluids spurted out of them. The shelves to one side collapsed, supports severed by the humming blue disc. He grinned at the wreckage; if he'd still been standing, the blue field would have cut him in half.

"Nice try, Doc," he said. The little doctor slumped to the floor like a pile of wet sand as the stun pistol hummed. Snack packets and drink cartons showered onto the floor from the demolished shelves; the ones falling through the blue beam hit the floor shredded; drink poured from the punctured containers in front of the door. There was a thumping noise coming from behind the containers.

He rather appreciated the heady smell of alcohol filling the storeroom, but hoped there weren't enough spirits involved to cause a fire. He spun the machine around, splashing through the drink gradually collecting on the floor of the small storeroom; the flickering blue half-disc cut through more shelves before sinking into the bulkhead opposite the door.

The machine shook; the air filled with a teeth-cracking whine, and black smoke spun round against the wrecked shelves as though propelled by the cutting blue light and then fell quickly to the surface of the sloshing drink filling the bottom decimeter of the store room, where it collected like a tiny dark fog bank. He started manipulating the controls on the machine; a little holo screen showed the shape of the field; he found a couple of tiny joysticks that altered it, producing an elliptical field. The machine thumped harder; the noise rose in pitch and black smoke poured out around him.

The thumping from behind the door got louder. The black smoke was rising in the room, and already he felt light-headed. He pushed hard against the machine with his shoulder; it trundled forward, howling; something gave.

He put his back against the machine and pushed with his feet; there was a bang from in front of the machine and it started to roll away from him; he turned, pushed with his shoulder again, staggering past smoking shelves through a glowing hole into a wrecked room full of tall metal cabinets. Drink spluttered through the gap. He held the machine steady for a moment; he opened one of the cabinets, to find a glittering mass of hair-fine filaments wrapped round cables and rods. Lights winked on a long thin control board, like some linear city seen at night.

He pursed his lips and made a kissing sound at the fibers. "Congratulations," he said to himself. "You have won a major prize." He hunkered down at the humming machine, adjusted the controls to something like the way Stap had had them, but producing a circular field, then switched it to full power.

The blue disc slammed into the gray cabinets in a blinding maelstrom of sparks; the noise was numbing. He left the machine where it was and waddled away under the blue disc, splashing back into the control room. He eased himself over the still unconscious doctor, kicked the containers away from the door and removed the metal tool from the door. The blue beam wasn't extending far through the gap from the control room, so he stood up, shoved the door open with his shoulder, and fell out into the arms of a startled ship's officer, just as the field machine blew up and blasted both of them across the bar and into the lounge.

All the lights in the lounge went out.

III

The hospital ceiling was white, like the walls and the sheets. Outside, on the surface of the berg, all was white as well. Today was a whiteout; a bright scour of dry crystals wheeling past the hospital windows. The last four days had been the same while the storm-wind blew, and the weather people said they expected no break for another two or three days. He thought of the troops, hunkered down in trenches and ice caves, afraid to curse the howling storm, because it meant there would probably be no fighting. The pilots would be glad too, but pretend they were not, and would loudly curse the storm that prevented them flying; having looked at the forecast, most would now be getting profoundly drunk.

He watched the white windows. Seeing the blue sky was supposed to be good for you. That was why they built hospitals on the surface; everything else was under the surface of the ice. The outer walls of the hospital were painted bright red, so that they would not be attacked by enemy aircraft. He had seen enemy hospitals from the air, strung out across the white glare of the berg's snow hills like bright drops of blood fallen frozen from some wounded soldier.

A whorl of whiteness appeared briefly at one window as the snow flurry circled on some vortex in the gale, then disappeared. He stared at the falling chaos beyond the layers of glass, eyes narrowing, as though by sheer concentration he might find some pattern in the inchoate blizzard. He put one hand up, touching the white bandage which circled his head.

His eyes closed, as he tried—again—to remember. His hand fell to the sheets over his chest.

"How are we today?" said the young nurse. She appeared at the bedside, holding a small chair. She placed the chair between his bed and the empty one to his right. All the other beds were empty; he was the only person in the ward. There hadn't been a big attack for a month or so.

She sat down. He smiled, glad to see her, and glad that she had the time to stop and talk. "Okay," he nodded. "Still trying to remember what happened."

She smoothed her white uniform over her lap. "How are your fingers today?"

He held up both hands, waggled the fingers on his right hand, then looked at his left; the fingers moved a little. He frowned. "About the same," he said, as though apologizing.

"You're seeing the doc this afternoon; he'll probably get the physics to take a look at you."

"What I need is a physio for my memory," he said, closing his eyes briefly. "I know there was something important I had to remember . . ." His voice trailed off. He realized he'd forgotten the nurse's name.

"I don't think we have such things," she smiled. "Did they have them where you came from?"

This had happened before; yesterday, hadn't it? Hadn't he forgotten her name yesterday too? He smiled. "I ought to say I don't remember," he said, grinning. "But no, I don't think they did."

He'd forgotten her name yesterday, and the day before, but he'd come up with a plan; he'd done something about it . . .

"Perhaps they didn't need them there, with that thick skull of yours."

She was still smiling. He laughed, trying to remember what the plan was he'd come up with. Something to do with blowing, with breath, with paper . . .

"Perhaps not," he agreed. His thick skull; that was why he was here. A thick skull, a skull thicker or at least more hardy than they were used to; a thick skull that had not quite shattered when somebody had shot him in the head. (But *why*, when he had not been fighting at the time, when he'd been among his own side, his fellow pilots?)

Fractured, instead; fractured, broken, but not smashed irretrievably . . .

. . . He looked to one side, where there was a little cabinet. A fold of paper lay on its surface.

"Don't tire yourself out trying to remember things," the nurse said. "Maybe you won't remember things; it doesn't matter very much. Your mind has to heal too, you know."

He heard her talk, took in what she was saying . . . but he was trying to remember what it was he'd told himself the day before; that little slip of paper; he had to do something to it. He blew at it; the top of the folded paper slip hinged up, so that he could see what was written underneath; TALIBE. The paper sank back again. He'd angled it—he remembered now—so that she couldn't see.

Her name was Talibe. Of course; it sounded familiar.

"I am healing," he said. "But there was something I had to remember, Talibe. It was important; I know it was."

She stood up, patted him on one shoulder. "Forget it. You mustn't worry yourself. Why not take a nap; shall I draw the curtains?"

"No," he said. "Can't you stay longer, Talibe?"

"You need your rest, Cheradenine," she said, putting one hand to his brow. "I'll be back soon, to take your temperature and change your dressings. Ring the bell if you need anything else." She patted his hand, and went away, taking the small white chair with her; she stopped at the doors, looked back. "Oh, yes; did I leave a pair of scissors here, last time I changed your dressing?"

He looked around him, and shook his head. "Don't think so."

Talibe shrugged. "Oh well." She went out of the ward; he heard her put the chair down on the corridor floor as the doors swung closed.

He looked at the window again.

Talibe took the chair away each time because he'd gone crazy when he'd first seen it, when he woke up for the first time. Even after that, when his mental state seemed more stable, he would shiver, wide-eyed with fear when he woke each morning, just because the white chair was sitting there at the side of his bed. So they had stacked the ward's few chairs out of his sight, in one corner, and Talibe, or the doctors, brought the chair in from the corridor with them when they came to see him.

He wished he could forget that; forget about the chair, and the Chairmaker, forget about the Staberinde. Why did that stay sharp and fresh, after so many years and so long a journey? And yet whatever had happened just a few days ago— when somebody had shot him, left him for dead in the hangar—that was dim and vague as something seen through the storm of snow.

He stared at the frozen clouds beyond the window, the amorphous frenzy of the snow. Its meaninglessness mocked him.

He slumped down in the bed, letting the piled bedclothes submerge him, like some drift, and slept, his right hand under the pillow, curled round one leg of the scissors he'd taken from Talibe's tray the day before.

"How's the head, old buddy-pal?" Saaz Insile tossed him a fruit which he failed to catch. He picked it up off his lap, where it had landed after hitting his chest.

"Getting better," he told the other man.

Insile sat on the nearest bed, threw his cap on the pillow, unfastened the top button of his uniform. His short, spiky black hair made his pale face look white as the blankness still filling the world beyond the ward windows. "How they treating you?"

"Fine."

"Damn good-looking nurse you've got out there."

"Talibe." He smiled. "Yes; she's okay."

Insile laughed and sat back on the bed, supporting himself with his arms splayed out behind. "Only 'okay'? Zakalwe, she's gorgeous. You get bed-baths?"

"No; I'm able to walk to the bathroom."

"Want me to break your legs?"

"Perhaps later." He laughed.

Insile laughed a little too, then looked at the storm beyond the windows. "How about your memory? Getting any better?" He picked at the doubled-over white sheet near where his cap lay.

"No," he said. In fact he thought it might be, but some-

how he didn't want to tell people; maybe he thought it would
be bad luck. "I remember being in the mess, and that card
game . . . then . . ." Then he remembered seeing the white
chair at his bedside and filling his lungs with all the air in
the world and screaming like a hurricane until the end of
time, or at least until Talibe came and calmed him (Livueta?
he'd whispered; Dar . . . Livueta?). He shrugged. ". . . then
I was here."

"Well," Saaz said, straightening the crease on his uniform trousers, "the good news is, we managed to get the
blood off the hangar floor."

"I expect it to be returned."

"Deal, but we're not cleaning it."

"How are the others?"

Saaz sighed, shook his head, smoothed the hair at the
back of his neck. "Oh, just the same dear lovable fine bunch
of lads they ever were." He shrugged. "The rest of the
squadron . . . said to send their best wishes for a rapid recovery. But you pissed them off that night." He looked sadly
at the man in the bed. "Cheri, old pal, nobody likes the war,
but there are ways of saying so . . . You just did it wrong. I
mean, we all appreciate what you've done; we know this isn't
really your battle, but I think . . . I think some of the guys
. . . even feel bad about that. I hear them sometimes; you
must have; at night, having nightmares. You can see that look
in their eyes sometimes, like they know how bad the odds
are, and they just aren't going to come through all this.
They're scared; they might try to put a bullet through *my* head
if I said so to their face, but scared is what they are. They'd
love a way out of this war. They're brave men, and they want
to fight for their country, but they want out, and nobody who
knew the odds would blame them. Any honorable excuse.
They wouldn't shoot themselves in the foot, and nowadays
they won't go for a walk outside in ordinary shoes and come
back with frostbite because too many did that early on; but
they'd love a way out of this. You don't have to be here, but
you are; you choose to fight, and a lot of them resent you for
it; it makes them feel like cowards, because they know that
if they were in your boots they'd be on land, telling the girls
what a brave pilot they have the chance to dance with."

"I'm sorry I upset them." He touched the bandages on
his head. "I'd no idea they felt *this* strongly though."

"They don't." Insile frowned. "That's what's weird."
He got up and walked over to the nearest window, looking
out at the blizzard.

"Shit, Cheri, half those guys would've gladly invited you
into the hangar and done their best to lose you a couple of
teeth, but a *gun*?" He shook his head. "There's not one of
those guys I'd trust behind me with a bread roll or a handful
of ice cubes, but if it was a gun . . ." He shook his head
again. "I wouldn't think twice. They just aren't like that."

"Maybe I imagined it all, Saaz," he said.

Saaz looked round, a worried expression on his face. It
melted a little when he saw his friend was smiling. "Cheri;
I admit I don't want to *imagine* I'm wrong about one of them,
but the alternative is . . . just somebody else. I don't know
who. The military police don't know either."

"I don't think I was much help to them," he confessed.

Saaz came back, sat down on the other bed again. "You
really have no idea who you talked to afterward? Where you
went?"

"None."

"You told me you were going to the briefing room, to
check out the latest targets."

"Yes, so I've heard."

"But when Jine went there—to invite you to step into the
hangar for saying such terrible things about our high command and our low tactics—you weren't there."

"I don't know what happened, Saaz; I'm sorry, but I
just . . ." He felt tears prick behind his eyes. The suddenness
surprised him. He put the fruit back down in his lap. He
made a very large sniffing noise, rubbed his nose, and
coughed, patted his chest. "I'm sorry," he repeated.

Insile watched the other man for a moment as he reached
for a handkerchief from the bedside table.

Saaz shrugged, grinned broadly. "Hey; never mind. It'll
come back to you. Maybe it was just some loony ground-
crewman pissed off because you'd stepped on his fingers once
too often. If you want to remember, don't try too hard."

"Yeah; 'Get some rest,' I've heard that before, Saaz."
He picked the fruit from his lap, placed it on the bedside
cabinet.

"Can I get you anything, for next time?" Insile asked.

"Apart from Talibe, on whom I may have designs myself if you refuse to rise to the occasion."

"No, thanks."

"Booze?"

"No, I'm saving myself for the mess-room bar."

"Books?"

"Really, Saaz; nothing."

"Zakalwe," Saaz laughed. "There isn't even anybody else here for you to talk to; what do you *do* all day?"

He looked at the window, then back at Saaz. "I think, quite a lot," he said. "I try to remember."

Saaz came over to the bed. He looked very young. He hesitated, then punched him gently in the chest. He glanced at the bandages. "Don't get lost in there, old buddy-pal."

He was expressionless for a moment. "Yeah; don't worry. But anyway, I'm a good navigator."

There was something he'd meant to tell Saaz Insile, but he couldn't remember what that was either. Something that would warn him, because there was something that he knew about that he hadn't known about before, and something that required . . . warning.

The frustration of it made him want to scream sometimes; to tear the white plump pillows in half and pick up the white chair and smash it through the windows to let the mad white fury out there inside.

He wondered how quickly he'd freeze if the windows were open.

Well, at least it would be appropriate; he'd arrived here frozen, so why not leave the same way? He entertained the thought that some cell-memory, some bone-remembered affinity had drawn him here, of all places, where the great battles were fought on the titanic crashing tabular bergs, calved from their vast glaciers and swirling like ice cubes in some planet-sized cocktail glass, a scatter of ever-shifting frozen islands, some of them hundreds of kilometers long, circling the world between pole and tropic, their broad backs a white wasteland spattered with blood and bodies, and the wrecks of tanks and planes.

To fight for what would inevitably melt and could never provide food or minerals or a permanent place to live, seemed an almost deliberate caricature of the conventional folly of war. He enjoyed the fight, but even the way the war was fought disturbed him, and he had made enemies among the other pilots, and his superiors, by speaking his mind.

But somehow he knew that Saaz was right; it had not been what he'd said in the mess that had led to somebody trying to kill him. At least (said something in him), not directly . . .

Thone, the squadron's CO, came to see him; no flunkies, for a change.

"Thank you, Nurse," he said at the door, then closed it, smiled, and came over to the bed; he had the white chair. He sat in it and drew himself up, so that his girth was made to look less. "Well, Captain Zakalwe, how are we coming along?"

A flowery smell, Thone's preferred scent, drifted over from the man. "I hope to be flying within a couple of weeks, sir," he said. He'd never liked the CO, but made the effort of smiling bravely.

"Do you?" Thone said. "Do you now. That's not what the doctors say, Captain Zakalwe. Unless they're saying different things to me than they are to you."

He frowned. "Well, it might be a . . . few weeks, sir . . ."

"It might be we have to send you home, I think, Captain Zakalwe," Thone said, with an insincere smile, ". . . or at least to the mainland, as I'm told your home is further afield, eh?"

"I'm sure I'll be able to return to my duties, sir. Of course, I realize there will be a medical, but . . ."

"Yes, yes, yes," Thone said. "Well, we'll just have to see, won't we. Hmm. Very good." He stood up. "Is there anyth—"

"There's nothing you can get—" He began, then saw the look on Thone's face. "I beg your pardon, sir."

"*As* I was saying, *Captain*; is there anything I can get you?"

He looked down at the white sheets. "No, sir. Thank you, sir."

"A speedy recovery, Captain Zakalwe," Thone said frostily.

He saluted Thone, who nodded, turned and left.

He was left looking at the white chair.

Nurse Talibe came in after a few moments, arms crossed, her round, pale face very calm and kind. "Try to sleep," she told him, and took the chair away.

He woke in the night and saw the lights shining through the snow outside; silhouetted against the floodlights, the falling flakes became translucent shadows, massing soft against the harsh, downward light. The whiteness beyond, in the black night, came compromised as gray.

He woke with the smell of flowers in his nostrils.

He clutched beneath the pillow, felt the single leg of the sharp, long-nosed scissor.

He remembered Thone's face.

He remembered the briefing room, and the four COs; they'd invited him for a drink, said they wanted a word.

In the room of one of them—he couldn't remember their names, but he would remember soon, and already he would recognize them—they asked him about what they'd heard he'd said in the mess.

And, a little drunk, and thinking he was very clever, thinking he might find out something interesting, he'd told them what he suspected they wanted to hear, not what he'd said to the other pilots.

And had discovered a plot. He wanted the new government to be true to its populist promises, and end the war. They wanted to stage a coup, and they needed good pilots.

High on the drink and his nerves, he'd left them thinking he was for them, and gone straight to Thone. Thone the hard but fair; Thone the dislikable and petty, Thone the vain, the perfumed, but Thone the man known to be pro-government. (Though Saaz Insile had once said the man was pro-government with the pilots, and anti-government with their superiors.)

And the look on Thone's face . . .

Not then; later. After Thone had told him to say nothing to anybody else, because he thought there might be traitors among the pilots too, and told him to go to bed as though nothing had happened, and he'd gone, and because he'd still been drunk, maybe, woken up that second too late as they came for him, shoved some impregnated rag over his face and held it there while he struggled, but eventually had to breathe, and the choking fumes took him.

Dragged through the corridors, socked feet sliding over the tiles; men on either side. They went to one of the hangars, and somebody went to the lift controls, and he still could only dimly see the floor in front of him and could not raise his head. But he could smell flowers, from the man on his right.

The clamshell doors opened overhead, cracking; he heard the noise of the storm, shrieking from the darkness. They dragged him over to the lift.

He tensed, swung round, grabbed at Thone's collar; saw the man's face; appalled, full of fear. He felt the man on the other side of him grab at his free arm; he wriggled, got his other arm free from Thone, saw the pistol in the CO's holster.

He got the gun; he remembered shouting, getting away but falling; he tried to shoot but the gun would not work. Lights flickered on at the far side of the hangar. It's not loaded! It's not loaded! Thone shouted to the others. They looked over to the far side of the hangar; there were planes in the way, but there was somebody there, shouting about opening the hangar doors at night with the lights on.

He never saw who shot him. A sledgehammer hit the side of his head and the next thing he saw was the white chair.

The snow boiled wildly beyond the floodlit windows.

He watched it until dawn, remembering and remembering.

"Talibe; will you send a message to Captain Saaz Insile. Tell him I need to see him, urgently; please send a message to my squadron, will you?"

"Yes, of course, but first your medication."

He took her hand in his. "No, Talibe; first phone the squadron." He winked at her. "Please, for me."

She shook her head. "Pest." She walked away through the doors.

"Well, is he coming?"

"He's on leave," she told him, taking up the clipboard to check off the medication he was receiving.

"Shit!" Saaz hadn't said anything about leave.

"Captain, tut tut," she said, shaking a bottle.

"The police, Talibe. Call the military police; do it now. This really is urgent."

"Medication first, Captain."

"Well as soon as I've taken it, you promise?"

"Promise. Open wide."

"Aaaah . . ."

Damn Saaz for being on leave, and damn him twice for not mentioning it. And Thone; the nerve of the man! Coming to see him, to check him out, to see if he remembered.

And what would have happened if he had?

He felt under the pillow again, for the scissor. It was there, cool and sharp.

"I told them it was urgent; they say they're on their way," Talibe said, coming in, not with the chair this time. She looked at the windows, where the storm still blew. "And I'm to give you something to keep you awake; they want you perky."

"I *am* perky; I *am* awake!"

"Quiet, and take these."

He took them.

He fell asleep clutching the scissor under the pillow, while the whiteness outside the windows went on and on and eventually penetrated the glass, layer by layer, by a process of discrete osmosis, and gravitated naturally to his head, and spun slowly in orbit round him, and joined with the white torus of bandages and dissolved them and unwound them and deposited the remains in one corner of the room where the white chairs gathered, muttering, plotting, and slowly pressed in against his head, tighter and tighter, whirling in the silly snowflake dance, faster and faster as they came closer and closer until eventually they became the bandage, cold and tight about his fevered head, and—finding the treated wound—slunk in through his skin and his skull, coldly and crisply and crystally into his brain.

Talibe unlocked the ward doors and let the officers in.

"You sure he's out?"

"I gave him twice the usual dose. If he isn't out he's dead."

"Still got a pulse. You take his arms."

"Okay . . . Hup! Hey: look at this!"

"Huh."

"My fault. I wondered where those had got to. Sorry."

"You did fine, kid. You better go. Thanks. This won't be forgotten."

"Okay . . ."

"What?"

"It . . . it will be quick, yes? Before he wakes up?"

"Sure. Oh, sure; yeah. He won't ever know. Won't feel a thing."

. . . And so he awoke in the cold snow, roused by the freezing blast inside him coming to the surface, piercing his skin at every pore, shrieking out.

He woke, and knew he was dying. The blizzard had already numbed one side of his face. One hand was stuck to the hard-packed snow beneath him. He was still in the standard-issue hospital pajamas. The cold was not cold; it was a stunning sort of pain, eating into him from every direction.

He raised his head, looking around. A few flat meters of snow, in what might have been morning light. The blizzard a little quieter than it had been, but still fierce. The last temperature he'd heard quoted had been ten below, but with the windchill, it was much, much worse than that. His head and hands and feet and genitals all ached.

The cold had woken him. It must have. It must have woken him quickly or he would already be dead. They must just have left him. If he could find which way they'd gone, follow them . . .

He tried to move, but could not. He screamed inside, to produce the most awesome surge of will he had ever attempted . . . and succeeded only in rolling over, and sitting up.

The effort of it was almost too much; he had to put his hands behind him to steady himself. He felt them both freeze there. He knew he would never stand up.

Talibe . . . he thought, but the blizzard swept that away in an instant.

Forget Talibe. You're dying. There are more important things.

He stared into the milky depths of the blizzard as it swept toward and past him, like tiny soft stars all packed and hurrying. His face felt pierced by a million tiny hot needles, but then started to go numb.

To have come all this way, he thought, just to die in somebody else's war. How silly it all seemed now. Zakalwe, Elethiomel, Staberinde; Livueta, Darckense. The names reeled off, were blown away by the sapping cold of the howling wind. He felt his face shrivel, felt the cold burrow through skin and eyeballs to his tongue and teeth and bones.

He ripped one hand away from the snow behind him; the cold already anesthetizing the flayed palm. He opened the jacket of the pajamas, tore off buttons, and exposed the puckered little mark on his chest over his heart to the cold blast. He put his hand on the ice behind him, and tipped his head up. The bones in his neck seemed to grate, clicking as his head moved, as though the cold was seizing up his joints. "Darckense . . ." he whispered to the boiling chill of the blizzard.

He saw the woman walking calmly toward him through the storm.

She walked on the surface of the hard-packed snow, dressed in long black boots and a long coat with a furry black collar and cuffs, and she wore a small hat.

Her neck and face were exposed, as were her gloveless hands. She had a long, oval face, and deep dark eyes. She walked easily up to him, and the storm behind her seemed to part at her back, and he felt himself in the lee of something more than just her tall body, and something like warmth seemed to seep through his skin, wherever it faced her.

He closed his eyes. He shook his head, which hurt a little, but he did it all the same. He opened his eyes again.

She was still there.

She had half knelt in front of him, her hands folded on one skirted knee, her face level with his. He peered forward, wrenched one hand free from the snow again (it was numb, but when he brought the hand round, he saw the raw flesh he'd torn from the snow). He tried to touch her face, but she took his hand in one of hers. She was warm. He thought he had never felt such glorious warmth in all his life.

He laughed, as she held his hand and the storm parted round her and her breath clouded the air.

"Goddamn," he said. He knew he sounded groggy with the cold and with the drug. "An atheist my entire fucking life, and it turns out the credulous assholes were right all along!" He wheezed, coughed. "Or do you surprise them too by *not* turning up?"

"You flatter me, Mr. Zakalwe," the woman said, in a superbly deep and sexy voice. "I am not Death, or some imagined Goddess. I am as real as you . . ." She stroked his torn, bleeding palm with one long, strong thumb. "If a little warmer."

"Oh, I'm sure you're real," he said. "I can feel you're rea . . ."

His voice faded; he looked behind the woman. There was a huge shape appearing inside the whirling snow. Gray-white like the snow, but a single shade darker, it floated up behind the woman, quiet and huge and steady. The storm seemed to die, just around them.

"That's called a twelve-person module, Cheradenine," the woman said. "It's come to take you away, if you want to be taken away; to the mainland, if you like. Or further afield, away with us if you'd prefer that."

He was tired of blinking and shaking his head. Whatever insane part of his mind wanted to play this bizarre game out would just have to be humored for as long as it took. What it had to do with the Staberinde and the Chair, he couldn't tell yet, but if that was what it was all about—and what else could it be about?—then there was still no point, in this weakened, dying state, trying to fight it. Let it happen. He had no real choice. "With you?" he said, trying not to laugh.

"With us. We'd like to offer you a job." She smiled. "But let's talk somewhere a little warmer, shall we?"

"Warmer?"

She made a single tossing motion with her head. "The module."

"Oh; yeah," he agreed. "That." He tried to pull his other hand away from the packed snow behind, failed.

He looked back at her; she had taken a small flask from her pocket. She reached round behind him, slowly poured

the flask's contents over his hand. It warmed, and came away
steaming gently.

"Okay?" she said, taking his hand, gently helping him
up. She pulled some slippers from her pocket. "Here."

"Oh." He laughed. "Yeah; thanks."

She put her arm under one of his, her hand under his other
shoulder. She was strong. "You seem to know my name,"
he said. "What's yours, if that isn't an impertinent question?"

She smiled as they walked through the few flakes of gently
falling snow, toward the slab-sided bulk of the thing she'd
called a module. It had got so quiet—despite the snow nearby,
streaking past—that he could hear their feet making the snow
creak.

"My name," she said. "Is Rasd-Coduresa Diziet Embless Sma da' Marenhide."

"No kidding!"

"But you may call me Diziet."

He laughed. "Yeah; right. Diziet."

She walked, he stumbled, into the orange warmth of the
module interior. The walls looked like highly polished wood,
the seats like burnished hide, the floor like a fur rug. It all
smelled like a mountain garden.

He tried to fill his lungs with the warm, fragrant air. He
swayed and turned, stunned, to the woman.

"This is *real*!" he breathed.

With enough breath, he might have screamed it.

The woman nodded. "Welcome aboard, Cheradenine
Zakalwe."

He fainted.

12

He stood in the long gallery and faced into the light. The tall white curtains billowed softly around him, quiet in the warm breeze. His long black hair was lifted only slightly by the gentle wind. His hands were clasped behind his back. He looked pensive. The silent, lightly clouded skies over the mountains, beyond the fortress and the city, threw a blank, pervasive light across his face, and standing there like that, in plain dark clothes, he looked somehow insubstantial, like some statue, or a dead man propped against the battlements to fool the foe.

Somebody spoke his name.

"Zakalwe. Cheradenine?"

"Whaa . . . ?" he came to. He looked into the face of an old man who looked vaguely familiar. "Beychae?" he heard himself say. Of course; the old man was Tsoldrin Beychae. Older-looking than he remembered.

He looked around, listening. He heard a hum and saw a small, bare cabin. Seaship? Spaceship?

Osom Emananish, a voice from his memory told him. Spaceship; clipper, bound for . . . somewhere near Impren (whatever and wherever that was). Impren Habitats. He had to get Tsoldrin Beychae to the Impren Habitats. Then he remembered the little doctor and his wonderful field machine with the cutting blue disc. Digging deeper, in a way that would not have been possible without the Culture's training and subtle changes, he found the little running loop of memory that took over from what his brain had already stored. The room with the fiber optics; blowing a kiss because it was just what he'd wanted; the explosion, sailing across the bar into the lounge; crashing, hitting his head. The rest was very vague; distant screams, and being picked up and carried. Nothing sensible from the voices he'd registered while he'd been unconscious.

He lay for a moment, listening to what his body was telling him. No concussion. Slight damage to his right kidney, lots of bruises, abrasions on both knees, cuts on right hand . . . nose still mending.

He raised himself up, looked again at the cabin; bare metal walls, two bunks, one small stool Beychae was sitting on. "This the brig?"

Beychae nodded. "Yes; the prison."

He lay back. He noticed he was wearing a disposable crew jumpsuit. The terminal bead had gone from his ear, and the lobe was raw and sore enough to make him suspect the transceiver hadn't relinquished its grip there without a struggle. "You too, or just me?" he asked.

"Just you."

"What about the ship?"

"I believe we are heading for the nearest stellar system, on the vessel's backup drive."

"What's the nearest system?"

"Well, the one inhabited planet is called Murssay. There's a war going on in part of it; one of those brush-fire conflicts you mentioned. Apparently the ship may not be allowed to land."

"Land?" He grunted, feeling the back of his head. Largish bruise. "This ship can't land; it's not built for in-atmosphere stuff."

"Oh," Tsoldrin said. "Well, perhaps they meant we wouldn't be able to go down to the surface."

"Hmm. Must have some sort of orbiter; a space station, yes?"

Beychae shrugged. "I suppose so."

He looked round the cabin, making it obvious he was looking for something. "What do they know about you?" He gestured round the cabin with his eyes.

Beychae smiled. "They know who I am; I've talked to the captain, Cheradenine. They did receive an order from the shipping company to turn back, though they didn't know why. Now they know why. The captain had the choice of waiting for Humanist naval units to pick us up, or heading for Murssay, and he chose the latter—despite some pressure, I believe—from Governance, via the shipping company. Apparently he insisted that the distress channel was used when he informed the shipping line of both what had happened to the ship, and who I was."

"So now everybody knows?"

"Yes. I imagine by now the whole Cluster knows exactly who both of us are. But the point is that I think the captain might not be entirely unsympathetic to our cause."

"Yeah, but what happens when we get to Murssay?"

"Looks like we get rid of you, Mr. Zakalwe." said a voice from a speaker overhead.

He looked at Beychae. "I hope you heard that too."

"I believe that might be the captain," Beychae said.

"It is," said the man's voice. "And we just got informed that we part company before we even get to Murssay Station." The man sounded peeved.

"Really, captain?"

"Yes, really, Mr. Zakalwe; I have just received a military communication from the Balzeit Hegemonarchy of Murssay. They want to uplift you and Mr. Beychae before we connect with the Station. As they're threatening to attack us if we don't comply, I intend to do as they ask; technically under protest, but frankly it will be a relief to be rid of you. I may add that the vessel they intend to take you off with must be a couple of centuries old, and was not thought to be spaceworthy until now. *If* it survives to make the rendezvous in a couple of hours, you ought to have an eventful journey through Murssay's atmosphere. Mr. Beychae; I believe if you reasoned with the Balzeit people they might let you continue with us to Murssay Station. Whatever you decide, sir, let me wish *you* a safe trip."

Beychae sat back on the small stool. "Balzeit," he said, nodding thoughtfully. "I wonder why they want us?"

"They want *you*, Tsoldrin," he said, swinging his feet off the bed. He looked uncertain. "They on the good guy's side? There's so damn many of these little wars . . ."

"Well, in theory they are," Beychae said. "I think they believe planets and machines can have souls."

"Yeah, I thought they were," he said, getting slowly to his feet. He flexed his arms, moved his shoulders. "If this Murssay Station is neutral territory, you'd be better going there, though I'd guess this Balzeit gang want you, not me."

He rubbed the back of his head again, trying to remember what the situation was on Murssay. Murssay was just the sort of place that could start a full-scale war. There was, in effect, a Consolidationist-Humanist war taking place between relatively archaic military forces on Murssay; Balzeit was on the consolidationist side, even though the high command was some sort of priesthood. Why they wanted Beychae, he wasn't sure, though he vaguely recalled that the priests were into hero-worship in a fairly serious way. Though, having heard that Beychae was nearby, maybe they just wanted to hold him to ransom.

Six hours later they rendezvoused with the ancient Balzeit spacecraft.

"They want *me*?" he said.

They stood by the airlock; him, Beychae, the *Osom Emananish*'s captain, and four suited figures with guns. The suited men wore visored helmets, their pale brown faces visible inside, foreheads marked with a blue circle. The circles actually seemed to glow, he thought, and he wondered if they were there because of some generous religious principle, to help snipers.

"Yes, Mr. Zakalwe," the captain said. He was a rotund little man with a shaved head. He smiled. "They want you, not Mr. Beychae."

He looked at the four armed men. "What are they up to?" he asked Beychae.

"I have no idea," Beychae admitted.

He waved his hands out, appealing to the four men. "Why do you want *me*?"

"Please come with us, sir," one of the suited men said, via a suit speaker, in what was obviously not his first language.

" 'Please'?" he said. "You mean I have a choice?"

The man looked uncomfortable in his suit. He talked for a while without any noise coming from the speaker, then said, "Sir Zakalwe, is very important you come. You must. Is very important."

He shook his head. "I must," he repeated seemingly to himself. He turned to the captain. "Captain, sir; could I have my earring back, please?"

"No," the captain said, with a beatific grin. "Now, get off my ship."

The craft was cramped and very low tech and the air was warm and smelled of electrics. They gave him an old suit to put on and he was shown to a couch, and belted in. It was a bad sign when they made you put a suit on *inside* a ship. The troopers who'd taken him from the clipper sat behind him. The three-man crew—also suited up—seemed suspiciously busy, and he had the disquieting impression that the manual controls in front of them were not just for emergencies.

The craft reentered the atmosphere spectacularly; buffeted, creaking, surrounded by gas glowing bright (seen through, he realized with a gut-wrenching shock, windows; crystal or glass, not screens), and with a gradually increasing howl. The air got even warmer. Flashing lights, hurried chatter between the crew, and some hurried movements and more excited talk, did not make him feel any happier. The glow disappeared and the sky turned from violet to blue; the buffeting returned.

They swept into the night, and plunged into cloud. The flashing lights all over the control panels looked even more worrying in darkness.

It was a rolling landing on some sort of runway, in a thunderstorm. The four troopers who'd boarded the *Osom Emananish* cheered weakly from behind him as the landing gear—wheels, he supposed—touched down. The craft trundled on for a worryingly long time, slewing twice.

When they finally rolled to a stop, the three crewmen all

sat back slumped in their seats, arms dangling over the edges, silent and staring out into the rain-filled night.

He undid the belts, took off the helmet. The troopers opened the interior airlock.

When they opened the outer door, it was to reveal rain and lights and trucks and tanks and some low buildings in the background, and a couple of hundred people, some in military uniforms, some in long robes, rain-slicked, some trying to hold umbrellas over others; all seemed to have the circular marks on their foreheads. A group of a dozen or so, all old, robed, white-haired, faces spattered with rain, walked to the bottom of the steps that led from the craft to the ground.

"Please, sir," one of the troopers held out a hand to indicate they should descend. The white-haired men in the robes gathered in an arrowhead formation at the foot of the steps.

He stepped out, stood on the little platform before the stairs. The rain battered into one side of his head.

A great shout went up, and the dozen old men at the foot of the steps each bowed their head and went down on one knee, into the puddles on the dark and wind-whipped runway. A blast of blue light ripped the blackness beyond the low buildings, its flickering brilliance momentarily illuminating hills and mountains in the distance. The assembled people started to chant. It took him a few moments to work out what it was, then realized they were yelling, "Za-kal-we! Za-kal-we!"

"Oh oh," he said to himself. Thunder bellowed in the hills.

"Yeah . . . could you just run that past me again?"

"Messiah . . ."

"I really wish you wouldn't use that word."

"Oh! Oh, well, Sir Zakalwe; what do you wish?"

"Ah . . . how about," he gestured with his hands. "Mister?"

"Sir Zakalwe, sir; you are preordained! You have been be-seen!" The high priest, sitting across the railway carriage, clenched his hands.

" 'Be-seen?' "

"Indeed! You are our salvation; our divine recompense! You have been sent!"

"Sent," he repeated, still trying to come to terms with what had happened to him.

They'd switched the floodlights off shortly after he'd set foot on the ground. The priests enveloped him, took him, many arms round his shoulders, from the concrete apron to an armored truck; the lights went out on the runway and they were left with the slit light from the truck and tank lights; cones made fans by blinkers clipped over the lights. He was bustled away down a track to a railway station where they transferred to a shuttered carriage that clattered into the night.

There were no windows.

"Why yes! Our faith has a tradition of finding outside influences, because they are always greater." The high priest—Napoerea, he'd said his name was—made a bowing motion. "And what can be greater than the man who was ComMil?"

ComMil; he had to dredge his memory for that one. ComMil; that was what he had been, according to the Cluster's media; director of military operations when he and Tsoldrin Beychae had been involved in the whole crazy dance the last time. Beychae had been ComPol, in charge of politics (ah, these fine divisions!).

"ComMil . . ." He nodded, not really much the wiser. "And you think I can help you?"

"Sir Zakalwe!" the high priest said, shifting down from his seat to kneel on the floor again. "You are what we believe in!"

He sat back in the upholstered cushions. "May I ask why?"

"Sir; your deeds are legend! Forever since the last unpleasantness! Our Guider, before he died, prophesied that our salvation would come from 'beyond the skies,' and your name was one of those mentioned; so coming to us in our hour of need, you must be our salvation!"

"I see," he said, seeing nothing. "Well, we'll see what we can do."

"Messiah!"

• • •

The train drew up in a station somewhere; they were escorted from it to an elevator, then to a suite of rooms that he was told looked out over the city beneath but it was all in black-out. The internal screens were closed. The rooms themselves were quite opulent. He inspected them.

"Yes. Very nice. Thank you."

"And here are your boys," the high priest said, sweeping aside a curtain in the bedroom to reveal a languorously displayed half-dozen or so young men lying on a very large bed.

"Well . . . I, uh . . . Thank you," he said, nodding to the high priest. He smiled at the boys, who all smiled back.

He lay awake in the ceremonial bed in the palace, hands behind his neck. After a while, in the darkness, there was a distinct "pop," and in a disappearing blue sphere of light there was a tiny machine about the size of a human thumb.

"Zakalwe?"

"Hi, Sma."

"Listen . . ."

"No. You listen; I would really like to know what the fuck is going on here."

"Zakalwe," Sma said, through the scout missile. "It's complicated, but . . ."

"But I'm in here with a gang of homosexual priests who think I'm going to solve all their military problems."

"Cheradenine," Sma said, in her winning voice. "These people have successfully incorporated a belief in your martial prowess into their religion; how can you deny them?"

"Believe me; it would be easy."

"Like it or not, Cheradenine, you've become a legend to these people. They think you can do things."

"So what am I supposed to do?"

"Guide them. Be their General."

"That's what they expect me to be, I think. But what should I really do?"

"Just that," Sma's voice said. "Lead them. Meanwhile Beychae's in the Station; Murssay Station. That counts as neutral territory for now, and he's making the right noises. Don't you see, Zakalwe?" Sma's voice sounded tense, exultant. "We've got them! Beychae's doing just what we wanted, and all you have to do is . . ."

"What?"

". . . Just be yourself; operate for these guys!"

He shook his head. "Sma; spell it out for me. What am I supposed to do?"

He heard Sma sigh. "Win their war, Zakalwe. We're putting our weight behind the forces you're working with. Maybe if they can win this, and Beychae gets behind the winning side here, we can—perhaps—swing the Cluster." He heard her take another deep breath. "Zakalwe; we need this. To a degree, our hands are tied, but we need you to make the whole thing settle out. Win their war for them, and we might just be able to get it all together. Seriously."

"Fine, seriously," he said to the scout missile. "But I've already had a quick look at their maps, and these guys are in deep shit. If they're going to win this war they're going to need a real miracle."

"Just try, Cheradenine. Please."

"Do I get any help?"

"Um . . . how do you mean?"

"Intelligence, Sma; if you could keep an eye on what the enemy's—"

"Ah, no, Cheradenine, I'm sorry we can't."

"What?" he said loudly, sitting up in the bed.

"I'm sorry, Zakalwe; really I am, but we've had to agree to that. This is a really delicate deal here, and we're having to keep strictly out of it. This missile shouldn't even be here; and it'll have to leave soon."

"So I'm on my own?"

"I'm sorry," Sma said.

"*You're* sorry!" he said, collapsing back dramatically on the bed.

No soldiering, he recalled Sma saying, some time ago now. "No fucking soldiering," he muttered to himself as he gathered his hair at the nape of his neck and pulled the little hide band over it. It was dawn; he patted the ponytail and looked out through thick, distorting glass to the mist-shrouded city, just starting to wake to the dawn-rouged mountain peaks and the blue-glowing skies above. He looked with distaste at the over-ornamented long robes the priests expected him to wear, then reluctantly put them on.

The Hegemonarchy and its opponents, the Glaseen Empire, had been fighting, on and off, for control of their modestly-sized subcontinent for six hundred years before the rest of the Cluster came calling in its strange floating sky-ships, a century ago. They'd been backward even then, compared to the other societies on Murssay, which were decades ahead in technology, and—arguably—several centuries ahead morally and politically. Before they'd been contacted, the natives had the crossbow and the muzzle-loading cannon. Now, a century later, they had tanks. Lots of tanks. Tanks and artillery and trucks and a few very inefficient aircraft. Each side also had one prestige system, partially brought from but mostly just donated by some of the Cluster's more advanced societies. The Hegemonarchy had its single sixth- or seventh-hand spacecraft; the Empire had a clutch of missiles which were generally reckoned to be inoperable, and probably were politically unusable anyway because they were supposed to be nuclear-tipped. Public opinion in the Cluster could tolerate the technologically enhanced continuation of a pointless war so long as men, women and children died in relatively small, regular batches, but the thought of a million or so being incinerated at once, nuked in a city, was not to be tolerated.

The Empire was winning a conventional war, then, being waged across two impoverished countries which left to themselves would probably just be harnessing steam power. Instead refugee peasants filled the roads, carts loaded with whole households swayed between hedgerows, while the tanks ploughed the crop fields and the droning planes dropping bombs took care of slum clearance.

The Hegemonarchy was retreating across the plains and into the mountains as its beleaguered forces fell back before the Empire's motorized cavalry.

He went straight to the map room after dressing; a few dozy general staff officers jumped to attention and rubbed sleep from their eyes. The maps didn't look any better in the morning than they had the previous evening, but he stood looking at them for a long time, sizing up the positions of their forces and the Empire's, asking the officers questions and trying to gauge how accurate their intelligence was and what level their own troops' morale was at.

The officers seemed to know more about the disposition of their enemy's forces than they did about the feelings of their own men.

He nodded to himself, scanned all the maps, then left for breakfast with Napoerea and the rest of the priests. He dragged them all back down into the map room afterward—they would normally have returned to their own apartments for contemplation—and asked even more questions.

"And I want a uniform like these guys," he said, pointing at one of the junior regular army officers in the map room.

"But, Sir Zakalwe," Napoerea said, looking worried. "Those would demean you!"

"And these will slow me down," he said, indicating the long, heavy robes he was wearing. "I want to take a look at the front myself."

"But, sir, this is the holy citadel; all our intelligence comes here, all our people's prayers are directed here."

"Napoerea," he said, putting his hand on the other man's shoulder. "I know; but I need to see things for myself. I only just got here, remember?" He looked round the unhappy faces of the other high priests. "I'm sure your ways work when circumstances are as they have been in the past," he told them, straight-faced. "But I'm new, and so I have to use new ways to discover what you probably already know." He turned back to Napoerea. "I want my own plane; a modified reconnaissance aircraft should do. Two fighters as an escort."

The priests had thought it the height of daring unorthodoxy to venture out to the space port, thirty kilometers away, by train and truck; they thought he was mad to want to start flying all over the subcontinent.

It was what he did for the next few days, however. There was a lull of sorts in the fighting just at that point—as the Hegemonarchy's forces fled and the Empire's consolidated—which made his task a little easier. He wore a plain uniform, without even the half dozen or so medal ribbons that even the most junior officer seemed to warrant just for existing. He spoke to the mostly dull, demoralized and thoroughly hidebound field generals and colonels, to their staff, and to the foot soldiers and tank crews, as well as to the cooks and the supply teams and the orderlies and doctors. Most of the time he needed an interpreter; only the top brass spoke the Cluster's common tongue, but even so he suspected the troops felt closer to somebody who spoke a different language but asked them questions than they did to somebody who shared their language and only ever used it to give orders.

He toured every major airfield in the course of that first week, sounding out the Air Force staff for their feelings and opinions. About the only person he tended to ignore on such occasions was the always watchful priest every squadron, regiment and fort had as its titular head. The first few of these priests he'd encountered had had nothing useful to say, and none of those he saw subsequently ever seemed to have anything interesting to add beyond the ritualized initial greetings. He had decided within the first couple of days that the main problem the priests had was themselves.

"Shenastri Province!" Napoerea exclaimed. "But there are a dozen important religious sites there! More! And you propose to surrender without a fight?"

"You'll get the temples back once we've won the war, and probably lots of new treasure to put inside them. They're going to fall whether we try to hold there or not, and they'll probably be damaged if not destroyed in the fighting. This way, they'll survive intact. And it stretches their supply lines like crazy. Look; the rains start in, what? A month? By the time we're ready to counterattack, they'll have even worse supply problems; the wetlands behind them mean they can't bring stuff that way, and they can't retreat there once we do attack. Nappy; old son; this is beautiful, believe me. If I was a commander on the other side and I saw this area being offered, I wouldn't go within a million klicks of it, but the Imperial Army boys are going to have to because the Court won't let them do anything else. But they'll know it's a trap. Terrible for the morale."

"I don't know, I don't know . . ." Napoerea shook his head, both his hands at his mouth, massaging his lower lip while he looked worriedly at the map.

(No, you don't know, he thought to himself, watching the

man's nervous body language. You lot haven't known anything very useful for generations, chum.) "It must be done," he said. "The withdrawal should start today." He turned to another map. "Aircraft; stop the bombing and strafing of the roads. Give the pilots two days' rest, then raid the oil refineries, here." He pointed. "A mass raid; use everything with the range that'll fly."

"But if we stop attacking the roads . . ."

"They'll fill with even more refugees," he told the man. "That'll slow the Imperial Army down more than our planes. I *do* want some of these bridges taken out." He tapped a couple of river crossings. He looked mystified at Napoerea. "You guys sign some sort of agreement not to bomb bridges or something?"

"It has always been felt that destroying bridges would hinder a counterattack, as well as being . . . wasteful," the priest said, unhappily.

"Well, these three have to go, anyway." He tapped the surface of the map. "That and the refinery raid should put some sand in their fuel lines," he said, clapping his hands together and rubbing them.

"But we believe the Imperial Army has great reserves of fuel," Napoerea said, looking very unhappy.

"Even if they have," he told the high priest, "commanders will move more cautiously knowing supplies have been interrupted; they're careful guys. But I bet they never did have the supplies you thought; they probably think you have bigger supplies than you do, and with the advance they've had to fund recently . . . believe me; they may panic a little if the refinery raid comes off the way I hope it will."

Napoerea looked downcast, rubbed his chin while he gazed forlornly at the maps. "It all sounds very . . ." he began, ". . . very . . . *adventurous*."

The high priest invested the word with a degree of loathing and contempt that might have been amusing in other circumstances.

Under great protest, the high priests were persuaded they must give up their precious province and its many important religious sites to the enemy; they agreed to the mass raid on the refinery.

He visited the retreating soldiers and the main airfields that would take part in the refinery raid. Then he took a couple of days traveling the mountains by truck, inspecting the defenses. There was a valley with a dam at its head that might also provide an effective trap if the Imperial Army made it that far (he remembered the concrete island, the sniveling girl and the chair). While he was driven along the rough roads between the hill forts, he saw a hundred or more aircraft drone overhead, heading out across the still peaceful-looking plains, their wings loaded with bombs.

The refinery raid was expensive; almost a quarter of the planes never came back. But the Imperial Army's advance halted a day later. He had hoped they would keep on coming for a bit—their supplies hadn't been supplied straight from the refinery, so they could have kept going for a week or so—but they'd done the sensible thing, and stopped for the moment.

He flew to the spaceport, where the lumbering spaceship—it looked even more dangerous and dilapidated in daylight—was being slowly patched up and repaired in case it was ever wanted again. He talked to the technicians, took a look round the ancient device. The ship had a name, he discovered; the *Hegemonarchy Victorious*.

"It's called decapitation," he told the priests. "The Imperial Court travels to Willitice Lake at the start of every Second Season; the high command comes to brief them. We drop the *Victorious* in on them, the day the general staff arrive."

The priests looked puzzled. "With what, Sir Zakalwe? A commando force? The *Victorious* is only able to hold . . ."

"No no," he said. "When I say drop it, I mean we bomb them with it. We put it into space and then bring it back in, down on top of the Lake Palace. It's a good four hundred tons; even traveling at only ten times the speed of sound it'll hit like a small nuke going off; we'll get the entire Court and the general staff in one go. We offer peace to the commoners' parliament immediately. With any luck at all we cause immense civil disturbance; probably the commoners' parliament will see this as their chance to grab real power; the army will want to take up the reins itself, and may even have to turn round and fight a civil war. Junior aristos filing competing claims should complicate the situation nicely.''

"But," Napoerea said, "this means destroying the *Victorious*, does it not?" The other priests were shaking their heads.

"Well, impacting at four or five kilometers a second wouldn't leave it totally undented, I suspect."

"But Zakalwe!" Napoerea roared, doing a reasonable impression of a small nuclear explosion himself, "That's absurd! You can't do it! The *Victorious* is a symbol of . . . it's our hope! All the people look at our . . ."

He smiled, letting the priest ramble on for a little while. He was fairly certain the priests looked on the *Hegemonarchy Victorious* as their escape route if things went badly in the end.

He waited until Napoerea had almost finished, then said, "I understand; but the craft is on its last legs already, gentlemen. I've talked to the technicians and the pilots; it's a death trap. It was more luck than anything else that it got me here safely." He paused, watching the men with the blue circles on their foreheads look wide-eyed at each other. The muttering increased. He wanted to smile. *That* had put the fear of god into them. "I'm sorry, but this is the one thing the *Victorious* is good for." He smiled. "And it could indeed produce Victory."

He left them to mull over the concepts of high-hypersonic dive-bombing (no, no suicide mission required; the craft's computers were perfectly capable of taking it up and bringing it straight down), symbol-trashing (a lot the peasants and factory workers would care about their piece of high-tech baublery getting junked), and decapitation (probably the most worrying idea of the lot for the high priests; what if the Empire thought of doing it to them?). He assured them the Empire would be in no state to retaliate; and when they offered peace, the priests would hint heavily they had used a missile of their own, not the spacecraft, and pretend there were more where that came from. Even though this would not be difficult to disprove, especially if one of the world's more sophisticated societies chose to tell the Empire what had really happened, it would still be *worrying* for whoever was trying to work out what to do on the other side. Besides, they could always just get out of the city. Meanwhile he went to visit more army units.

The Imperial Army started its advance again, though slower than before. He had drawn his troops back almost to the foothills of the mountains, burning the few unharvested fields and razing the towns behind them. Whenever they abandoned an airfield they planted bombs under the runways with days-long time delays, and dug plenty of other holes that looked like they might contain bombs.

In the foothills he supervised much of the layout of their defensive lines himself, and kept up his visits to airfields, regional headquarters and operational units. He kept up, too, the pressure on the high priests at least to consider using the spacecraft for a decapitation strike.

He was busy, he realized one day, as he lay down to sleep in an old castle that had become operational HQ for this section of the front (the sky had bloomed with light on the tree-lined horizon, and the air shaken with the sound of a bombardment, just after dusk). Busy and—he had to admit, as he put the last reports on the floor under the camp bed, and put the light out and was almost instantly asleep—happy.

Two weeks, three weeks from his arrival; the little news that came in from outside seemed to indicate that there was an awful lot of nothing going on. He suspected there was a lot of intense politicking taking place. Beychae's name was mentioned; he was still on the Murssay Station, in touch with the various parties. No word of the Culture, or from it. He wondered if they ever just forgot things; maybe they'd forget about him, leave him here, struggling forever in the priests' and the Empire's insane war.

The defenses grew; the Hegemonarchy's soldiers dug and built, but were mostly not under fire, and the Imperial Army gradually lapped against the foothills and paused. He had the Air Force harry the supply lines and the front line units, and pound the nearest airfields.

"There are far too many troops stationed here, round the city. The best troops should be at the front. The attack will come soon, and if we're to counterattack successfully—and it could be *very* successfully, if they're tempted to go for a knockout; they've little left in reserve—then we need those elite squads where they can do some good."

"There is the problem of civil unrest," Napoerea said.
He looked old and tired.

"Keep a few units here, and keep them in the streets, so
people don't forget they're here, but dammit, Napoerea, most
of these guys spend all their time in barracks. They're needed
at the front. I have just the place for them, look . . ."

Actually he wanted to tempt the Imperial Army to go for
the knockout, and the city was to be the bait. He sent the
crack troops into the mountain passes. The priests looked at
how much territory they'd now lost, and tentatively gave the
go-ahead for preparing for decapitation; the *Hegemonarchy
Victorious* would be readied for its final flight, though not
used unless the situation appeared genuinely desperate. He
promised he would try to win the war conventionally first.

The attack came; forty days after he had arrived on Murssay, the Imperial Army crashed into the foothill forests. The
priests began to panic. He had the Air Force attack the supply
lines the majority of the time, not the front. The defensive
lines gradually gave way; units retreated, bridges were blown.
Gradually, as the foothills led into the mountains, the Imperial Army was concentrated, funneled into the valleys. The
trick with the dam didn't work this time; the charges placed
under it just didn't go off. He had to move fast to shift two
elite units to cover the pass above that valley.

"But if we leave the city?" The priests looked stunned. Their
eyes looked as empty as the painted blue circle on their foreheads. The Imperial Army was slowly moving up the valleys,
forcing their soldiers back. He kept telling them things would
be all right, but things just got worse and worse. There was
nothing else for them to do; it all seemed too hopeless, and
too late to take things back into their own hands. Last night,
with the wind blowing down from the mountains to the city,
the sound of distant artillery had been audible.

"They'll try to take Balzeit City if they think they can,"
he said. "It's a symbol. Well fine, but it doesn't actually have
much military importance. They'll grab at it. We let just so
many through, then we close the passes; here," he said, tapping the map. The priests shook their heads.

"Gents, we are not in disarray! We are falling back. But
they are in much worse shape than we are, taking far heavier

casualties; each meter is costing them blood. And, all the time, their supply lines get longer. We must take them to the point where they start to think about pulling back, then present them with the possibility—the seeming possibility—of a knockout blow. But it won't knock us out; it knocks them out.'' He looked round them. ''Believe me; it'll work. You may have to leave the citadel for a while, but when you return, I guarantee it will be in triumph.''

They did not look convinced, but—possibly because they were just too stunned to fight—they let him have his way.

It took a few days, while the Imperial Army struggled up the valleys, and the Hegemonarchy's forces resisted, retreated, resisted, retreated, but eventually—watching for signs that the Imperial soldiers were tiring, and the tanks and trucks not always moving when they might have wanted to, starved of fuel—he decided that were he on the other side, he'd be thinking about halting the advance. That night, in the pass which led down to the city, most of the Hegemonarchy troops left their positions. In the morning the battle resumed, and the Hegemonarchy's men suddenly retreated, shortly before they would have been overrun. A puzzled, excited but still exhausted and worried General in the Imperial High Command watched through field glasses as a distant convoy of trucks crawled away down the pass toward the city, occasionally strafed by Imperial aircraft. Reconnaissance suggested the infidel priests were making preparations to leave their citadel. Spies indicated that their spacecraft was being readied for some special mission.

The General radioed the Court High Command. The order to advance on the city was given the following day.

He watched the terminally worried-looking priests leave from the train station under the citadel. In the end he had to dissuade them from ordering the decapitation attack. Let me try this first, he'd told them.

They could not understand each other.

The priests looked at the territory they had lost, and the fraction they had left, and thought it was all over for them. He looked at his relatively unscathed divisions, his fresh units, his crack squads, all positioned just where they should be, knives laid against and inside the body of an over-extended, worn-out enemy, just ready to cut . . . and thought it was all over for the Empire.

The train pulled out, and—unable to resist—he waved cheerily. The high priests would be better out of the way, in one of their great monasteries in the next mountain range. He ran back upstairs to the map room, to see how things were going.

He waited until a couple of divisions had made it through the pass, then had the units that had held it—and mostly retreated into the forests around the pass, not gone down the pass at all—take it again. The city and the citadel were bombed, though not well; the Hegemonarchy's fighters shot most of the bombers down. The counterattack finally began. He started with the elite troops, then brought in the rest. The Air Force still concentrated on the supply lines for the first couple of days, then switched to the front line. The Imperial Army wavered, line crinkling; it seemed to hesitate like some wash of water almost but not quite capable of overspilling the damming line of mountains save in one place (and that trickle was drying, still pushing for the city, leaving the pass, fighting through the forests and fields for the shining goal they still hoped might win the war . . .), then the line fell back; the soldiers too exhausted, their supplies of ammunition and fuel too sporadic.

The passes stayed with the Hegemonarchy, and slowly they pushed down from them again, so that it must have seemed to the Imperial soldiers that they were forever shooting uphill, and that while advancing had been a heavy, dangerous slog, retreating was only too easy.

The retreat became a rout in valley after valley. He insisted on keeping the counterattack going; the priests cabled that more forces ought to be deployed to stop the advance of the two Imperial divisions on the capital. He ignored them. There was barely enough left of the two tattered divisions to make one whole one, and they were being gradually eroded further all the time. It was possible they might make it to the city, but after that they would have nowhere to go. He thought it might be satisfying to accept their eventual surrender personally.

The rains came on the far side of the mountains, and as

the bedraggled Imperial forces made their way through the dripping forests, their Air Force was all too often grounded by bad weather, while the Hegemonarchy's planes bombed and strafed them with impunity.

People fled to the city; artillery duels thundered nearby. The remnants of the two divisions that had broken through the mountains fought desperately on toward their goal. On the distant plains on the far side of the mountains, the rest of the Imperial Army was retreating as fast as it could. The divisions trapped in Shenastri Province, unable to retreat through the quagmire behind them, surrendered en masse.

The Imperial Court signaled its desire for peace the day what was left of its two divisions entered Balzeit City. They had a dozen tanks and a thousand men, but they left their artillery in the fields, bereft of ammunition. The few thousand people left in the city sought refuge in the wide parade grounds of the citadel. He watched them stream in through the gates in the high walls, far in the distance.

He'd been going to quit the citadel that day—the priests had been screaming at him to do so for days, and most of the general staff had already left—but now he held the transcript of the message they'd just received from the Imperial Court.

Two Hegemonarchy divisions were, anyway, on their way out of the mountains, coming to the aid of the city.

He radioed the priests. They decided to accept a truce; fighting would stop immediately, if the Imperial Army withdrew to the positions it had held before the war. There were a few more radio exchanges; he left the priests and the Imperial Court to sort it all out. He took off his uniform and for the first time since he'd arrived, dressed as a civilian. He went to a high tower with some field glasses, and watched the tiny specks that were enemy tanks as they rolled down a street, far away. The citadel gates were closed.

A truce was declared at midday. The weary Imperial soldiers outside the citadel gates billeted themselves in the bars and hotels nearby.

He stood in the long gallery and faced into the light. The tall white curtains billowed softly around him, quiet in the warm breeze. His long black hair was lifted only slightly by the gentle wind. His hands were clasped behind his back. He looked pensive. The silent, lightly clouded skies over the mountains, beyond the fortress and the city, threw a blank, pervasive light across his face, and standing there like that, in plain dark clothes, he looked insubstantial, like some statue, or a dead man propped against the battlements to fool the foe.

"Zakalwe?"

He turned. His eyes widened in surprise. "Skaffen-Amtiskaw! This is an unexpected honor. Sma letting you out alone these days, or is she about too?" He looked the length of the citadel's long gallery.

"Good day, Cheradenine," the drone said, floating toward him. "Ms. Sma is on her way, in a module."

"And how is Dizzy?" He sat down on a small bench set against the wall which faced the long line of white-curtained windows. "What's the news?"

"I believe it is mostly good," Skaffen-Amtiskaw said, floating level with his face. "Mr. Beychae is on his way to the Impren Habitats, where a summit conference between the Cluster's two main tendencies is to be held. It would appear the danger of war is lessening."

"Well, isn't this all very wonderful," he said, sitting back with his hands behind his neck. "Peace here; peace out there." He squinted at the drone, his head to one side. "And yet, drone, somehow you do not seem to be overflowing with joy and happiness. You seem—dare I say it?—positively somber. What's the matter? Batteries low?"

The machine was silent for a second or two. Then it said, "I believe Ms. Sma's module is about to land; shall we go to the roof?"

He looked puzzled for a moment, then nodded, stood smartly and clapped his hands once, indicating the way forward. "Certainly; let's go."

They went to his apartments. He thought Sma seemed rather subdued, too. He'd imagined she'd be bubbling over with excitement because the Cluster looked like it wasn't going to go to war after all.

"What's the problem, Dizzy?" he asked, pouring her a drink. She was pacing up and down in front of the room's shuttered windows. She took the drink from him, but didn't seem interested in it. She turned to face him, her long, oval face looking . . . he wasn't sure. But there was a cold feeling somewhere in his guts.

"You have to leave, Cheradenine," she told him.

"Leave? When?"

"Now; tonight. Tomorrow morning at the latest."

He looked confused, then laughed. "Okay; I confess; the catamites were starting to look attractive, but . . ."

"No," Sma said. "I'm serious, Cheradenine. You have to go."

He shook his head. "I can't. There's no guarantee the truce will hold. They might need me."

"The truce isn't going to hold," Sma told him, looking away. "Not on one side, anyway." She put her glass down on a shelf.

"Eh?" he said. He glanced at the drone, which was looking noncommittal. "Diziet, what are you talking about?"

"Zakalwe," she said, eyes blinking rapidly; she tried to look at him. "A deal's been done; you have to leave."

He stared at her.

"What's the deal, Dizzy?" he said softly.

"There was some . . . fairly low-level help being given to the Empire by the Humanist faction," she told him, walking toward one wall, then returning, talking not to him but to the tile and carpet floor. "They had . . . face invested in what's been happening here. The whole delicate structure of the deal did rather depend on the Empire triumphing here." She stopped, glanced at the drone, looking away again. "Which is what everybody agreed was going to happen, up until a few days ago."

"So," he said slowly, putting aside his own drink, sitting down in a great chair that looked like a throne. "I messed things up by turning the game against the Empire, did I?"

"Yes," Sma said, swallowing. "Yes, you did. I'm sorry. And I know it's crazy, but that's the way things are here, the way the people are here; the Humanists are divided at the moment, and there are factions within them that would use any excuse to argue for getting out of the deal, however insignificant that excuse might be. They might just be able to pull the whole thing down. We can't take that risk. The Empire has to win."

He sat, looking at a small table in front of him. He sighed. "I see. And all I have to do is leave?"

"Yes; come with us."

"What happens after that?"

"The high priests will be kidnapped by an Imperial commando squad brought in by Humanist controlled aircraft. The citadel here will be taken over by the troops outside; there are raids planned on the field HQs; they should be pretty bloodless. If necessary, the Hegemonarchy planes, tanks, artillery pieces and trucks will be put out of action, should the armed forces ignore the call put out by the high priesthood to surrender their arms. Once they've seen a few planes and tanks laser-blasted from space, it's expected the fight will go out of the army."

Sma stopped pacing, came to stand in front of him, on the far side of the little table. "It all happens at dawn tomorrow. It should be fairly bloodless, really, Zakalwe. You might as well leave now; it would be best." He heard her exhale. "You've done . . . brilliantly, Cheradenine. It's worked; you did it; brought Beychae out, got him . . . motivated or whatever. We're grateful. We're very grateful, and it's not easy . . ."

He raised one hand to stop her. He heard her sigh. He looked up from the small table, up to her face. "I can't leave right away. There are a few things I have to do. I'd rather you left now and then came back. Pick me up tomorrow; at dawn." He shook his head. "I won't desert them until then."

Sma opened her mouth, then closed it, glanced at the drone. "All right; we'll be back tomorrow. Zakalwe, I—"

"It's all right, Diziet," he interrupted calmly, and slowly stood up. He looked into her eyes; she had to look away. "It'll be as you say. Goodbye." He didn't hold out his hand.

Sma walked to the door; the drone followed her.

The woman looked back. He nodded once; she hesitated, seemed to think the better of saying anything, and went out.

The drone stopped there too. "Zakalwe," it said. "I just want to add—"

"Out!" he screamed, and in one movement turned, swooped, caught the small table between the legs and threw it with all his might at the floating machine. The table bounced off an invisible field and clattered to the floor; the drone swept out and the door closed.

He stood staring at it for some time.

II

He was younger then. The memories were still fresh. He discussed them with the frozen, seemingly sleeping people sometimes, on his wanderings through the cold, dark ship, and wondered, in its silence, if he really was mad.

The experience of being frozen and of then being woken up had done nothing to dull his memories; they remained keen and bright. He had rather hoped that the claims they made for freezing were over-optimistic, and the brain did indeed lose at least some of its information; he'd secretly desired that attrition, but been disappointed. The process of warming and revival was actually rather less traumatic and confusing than coming round after being knocked unconscious, something that had happened to him a few times in his life. Revival was smoother, took longer, and was really quite pleasant; in truth quite like waking up after a good night's sleep.

They left him alone for a couple of hours after they'd run the medical checks and pronounced him fit and well. He sat, wrapped in a big thick towel, on the bed, and—like somebody probing a diseased tooth with tongue or finger, unable to stop checking that it really does hurt every now and again—he called up his memories, going through the roll call of those old and recent adversaries he'd hoped he might have lost somewhere in the darkness and the cold of space.

All his past was indeed present, and everything that had been wrong present too, and correct.

The ship was called the *Absent Friends*; its journey would take it over a century. It was a mercy voyage, in a way; its services donated by its alien owners to help assuage the aftereffects of a terrible war. He had not really deserved his place, and had used false papers and a false name to secure his escape. He'd volunteered to be woken up near the middle of the journey to provide part of the human crew because he thought it would be a shame to travel in space and never really know it, never appreciate it, never look out into that void. Those who did not choose to do crew duty would be drugged on planet, taken into space unconscious, frozen out there, and then wake up on another planet.

This seemed undignified, to him. To be treated so was to become cargo.

The two other people on duty when he was woken were Ky and Erens. Erens had been supposed to return to the ranks of the frozen people five years earlier, after a few months of duty on the ship, but had decided to stay awake until they arrived at their destination. Ky had been revived three years later and should also have gone back to sleep, to be replaced after a few months by the next person on the crew rota, but by then Erens and Ky had started to argue, and neither wanted to be the first to return to the stasis of the freeze; there had been stalemate for two and a half years while the great slow ship moved, quiet and cold, past the distant pinprick lights that were the stars. Finally they'd woken him up, at last, because he was next on the rota and they wanted somebody else to talk to. As a rule, however, he just sat in the crew section and listened to the two of them argue.

"There's still *fifty years* to go," Ky reminded Erens.

Erens waved a bottle. "I can wait. It isn't forever."

Ky nodded at the bottle. "You'll kill yourself with that stuff, and all the other junk you take. You'll never make it. You'll never see real sunlight again, or taste rain. You won't last one year let alone fifty; you should go back to sleep."

"It isn't sleep."

"You should go back to it, whatever you want to call it; you should let yourself be frozen again."

"And it isn't literally frozen . . . freezing, either." Erens looked annoyed and puzzled at the same time.

The man they'd woken up wondered how many hundreds of times the two had been through this argument.

"You should go back into your little cold cubicle like you were supposed to, five years ago, and get them to treat you for your addictions when they revive you," Ky said.

"The ship already treats me," Erens told Ky, with a kind of slow drunken dignity. "I am in a state of grace with my enthusiasms; sublimely tensioned grace." So saying, Erens tipped the bottle back and drained it.

"You'll kill yourself."

"It's my life."

"You might kill us all; everybody on the whole ship, sleepers too."

"The ship looks after itself," Erens sighed, looking round the Crew Lounge. It was the only dirty place on the ship. Everywhere else, the ship's robots tidied, but Erens had worked out how to delete the Crew Lounge from the craft's memory, and so the place could look good and scruffy. Erens stretched, kicking a couple of small recyclable cups off the table.

"Huh," Ky said. "What if you've damaged it with all your messing around?"

"I have not been 'messing around' with it," Erens said, with a small sneer. "I have altered a few of the more basic housekeeping programs; it doesn't talk to us anymore, and it lets us keep this place looking lived-in; that's about it. Nothing that's going to make the ship wander into a star or start thinking it's human and what are these intestinal parasites doing in there. But you wouldn't understand. No technical background. Livu, here; he might understand, eh?" Erens stretched out further, sliding down the grubby seat, boots scraping on the filthy surface of the table. "You understand, don't you, Darac?"

"I don't know," he admitted (he was used to answering to Darac, or Mr. Livu, or just Livu, by now). "I suppose if you know what you're doing, there's no real harm." Erens looked pleased. "On the other hand, a lot of disasters have been caused by people who thought they knew what they were doing.''

"Amen," Ky said, looking triumphant, and leaned aggressively toward Erens. "See?''

"As our friend said," Erens pointed out, reaching for another bottle. "He doesn't know.''

"You should go back with the sleepers," Ky said.

"They're not sleeping.''

"You're not supposed to be up right now; there's only supposed to be two people up at any point.''

"You go back then.''

"It isn't my turn. You were up first.''

He left them to argue.

Sometimes he would put a spacesuit on and go through the airlock into the storage sections, which were in vacuum. The storage sections made up most of the ship; over ninety-nine percent of it. There was a tiny drive unit at one end of the craft, an even tinier living unit at the other, and—in between—the bulging bulk of the ship, packed with the undead.

He walked the cold, dark corridors, looking from side to side at the sleeper units. They looked like drawers in a filing cabinet; each was the head end of something very like a coffin. A little red light glowed faintly on each one, so that standing in one of the gently spiraling corridors, with his own suit lights switched off, those small and steady sparks curved away in a ruby lattice folded over the darkness, like some infinite corridor of red giant suns set up by some obsessively tidy-minded god.

Spiraling gradually upward, moving away from the living unit at what he always thought of as the head of the ship, he walked up through its quiet, dark body. Usually he took the outermost corridor, just to appreciate the scale of the vessel. As he ascended, the pull of the ship's fake gravity gradually decreased. Eventually, walking became a series of skidding leaps in which it was always easier to hit the ceiling than make any forward progress. There were handles on the coffin-drawers; he used them once walking became too inefficient, pulling himself along toward the waist of the ship, which—as he approached it—turned one wall of coffin-drawers to a floor and the other to a ceiling, in places. Standing under a radial corridor, he leapt up, floated toward what was now the ceiling with the radial corridor a chimney up through it. He caught a coffin-drawer handle, and used a succession of them as rungs, climbing into the center of the ship.

Running through the center of the *Absent Friends* there was an elevator shaft that extended from living unit to drive unit. In the very center of the whole ship, he would summon the elevator, if it wasn't already waiting there from last time.

When it came, he would enter it, floating inside the squat, yellow-lit cylinder. He would take out a pen, or a small torch, and place it in the center of the elevator car, and just float there, watching the pen or torch, waiting to see if he had stationed it so exactly in the center of the whole slowly spinning mass of the ship that it would stay where he'd left it. He got very good at doing this, eventually, and could spend hours sitting there, with the suit lights and the elevator lights on sometimes (if it was a pen) or off (if it was a torch), watching the little object, waiting for his own dexterity to prove greater than his patience, waiting for—in other words, he could admit to himself—one part of his obsession to win over the other.

If the pen or torch moved and eventually connected with the walls or floor or ceiling of the elevator car, or drifted through the open door, then he had to float, climb (down) and then pull and walk back the way he had come. If it stayed still in the center of the car, he was allowed to take the elevator back to the living unit.

"Come on, Darac," Erens said, lighting up a pipe. "What brought you along on this one-way ride, eh?"

"I don't want to talk about it." He turned up the ventilation to get rid of Eren's drug fumes. They were in the viewing carousel, the one place in the ship where you could get a direct view of the stars. He came up here every now and again, opened the shutters and watched the stars spin slowly overhead. Sometimes he tried to read poetry.

Erens still visited the carousel alone as well, but Ky no longer did; Erens reckoned Ky got homesick, seeing the silent nothingness out there, and the lonely specks that were other suns.

"Why not?" Erens said.

He shook his head and sat back in the couch, looking out into the darkness. "It isn't any of your business."

"I'll tell you why I came along if you tell me why you did," Erens grinned, making the words sound childish, conspiratorial.

"Get lost, Erens."

"Mine is an interesting story; you'd be fascinated."

"I'm sure," he sighed.

"But I won't tell you unless you tell me first. You're missing a lot; mm-hmm."

"Well, I'll just have to live with that," he said. He turned down the lighting in the carousel until the brightest thing in it was Erens' face, glowing red with reflected light on each draw of the pipe. He shook his head when Erens offered him the drug.

"You need to loosen up, my friend," Erens told him, slumping back in the other seat. "Get high; share your problems."

"What problems?"

He saw Erens' head shake in the darkness. "Nobody on this ship hasn't got problems, friend. Nobody out here not running away from something."

"Ah; ship psychiatrist now are we?"

"Hey, come on; nobody's going back, are they? Nobody on here's ever going back home. Half the people we know are probably dead already, and the ones that aren't will be, by the time we get where we're going. So if we can't ever see the people we used to know again, and probably never see home again, it has to be something pretty damn important and pretty damn bad, pretty damn *evil* to make a body up and leave like that. We all *got* to be running from something, whether it's something we did or something we had done to us."

"Maybe some people just like traveling."

"That's crap; nobody likes traveling that much."

He shrugged. "Whatever."

"Aw, Darac, come on; argue, dammit."

"I don't believe in argument," he said, looking out into the darkness (and saw a towering ship, a capital ship, ringed with its layers and levels of armament and armor, dark against the dusk light, but not dead).

"You don't?" Erens said, genuinely surprised. "Shit, and I thought I was the cynical one."

"It's not cynicism," he said flatly. "I just think people overvalue argument because they like to hear themselves talk."

"Oh well, thank *you*."

"It's comforting, I suppose." He watched the stars wheel, like absurdly slow shells seen at night; rising, peaking, falling . . . (And reminded himself that the stars too would explode, perhaps, one day.) "Most people are not prepared to have their minds changed," he said. "And I think they know in their hearts that other people are just the same, and one of the reasons people become angry when they argue is that they realize just that, as they trot out their excuses."

"*Excuses*, eh? Well, if this ain't cynicism, what is?" Erens snorted.

"Yes, excuses," he said, with what Erens thought might just have been a trace of bitterness. "I strongly suspect the things people believe in are usually just what they instinctively feel is right; the excuses, the justifications, the things you're supposed to argue about, come later. They're the least important part of the belief. That's why you can destroy them, win an argument, prove the other person wrong, and still they believe what they did in the first place." He looked at Erens. "You've attacked the wrong thing."

"So what do you suggest one does, Professor, if one is not to indulge in this futile . . . arguing stuff?"

"Agree to disagree," he said. "Or fight."

"*Fight?*"

He shrugged. "What else is left?"

"Negotiate?"

"Negotiation is a way to come to a conclusion; it's the type of conclusion that I'm talking about."

"Which basically is disagree or fight?"

"If it comes to it."

Erens was silent for a while, drawing on the pipe until its red glow faded, then saying, "You have a military background, at all, yeah?"

He sat and watched the stars. Eventually he turned his head and looked at Erens. "I think the war gave us all a military background, don't you?"

"Hmm," Erens said. They both studied the slowly moving star field.

Twice, in the depths of the sleeping ship, he almost killed somebody. One of those times, it was somebody else.

He stopped on the long, spiraling outer corridor, about halfway to the waist of the ship, where he felt very light on his feet, and his face was a little flushed with effects of normal blood pressure working against the reduced pull. He hadn't intended to look at any of the stored people—the truth was, he never really thought about them in any but the most abstract way—but suddenly he wanted to see something more of a sleeper than just a little red light. He stopped at one of the coffin-drawers.

He had been shown how to work them after he'd volunteered to act as a crew, and had another, rather perfunctory, run through the procedures shortly after being revived. He turned the suit lights on, flipped out the drawer's control pad, and carefully—using one bulky, gloved finger—keyed in the code that Erens said turned off the ship's monitoring system. A little blue light came on. The red light stayed steady; if it flashed the ship knew there was something wrong.

He unlocked the cabinet, drew the whole device sliding out.

He looked at the woman's name, printed on a plastic strip stuck to the head unit. No one he knew, anyway, he thought. He opened the inner cover.

He looked in at the woman's calm, deathly pale face. His lights reflected on the crinkled transparent plastic wrapping covering her like something you'd buy in a shop. Tubes in her nose and mouth, leading away beneath her. A small screen flashed on above her tied-up hair, on the head unit. He looked; she seemed in good shape, for somebody so nearly completely dead. Her hands were crossed across the chest of the paper tunic she wore. He looked at her fingernails, like Erens had said. Quite long, but he'd seen people grow them longer.

He looked at the control pad again, entered another code. Lights flashed all over the control surface; the red light did not start flashing, but almost everything else did. He opened a little red and green door set in the top of the head unit. Out of it he took a small sphere of what looked like fine green wires, containing an ice blue cube. A compartment alongside gave access to a covered switch. He pushed the cover back, put his finger down to the switch.

He held the woman's recorded brain patterns, backed up onto the little blue cube. Easily crushable. His other hand, finger resting on the small switch, could turn off her life.

He wondered if he would do it, and seemed to wait for a while, as if expecting some part of his own mind to assume control for him. A couple of times it seemed to him that he felt the start of the impulse to throw the switch, and could have started to do so just an instant later, but each time suppressed the urge. He left his finger there, looked at the small cube inside its protective cage. He thought how remarkable and at the same time how oddly sad it was that all of a human mind could be contained in something so small. Then he reflected that a human brain was not so very much bigger than the little blue cube, and used resources and techniques far more ancient, and so was no less impressive (and still as sad).

He closed the woman up again in her chill sleep, and continued on his slow-motion walk to the center of the ship.

"I don't know any stories."

"Everybody knows stories," Ky told him.

"I don't. No proper stories."

"What's a 'proper' story?" Ky sneered. They sat in the Crew Lounge, surrounded by their debris.

He shrugged. "An interesting one. One people want to listen to."

"People want to listen to different things. What one person would call a proper story might not please somebody else."

"Well, I can only go by what I think would be a proper story, and I don't have any. Not stories that I want to tell, anyway." He grinned coldly at Ky.

"Ah; that's different," Ky nodded.

"Indeed it is."

"Well, tell me what you believe in, then," Ky said, leaning toward him.

"Why should I?"

"Why shouldn't you? Tell me because I asked."

"No."

"Don't be so stand-offish. We're the only three people for billions of kilometers and the ship's a bore; who else is there to talk to?"

"Nothing."

"Exactly. Nothing and nobody." Ky looked pleased.

"No; I meant that's what I believe in; nothing."

"At *all*?"

He nodded. Ky sat back, thoughtful, nodding. "They must have hurt you bad."

"Who?"

"Whoever robbed you of whatever it was you used to believe in."

He shook his head slowly. "Nobody ever robbed me of anything," he said. Ky was silent for a while, so he sighed and said, "So, Ky, what do you believe in?"

Ky looked at the blank screen that covered most of one wall of the lounge. "Something other than nothing."

"Anything with a name is other than nothing," he said.

"I believe in what's around us," Ky said, arms crossed, sitting back in the seat. "I believe in what you can see from the carousel, what we'd see if that screen was on, although what you'd see wouldn't be the only *sort* of what I believe in that I believe in."

"In a word, Ky," he said.

"Emptiness," Ky said with a flickering, jittery smile. "I believe in emptiness."

He laughed. "That's pretty close to nothing."

"Not really," Ky said.

"Looks it to most of us."

"Let me tell you a sort of story."

"Must you?"

"No more than you must listen."

"Yeah . . . okay, then. Anything to pass the time."

"The story is this. It's a true story, by the way, not that that matters. There is a place where the existence or non-existence of souls is taken very seriously indeed. Many people, whole seminaries, colleges, universities, cities and even states devote almost all their time to the contemplation and disputation of this matter and related topics.

"About a thousand years ago, a wise philosopher-king

who was considered the wisest man in the world announced that people spent too much time discussing these things, and could, if the matter was settled, apply their energies to more practical pursuits which would benefit everybody. So he would end the argument once and for all.

"He summoned the wisest men and women from every part of the world, and of every known persuasion, to discuss the matter.

"It took many years to assemble every single person who wished to take part, and the resulting debates, papers, tracts, books, intrigues and even fights and murders took even longer.

"The philosopher-king took himself off to the mountains to spend these years alone, emptying his mind of everything so that he would be able, he hoped, to come back once the process of argument was ended and pronounce the final decision.

"After many years they sent for the king, and when he felt ready he listened to everyone who thought they had something to say on the existence of souls. When they had all said their piece, the king went away to think.

"After a year, the king announced he had come to his decision. He said that the answer was not quite so simple as everybody had thought, and he would publish a book, in several volumes, to explain the answer.

"The king set up two publishing houses, and each published a great and mighty volume. One repeated the sentences, 'Souls do exist. Souls do not exist,' time after time, part after part, page after page, section after section, chapter after chapter, book after book. The other repeated the words, 'Souls do not exist. Souls do exist,' in the same fashion. In the language of the kingdom, I might add, each sentence had the same number of words, even the same number of letters. These were the only words to be found beyond the title page in all the thousands of pages in each volume.

"The king had made sure that the books began and finished printing at the same time, and were published at the same time, and that exactly the same number were published. Neither of the publishing houses had any perceivable superiority or seniority over the other.

"People searched the volumes for clues; they looked for a single repetition, buried deep in the volumes, where a sentence or even a letter had been missed out or altered, but they found none. They turned to the king himself, but he had taken a vow of silence, and bound up his writing hand. He would still nod or shake his head in reply to questions concerning the governing of his kingdom, but on the subject of the two volumes, and the existence or otherwise of souls, the king would give no sign.

"Furious disputes arose, many books were written; new cults began.

"Then a half year after the two volumes had been published, two more appeared, and this time the house that had published the volume beginning, 'Souls do not exist,' published the volume which began, 'Souls do exist.' The other publisher followed suit, so that theirs now began, 'Souls do not exist.' This became the pattern.

"The king lived to be very old, and saw several dozen volumes published. When he was on his death bed, the court philosopher placed copies of the book on either side of him, hoping the king's head would fall to one side or the other at the moment of death, so indicating by the first sentence of the appropriate volume which conclusion he had really come to . . . but he died with his head straight on the pillow and with his eyes, under the eyelids, looking straight ahead.

"That was a thousand years ago," Ky said. "The books are published still; they have become an entire industry, an entire philosophy, a source of unending argument and—"

"Is there an ending to this story?" he asked, holding up one hand.

"No," Ky smiled smugly. "There is not. But that is just the point."

He shook his head, got up and left the Crew Lounge.

"But just because something does not have an ending," Ky shouted, "doesn't mean it doesn't have a . . ."

The man closed the elevator door, outside in the corridor; Ky rocked forward in the seat and watched the lift-level indicator ascend to the middle of the ship. ". . . conclusion," Ky said, quietly.

He'd been revived nearly half a year when he almost killed himself.

He was in the elevator car, watching a torch he had left in the center of the car as it slowly spun. He had left the torch switched on, and put out all the other lights. He watched the tiny spot of light move slowly around the circular wall of the car, slow as any clock hand.

He remembered the search lights of the Staberinde, and wondered how far they were away from it now. So far that even the sun itself must be weaker than a searchlight seen from space.

He did not know why that made him think of just taking off the helmet, but found himself starting to do it, nevertheless.

He stopped. It was quite a complicated procedure to open the suit while in vacuum. He knew each of the steps, but it would take some time. He looked at the white spot of light which the torch was shining on the wall of the lift, not far from his head. The white spot was gradually coming closer as the torch spun. He would start to ready the suit to take the helmet off; if the torch beam hit his eye—no, his face, any part of his head—before that, then he would stop, and go back as though nothing had happened. Otherwise, if the spot of light did not strike his face in time, he would take the helmet off and die.

He allowed himself the luxury of letting the memories wash over him, while his hands slowly began the sequence that would end, unless interrupted, with the helmet being blasted off his shoulders by the air pressure.

Staberinde, the great metal ship stuck in stone (and a stone ship, a building stuck in water), and the two sisters. Darckense; Livueta (and of course he'd realized at the time that he was taking their names, or something like their names, in making the one he masqueraded under now). And Zakalwe, and Elethiomel. Elethiomel the terrible, Elethiomel the Chairmaker . . .

The suit beeped at him, trying to warn him he was doing something very dangerous. The spot of light was a few centimeters from his head.

Zakalwe; he tried to ask himself what the name meant to him. What did it mean to anybody? Ask them all back home; what does this name mean to you? War, perhaps, in the immediate aftermath; a great family, if your memory was long enough; a kind of tragedy. If you knew the story.

He saw the chair again. Small and white. He closed his eyes, tasting bitterness in his throat.

He opened his eyes. Three final clips to go, then one quick twist . . . he looked at the spot of light. It was invisible, so close to the helmet, so close to his head. The torch in the center of the elevator car was facing almost straight at him, its lens bright. He undid one of the three final helmet clips. There was a tiny hiss, barely noticeable.

Dead, he thought, seeing the girl's pale face. He undid another clip. The hiss grew no louder.

There was a sense of brightness at the side of the helmet, where the light would be shining.

Metal ship, stone ship, and the unconventional chair. He felt tears come to his eyes, and one hand—the one not un-doing the third helmet clip—went to his chest, where, under the many synthetic layers of the suit, beneath the fabric of the undersuit, there was a small puckered mark on the skin just over his heart; a scar that was two decades old, or seven decades old, depending how you measured time.

The torch swung, and just as the final clip came undone, and the spot of light started to leave the inside edge of the suit, to shine on his face, the torch flickered and went out.

He stared. It was almost totally dark. There was the hint of light from outside the car; the faintest of red glows, produced by all the near-dead people and the quietly watching equipment.

Out. The torch had gone out; charge exhausted or just a fault, it didn't matter. It had gone out. It hadn't shone on his face. The suit beeped again, plaintive above the quiet hiss of escaping air.

He looked down, at the hand that lay over his chest.

He looked back up at where the torch must be, unseen in the center of the car in the center of the ship, in the middle of its journey.

How do I die now? he thought.

He did go back to his chill sleep, after a year. Erens and Ky, their sexual predilections forever estranging them despite the fact they seemed like a well-matched couple otherwise, were still arguing when he left.

He ended up in another lo-tech war, learning to fly (be-cause he knew now that aircraft would always win against a battleship), and flying the frosty vortices of air above the vast white islands that were the colliding tabular icebergs.

13

Where they lay, the discarded robes looked like the just-shed skin of some exotic reptile. He had been going to wear those, but then changed his mind. He would wear the clothes he had come here in.

He stood in the bathroom, in its steams and smells, stopping the razor again, then putting it to his head, slowly and carefully as though pulling a comb through his hair in slow motion. The razor scraped through the foam on his skin, catching a last few stubbly hairs. He swept the razor past the tops of his ears, then took up a towel, wiped the gleaming skin of his skull, inspecting the baby-smooth landscape he had revealed. The long dark hair lay scattered on the floor, like plumage scattered during a fight.

He looked out to the citadel parade grounds, where a few weak fires glowed. Above the mountains, the sky was just starting to become light.

From the window, he could see a few craggy levels of the citadel's curbed wall and jutting towers. In that first outlining light, it looked, he thought—though trying hard not to feel maudlin—poignant, even noble, now that he knew it was doomed.

He turned from the sight and went to put on his shoes.

The air moved over his shaven skull, feeling very strange. He missed the feel and sweep of his hair on the nape of his neck. He sat on the bed, pulled on the shoes and clasped them, then looked at the telephone sitting on the bedside cabinet. He lifted the device.

He recalled (he seemed to remember) contacting the space port last night, after Sma and Skaffen-Amtiskaw had gone. He had been feeling bad, dissociated and remote somehow, and he was not at all certain he really did remember calling the technicians there, but he thought he probably had. He'd told them to ready the ancient spacecraft, for the Decapitation strike, some time that morning. Or he hadn't. One of the two. Maybe he had been dreaming.

He heard the citadel operator asking him who he wanted. He asked for the space port.

He talked to the technicians. The chief flight engineer sounded tense, excited. The craft was ready, fueled up, co-ordinates locked in; it could be launched within a few minutes as soon as he gave the word.

He nodded to himself as he listened to the man. He heard the chief flight engineer pause. The question was unasked, but there.

He watched the skies outside the window. They still looked dark, from inside here. "Sir?" the chief flight engineer said. "Sir Zakalwe? What are your orders, sir?"

He saw the little blue cube, the button; he heard the whisper of escaping air. There was a shudder, just then. He thought it was his own body, reacting involuntarily, but it was not; the shudder ran through the fabric of the citadel, through the walls of the room, through the bed beneath him. Glass rattled in the room. The noise of the explosion rumbled through the air beyond the thick windows, low and unsettling.

"Sir?" the man said. "Are you still there?"

They would probably intercept the spacecraft; the Culture itself—the *Xenophobe*, probably—would use effectors on it . . . the decapitation strike was bound to fail . . .

"What should we do, sir?"

But there was always a possibility . . .

"Hello? Hello, sir?"

Another explosion shook the citadel. He looked at the handset he held. "Sir, do we go ahead?" he heard a man say, or remembered a man saying, from long ago and far

away . . . And he had said yes, and taken on a terrible cargo
of memories, and all the names that might bury him . . .

"Stand down," he said quietly. "We won't need the strike
now," he said. He put the handset down, and left the room
quickly, taking the rear stairs, away from the main entrance
to his apartments, where he could already hear a commotion
building.

More explosions shook the citadel, dislodging dust around
him as the curtain wall was breached and breached again. He
wondered how it would be with the regional headquarters, how
they would fall, and whether the raid to capture the high priests
would be as bloodless as Sma had hoped. But he realized even
as he thought about it that he no longer really cared.

He left the citadel via a postern and entered the great
square that was the parade ground. The small fires still burned
outside the tents of the refugees. In the distance, great clouds
of dust and smoke floated slowly into the gray dawn sky
above the curtain wall. He could see a couple of gaps in the
wall from here. The people in the tents were starting to wake
up and come out. From the citadel walls at his back and
above him, he could hear the crackle of gunfire.

A heavier gun fired from the breached walls, and a huge
explosion shook the ground, ripping a great hole in the cliff
that was the citadel; an avalanche of stone thundered into the
parade ground, burying a dozen tents. He wondered what sort
of ammunition the tank was firing; not a type they'd had until
this morning, he suspected.

He walked on through the tent city, as the people appeared, blinking, from their sleep. Scattered firing continued
from the citadel; the vast cloud of dust rolled over the parade
ground from the great tumbled breach in the towering walls.
Another shot from near the curtain walls; another ground-
quaking detonation that brought a whole side of the citadel
down, the stone bursting from the wall as though with relief,
falling and tumbling in their own rolling dust; released, returning to the earth.

There was less firing from the citadel ramparts now, as
the dust drifted and the sky slowly lightened and the frightened people clutched at each other outside their tents. More
firing came from the breached curtain walls, and from inside
the parade ground, within the tent city.

He walked on. Nobody stopped him; few people really

seemed to notice him. He saw a soldier fall from the curtain
wall to his right, tumbling into the dust. He saw the people
running this way and that. He saw the Imperial Army soldiers, in the distance, riding on a tank.

He walked through the clustered tents, avoiding people
running, stepping over a couple of the smoldering fires. The
huge breaches in the curtain wall and the citadel itself smoked
in the increasing gray light, which was just starting to take
on color as the sky burned pink and blue.

Sometimes, as the people milled and streamed around
him, running past, clutching babies, dragging children, he
thought he saw people he recognized, and several times was
on the point of turning and talking to them, putting out his
hand to stop the snowfall of faces rushing past him, shouting
after them . . .

Suddenly aircraft screamed overhead, tearing through the
air over the curtain wall, dropping long canisters into the
tents, which erupted in flame and black, black smoke. He
saw burning people, heard the screams, smelled the roasting
flesh. He shook his head.

Terrified people jostled him, bumped into him, once
knocked him down so that he had to pick himself up, dust
himself down, and suffer the knocks and the shouts and
screams and curses. The aircraft came back, strafing, and he
was the only one who stayed upright, walking while the rest
fell to the ground; he watched the puffs and bursts of dust
fountain in lines around him, saw the clothing of a few of the
fallen people suddenly jerk and flap as a round hit home.

It was getting lighter as he encountered the first troops.
He dodged behind a tent and rolled as a trooper fired at
him, then got back on his feet and ran round the rear of a
tent, almost bumping into another soldier, who swung his
carbine round too late. He kicked it away. The soldier drew
a knife. He let him lunge and took the knife, throwing the
soldier to the ground. He looked at the blade he held in his
hand, and shook his head. He threw the knife away, looked
at the soldier—lying on the ground staring fearfully up at
him—then shrugged and walked away.

Still people rushing past; soldiers shouting. He saw one
take aim at him, and could not see anywhere to go for cover.
He raised his hand to explain, to say there was really no need,
but the man shot him anyway.

Not a very good shot, considering the range, he thought as he was kicked back and spun round by the force of the impact.

Upper chest near the shoulder. No lung damage, and possibly not even a chipped rib, he thought as the shock and pain burst through him, and he fell.

He lay still in the dust, near the staring face of a dead city guardsman. As he'd spun round, he'd seen the Culture module; a clear shape hovering uselessly over the remains of his apartments high in the ruined citadel.

Somebody kicked him, turning him over and bursting a rib at the same time. He tried not to react to the stab of pain, but looked through cracked eyes. He waited for the coup de grace, but it did not come.

The shadow-figure above him, dark against light, passed on.

He lay a while longer, then got up. It wasn't too difficult to walk at first, but then the planes came back again, and though he didn't get hit by a bullet, something splintered somewhere nearby, as he passed by some tents that shook and rippled as the bullets hit them, and he wondered if the sharp, puncturing pain in his thigh was a bit of wood or stone, or even bone, from somebody in one of the tents. "No," he muttered to himself as he limped away, heading for the biggest breach in the wall. "No; not funny. Not bone. Not funny."

An explosion blew him off his feet, into and through a tent. He got up, head buzzing. He looked round and up at the citadel, its summit starting to glow with the first direct sunlight of the day. He couldn't see the module anymore. He took a shattered wooden tent pole to use as a crutch; his leg was hurting.

Dust wrapped him, screams of engines and aircraft and human voices pierced him; the smells of burning and stone dust and exhaust fumes choked him. His wounds talked to him in the languages of pain and damage, and he had to listen to them, but paid them no further heed. He was shaken and pummeled and tripped and stumbled and drained and fell to his knees, and thought perhaps he was hit by more bullets, but was no longer sure.

Eventually, near the breach, he fell, and thought he might just lie here for a while. The light was better, and he felt tired. The dust drifted like pale shrouds. He looked up at the sky, pale blue, and thought how beautiful it was, even through all this dust, and, listening to the tanks as they came crunching up through the slope of wrecked stones, reflected that, like tanks everywhere, they squeaked more than they roared.

"Gentlemen," (he whispered to the rabid blue sky) "I am reminded of something the worshipful Sma said to me once, on the subject of heroism, which was something like: 'Zakalwe, in all the human societies we have ever reviewed, in every age and every state, there has seldom if ever been a shortage of eager young males prepared to kill and die to preserve the security, comfort and prejudices of their elders, and what you call heroism is just an expression of this simple fact; there is never a scarcity of idiots.' " He sighed. "Well, no doubt she didn't say *every* age and *every* state, because the Culture just loves there to be exceptions to everything, but . . . that was the gist of it . . . I think . . ."

He rolled over, away from the achingly blue sky, to stare at the blurred dust.

Eventually, reluctantly, he pushed himself over, and then half up, then to his knees, then clutched at the tent-pole crutch and forced down on it, and got to his feet, ignoring all the pestering aches and pains, and staggered for the piled wreckage of the walls, and somehow dragged and hauled and scraped his way to the top, where the walls ran smooth and wide for a way, like roadways in the sky, and the bodies of a dozen or so soldiers lay, blood pooling, the ramparts around them scarred with bullet holes and gray with dust.

He staggered toward them, as though anxious to be one of their number. He scanned the skies for the module.

It was some time before they spotted the "Z" sign he made from the bodies on the top of the walls, but in that language it was a complicated letter, and he kept getting mixed up.

I

No lights burned on the *Staberinde*. It sat squat against the gray leechings of the false dawn, its dim silhouette a piled cone which only hinted at the concentric loops and lines of its decks and guns. Some effect of the marsh mists between him and the ziggurat of the ship made it look as though its black shape was not attached to the land at all, but floated over it, poised like some threatening dark cloud.

He watched with tired eyes, stood on tired feet. This close to the city and the ship, he could smell the sea, and—nose this close to the concrete of the bunker—a limy scent, acrid and bitter. He tried to remember the garden and the smell of flowers, the way he sometimes did whenever the fighting started to seem just too futile and cruel to have any point whatsoever, but for once he could not conjure up that faintly remembered, beguilingly poignant perfume, or recall anything good that had come out of that garden (instead he saw again those suntanned hands on his sister's pale hips, the ridiculous little chair they'd chosen for their fornication . . . and he remembered the last time he'd seen the garden, the last time he'd been to the estate; with the tank corps, and he'd seen the chaos and ruin Elethiomel had visited upon the place that had been the cradle for both of them; the great house gutted, the stone boat wrecked, the woods burned . . . and his last glimpse of the hateful little summerhouse where he'd found them, as he took his own retaliatory action against the tyranny of memory; the tank rocking beneath him, the already flare-lit clearing whiting out with bright flame, his ears ringing with a sound that was no sound, and the little house . . . was still there; the shot had gone right through, exploded somewhere in the woods behind, and he'd wanted to weep and scream and tear it all down with his own hands . . . but then had remembered the man who had sat there, and thought how he might treat something like this, and so had gathered the strength to laugh at it, and ordered the gunner to aim at the top step beneath the little house, and saw it all finally lift and burst into the air. The debris fell around the tank, sprinkling him with earth and wood and ripped bundles of thatch).

The night beyond the bunker was warm and oppressive, the land's daytime heat trapped and pressed to the ground by the weight of clouds above, sticking against the skin of the land like some sweat-soaked shirt. Perhaps the wind changed then, for he thought he detected the smell of the grass and the hay in the air, swept hundreds of kilometers from the great prairies inland by some wind since spent, the old fragrance going stale now. He closed his eyes and leaned his forehead against the rough concrete of the bunker wall, beneath the slit he'd been looking through; his fingers splayed out lightly on the hard, grainy surface, and he felt the warm material press into his flesh.

Sometimes all he wanted was for it all to be over, and the way of it did not really seem to matter. Cessation was all, simple and demanding and seductive, and worth almost anything. That was when he had to think of Darckense, trapped on the ship, held captive by Elethiomel. He knew she didn't love their cousin anymore; that had been something brief and juvenile, something she'd used in her adolescence to get back at the family for some imagined slight, some favoring of Livueta over her. It might have seemed like love at the time, but he suspected even she knew it was not, now. He believed that Darckense really was an unwilling hostage; many people had been taken by surprise when Elethiomel attacked the city; just the speed of the advance had trapped half the population, and Darckense had been unlucky to be discovered trying to leave from the chaos of the airport; Elethiomel had had agents out looking for her.

So for her he had to go on fighting, even if he had almost worn away the hate in his heart for Elethiomel, the hate that had kept him fighting these last years, but now was running out, just worn down by the abrading course of the long war.

How could Elethiomel do it? Even if he didn't still love her (and the monster claimed that Livueta was his real desire), how could he use her like another shell stored in the battleship's cavernous magazines?

And what was *he* supposed to do in reply? Use Livueta against Elethiomel? Attempt the same level of cunning cruelty?

Already Livueta blamed *him*, not Elethiomel, for all that had happened. What was he supposed to do? Surrender? Barter sister for sister? Mount some mad, doomed rescue attempt? Simply attack?

He had tried to explain that only a prolonged siege guaranteed success, but argued about it so often now that he was starting to wonder if he was right.

"Sir?"

He turned, looked at the dim figures of the commanders behind him. "What?" he snapped.

"Sir,"—it was Swaels—"Sir, perhaps we should be setting off now, back to headquarters. The cloud is breaking from the east, and it will be dawn soon . . . we shouldn't be caught in range."

"I know that," he said. He glanced out at the dark outline of the *Staberinde*, and felt himself flinch a little, as though he expected its huge guns to belch flame right there and then, straight at him. He drew a metal shutter across the concrete slit. It was very dark in the bunker for a second, then somebody switched on the harsh yellow lights and they all stood there, blinking in the glare.

They left the bunker; the long mass of the armored staff car waited in the darkness. Assorted aides and junior officers leapt to attention, straightened caps, saluted and opened doors. He climbed into the car, sitting on the fur-covered rear bench, watching as three of the other commanders followed, sitting in a line opposite him. The armored door clanged shut; the car growled and moved, bumping over the uneven ground and back into the forest, away from the dark shape resting in the night behind.

"Sir," Swaels said, exchanging looks with the other two commanders. "The other commanders and I have discussed—"

"You are going to tell me that we should attack; bomb and shell the *Staberinde* until it is a flaming hulk and then storm it with troop hovers," he said, holding up one hand. "I know what you've been discussing and I know what . . . decisions you think you've arrived at. They do not interest me."

"Sir, we all realize the strain you are under because your sister is held on the ship, but—"

"That has nothing to do with it, Swaels," he told the other man. "You insult me by implying that I even consider that a reason for holding off. My reasons are sound military reasons, and foremost of those is that the enemy has succeeded in creating a fortress that is, at the moment, almost impregnable. We must wait until the winter floods, when the fleet can negotiate the estuary and the channel, and engage the *Staberinde* on equal terms; to send in aircraft or attempt to engage in an artillery duel would be the height of folly."

"Sir," Swaels said. "Much as we are distressed at having to disagree with you, we nevertheless—"

"You will be silent, Commander Swaels," he said icily. The other man swallowed. "I have sufficient matters to worry about without having to concern myself with the drivel that passes for serious military planning between my senior officers, or, I might add, with replacing any of those senior officers."

For a while there was only the distant grumbling noise of the car engine. Swaels looked shocked; the other two commanders were staring at the rug floor. Swaels' face looked shiny. He swallowed again. The voice of the laboring car seemed to emphasize the silence in the rear compartment as the four men were jostled and shaken; then the car found a metaled road, and roared off, pressing him back in the seat, making the other three sway toward him before sitting back again.

"Sir, I am ready to lea—"

"Must this go on?" he complained, hoping to stop

Swaels. ''Can't you lift even this small burden from me? All I ask is that you do as you ought. Let there be no disagreement; let us fight the enemy, not among ourselves.''

''. . . to leave your staff, if you so wish,'' Swaels continued.

Now it was as though the noise of the engine did not intrude inside the passenger cell at all; a frozen silence—held not in the air, but in the expression of Swaels' face and the still, tensed bodies of the other two commanders—seemed to settle over the four, like some prescient breath of a winter that was still half a year away. He wanted to close his eyes, but could not show such weakness. He kept his gaze fixed on the man directly across from him.

''Sir, I have to tell you that I disagree with the course you are pursuing, and I am not alone. Sir, please believe me that I and the other commanders love you as we love our country; with all our hearts. But because of that love, we cannot stand by while you throw away everything you stand for and all we believe in trying to defend a mistaken decision.''

He saw Swaels' hands knit together, as though in supplication. No gentleman of breeding, he thought, almost dreamily, ought to begin a sentence with the unfortunate word ''but'' . . .

''Sir, believe me; I wish that I was wrong. I and the other commanders have done everything to try to accommodate your views, but we cannot. Sir, if you have any love for any of your commanders, we beseech you; think again. Remove me if you feel you must, sir, for having spoken like this; court-martial me, demote me, execute me, forbid my name, but, sir; reconsider, while there is still time.''

They sat still, as the car hummed along the road, swerving occasionally for corners, jiggling left-right or right-left to avoid craters, and . . . and we must all look, he thought, as we sit here, frozen in the weak yellow light, like the stiffening dead.

''Stop the car,'' he heard himself saying. His finger was already depressing the intercom button. The car rumbled down through the gears and came to a halt. He opened the door. Swaels' eyes were closed.

''Get out,'' he told him.

Swaels looked suddenly like an old man hit by the first of many blows. It was as though he had shrunk, collapsed inside. A warm gust of wind threatened to close the door again; he held it open with one hand.

Swaels bent forward and got slowly out of the car. He stood by the dark roadside for a moment; the cone of light thrown out by the staff car's interior lights swept across his face, then disappeared.

Zakalwe locked the door. "Drive on," he told the driver.

They raced away from the dawn and the *Staberinde*, before its guns could find and destroy them.

They had thought they'd won. In the spring they'd had more men and more matériel and in particular they had more heavy guns; at sea the *Staberinde* lurked as a threat but not a presence, famished of the fuel it needed for effective raids against their forces and convoys; almost more of a liability. But then Elethiomel had had the great battleship tugged and dredged through the seasonal channels, over the ever-changing banks to the empty drydock, where they'd blasted the extra room and somehow got the ship inside, closed the gates, pumped out the water and pumped in concrete, and—so his advisors had suggested—probably some sort of shock-absorbing cushion between the metal and the concrete, or the half-meter caliber guns would have shaken the vessel to pieces by now. They suspected Elethiomel had used rubbish; junk, to line the sides of his improvised fortress.

He found that almost amusing.

The *Staberinde* was not really impregnable (though it was, now, quite literally unsinkable); it could be taken, but it would exact a terrible price in the taking.

And of course, having had their breathing space, and time to reequip, perhaps the forces in and around the ship and the city would break out; that possibility had been discussed, too, and Elethiomel was quite capable of it.

But whatever he thought about it, however he approached the problem, it always came back to him. The men would do as he asked; the commanders would too, or he'd have them replaced; the politicians and the church had given him a free hand and would back him in anything he did. He felt secure in that; as secure as any commander ever could. But what *was* he to do?

He had expected to inherit a perfectly drilled peacetime

army, splendid and impressive, and eventually to hand that
over to some other young scion of the Court in the same
creditable condition, so that the traditions of honor and obe-
dience and duty could be continued. Instead he found himself
at the head of an army going to furious war against an enemy
he knew was largely made up of his own countrymen, and
commanded by a man he had once thought of as a friend as
well as almost a brother.

So he had to give orders that meant men died, and sometimes sacrifice hundreds, thousands of them, knowingly sending them to their near-certain deaths, just to secure some
important position or goal, or protect some vital position.
And always, whether they liked it or not, the civilians suffered too; the very people they both claimed to be fighting
for made up perhaps the bulk of the casualties in their bloody
struggle.

He had tried to stop it, tried to bargain, from the beginning, but neither side wanted peace on anything except its
own terms, and he had no real political power, and so had
had to fight. His success had amazed him, as it had others,
probably not least Elethiomel, but now, poised on the brink
of victory—perhaps—he just did not know what to do.

More than anything else now, though, he wanted to save
Darckense. He had seen too many dead, dry eyes, too much
air-blackened blood, too much fly-blown flesh, to be able to
relate such ghastly truths to the nebulous ideas of honor and
tradition that people claimed they were fighting for. Only the
well-being of one loved person seemed really worth fighting
for now; it was all that seemed real, all that could save his
sanity. To acknowledge the interest millions of other people
had in whatever happened here was to place too great a burden on him; it would be to admit, by implication, that he was
at least partially responsible for the deaths already of hundreds of thousands, even if nobody else could have fought
more humanely.

So he waited; held back the commanders and the squadron leaders, and waited for Elethiomel to reply to his signals.

The two other commanders said nothing. He put out the
lights in the car, unshuttered the doors, and looked out at the
dark mass of the forest, racing past under dull dawn skies the
color of steel.

They moved past dim bunkers, dark trenches, still figures,

stopped trucks, sunken tanks, taped windows, hooded guns, raised poles, gray clearings, wrecked buildings and slitted lamps; all the paraphernalia of the outskirts of the headquarters camp. He watched it all and wished—as they moved closer to the center, to the old castle that had become his home in all but name over the last couple of months—he wished that he did not have to stop, and could just go on driving through the dawn and the day and the night again forever, cleaving the finally unyielding trees toward nothing and nowhere and no one—even if it was in an icy silence—secure in the nadir of his sufferings, perversely content that at least now they could grow no worse; just to go on and on and never have to stop and make decisions that would not wait but which might mean he would commit mistakes he could never forget and would never be forgiven for . . .

The car reached the castle courtyard and he got out. Surrounded by aides, he swept into the grand old house that had, once, been Elethiomel's HQ.

They pestered him with a hundred details of logistics and intelligence reports and skirmishes and small amounts of ground lost or gained; there were requests from civilians and the foreign press for this and that. He dismissed them all, told the junior commanders to deal with them. He took the stairs to his offices two at a time, handed his jacket and cap to his ADC, and closed himself in his darkened study, his eyes closed, his back against the double doors, the brass handles still clutched in his hands at the small of his back. The quiet, dark room was a balm.

"Been out to gaze upon the beast, have you?"

He started, then recognized Livueta's voice. He saw her by the windows, a dark figure. He relaxed. "Yes," he said. "Close the drapes."

He turned on the room lights.

"What are you going to do?" she said, walking slowly closer, her arms folded, her dark hair gathered up, her face troubled.

"I don't know," he admitted, going to the desk and sitting. He put his face in his hands and rubbed it. "What would you have me do?"

"Talk with him," she said, sitting on the corner of the desk, arms still crossed. She was dressed in a long dark skirt, dark jacket. She was always in dark clothes nowadays.

"He won't talk to me," he said, sitting back in the ornate chair he knew the junior officers called his throne. "I can't make him reply."

"You can't be saying the right things," she said.

"I don't know what to say, then," he said, closing his eyes again. "Why don't you compose the next message?"

"You wouldn't let me say what I'd want to say, or if you let me say it, you wouldn't live up to it."

"We can't just all lay down our weapons, Livvy, and I don't think anything else would work; he wouldn't pay any attention."

"You could meet face to face; that might be the way to settle things."

"Livvy; the first messenger we sent personally came back without his SKIN!" He screamed the last word, suddenly losing all patience and control. Livueta flinched, and stepped away from the desk. She sat in an ornamental winged couch, her long fingers rubbing at the gold thread sewn into an arm.

"I'm sorry," he said quietly. "I didn't mean to shout."

"She's our sister, Cheradenine. There must be more we can do."

He looked about the room, as though for some fresh inspiration, "Livvy; we have been over this and over this and over this; don't you . . . can't I get it through? Isn't it clear?" He slapped both hands on the desk. "I am doing all I can. I want her out of there as much as you do, but while he has her, there is just nothing more I can do; except attack, and that probably would be the death of her."

She shook her head. "What is it between you two?" she asked. "Why won't you talk to each other? How can you forget everything from when we were children?"

He shook his head, pushed himself up from the desk, turned to the book-lined wall behind, gaze running over the hundreds of titles without really seeing them. "Oh," he said tiredly, "I haven't forgotten, Livueta." He felt a terrible sadness then, as though the extent of what he felt they had all lost only became real to him when there was somebody else there to acknowledge it. "I haven't forgotten anything."

"There must be something else you can do," she insisted.

"Livueta, please believe me; there isn't."

"I believed you when you told me she was safe and well,"

the woman said, looking down at the arm of the couch, where her long nails had started to pick at the precious thread. Her mouth was a tight line.

"You were ill," he sighed.

"What difference does that make?"

"You might have died!" he said. He went to the curtains and began straightening them. "Livueta; I couldn't have told you they had Darckle; the shock—"

"The shock for this poor, weak woman," Livueta said, shaking her head, still tearing at the threads on the couch arm. "I'd rather you spared me that insulting nonsense than spare me the truth about my own sister."

"I was only trying to do what was best," he told her, starting toward her, then stopping, retreating to the corner of the desk where she had sat.

"I'm sure," she said laconically. "The habit of taking responsibility comes with your exalted position, I suppose. I am expected to be grateful, no doubt."

"Livvy, please, must you—?"

"Must I what?" She looked at him, eyes sparkling. "Must I make life difficult for you? Yes?"

"All I want," he said slowly, trying to control himself. "Is for you to try . . . and understand. We need to . . . to stick together, to support each other right now."

"You mean I have to support you even though you won't support Darckle," Livueta said.

"Dammit, Livvy!" he shouted. "I am doing my best! There isn't just her; there's a lot of other people I have to worry about. All my men; the civilians in the city; the whole damn country!" He went forward to her, knelt in front of the winged couch, put his hand on the same arm that her long-nailed hand picked at. "Livueta; please. I am doing all it is possible to do. Help me in this. Back me up. The other commanders want to attack; I'm all there is between Darckense and—"

"Maybe you should attack," she said suddenly. "Maybe that's the one thing he isn't expecting."

He shook his head. "He has her in the ship; we'd have to destroy that before we can take the city." He looked her in the eye. "Do you trust him not to kill her, even if she isn't killed in the attack?"

"Yes," Livueta said. "Yes, I do."

He held her gaze for a while, certain that she would recant or at least look away, but she just kept looking straight back at him. "Well," he said eventually, "I can't take that risk." He sighed, closing his eyes, resting his head against the arm of the couch. "There's so much . . . pressure on me." He tried to take her hand, but she pulled it away. "Livueta, don't you think I *feel*? Don't you think I care about what happens to Darckle? Do you think that I'm not still the brother you knew as well as the soldier they made me? Do you think that because I have an army to do my bidding, and ADCs and junior officers to obey every whim, I don't get *lonely*?"

She stood up suddenly, without touching him. "Yes," she said, looking down at him, while he looked at the threads of gold on the couch arm. "You are lonely, and I am lonely, and Darckense is lonely, and he is lonely, and everybody is *lonely*!"

She turned quickly, the long skirt briefly belling, and walked to the door and out. He heard the doors slam, and stayed where he was, kneeling in front of the abandoned couch like some rejected suitor. He pushed his smallest finger through a loop in the gold thread Livueta had teased from the couch arm, and pulled at it until it burst.

He got up slowly, walked to the window, slipped through the drapes and stood looking out at the gray dawn. Men and machines moved through the vague wisps of mist, gray skeins like nature's own gauzy camouflage nets.

He envied the men he could see. He was sure most of them envied him, in return; he was in control, he had the soft bed and did not have to tread through trench mud, or deliberately stub his toes against rocks to keep awake on guard duty . . . But he envied them, nevertheless, because they only had to do what they were told. And—he admitted to himself—he envied Elethiomel.

Would that he were more like him, he thought, all too often. To have that ruthless cunning, that extemporizing guile; *he* wanted that.

He slunk back through the drapes, guilty at the thought.

At the desk he turned the room lights off and sat back in the seat. His throne, he thought and, for the first time in days, laughed a little, because it was such an image of power and he felt so utterly powerless.

He heard a truck draw up outside the window, where it

was not supposed to. He sat still, suddenly thinking; a massive bomb, just out there . . . and was suddenly terrified. He heard a sergeant barking, some talk, and then the truck moved a little way off, though he could still hear its engine.

After a while, he heard raised voices in the hall stairwell. There was something about the tone of the voices that chilled him. He tried to tell himself he was being foolish, and turned all the lights back on, but he could still hear them. Then there was something like a scream, cut off abruptly. He shook. He unholstered his pistol, wishing he had something more lethal than this slim little dress-uniform gun. He went to the door. The voices sounded odd; some were raised, while some people were apparently trying to keep theirs quiet. He opened the door a crack, then went through; his ADC was at the far door, onto the stairs, looking down.

He put the pistol back in his holster. He walked out to join the ADC, and followed his gaze, down into the hall. He saw Livueta, staring wide-eyed back up at him; there were a few other soldiers, one of the other commanders. They stood round a small white chair. He frowned; Livueta looked upset. He went quickly down the steps; Livueta suddenly came bounding up to meet him, skirt hem flying. She pushed into him, both hands against his chest. He staggered back, amazed.

"No," she said. Her eyes were bright and staring; her face looked more pale than he'd ever seen before. "Go back," she said. Her voice sounded thick, like it was not her own.

"Livueta . . ." he said, annoyed, and pushed himself away from the wall, trying to glance round her at whatever was happening in the hall round the little white chair.

She pushed him again. "Go back," the thick, strange voice said.

He took her wrists in his hands, *"Livueta,"* he said, voice low, eyes flicking to indicate the people standing beneath in the hall.

"Go back," the strange, terrifying voice said.

He pushed her away, annoyed at her, tried to go past her. She attempted to grab him from behind. "Back!" she gasped.

"Livueta, stop this!" he shook her off, embarrassed now. He clattered quickly down the steps before she could grab him again.

Still she threw herself down after him, clutched at his waist. "Go *back*!" she wailed.

He turned round. "Get off me! I want to see what's going on!" He was stronger than her; he tore her arms free, threw her down on the stairs. He went down, walked across the flagstones to where the silent group of men stood round the little white chair.

It was very small; it looked so delicate that an adult might have broken it. It was small and white, and as he took a couple of more paces forward, as the rest of the people and the hall and the castle and the world and the universe disappeared into the darkness and the silence and he came closer and slowly closer to the chair, he saw that it had been made out of the bones of Darckense Zakalwe.

Femora formed the back legs, tibiae and some other bones the front. Arm bones made the seat frame; the ribs were the back. Beneath them was the pelvis; the pelvis that had been shattered years earlier, in the stone boat, its bone fragments rejoined; the darker material the surgeons had used quite visible too. Above the ribs, there was the collar bone, also broken and healed, memoir of a riding accident.

They had tanned her skin and made a little cushion out of it; a tiny plain button in her navel, and at one corner, just the hint, the start of some dark but slightly red-tinged hair.

There were stairs, and Livueta, and the ADC, and the ADC's office, between there and here, he found himself thinking, as he stood at his desk again.

He tasted blood in his mouth, looked down at his right hand. He seemed to recall having punched Livueta on his way up the stairs. What a terrible thing to do to one's own sister.

He looked about, distracted, for a moment. Everything looked blurred.

Intending to rub his eyes, he raised one hand and found the pistol in it.

He put it to his right temple.

This was, of course, he realized, exactly what Elethiomel wanted him to do, but then, what chance did one have against such a monster? There was only so much a man could take, after all.

He smiled at the doors (somebody was thumping on them, calling out a word that might have been his name; he couldn't remember now). So silly. Doing the Right Thing; the Only Way Out. The Honorable Exit. What a load of nonsense. Just despair, just the last laugh to have, opening a mouth through the bone to confront the world direct; here.

But such consummate skill, such ability, such adaptability, such numbing ruthlessness, such a use of weapons when anything could become *weapon* . . .

His hand was shaking. He could see the doors starting to give way; somebody must be hitting them very hard. He supposed he must have locked them; there was nobody else in the room. He ought to have chosen a bigger gun, he realized; this one might not be big enough to do the job.

His mouth was very dry.

He pressed the gun hard against his temple and pulled the trigger.

The besieged forces round the *Staberinde* broke out within the hour, while the surgeons were still fighting for his life.

It was a good battle, and they nearly won.

14

"Zakalwe . . . ."
    "No."
    Still the same refusal. They stood in a park, at the edge of a large, neatly mown lawn, under some tall, pollarded trees. The warm breeze carried the ocean scent and a hint of flowers, whispering through the copse. The clearing morning mist still veiled two suns. Sma shook her head in exasperation, and walked off a little way.

    He leaned against a tree, clutching at his chest, breathing with difficulty. Skaffen-Amtiskaw hovered nearby, keeping a watch on the man, but playing with an insect on the trunk of another tree.

    Skaffen-Amtiskaw thought the man was mad; certainly he was weird. He had never really explained why he'd gone wandering through the mayhem of the citadel-storming. When Sma and the drone had finally found him and picked him up, bullet-riddled, half-dead and raving from the top of the curtain wall, he had insisted they stabilize his condition; no more. He did not want to be made well. He would not listen to sense, and still the *Xenophobe*—when it had picked them all up—had refused to pronounce the man insane and incapable of making up his own mind, and so had dutifully put him into a low-metabolism sleep for the fifteen day journey to the planet where the woman called Livueta Zakalwe now lived.

He'd come out of his slow-sleep as ill as he'd gone into it. The man was a walking mess and there were still two bullets inside him, but he refused to accept any treatment until he'd seen this woman. Bizarre, Skaffen-Amtiskaw thought, using an extended field to block the path of a small insect as it felt and picked its way up the trunk of the tree. The insect changed direction, feelers waving. There was another type of insect further up the trunk, and Skaffen-Amtiskaw was trying to get them to meet, to see what would happen.

Bizarre, and even—indeed—perverse.

"Okay." He coughed (one lung, the drone knew, filling up with blood). "Let's go." He pushed himself away from the tree. Skaffen-Amtiskaw abandoned its game with the two insects regretfully. The drone felt odd, being here; the planet was known about but had not yet been fully investigated by Contact. It had been discovered through research rather than physical exploration, and—while there was nothing obviously outlandish about the place, and a very rudimentary survey had been carried out—technically it was still terra incognita, and Skaffen-Amtiskaw was on a relatively high state of alert, just in case the place held any nasty surprises.

Sma went to the bald-headed man and put her arm round his waist, helping to support him. Together they walked up the small slope of lawn toward a low ridge. Skaffen-Amtiskaw watched them go, from the cover of the treetops, then swooped slowly down toward them as they walked to the summit of the gentle slope.

The man staggered when he saw what was on the far side, in the distance. The drone suspected he would have fallen to the grass if Sma hadn't been there to hold him up.

"Shiiit," he breathed, and tried to straighten, blinking in a sudden slant of sunlight as the mists continued to evaporate.

He stumbled another couple of steps, shook Sma off, and turned round once, taking in the parkland; shaped trees and manicured lawns, ornamental walls and delicate pergolas, stone-bordered ponds and shady paths through quiet groves. And, in the distance, set among mature trees, the tattered black shape of the *Staberinde*.

"They've made a fucking park out of it," he breathed,

and stood, swaying, bent slightly at the waist, looking at the battered silhouette of the old warship. Sma walked to his side. He seemed to sag a little, and she put her arm round his waist again. He grimaced with pain; they walked on, down toward a path which led to the ship.

"Why did you want to see this, Cheradenine?" Sma said quietly as they crunched along the gravel. The drone floated behind and above.

"Hmm?" the man said, taking his eyes off the ship for a second.

"Why did you want to come here, Cheradenine?" Sma asked. "She isn't here. This isn't where she is."

"I know," he breathed. "I know that."

"So why do you want to see this wreck?"

He was silent for a little while. It was as though he hadn't heard, but then he took a deep breath—flinching with pain as he did so—and shook his sweat-sheened head as he said, "Oh; just for . . . old times' sake . . ." They passed through another copse of trees. He shook his shaved head again as they came out of the grove, and saw the ship better. "I just didn't think . . . they'd do this to it," he said.

"Do what?" Sma asked.

"This." He nodded at the blackened hulk.

"What have they done, Cheradenine?" Sma said patiently.

"Made it." He began, then stopped, coughed, body tense with pain. "Made the damn thing . . . an ornament. Preserved it."

"What, the ship?"

He looked at her as though she were crazy. "Yes," he said. "Yes; the ship."

Just a big old battleship hulk cemented into a dock, as far as Skaffen-Amtiskaw could see. It contacted the *Xenophobe*, which was passing the time by making a detailed map of the planet.

—Hello, ship. This ship-ruin in the park; Zakalwe seems very interested. Just wondering why. Care to do some research?

—In a while; I've still got one continent, the deep sea beds and the subsurface to do.

—They'll still be there later; this could prove interesting now.

—Patience, Skaffen-Amtiskaw.

Pedant, thought the drone, breaking off.

The two humans walked down twisty paths past litter bins and benches, picnic tables and information points. Skaffen-Amtiskaw activated one of the old information points as it passed. A slow and crackly tape started up. "The vessel you see before you . . ." This was going to take ages, Skaffen-Amtiskaw thought. It used its effector to speed the machine up, winding the voice up into a high-pitched warble. The tape broke. Skaffen-Amtiskaw delivered the effector equipment of an annoyed slap, and left the information machine smoking and dripping burning plastic onto the gravel beneath, as the two humans walked into the shadow of the battered ship.

The ship had been left as it was; bombed, shelled, strafed, blasted and ripped but not destroyed. Where hands could not reach and rain did not strike, traces of the original soot from flames two centuries old still marked the armor plate. Gun turrets lay peeled open like tin cans; gun barrels and range-finders bristled askew all over the mounting levels of deck; tangled stays and fallen aerials lay strewn over shattered searchlights and lopsided radar dishes; the single great funnel looked tipped and subsided, metal pitted and flayed.

A little awning-covered stairway led up to the ship's main deck; they followed a couple with two young children. Skaffen-Amtiskaw floated, almost invisible, ten meters away, rising slowly with them. One of the toddlers cried when she saw the hobbling, bald-headed man with the staring eyes behind her. Her mother lifted her up and carried her.

He had to stop and rest when they got to the deck. Sma guided him to a bench. He sat doubled up for a while, then looked at the ship above, taking in the blackened rusted wreckage all around. He shook his shaven head, muttered to himself once, then ended up laughing quietly, holding his chest and coughing.

"Museum," he said. "A museum . . ."

Sma put her hand on his damp brow. She thought he looked terrible, and the baldness didn't suit him. The simple dark clothes they'd found him wearing when they picked him up from the citadel's curtain wall had been torn and crusted with blood; they'd been cleaned and repaired on the *Xenophobe* but they looked out of place here, where everybody seemed to be dressed in bright colors. Even Sma's culottes and jacket were somber compared to the gaily decorated dresses and smocks most of the people were wearing.

"This is an old haunt of yours, Cheradenine?" she asked him.

He nodded. "Yes," he breathed, looking up at a last few tendrils of mist flowing and disappearing like gaseous pennants from the tilted main mast. "Yes," he repeated.

Sma looked round at the park behind and the city off to one side. "This where you came from?"

He seemed not to hear. After a while, he stood slowly, and looked, distracted, into Sma's eyes. She felt herself shiver, and tried to remember exactly how old Zakalwe was. "Let's go, Da— . . . Diziet." He smiled a watery sort of smile. "Take me to her, please?"

Sma shrugged and supported the man by one shoulder. They went back to the steps that led back down to the ground.

"Drone?" Sma said to a brooch on her lapel.

"Yep?"

"Our lady still where we last heard?"

"Indeed," said the drone's voice. "Want to take the module?"

"No," he said, stumbling down a stair, until Sma caught him. "Not the module. Let's . . . take a train, or a cab or . . ."

"You sure?" Sma said.

"Yes; sure."

"Zakalwe," Sma sighed. "*Please* accept some treatment."

"No," the man said, as they reached the ground.

"There's an underground station right and right again," the drone told Sma. "Alight Central Station; platform eight for trains to Couraz."

"Okay," Sma said reluctantly, glancing at him. He was looking down at the gravel path as though concentrating on working out which foot to put in front of another. He swung his head as they passed under the stem of the ruined battleship, squinting up at the tall curving V of the bows. Sma watched the expression on his sweating face, and could not decide whether it was awe, disbelief, or something like terror.

The underground train whisked them into the city center down concrete-lined tunnels; the main station was crowded, tall, echoing and clean. Sunlight sparkled on the vault of the arched glass roof. Skaffen-Amtiskaw had done its suitcase impression, and sat lightly in Sma's hand. The wounded man was a heavier weight on her other arm.

The Maglev train drew in, disgorged its passengers; they boarded with a few other people.

"You going to make it, Cheradenine?" Sma asked him. He was slumped in the seat, resting his arms on the table in a way that somehow made them look as though they were broken, or paralyzed. He stared at the seat across from him, ignoring the cityscape as it slid by, the train accelerating along viaducts toward the suburbs and the countryside.

He nodded. "I'll survive."

"Yes, but for how much longer?" said the drone, sitting on the table in front of Sma. "You are in terrible shape, Zakalwe."

"Better than looking like a suitcase," he said, glancing at the machine.

"Oh, how droll," the machine said.

—You finished drawing things yet? it asked the *Xenophobe*.

—No.

—Can't you devote just a *little* of your supposedly bogglingly fast Mind to finding out why he was so interested in that ship?

—Oh, I suppose so, but—

—Wait a minute; what have we here? Listen to this:

". . . You'll find out, I suppose. Past time I told you," he said, looking out of the window but talking to Sma. The city slid by beyond, bright in the sunlight. His eyes were wide, pupils dilated, and somehow Sma got the impression he was looking at one city, but seeing another, or seeing the same one but long ago, as though in some time-polarized light only his distressed, enfevered eyes could see.

"This is where you come from?"

"Long time ago, now," he said, coughing, doubling up, holding one arm tight to his side. He took a long slow breath. "I was born here . . ."

The woman listened. The drone listened. The ship listened.

While he told them the story, of the great house that lay halfway between the mountains and the sea, upstream from the great city. He told them about the estate surrounding the house, and the beautiful gardens, and about the three, later four, children who were brought up in the house, and who played in the garden. He told them about the summerhouses and the stone boat and the maze and the fountains and the lawns and the ruins and the animals in the woods. He told them about the two boys and the two girls, and the two mothers, and the one strict father and the one unseen father, imprisoned in the city. He told them about the visits to the city, which the children always thought lasted too long, and about the time when they were no longer allowed to go into the garden without guards to escort them, and about how they stole a gun, one day, and were going to take it out into the estate to shoot it, but only got as far as the stone boat, and surprised an assassination squad come to kill the family, and saved the day by alerting the house. He told them about the bullet that hit Darckense, and the sliver of her bone that pierced him almost to his heart.

He started to dry up, voice croaking. Sma saw a waiter pushing a trolley into the far end of the coach. She bought a couple of soft drinks; he gulped at first, but coughed painfully, and then just sipped his.

"And the war did start," he said, looking at but not seeing the last of the suburbs flow past; the countryside was a green blur as they accelerated again. "And the two boys, that had become men . . . ended up on different sides."

—Fascinating, the *Xenophobe* communicated to Skaffen-Amtiskaw. I think I will do a little quick research.

—About time too, the drone sent back, listening to the man talk at the same time.

He told them about the war, and the siege that involved the *Staberinde*, and the besieged forces breaking out . . . and he told them about the man, the boy who'd played in the garden who, in the depths of one terrible night, had caused the thing to be done which led to him being called the Chairmaker, and the dawn when Darckense's sister and brother had found what Elethiomel had done, and the brother trying to take his own life, giving up his generalship, abandoning the armies and his sister in the selfishness of despair.

And he told them about Livueta, who had never forgiven, and had followed him—though he did not know it at the time—on another cold ship, for a century through the intractable calm slowness of real space, to a place where the ice-bergs swirled round a continental pole, forever calving and crashing and shrinking . . . But then she had lost him, the trail gone appropriately cold, and she had stayed there, searching, for years, and could not have known that he had left for another life entirely, taken away by the tall lady who walked through the blizzard as though it wasn't there, a small spaceship at her back like a faithful pet.

And so Livueta Zakalwe gave up, and took another long journey, to get away from the burden of her memories, and where she had ended up—(the ship quizzed the drone for the location; Skaffen-Amtiskaw gave it the name of the planet and the system, a few decades away)—that had been where she'd finally been tracked down, after his last job for them.

Skaffen-Amtiskaw remembered. The gray-haired woman, in her early late-years, working in a clinic in the slums, a delicate shanty town strewn like trash across the mud and tree-lined slopes above a tropical city looking out across spar-kling lagoons and golden sandbars to the rollers of a vast ocean. Thin, marks under her eyes, a pot-bellied child on each hip when they first went to see her, standing in the middle of the crowded room, wailing children tugging at her hems.

The drone had learned to appreciate the full range of pan-human facial expression, and thought that, in witnessing the one that appeared on Livueta Zakalwe's face when she saw Zakalwe, it had experienced something close to unique. Such surprise; but such hatred!

"Cheradenine . . ." Sma said tenderly, gently laying one hand on his. She put her other hand to the nape of his neck, stroking him there as his head bent lower to the table. He turned and watched the prairie stream past like a sea of gold.

He put one hand up, smoothing it slowly over his brow and shaved scalp, as though through long hair.

Couraz had been everything; ice and fire, land and water. Once, the broad isthmus had been a place of rock and gla-ciers, then a land of forests as the world and its continents shifted and the climate altered. Later it became a desert, but then suffered something beyond the capacity of the globe itself to provide. An asteroid the size of a mountain hit the isthmus, like a bullet striking flesh.

It burst into the granite heart of the land, ringing the planet like a bell. Two oceans met for the first time; the dust of the immense explosion blocked out the sun, started a small ice age, wiped out thousands of species. The ancestors of the species that later came to rule the planet took their initial opportunity from that cataclysm.

The crater became a dome as the planet reacted over the millennia; the oceans were separated again when the rocks—even the seemingly solid layers flowing and warping, over those great scales of time and distance—pushed back, like an aeons late bruise forming on the skin of the world.

Sma had found the information brochure in a seat pocket. She looked up from it for a moment at the man in the seat beside her. He'd fallen asleep. His face looked drawn and gray and old. She could not remember ever having seen him look so ancient and ill. Dammit, he'd looked healthier when he'd been beheaded. "Zakalwe," she whispered, shaking her head. "What's wrong with you?"

"Death-wish," the drone muttered, quietly. "With extrovert complications."

Sma shook her head and went back to the brochure. The man slept fitfully and the drone monitored him.

Reading about Couraz, Sma suddenly recalled the great fortress she had been picked up from by the *Xenophobe*'s module, on a sunny day that now seemed as long ago as it was far away. She looked up, sighing, from a photograph of the isthmus taken from space, and thought back to the house under the dam, and felt homesick.

. . . Couraz had been a fortified town, a prison, a fortress, a city, a target. Now—perhaps appropriately, Sma thought, looking at the injured, shivering man at her side—the great dome of rock held a small city that was mostly taken up with the biggest hospital in the world.

The train hurtled into a tunnel carved from naked rock.

They passed through the station, took an elevator to one of the hospital reception levels. They sat on a couch, surrounded by potted plants and soft music, while the drone, sitting on the floor at their feet, plundered the nearest computer work station for information.

"Got her," it announced quietly. "Go to the receptionist

and tell her your name; I've ordered you a pass; no verification required.''

"Come on, Zakalwe.'' Sma rose, collected her pass, and helped him to his feet. He staggered. "Look,'' she said, "Cheradenine, let me at—''

"Just take me to her.''

"Let me talk to her first.''

"No; take me to her. Now.''

The ward was up another few levels, in the sunlight. The light came through clear, high windows. The sky was white with scudding cloud outside, and way in the distance, beyond the dappled fields and woodland, the ocean was a line of blue haze beneath the sky.

Old men lay quietly in the broad, partitioned ward. Sma helped him toward the far end, where the drone said Livueta must be. They entered a short, broad corridor. Livueta came out of a side room. She stopped when she saw them.

Livueta Zakalwe looked older; white-haired, skin soft and lined with age. Her eyes were undulled. She drew herself up a little. She was holding a deep-sided tray full of little boxes and bottles.

Livueta looked at them; the man, the woman, the little pale suitcase that was the drone.

Sma glanced to one side, hissed, "Zakalwe!'' She hauled him more upright.

His eyes had been shut. They blinked open and he squinted uncertainly at the woman standing in front of them. He appeared not to recognize her at first, then, slowly, understanding seemed to filter through.

"Livvy?'' he said, blinking quickly, squinting at her. "Livvy?''

"Hello, Ms. Zakalwe,'' Sma said, when the woman did not reply.

Livueta Zakalwe turned contemptuous eyes from the man half hanging from Sma's right arm. She looked at Sma and shook her head, so that just for an instant, Sma thought she was going to say no, she wasn't Livueta.

"Why do you keep doing this?'' Livueta Zakalwe said softly. Her voice was still young, the drone thought, just as the *Xenophobe* came back with some fascinating information it had gleaned from historical records.

(—*Really?* the drone signaled. Dead?)

"Why do you do this?" she said. "Why do you do this
. . . to him; to me . . . why? Can't you just leave us all
alone?"

Sma shrugged, a little awkwardly.

"Livvy . . ." he said.

"I'm sorry, Ms. Zakalwe," Sma said. "It's what he
wanted; we promised."

"Livvy; please; talk to me; let me ex—"

"You shouldn't do this," Livueta told Sma. Then she
turned her gaze to the man, who was rubbing one hand over
his shaved scalp, grinning inanely at her, blinking. "He looks
sick," she said flatly.

"He is," Sma said.

"Bring him in here." Livueta Zakalwe opened another
door; a room with a bed. Skaffen-Amtiskaw, still wondering
exactly what was going on in the light of the information it
had just received from the ship, still found the time to be
mildly surprised that the woman was taking it all so calmly
this time. Last time she'd tried to kill the fellow and it had
had to move in smartly.

"I don't want to lie down," he protested, when he saw
the bed.

"Then just sit, Cheradenine," Sma said. Livueta Zakalwe made a shaking motion with her head, muttered something even the drone could not make out. She placed the tray
of drugs down on a table, stood in one corner of the room,
arms crossed, while the man sat down on the bed.

"I'll leave you alone," Sma said to the woman. "We'll
be just outside."

Close enough for me to hear, thought the drone, and to
stop her trying to murder you again, if that's what she decides
to do.

"No," the woman said, shaking her head, looking with
an odd dispassion at the man on the bed. "No; don't leave.
There's nothing—"

"But I want them to leave," he said, and coughed, doubling over and almost falling off the bed. Sma went to help
him, and pulled him a little further on to the bed.

"What can't you say in front of them?" Livueta Zakalwe
asked. "What don't they know?"

"I just want to have a . . . a talk in private, Livvy,
please," he said, looking up at her. "Please . . ."

"I have nothing to say to you. And there is nothing you can say to me."

The drone heard somebody in the corridor outside; there was a knock at the door. Livueta opened it. A young female nurse, who called Livueta Sister, told her that it was time to prepare one of the patients.

Livueta Zakalwe looked at her watch. "I have to go," she told them.

"Livvy! Livvy, please!" He leaned forward on the bed, both elbows tight by his sides, both hands clawed out, palm up, in front of him. *"Please!"* There were tears in his eyes.

"This is pointless," the old woman shook her head. "And you are a fool." She looked at Sma. "Don't bring him to me again."

"LIVVY!" He collapsed on the bed, curled up and quivering. The drone sensed heat from the shaven head, could see blood vessels throb on his neck and hands.

"Cheradenine, it's all right," Sma said, going to the bed and down on one knee, taking his shoulders in her hands.

There was a crack as one of Livueta Zakalwe's hands thumped down onto the top of a table she stood beside. The man wept, shaking. The drone sensed odd brain-wave patterns. Sma looked up at the woman.

"Don't call him that," Livueta Zakalwe said.

"Don't call him what?" Sma said.

Sma could be pretty thick, the drone thought.

"Don't call him Cheradenine."

"Why not?"

"It isn't his name."

"It isn't?" Sma looked mystified. The drone monitored the man's brain activity and blood flow and thought there was trouble coming.

"No, it isn't."

"But . . ." Sma began. She shook her head suddenly. "He's your brother; he's Cheradenine Zakalwe."

"No, Ms. Sma," Livueta Zakalwe said, taking the drug tray up again and opening the door with one hand. "No, he isn't."

"Aneurysm!" the drone said quickly, and slipped through the air, past Sma to the bed, where the man was shaking spastically. It scanned him more thoroughly; found a massive blood vessel leakage pouring into the man's brain.

It whirled him round, straightened him out, using its effector to make him unconscious. Inside his brain, the blood continued to pump through the tear into the surrounding tissue, invading the cortex.

"Sorry about this, ladies," the drone said. It produced a cutting field and sliced through his skull. He stopped breathing. Skaffen-Amtiskaw used another aspect of its force field to keep his chest moving in and out, while its effector gently persuaded the muscles that opened his lungs to work again. It took the top of his skull off; a quick low-powered CREW blast, mirrored off another field component, cauterized all the appropriate blood vessels. It held his skull to one side. Blood was already visible, welling through the folded gray geography of the man's brain tissue. His heart stopped; the drone kept it going with its effector.

Both women had stopped, fascinated and appalled at the actions of the machine.

It stripped away the layers of the man's brain with its own senses; cortex, limbic, thalamus/cerebellum, it moved through his defenses and armaments, down his thoroughfares and ways, through the stores and the lands of his memories, searching and mapping and tapping and searing.

"What do you mean?" Sma said, in an almost dreamlike way to the elderly woman just about to quit the room. "What do you mean, 'no'? What do you mean he isn't your brother?"

"I mean he is not Cheradenine Zakalwe," Livueta sighed, watching the drone's bizarre operation upon the man.

She was . . . She was . . . She was . . .

Sma found herself frowning into the woman's face. "What? Then . . ."

Go back; go right back. What was I to do? Go back. The point is to win. Go back! Everything must bend to that truth.

"Cheradenine Zakalwe, my brother," Livueta Zakalwe said, "died nearly two hundred years ago. Died not long after he received the bones of our sister made into a chair."

The drone sucked the blood from the man's brain, teasing a hollow field-filament through the broken tissue, collecting the red fluid in a little transparent bulb. A second filament tube spun-knit the torn tissue back together. It sucked more blood to decrease the man's blood pressure, used its effector to alter the settings in the appropriate glands, so that the pressure would not grow so great again for a while. It sent a narrow tube of field over to a small sink under the window, jetting the excess blood down the drain hole, then briefly turning on the tap. The blood flushed away, gurgling.

"The man *you* know as Cheradenine Zakalwe—"

Facing it by facing it, that's all I ever did; Staberinde, Zakalwe; the names hurt, but how else could I—

"—is the man who took my brother's name just as he took my brother's life, just as he took my sister's life—"

But she—

"—*He* was the commander of the *Staberinde*. *He* is the Chairmaker. He is Elethiomel."

Livueta Zakalwe walked out, closing the door behind her.

Sma turned, face almost bloodless, to look at the body of the man lying on the bed . . . while Skaffen-Amtiskaw worked on, engrossed in its struggle to make good.

EPILOGUE

Dust, as usual, followed them, though the young man said several times he thought it might rain. The old man disagreed and said the clouds over the mountains were deceptive. They drove on through the deserted lands, past blackened fields and the shells of cottages and the ruins of farms and the burned villages and the still smoking towns, until they came to the abandoned city. In the city they drove resoundingly through the wide empty streets, and once took the vehicle crashing and careering up a narrow alley crammed with bare market stalls and rickety poles supporting tattered shade-cloths, demolishing it all in a fine welter of splintering wood and wildly flapping fabric.

They chose the Royal Park as the best place to plant the bomb, because the troops could be comfortably accommodated in the Park's wide spaces, and the high command would likely take to the grand pavilions. The old man thought that they'd want to occupy the Palace, but the young man was convinced that in their hearts the invaders were desert people, and would prefer the spaces of the Park to the clutter of the Citadel.

So they planted the bomb in the Great Pavilion, and armed it, and then argued about whether they'd done the right thing. They argued about where to wait things out, and what to do if the army ignored the city altogether and just went on by, and whether after the prospective event the other armies would retire in terror, or split up into smaller units to continue the invasion, or know the weapon used had been unique, and so maintain their steady progress, doubtless in an even more ruthless spirit of vengeance than before. They argued about whether the invaders would bombard the city first, or send in scouts, and—if they did shell—where they would target. They had a bet on that.

About the only thing they agreed on was that what they were doing was a waste of the one nuke their side—indeed either side—possessed, because even if they had guessed correctly, and the invaders behaved as they'd anticipated, the most they could hope to do was wipe out one army, and that would still leave three more, any one of which could probably complete the invasion. So the warhead, like the lives, would be wasted.

They radioed their superiors and with a code word told them what they had done. After a little while they received the blessing of the high command, in the form of another single word. Their masters didn't really believe the weapon would work.

The older man was called Cullis, and he won the argument about where they ought to wait, and so they settled into their high, grand citadel, and found lots of weapons and wine and got drunk and talked and told jokes and swapped outrageous stories of derring-do and conquest, and at one point one of them asked the other what happiness was, and received a fairly flippant reply, but later neither could remember which one had asked and which one had answered.

They slept and they woke and they got drunk again and they told more jokes and lies, and a light shower of rain blew softly over the city at one point, and sometimes the young man would move his hand over his shaved head, through long, thick hair that was not there anymore.

Still they waited, and when the first shells started to fall they found they'd picked the wrong place to wait, and so went scrambling out of it, down the steps and into the courtyard and into the half-track and then away, out into the desert and the wasteland beyond, where they camped at dusk and got drunk again and stayed up specially that night, to watch the flash.

ZAKALWE'S SONG

Watching from the room
As the troops go by.

You ought to be able to tell, I think,
Whether they are going or coming back
By just leaving the gaps in the ranks.

You are a fool, I said,
And turned to leave,
Or maybe only mix a drink
For that deft throat to swallow
Like all my finest lies.

I faced into the shadows of things,
You leaned against the window,
Gazing at nothing.

When are we going to leave?
We could get stuck here,
Caught
If we try to stay too long.   (turning)
Why don't we *leave*?

I said nothing,
Stroked a cracked glass,
Exclusive knowledge in the silence;

The bomb lives only as it is falling.

—Shias Engin.
Complete Collected Works (Posthumous Edition).
Month 18, 355th Great Year (Shtaller, Prophetican calendar).
Volume IX: "Juvenilia and Discarded Drafts"

STATES
OF
WAR

PROLOGUE

The path up to the highest cultivation terrace followed an extravagantly zigzag route, to allow the wheelchairs to cope with the gradient. It took him six and a half minutes of hard work to get to the highest terrace; he was sweating when he got there, but he had beaten his previous record, and so he was pleased. His breath smoked in the cold air as he undid the heavy quilted jacket and wheeled the chair along to one of the raised beds.

He lifted the basket out of his lap and balanced it on the retaining wall, took the cutters from his jacket pocket and looked carefully at the selection of small plants, trying to gauge which cuttings had fared best since their planting. He hadn't chosen the first one when some movement up-slope attracted his attention.

He looked through the high fence, to the dark green forest. The distant peaks were white against the blue sky above. At first he thought it was an animal, then the figure moved out of the trees and walked over the frost-whitened grass toward the gate in the fence.

The woman opened the gate, closed it behind her; she wore a thin-looking coat and trousers. He was mildly surprised to see that she didn't have a rucksack. Perhaps she had walked up through the grounds of the institute earlier, and was now returning. A visiting doctor, maybe. He had been going to wave, if she looked at him as she took the steps down to the institute buildings, but she left the gate and walked straight toward him. She was tall; dark hair and a light brown face under a curious looking fur hat.

"Mr. Escoerea," she said, extending a hand. He put down the cutters, shook her hand.

"Good morning, Ms. . . ?"

She didn't reply, but sat down on the wall, clapped ungloved hands together, looked around the valley, at the mountains and the forest, the river, and the institute buildings down-slope. "How are you, Mr. Escoerea? Are you well?"

He looked down at what was left of his legs, amputated above the knees. "What is left of me is well, ma'am." It had become his usual reply. He knew it might sound bitter to some people, but really it was his way of showing he did not want to pretend that there was nothing wrong with him.

She looked at the trousered stumps with a frankness he had only known before from children. "It was a tank, wasn't it?"

"Yes," he said, taking up the clippers again. "Tried to trip it up on the way to Balzeit City; didn't work." He leaned over, took a cutting and placed it in the basket. He made a note of which plant he'd taken it from, and attached it to the twig. "Excuse me . . ." He moved the wheelchair along a little, and the woman got out of his way as he took another cutting.

She stepped round in front of him again. "Story I heard said you were dragging one of your comrades out of its—"

"Yes," he interrupted. "Yes, that's the story. Of course I didn't know then the price of charity is developing extremely strong arm muscles."

"You get your medal yet?" She squatted down on her haunches, putting one of her hands on a wheel of his chair. He looked at the hand, then at her face, but she just grinned.

He opened his quilted jacket, showed the uniform tunic underneath, with all its ribbons. "Yes, I got my medal." He ignored her hand, pushed the chair along again.

The woman rose, squatted down again, beside him. "Impressive display for one so young. Surprised you weren't promoted faster; is it true you didn't show the right attitude to your superiors? That why—''

He threw the clippers down in the basket, wheeled the chair round to face her. "Yeah, lady," he sneered. "I said the wrong things, my family were never very well connected even when they were alive and now they're not even that, thanks to the Imperial Glaseen Air Force, and *these* . . ." He clutched at the chest of the tunic, hauling at the medal ribbons, brandishing them. "These I'd trade you; all of them for a pair of shoes I could wear. Now," he leaned forward at her, took up the clippers. "I have work to do. There's a guy down in the institute who stepped on a mine; he hasn't got any legs at all *and* he lost an arm. Maybe you'd find it even more fun to go and patronize him. Excuse me."

He whirled the chair around, moved off a few meters, and took a couple of cuttings, tearing at two plants almost at random. He heard the woman on the path behind him, and put his hands on the wheels, pushing himself away.

She stopped him. Her hand held the back of the wheel-chair and she was stronger than she looked. His arms strained against the wheels; the rubber buzzed against the stone path, wheels turning but not propelling him anywhere. He relaxed, looked up at the sky. She came round in front of him, squatted down again.

He sighed. "What exactly do you want, lady?"

"You, Mr. Escoerea." The woman smiled her beautiful smile. She nodded at the stumps. "By the way; the deal with the medals and the shoes; fair enough." She shrugged. "Except you can keep the medals." She reached into the basket, took out the clippers and stuck them into the earth under the plants, then put her hands, clasped, on the front of the seat. "Now, Mr. Escoerea," Sma said, shivering. "How would you like a proper job?"